ELEVATOR PITCH

EVELYN LEIGH

elevator pitch

The Hapless In Love Series
Book One

evelyn leigh

ISBN: 979-8-9915358-0-9

Editing by Cassidy Hudspeth (Cassidy Hudspeth Editing and Proofreading)

Proofreading by Cassidy Hudspeth (Cassidy Hudspeth Editing and Proofreading)

Cover art by Treshell Fisher

Typography by DisturbedValkyrieDesigns

Interior Formatting by Kath Richards

Internal images by Sam (Ink & Velvet Designs)

1st edition 2024

author's note

Welcome to the Hapless In Love Book Club!

I am writing this on my thirtieth birthday. One day I wasn't sure I'd be able to see, but I'm grateful I'm here writing my first novel. It is fitting for me to be a writer since I am a homebody who can go days without human contact, enjoy my own company and daydream about imaginary friends. Prior to writing this series, I had writer's block for seven years. I accepted that it was likely I would never write again, but from the moment I opened a fresh document for this story, I haven't been able to stop. So, I hope you like me, because I have a hell of a lot more to share with you all.

I had believed I wasn't an interesting enough person to write a book about. Your overwhelming support, kindness and love has proven me wrong. So wrong. When I originally set out to write 'Elevator Pitch' my intent was to write a silly romantic comedy. However, once I began writing it, I was inspired to tell a different story. One that was much more realistic and difficult to share. *My own.* I am a survivor of domestic violence, so are my mother and grandmother. I have never said that out loud or admitted it publicly before now. I was always afraid to tell my story, but the need to write 'Elevator Pitch' was far greater than living in fear, and to that I said, "fuck it." ;)

It was important to tell a story about a woman finding her freedom and the community that rallied behind her when she lost it all because that was my story. I found community, peace and love in ruin and I watered that soil every single day–sometimes with tears. The vibrant garden that blossomed from it, you will experience right now. I ask that you enter this story with empathy for both Greyson and Selah. As the internal battles they face are far too common and while some are cultural, others are not. Thank you for picking up this story and taking a chance on me. I hope this love story changes your lives as much as it has mine.

Selah is a neurodivergent Black woman with ADHD. And while that is my lived experience, I thoroughly enjoyed collaborating with my team of advisors, both in the medical field and fellow neurodivergent friends. I cannot thank my advisors and sensitivity readers enough for their dedication and sharing their expertise. I ensured she was captured in a light that truly expresses what it is like to be both Black and neurodivergent.

Greyson is a second-generation Korean American man. It was incredibly rewarding to research Korean culture through immersing myself, as well as consulting my advisors and sensitivity readers. I sincerely cannot thank them enough for their countless hours working on this project and for sharing their culture/experiences with me. I am so grateful for your graciousness.

I recognized the importance of writing an Asian-American hero in romance and handled Greyson with the utmost care. While he is a fictional character, it was crucial he was represented accurately. With this being said, I have not altered his or Selah's experiences to make them more palatable to the masses.

For any readers out there, who are also DV survivors, I am so proud of you for choosing yourself and grateful you are still here. We endured a lot that we shouldn't have and for that we've earned a slice of heaven on Earth, if not the whole damn pie. You all deserve a beautiful love story for the books, so I wrote one just for you.

If you or someone you know is experiencing abuse, help is available and your story matters just as much as this one. Please get to a safe space before reaching out.

The National Domestic Violence Hotline: 1-800-799-7233
Text 'START' to 88788
www.thehotline.org

There are mentions of panic attacks, anxiety, depression, PTSD, infertility, domestic violence, alcohol use, death of a parent, therapy sessions, marijuana use, nightmares, and explicit language.

This is an open door romance with a generous amount of consensual sex. If that isn't your cup of tea, this book may not be for you. I would also recommend reviewing the Dick-tionary on the following page to know what chapters to avoid if you would still like to enjoy this story without the sexually explicit scenes. For a detailed list of events, please feel free to contact the author via Instagram DMs @evelynleighauthor or email at contact@authorevelynleigh.com with any specific questions you may have about the contents of this book. *Elevator Pitch* is a contemporary romance that contains topics that may be triggering to some. Please do not hesitate to reach out if you would like to inquire about specific chapters to avoid or avoid reading this novel entirely. Your mental health is far more important.

dick-tionary

If you would like to jump straight into the spice, know how far ahead the fun times are or if you would like to skip the spice entirely. Chapters with an asterisk * are partial scenes.

- Chapter 21*
- Chapter 22
- Chapter 23
- Chapter 26
- Chapter 27*
- Chapter 40
- Chapter 41*
- Chapter 42
- Chapter 47*
- Chapter 48*
- Chapter 51
- Chapter 56*
- Chapter 57
- Chapter 61
- Chapter 74*
- Chapter 75
- Chapter 76*

If you've ever been told "you'll never find love if you don't leave the house," this one's for you.

&

For those who need a reminder that they are worthy of love.

playlist

Forgiveless – SZA (feat. Ol' Dirty Bastard)
I Been - Ari Lennox
When I Get You Alone – Robin Thicke
Coffee – Tori Kelly
Sunflower Vol. 6 – Harry Styles
Strings – MAX (feat. JVKE & Bazzi)
Method Man – Wu-Tang Clan
The Jump Off – Lil Kim
L.M.F. - Smino
Garden (Say It Like That) – SZA
Cruisin' – Smokey Robinson
I Put A Spell On You – Nina Simone
Soundproof Room – Elle Varner
Kiss U Right Now – Duckwrth
N Side – Steve Lacy
40 Shades Of Choke – Ari Lennox
Long Night – Gwen Bunn
Some – Steve Lacy
Ooh Nah Nah – SiR, Masego
Stop By – Ari Lennox
Adore You – Harry Styles

I Wantcha' – Be.Be The Neosoul
Lights Up – Harry Styles
Brown Eyed Lover – Allen Stone
POV – Ariana Grande
Find Someone Like You – Snoh Aalegra
Give You Blue – Allen Stone
LOVE AGAIN – Daniel Caesar, Brandy
Anita – Smino
Freefall – KAYTRANADA, Durand Bernarr
Lay It Down – Allen Stone
Let The Light In – Lana Del Rey (feat. Father John Misty)
Moon and Back – JVKE
Lee & Lovie - Smino (feat Reggie)

Listen on Spotify
Listen on Apple Music

selah's fuck it list

1. Have multiple orgasms in one session
2. Have sex in a public place
3. Make pot brownies
4. Recreate a favorite spicy scene from a book
5. Experience an earth-shattering kiss
6. See Niagara Falls
7. Host a successful gathering
8. Explore kink
9. Fly first class
10. Learn to bake
11. Movie Night at the park
12. Have a picnic

1
egg on your foot
Selah

Manhattan, NY | September 2, 2023

WHEN I SPRAYED perfume on my ankles tonight, I obviously had other plans. Instead, I ended up with my ankles in a public sink while I scrubbed raw egg off my foot. After the worst date I've ever had, I'd just like to go home, curl up with a book, and forget this ever happened. I've tried giving real men a chance, but that's it. I'm deleting my dating profile and going back to fictional men.

I've committed to a date or two a week, and while I haven't been successful, it's been eventful, to say the least. I can't say I wasn't warned about the water conditions. If this is *the* dating pool, it's a lazy fucking river. My girls have been very transparent about their experiences with dating, and I figured it wouldn't be so damn bad since I wasn't looking for love. I was sorely mistaken.

Last year, I created a version of a bucket list that I call a *"Fuck It List."* My goal has been to force myself out of my comfort zone, and that includes sexual fantasies. After wasting my twenties with my abusive ex-fiancé, Jourdan, this list has allowed me to embrace my newfound freedom, and I hope to complete it all by my thirtieth birthday. I have accomplished a great deal, but I'm cutting it close with eight months left and a handful of tasks uncompleted.

I met the guy I just went out with on an app called *SoulBlend*, which is advertised as the most successful dating app for finding your perfect match. I personally haven't seen any positive results, considering this is the twelfth date I've matched with, and I haven't yet struck gold.

I've been transparent in therapy about what I'm doing here. It's been two years since Jourdan, and I'm still not ready for a relationship, but I do have needs. Needs that a man hasn't fulfilled in 788 days, but who's counting? Surely, my friends are, who refer to me as "Cobweb Queen."

I'll admit it is funny.

While I'm very proud of my toy collection, and there isn't much it *can't* do, I'll need human interaction to check the more suggestive things off my list. That's why I'm dating.

My Uber is ten minutes away. As I recount the events of this evening, I'm wondering when the exact moment I should've hidden in the bathroom or made up a fake emergency was. Was it when he interrupted me every time I spoke? Maybe when he called me Layla multiple times? Or better yet, when he tipped the chef forty fucking dollars after he dropped a raw egg on my foot, but the meal *I* wanted was too expensive? Either way, it was a train wreck, and I was chained to my seat with no choice but to sit and watch.

His name was Keith, and he was very handsome with dimples and a devilish smile. He had a *really* nice voice—the kind that would sound amazing in your ear, guiding you over the edge. Our love for music was one of the few things we had in common. He didn't cross off many boxes, but he looked the part, and since I wasn't seeking any other connection aside from his parts fitting into mine, I gave him a shot.

We had dinner at a hibachi grill. Nothing wrong with that, except when you're on a first date, things are already awkward enough. Let's add flair by sitting at a table beside strangers while trying to get to know each other. Fun.

The cook introduced himself, asking us to go easy on him since it was his first night on the floor. We cheered, and he started making the rice. He went around asking everyone what they'd like, and I wanted egg with my rice. You know how the cooks engage with the audience by making small talk while creating actual flames in front of you?

I did my best to ignore the fire dancing across the grill and focus on my date.

He started throwing food for people to catch in their mouths —*count me out.* My date, however, was catching loads of shrimp in his. I should mention that I hate shrimp. He had to be *that* person. He caught about eight pieces back-to-back. I'm sure he didn't even take breaths in between. I was equally impressed and annoyed at the attention being directed my way. I wouldn't be kissing him tonight, and he wouldn't be using that mouth on me.

After the cook played *catch the food,* he started doing tricks with the eggs. Facing me, he threw an egg in the air and caught it with the side of his spatula, making a clean crack before placing it on the grill to cook. He grabbed another egg to repeat the trick, except the egg didn't fall on his spatula. It slipped through an open slot between the table and the grill…landing on my *open toes.* I wanted to scream, vomit, and commit assault. The internal panic was like a hundred fire alarms going off at once.

If there was ever a real-life moment to redeem a get-out-of-jail-free card, that was it.

6

My phone vibrates as I stand near the curb, waiting for my

Uber. I'm shocked to see a Venmo request from Keith for twenty-five dollars. I assume he'd like to be reimbursed for that rubber dog toy of a steak he ordered me. Well-done steak and dog toys are basically the same thing. He left a note that simply states, "You are a bitch."

This is why you don't have to be nice to men.

I deny the request and send him fifty dollars instead. He obviously needs it, and I'm impressed at his audacity. I added a note: *Take Layla somewhere that doesn't serve eggs*. I roar a laugh that would've surely earned me some stares back in St. Louis or West Chester. However, this is New York, and nobody gives a fuck. The city of minding your own damn business.

I should've moved here sooner.

A notification flashes on my screen: my driver, Deena, is approaching in a blue SUV. My Uber driver isn't very social, which is fine by me. I settle in, block Keith's contact, and screenshot the Venmo requests. The girls will have a good laugh about that.

I've still got a few more minutes before getting back to my place, so of course, I'm using that time to overthink. My therapist wants me to journal more, so I'm making bullet points to summarize the eventful date in my notes app. I was so considerate of Keith until it was painful, and I was called a 'bitch' anyway. I wasn't even rude when I spoke up. I can't win. I'm a people pleaser in recovery. We prioritize everyone else's happiness, even strangers who don't mean anything to us. It's just in our nature. Externally, I'm too fucking nice. Internally, I'm a badass like the women in my family. I struggle with displaying both sides in a way that is healthy for me.

Something about Keith made me shut down like I was with Jourdan again. I think that's why I couldn't just fucking leave the restaurant, even with the strike system. Which is a guiltless system I created to give myself the green light to do something mean or inconsiderate whenever I feel unsafe, unhappy, or uncomfortable. If a date hits three strikes, I can lie, make an excuse, or tell the truth. It doesn't fucking matter if I abide by the rules and *leave*.

I considered how I could've handled tonight differently. Like sending a text from the bathroom and sneaking out. It wouldn't have been the first time, and I'm no stranger to bailing over a call or text. I even paused *Harry's House* to dump my fiancé over the phone.

What? Harry told us to leave our boyfriends, and I listened.

If anything, a phone call was all he deserved after wasting five years of my life.

6

Acknowledging my tendency to please others and making a conscious effort to unlearn that behavior has been one of the most challenging aspects of my personal development. It takes some work to grow and unlearn this habit, but I'm progressing. I'm creating a life I'm pleased with by putting myself first. I refuse to apologize for who I've become because I'll never be an afterthought again. I also believe that if I ever "settle down", I won't be settling in the least. Someone is out there waiting to love *me*. Someone will see all that I am and provide ample space for me to just *be*. Someone will contribute to the life I've created for myself without dimming my light.

I'd consider letting love in if I ever found someone like that. I understand that person is not on a dating app. After twelve doozies, I'm throwing in the towel and revising my list. I don't need a partner, nor do I want one. I pull up my *SoulBlend* profile, and my thumb hovers over the deactivate button.

I am distracted when my Uber driver says, "We're here."

I grab my things and open the door.

"Thank you! Have a great night."

She gives me a soft smile and a wave goodbye. I step onto the curb and head toward the entrance of my building. I'm greeted by our door attendant, David, and chat with him for a moment before I step through the doors, accidentally dropping my keys and bending to pick them up. As I rise, I see a tall figure heading toward the entrance out of the corner of my eye. I turn around and walk further into the lobby. It's a dead zone, so I grab my e-reader, open to the chapter I left off on, and read it as I walk. I would've much rather spent my evening doing this than having a front-row seat at a shit show.

I hear the entrance door beep as someone enters the building and focus on my story, which is heating up, and I can't wait for the spice. I stop once I'm close enough to the elevator and press the up button. Stepping aside, I read as I wait. Footsteps approach, from the person who came in behind me. Once they stand beside me, I'm enveloped in a heady scent. It's intoxicating and sensual. Very masculine.

Judging by the scent, I'd imagine it's something a man who goes for exactly what he wants would wear. He smells *sexy. Very sexy.* I don't bother looking up from my book to see his face because I no longer have the energy to converse with anyone. E*specially* not a man.

2
out of service

Greyson

Manhattan, NY | September 2, 2023

WHEN I ATTENDED my ex-wife's engagement party, I hadn't expected to learn that she met her fiancé, Daniel, on the dating app I founded. I thought inviting me to the engagement party was far from normal, but Aileen insisted because 'we're just friends who used to be married, it was fine.'

We met freshman year at NYU and dated all through college, then I proposed after graduation, and we eloped soon after. Once I got the degree and the girl, I became stagnant. After all those years of seeking approval from my parents, I felt like I could finally breathe. We were married for two years before she filed for divorce, and while I was devastated, I knew I failed her. Before Aileen, I hadn't failed at anything.

We struggled with communication, and it trickled into our sex life. It was evident once you took friendship out of it that Aileen and I didn't make sense as a couple. We were polar opposites in many areas, mainly the bedroom, and she wasn't open-minded. I didn't fight to break down those barriers. Instead, I poured all my focus into work because that was easier than getting my wife to open up to me. I once made an effort to notice all the little things and cater to her every need, but then I became obsessed with the money I was making and the opportunities that came along. I was finally experiencing what validation felt like after years of feeling like I wasn't good enough, but I lost sight of *her* in the process.

Five years ago, I founded a dating app called *SoulBlend, which has* been wildly successful in helping users worldwide find their person. I've lost count of how many weddings and baby showers I'm invited to each year, but when my schedule allows, I attend.

Here's a fun fact about me: I love weddings. Though, when Aileen and I got married, we didn't have one. We couldn't afford one fresh out of college and we could've involved our parents, but we didn't want to wait or have a big ceremony.

After the divorce, I went out to find myself, and I did everything you should to 'find your peace.' I've eaten on nearly every continent and prayed to many gods, but love? I'd like to think that if love knocks again, I'll answer the door. Now, I don't expect to find a billionaire like Aileen did, but I wouldn't complain.

Thanks to my best friends, Alex and Elena, I didn't have to endure this party solo. Then there's my brother Henry, who couldn't care less about my ex remarrying. He desperately needed a night out of his dorm, and the free liquor was a bonus. I can't say I blame the kid. To be fair, he was thirteen when we split, and they stayed close. She was the big sister he never had.

We're leaving early because Henry had a little too much to drink. Alex helps me get Henry in the backseat with ease. Elena offers to sit with him in the back, but Alex protests, saying she looks too pretty tonight to be covered in vomit. Elena laughs and hops in the passenger seat. Once everyone is boarded up, I round the car and hop in. As I pull out of the parking lot, I hear rustling and notice Alex digging through the food bags Daniel left us.

"Coffee Buns, Fresh Cream Cake, and Yakgwa cookies," he

sings, before adding begrudgingly, "We could've had some bingsu too if Henry could hold his liquor."

I chuckle softly. "Hey. Save some for us."

"There's more than enough. Daniel was very generous with the desserts."

"Did *you* have fun?" I ask Alex.

"I didn't expect to, but I did. I also didn't mind babysitting. You know our boy Henry got some numbers tonight?"

"Oh, really?" I ask with raised brows.

"Yup. Our little boy is becoming a man," he says with pride.

I snort.

As we get closer to Alex's place, he asks if we're all staying the night, and I decline. They suggest letting Henry stay over. I know it's to let me process the night I just had, and I'm grateful. I look through my rearview and see Henry has fallen asleep.

I start thinking about the uncomfortable conversation with Aileen.

You're a romantic, always have been. A flower buying, slow dancing, stargazing romantic. You're in the business of matchmaking. I don't believe that a man like you truly prefers casual dating over commitment.

I wonder if Elena can read my thoughts when she asks, "So, what were you talking about when she came over to the table?"

"Well, she said a lot while devouring the desserts on my plate." I chuckle. "Oh, and she was wearing those pearl earrings I bought her when I landed my first job out of college. The ones you helped me pick out." I nod to Elena.

"Noooo. I knew they looked familiar," she whines.

"I hope you know I am trying so hard to keep my mouth shut," Alex adds.

"I know, man. She gave me shit about not bringing a date, and she doesn't believe I'm happy single. Went on a tangent about how I was when we were in love. Talked about how I'm a romantic at heart, and I'm not getting any younger…it was fucking awful."

Elena and Alex collectively groan.

"Oh, she had more to say. She met Daniel on *SoulBlend*."

"Fuck out of here!" Alex exclaims, startling sleeping Henry.

"Yeah. That was my thought too. She didn't want to tell me because of how strange it was. She met her future husband on an app *I* created to move on from *her*."

"That's fucked up. If any person deserves to find love on that app, it should be you."

"The success of the app aided me through the divorce, and I'm proud of that. I didn't create *SoulBlend* solely for me. I did it for everyone."

Elena rubs my arm to reassure me.

"It's alright, really."

"It's really not. I'm sure you don't want to talk about this shit anymore, so we'll drop it. You know we're always here for you."

"Of course. I love you fools."

"We love you too," they say in unison.

"And don't think you're getting out of a hug tonight. *You need one* and we're doing a group hug."

"Since when did you become so affectionate?"

Elena chortles beside me before saying, "Alex *is* affectionate. His love language is physical touch."

"Did he tell you that?" I lock eyes with Alex in the rearview, and he glares at me.

"I just have a way of knowing things," she says matter-of-factly.

I raise my eyebrows at Alex through the mirror, and he flips me off.

Classy.

12

I flick off the light and close the door behind me, leaving Hen to rest. When I was Henry's age, I was married and worked tirelessly. The fact that he enjoyed himself tonight while he's been busting his ass in med school fills me with pride. I'm grateful he's so different from me.

I gather my things so I can get back home to Clifford. I enter the kitchen to find Alex reenacting his favorite Henry dance moves of the night, and we erupt into laughter.

"Thanks for coming with me. I really appreciate it."

"Don't mention it."

"Anytime," Elena chimes.

She bags up my desserts when Alex strides closer with a devious grin.

"About that group hug."

I snort. "Oh, you were serious?"

"Bring it in." He pats his chest. "Come get it while it's hot."

"What does that even mean?"

"I've heard Elena say it on the food truck before."

She bursts out laughing. "That means someone's order is ready."

He opens his arms, wrapping them around us tightly.

He sighs, "I love you fools."

"Love you too," we say collectively before pulling apart.

Elena walks me to the door, asking about brunch tomorrow and to bring Cliff because she misses him. I let her know I'll be back tomorrow, and she knows how much I love her cooking. I say goodnight to them both and listen for the door to lock before I head to my SUV.

After scrolling the *Kiwi Music* app, I chose a playlist for the drive. I recap the night as *When I Get You Alone* comes through my speakers. I soon recall the conversation with Aileen's wedding planner, who was trying to set me up with a friend of hers. I had to get Henry out of there, so I didn't get her name or her friend's.

She's beautiful like the Summertime.

Radiant, like a field of sunflowers when she feels safe enough to shine.

Maybe it wasn't meant to be.

When I get back to my place and walk up to the garage elevator, I notice an out-of-service sign taped to the doors.

This Elevator is temporarily out of service. We apologize for the inconvenience. Please reach out to the front desk if you have any questions.
- Management

I consider taking the stairs because it's on the same level as my apartment, but I remember to check my mailbox. I refuse to take twelve flights of stairs to the lobby and back, so I park on the ground floor. Approaching the entrance, I spot a shapely woman in a silk, burnt orange dress bending to pick something off the ground. I slow my steps to put more distance between us as I don't wish to startle her.

She returns to her height, with brown skin and long dark hair straightened—stopping at her lower back. I watch her converse with our door attendant for a moment, so she must live here. I greet David and head over to my mailbox on the opposite side of the lobby. I lock the box, tuck the mail into my camera bag, and turn around to see if the mystery woman is still here, and to my surprise, she is. She's holding an e-reader and appears to be reading something interesting because she's not paying attention to her surroundings. There's no one here but me and Barb at the front desk.

I'd like to read something that captures my attention like that.

I pad towards the elevator, careful not to disturb her. Planting my feet a respectful distance, I glance over my shoulder, but she doesn't notice me. I take a deep breath when her scent hits me violently: jasmine and tuberose. I'm enthralled. She smells like *sex*.

Does she know it?

I give her my full attention, and she is so wrapped up in that book that I can't see much of her face, but her side profile is divine. Her full, glossy lips are reminiscent of lava cake. She has a cute button nose and full brows. She wears two gold necklaces, hoop earrings, and various gold bands spread across her fingers. Fine-line tattoos are scattered over her curvaceous frame. I imagine her as a force to be reckoned with and am determined to earn her attention.

The ding sounds, she rushes onto the platform, and I follow behind. Once we're inside, she stands opposite me, immersed in that book.

She didn't even press a button for her floor.

I challenge myself to distract her at least once on this elevator ride. I'm not sure why this is so important to me, but it is.

I break the silence to ask, "what floor?"

3
what floor?

Selah

Manhattan, NY | September 2, 2023

"WHAT FLOOR?"

My book is getting good, and now I'm trapped in the elevator with the 'Smell Good Man.'

Is he talking to me? If so, that's just my luck.

"I'm sorry?" I ask without looking up.

I swear I'm not usually this rude. I'm just on the last two pages of this chapter, and I must know what happens.

The enemies are about to become lovers, dammit!

His voice is smooth and husky.

"Excuse me, Miss. I don't mean to interrupt, but I'm not sure where you're headed?" I see his hands motion to the buttons beside the door from the corner of my eye. "You didn't press a button, so we're sitting in limbo here. Not that you aren't good company," he chuckles.

My eyes are still focused on my book.

"Why didn't you press your floor? You could've left me in limbo while you went home."

"Ladies first."

I snort, reading the end of the chapter.

"I'm sure limbo would be better if I could see your face, but I'm not as interesting as your book."

"Sir," I say flatly.

"Ma'am," he says sternly.

I finally glance at him, and I wasn't prepared *at all*. He's in an all-black suit that's tailored to perfection, and I wonder where he just came from.

What's his story?

He's tall with broad shoulders and bulging arms. He obviously works out often.

I bet he could pick me up.

His hair is dark and tousled like he'd been running his fingers through it. His face is incredibly chiseled, and his skin is glowing.

I'm almost certain he could cut glass with that jaw.

What's his skincare routine?

His striking brown eyes sparkle with warmth. I usually avoid eye contact, but my curiosity takes the lead. I can't pinpoint what it is about him, nor can I look away.

This man is gorgeous.

He stares at me with confusion before he notices what I'm doing. He's so expressive that you can see his thought process on his face. He focuses on my mouth. Instinctively, I start swiping at my lip in case I'm drooling, and he smirks.

"You're not drooling. If that's why you keep wiping your mouth."

"I know I'm not," I say defensively.

"Listen, ma'am. I don't have anywhere to be, *but* if you're going to keep eye fucking me…I'd appreciate it if you'd ask me my name."

My jaw drops, and I cover my face with my hand.

"Don't be shy now," he says in a playful voice.

I smile wider, shaking my head.

It's annoying that I'm enjoying this interaction.

"What floor?" he asks again.

"Six."

He doesn't move and holds my gaze. He's intense, and I'm curious about him. I ask if he's going to press the button, and he tells me he'd like to know more about the book I'm reading.

He can't be serious.

"Why is that important?"

"I'd like to know what captivates you."

"Hmm. Okay," I say. "It's a romance. Enemies-to-lovers. They meet in traffic when the woman is running late for her first day at a new job. She initiates a road rage incident with a man, where they exchange words and part ways. She makes it to work on time and learns the man she just snapped at in traffic is her new boss."

He listens with intent and asks about the author. I tell him this is her debut, and she's anonymous. He pulls out his phone and claims to order the book. Says he's intrigued and hasn't read a romance before.

This man is *different,* to say the least.

I snort. "Surely you're joking."

He raises an eyebrow. "I'm not," he replies matter-of-factly and puts his phone away.

He turns around and presses two buttons: six and twelve. The elevator jostles beneath our feet, startling me after being still for so long, and begins moving upwards.

"I would say that you look beautiful tonight, but you probably get that a lot."

I tilt my head and respond, "So you won't pay me a compliment because I'm used to them?"

"Did I say that? For someone who reads, I'd expect you to wait for the words *before* you reacted to them." I scoff.

I think I may be turned on right now.

We'll circle back to that.

"I was saying, before you *rudely* interrupted me, that you're enchanting." His eyes meet mine. "I'll admit I was trying to distract you. You grabbed my attention and held onto it, all while you were focused on that novel. I wanted to earn your gaze."

How the hell do I respond to that?

I am not prepared, and why are my cheeks hot?

"You wanted to *captivate* me?" I say curiously.

"Absolutely," he responds confidently.

I was right. A man who goes after exactly what he wants.

"How do you feel now that you got to see *me*?"

He stares adoringly.

"Very fucking fortunate."

Well, shit.

I try hiding my smile and fail miserably.

"My name is Greyson, but you can call me Grey *if* you're nasty," he adds with a disarming smile.

The audacity of this man.

My eyebrows shoot up, and I chuckle to myself.

"Well, it's nice to meet you, Greyson," I say, drawing out his name.

His smile falters.

"What? Disappointed that I'm not nasty?" I say in a mocking tone.

"No, I'm certain that book you're reading is *nasty,* and I'll know soon enough," he states with a wink.

I throw my head back in laughter.

Alright. He's cute and funny.

"I'd only be disappointed if I didn't get your name."

"It's Selah, if you're naughty *or* nice," I tease.

I reach out my hand awkwardly to shake his. He zeroes in on it before returning my handshake. Looks like he's curious about my tattoo. *Happier than ever* inked on the side of my right thumb. His large hand engulfs mine in a firm shake.

"Selah," he repeats to himself in a softer tone.

Testing it on his tongue, savoring it. I feel goosebumps erupt throughout my body at the sound of my name on his lips.

Fuck.

"Did you move in recently? I've never seen you before."

"Yeah, I moved in about three months ago. I work from home and don't leave the house much."

He looks intrigued. "What got you out of the house tonight?"

"A date," I respond flatly.

"Wasn't a good one?"

I shake my head and say, "they never are."

The elevator stops on the sixth floor.

"That's me." I chuckle nervously.

I get off, take a few steps, and stop in my tracks. For some reason, I'm not ready to part with him just yet. *Weird.* Once he notices me, he holds the doors open and waits.

"I know you were just making conversation, but thanks for asking about my book. I know you're not going to read it." I stare down at my feet.

"You thought I was just saying that? You sold me. We'll discuss it when I see you again."

I look up at him with a playful smile.

"What makes you think you'll be seeing me again?"

He stares at me deadpan.

"You live here. I'll have the pleasure of running into you again."

I stifle a laugh.

"I suppose you're right about that. Not that a man could be right about anything."

"Of course not. I wouldn't dream of being right," he responds sarcastically with a smile. "Have a good night."

"You too, *Greyson*." I add extra emphasis on his name again.

He takes a step back and reduces his grip on the door.

"See you around, Selah. I hope to hear you calling me *Grey* sometime soon." He flashes a kilowatt smile before the elevator doors close.

My eyes widen as I stand there for a moment processing that encounter.

This man.

Greyson.

Once I'm inside my apartment, I sink to the floor, holding my knees. My cat, Peach, saunters up to me, rubbing her head against my legs and meowing loudly. I remove my shoes and lean up against the door while she snuggles up to me.

Home.

I text the group chat, telling them that I made it back safely. I fully intended to have a good cry once I returned, but I don't feel the urge anymore. Greyson's words replay in my head.

I'd like to know what captivates you.

I wanted to earn your gaze.

I hope to hear you calling me Grey sometime soon.

I wonder when I'll run into Greyson again.

Maybe I won't throw in the towel just yet.

4
brunch games

Selah

Brooklyn, NY | September 3, 2023

WEEKLY BRUNCH always serves as a much-needed reset to get through the upcoming week. The girls can't wait for the juicy details about my recent *SoulBlend* date—even if there were just strikes and no home runs. Since we all had dates this week, we're participating in the "brunch games." The rules are simple: talk about your bad date or hookup, the table votes for the worst date, and the winner eats for free. It's become an interesting tradition among us. Fortunately, I'm not the only one dating. We all are, except Audrey. She successfully found a book boyfriend out in the wild, and she restored our faith. We've all been unlucky in our romantic endeavors but are still suckers for a good love story. So, it was only fitting that we named our book club "Hapless In Love."

Our founder, Audrey, is a multitude of things. More than meets the eye describes her best. She's the big sister, the eldest at thirty-four, and a chaotic Sagittarius. She's more known for being a billionaire hotel heiress and successful event planner, doubling as a social butterfly. Far from a party animal but can throw one hell of a party. She'll often throw an event, make sure everything is running smoothly, and leave early to protect her peace.

In her twenties, Audrey got into a bit of trouble for not keeping her hands to herself. And by not keeping her hands to herself, I mean, she was breaking people's bones in broad daylight.

Allegedly.

She gave absolutely no fucks, and if *you* started it, she *finished* it. Sometimes, in public with witnesses.

Allegedly.

The only reason I can talk about this now is because she got off multiple times. I should mention that her boyfriend, Roman, who also goes by 'Rome,' is a defense attorney and a damn good one. This behavior led to Rome convincing her family that she needed a bodyguard. That's where Eric came in. While she's *very* capable of handling herself, it's for the best.

Eric is quiet about his life before moving to New York, which I can relate to. He's been Audrey's bodyguard for the past four years, and they're inseparable. I do wonder if he ever gets lonely, though. I know he takes his job seriously, but I hope one day he gets his own happily ever after too. Reading romance is amazing, but eventually, you start to wonder if your main character moment will ever come along. I can't be the only one who feels that way.

Neither of them will say it, but they're like siblings. Not that she needs any more brothers; Avery and August keep her busy. She also has an older brother she refuses to talk about. We know that he lives in Chicago, they don't get along, and he owns *Blood Orange*, our favorite brunch spot.

Speaking of *Blood Orange*, we're seated on the patio, enjoying the last few days of summer before fall swoops in and the darkness that accompanies it. I don't enjoy the colder months, but I can't complain too much as someone who's lived in states with terrible winters. What concerns me most about the season change is Francesca. She seems to be in better spirits than before.

The anniversary of her dad's passing is approaching, and I've noticed her drawing back. She would fight every battle alone, and we're just not the kind of friends to let that happen.

Our co-founder, Francesca, better known as "Chess", is our resident wild child from Staten Island. She and Audrey met a while back and started the book club. She'll be turning thirty-two soon, and she's our lover girl Libra. Chess is fascinating and an excellent storyteller. That has a lot to do with the fact that she graduated from Columbia with a master's in journalism. She's now a hairstylist who owns *Chessboard*, a popular salon in Brooklyn, along with her sister Evangeline.

When she's not at work, she plays around. That's precisely where her nickname came from, after Audrey's favorite game. Chess loves game night and wouldn't miss it for the world. Her competitive side comes out in full force. And if we're playing Monopoly, all bets are off. Seeing her win is hilarious because she has a money gun to make it rain Monopoly money on us. The cleanup is annoying, but we all pitch in. Plus, it's worth it to see her light up over her favorite board game, especially after all that's happened.

When her dad passed last year, she lost her spark. Just recently, I've seen her smiling a bit more, and it doesn't seem forced. Then again, as someone accustomed to putting on a brave face, I keep a close eye on her. Having her birthday so close to the anniversary and the holidays is just an awful time. I'm surprised to hear she went on a date this week and am hoping it was a good one. Chess could use a fucking break.

"So, I met him on *SoulBlend*. We agreed to meet and get drinks after work, and after hitting it off, we decided to go back to his place. We're hooking up, and everything's fine until I start hearing a squeaking noise. It wasn't the bedsprings. This was different."

"Oh, shit," I say nervously.

"Just wait," she says with a chuckle. "I stop hearing it, and we change positions. We get back to it, still having a good time.

A great time, actually. I grab a pillow to put my face in and scream a bit. Then I feel a light tugging on my hair, which I don't mind, so I think nothing of it at first. But the tugging continues, and where it's being tugged doesn't make sense for how he's positioned behind me. Since I'm bent over, I can look around from there, and I do. To my surprise, I find exactly what is yanking on my hair, and it was…um…a tiny foot."

"What?" Audrey exclaims.

She takes a deep breath. "Hold on. I don't want to get sick."

"Take your time," Eric urges, scooting his chair to our table.

She takes sips of water before she continues.

"It was a tiny rodent foot. It was a rat in his bed, but it wasn't a typical New York rat. It wasn't *Ratatouille. It* was more like Ravioli. He was on the bed walking across my hair when his foot got tangled in it.

I screamed so loud, and the idiot thought that since I had been screaming before, it was because of him, but no. I couldn't get much out other than the word *rat*, so I just yelled that and froze. Scared if I moved too much, it would bite me. So, he stills while he's inside me and says, 'Oh, that's just my pet rat, Martell.'"

"Oh no," I whisper.

"I tell him I'm going home, and he makes no attempt to pull out. So, I grab the clump of hair and shake it gently to free Ravioli. He scurries away, and I resist the urge to barf because I had my face in that pillow, and this rat was walking all over it *and* the bed at his leisure. Pet or not, I don't give a shit. He had company over and should've mentioned it. I turn around and tell the guy who's still inside me, 'you have two seconds to pull out, or I will dislocate your jaw.' I heard him gasp, and he pulled out immediately."

"Oh. This was a WWAD situation," Dayanara says.

"Absolutely," she agrees.

WWAD stands for "What would Audrey Do?"

Anytime we need to be brave, she comes to mind.

"He's throwing on boxers and apologizing profusely while I'm getting dressed. I zero in on the floor to make sure I don't step on it, but I don't see it anywhere. All I know is I can't get out of there fast enough. Once I find my purse, I take off and head straight home to shower. It was all I could think of," she says with a chuckle.

Eric bursts out laughing, and we join him.

I notice Chess' tattooed hands beside me are rubbing the condensation from her glass onto her ripped jeans. She's wearing a coral-cropped tank that compliments her tan olive skin and displays the tattooed sleeve on her right arm. Her long, dark hair is pulled into an elegant updo with curtain bangs framing her face.

"I don't know whether to laugh or cry," I say.

"Evangeline couldn't stop laughing when I told her," she says before taking another sip from her mimosa.

"You're up," she says over her shoulder.

"I'm not sure how I can follow that, but I'll try," Dayanara says as she moves her curls out of her face.

Dayanara is the newest addition to our friend group, the youngest of us at twenty-six and a Scorpio. She's a tattoo artist from the Bronx, and like me, she started over in Manhattan after a bad breakup. She joined our book club last summer and recommends great authors. So naturally, we couldn't stop talking about books and are all friends now.

There's never a dull moment with her, and she brings a lot of laughs, giving Eric a run for his money. She also loves good pranks, won't turn down a dare, and is no stranger to getting in trouble, and we don't judge 'cause we've all done stupid shit. She will pull up anytime, anyplace if you need her, and she'll wait up until she knows we've all made it home safely. I've never met anyone quite like her. She prefers to be called 'Daya,' and how we all met is a hilarious story that I won't be sharing until the statute of limitations wears off. If anyone asks, we met when she tattooed us. It's a believable lie if Audrey doesn't tell it. She only gets tattooed by her cousins, and everyone knows it.

"My night starts off similar to yours," she says to Chess. "We met on *SoulBlend* and agreed to a hookup, but I swear this guy misunderstands the concept. He looks at me the whole night like he's planning the rest of our lives together. The sex isn't bad. He's doing a bit too much with the romance, but I'm not judging. I get irritated when he grabs me to cuddle after and immediately falls asleep holding me," she says with a huff.

We're on the edge of our seats because cuddling is a no-no for her. She hates it. We don't know why, but she does.

"I'm stuck in his grip, and he's snoring hard in my ear. My blood is boiling. Eventually, he rolls over, and I climb out of the bed to get dressed. I don't make a sound. I'm tiptoeing down the stairs, and you know what happens? This loud, deep-ass bark from the pits of hell roars through the fucking house, and it scares the fuck out of me. I hold in a scream and can't see shit because it's dark. I use the flashlight on my phone and find his dog staring at me at the foot of the stairs. I wouldn't even call it a dog. Marshall is a dog—that *thing* has done time at Riker's. Anyway, he was so loud that he woke the guy up, and he caught me trying to escape. I froze on the steps because I wasn't going to try walking past that thing."

The table erupts in laughter, and Daya can't even keep a straight face.

"Holy shit," Eric wheezes.

"Fucking loudmouth Doberman. At least my dog is quiet," she grumbles. "Anyway, he wakes him up, and it's awkward, okay? I let him down easy 'cause I'm leaving. I was very clear about it being a hookup. He handles it well and goes back to bed after reassuring me the dog is friendly. Once the shock wears off, I realize he's a cute little menace. Still a snitch, though. He even licks my hand when I pass him to walk out the door," she adds with an eye roll.

"He wanted you to be his new mommy," Chess teases.

She covers her face and shakes her head. "Who's next?"

I tell them all about my hibachi hell date, starting with the shrimp catching and the egg on my foot. I tell them about him ordering my well-done steak, rapping at the table, and calling me his ex's name all night.

Then he had the audacity to assume we'd be going out again and tried to kiss me at the end of the night. He ended up with six strikes instead of three because I couldn't bring myself to get up and leave. I didn't want to hurt his feelings, and I let him down relatively easily compared to what he deserved. Then he went on to request the funds for my share of the bill because I was being a 'bitch.'

By the looks on their faces, I think I may have won this week. However, I don't want a pity vote, and Chess had it worse. Eric stopped laughing a while ago and looks like he's ready to pay Keith a visit once brunch is over. He always sits at another table close by, letting us have Aud to ourselves. Then he'll tell us not to disturb him while he's reading, but he'll jump into our conversations anyway. By the end of brunch, we all moved around to make room for his chair. You've gotta love him.

"Ready to vote for our winner?" Audrey asks the table.

Everyone nods and says 'Selah' in unison.

I won't argue with that.

5
the dreaded 'v-word'

Selah

Manhattan, NY | September 6, 2023

I'VE SET up my iPad on my island, along with my usual supplies for therapy—tissues, water, a notepad and a pen. I sit and stare at the clock as I wait for the call. I think of what's happened over the last week and what I'd like to discuss today. Moments later, Dr. Garnett's name flashes on the screen, and I swipe to answer. She appears with a soft smile. Her burgundy hair is styled in a short, layered bob with a side bang. When she reaches up to adjust her square-framed glasses, I notice how her olive blouse compliments her brown skin.

It was important for me to find a fellow Black woman as a therapist. I wanted to open up to someone who looked like me and would have a better understanding of my daily challenges as a Black woman.

"Good Afternoon, Selah. How are you feeling today?"

"I'm feeling better, Doc. It was an okay week. I had a bad date, so I won the brunch games, met some neighbors, and made no progress on my list."

"What about the date was bad?"

"Everything. It was awful, and I didn't leave when I

should've. The cook dropped a raw egg on my foot. My date couldn't pronounce my name and eventually started calling me his ex's name. He refused to order what I wanted, so he ordered for me. He didn't have a job and is a rapper who sent me his music once I told him where I worked. He interrupted me whenever I spoke and got six strikes." I let out a resigned sigh.

She starts jotting down notes before she looks back into the camera.

"It sounds like you weren't comfortable at any point of the date. You implemented the strike system for these exact situations. To have an excuse to remove yourself. Take a moment to think about that."

I think about it, and I'm not sure what it was about this date that made me feel stuck. It was as if everything I'd been working toward left me in that moment. It returned when I got angry at the end of the night.

"Simple answer. I'm still people-pleasing. I'm struggling with taking control of situations and removing myself when I'm uncomfortable because I'm still considering everyone's feelings over my own."

"Did you stay the entire time?"

I nod. "At the end of the date, he called me 'Sara,' tried to kiss me, and suggested that I'd be paying the next time. I finally got angry and found my voice."

"How did that make you feel?"

"Not as good as I expected. Probably because I should've spoken up sooner. When I left the date, I was disappointed, mostly with myself, and I was hurt. He even Venmoed me for my meal because I was a 'bitch.' His words. It felt like a sick joke by how much worse it got. I just wanted to go home so I could cry. I even contemplated deleting the *SoulBlend* app."

"Did you?"

I shake my head. "I got distracted when my Uber pulled up in front of my building. I realized how close I was to the comfort of my home, and I could let it all out. I grabbed my e-reader to get a little further into my book and hide my face if I looked like I was going to start crying."

"You know, we often talk about the 'strong Black woman trope,' and when you hide your vulnerability, you're adhering to it. What would happen if you let go and allowed yourself to just be 'Selah?' Feel whatever you were feeling in that moment?"

Fuck.

Here come the tears.

She always clocks me.

I love and hate her for it.

"I don't know how to let go publicly as I do in private. I'm not comfortable doing that. The last time I let anyone see me break down…I had that panic attack. I met Audrey and Eric in that elevator."

"No consequences came from that. You made friends, and that led to a lot more. You allowed yourself to be vulnerable with no regard for what anyone around you thought, and how did it feel?"

"It was embarrassing. The only reason I didn't have time to harp on it was because I had more important things to worry about than what two strangers thought about me crying in public."

She jots down more in her notebook, and I know that means we'll be digging deeper into that one.

Great.

"We're going to circle back and dive further into that, but I'd like to cover everything you mentioned before we run out of time. Now, did you allow yourself to cry when you got home?"

"No. I didn't feel the need to once I settled in."

"What happened in between the walk from the car to your door?"

"Greyson," I say in a low voice.

She raises a brow. "You've never mentioned him. Who is he?"

"A neighbor I met in the elevator."

"How was meeting Greyson?"

"Annoying at first, he interrupted my reading to talk to me. *Intentionally*. I was rude and didn't give him eye contact initially, but when I did, I was…stunned. He's attractive. I'll say that," I add with an eye roll.

She stares deadpan over her glasses. "What else?"

"It was a positive interaction, and he was amusing. He inquired about the book I was reading and said he'd like to discuss it when we saw each other again."

She gives me a look that says '*girl*.'

"So, when I got home, I didn't want to cry anymore. I read my book until I fell asleep."

"And have you seen him again?"

"No. I haven't left my apartment since Sunday besides getting the mail and taking out the trash."

She looks down to scribble something in her notebook.

"And you said you met new people this week. Who else?"

"Estelle. A neighbor who lives on my floor. She's an older Black woman who's growing out her gray, just like my mom. Movie star gorgeous, and I have no idea how old she is. She's got a big personality, and she's hilarious. I learned she grew up in St. Louis too, but she's lived in New York for the past twenty years."

"How did you meet?"

"I got some of her mail by accident, and I brought it to her. She answered the door with a wine glass, looking like she'd had a rough day. She was expecting that card and thought it was lost in the mail. Before her husband passed, he wrote her a bunch of love letters and arranged for them to be sent in the future on their anniversaries and birthdays. He got really sick a few years ago and said he didn't want her to forget how much he loved her when he was gone." I pause as tears start to fall, and I snatch a tissue to dab at them. I take a deep breath before I continue. "She told me that, and I sobbed on her doorstep."

"I understand why." She nods.

"Yeah. She felt bad for making me cry, so she invited me in

for wine and cookies. Then we watched the *Housewives* marathon for a bit." I chuckle.

"It's good to hear that you are finally settling in and meeting your neighbors. I would like to challenge you a bit. I don't think you'll like this, but I hope you'll give it a shot."

"Okay."

She sits up in her chair and adjusts her glasses. "I'd like for you to try immersion therapy soon. Your dates are a version of this. You are still fearful of dating and relationships, yet you are trying to connect with people. I know the goal is to find partners for things on your list, but it matters no less.

"I know how you feel about working in the office, and I understand it's optional. However, I'd like to suggest an experiment. How would you feel about working from a coffee shop for a few hours once or twice a week? Just to get out of the house and be around other people?"

I frown and exhale as I consider it.

"I don't love the way it sounds, but I will give it a try."

The timer sounds, signaling the end of our session. I couldn't be happier because I want to climb in bed before I try to work on anything I learned today.

"Let's recap. What is your homework for the next week?"

"Follow the rules of the strike system. Allow myself to be vulnerable. Try working outside the house once a week and meet new people."

"Sounds good to me. I'll see you next week, same time. Take care, Selah."

"You too, Doc."

The screen goes black as the session ends. I take the tissues with me as I head to my bedroom. I call out for Peach to see if she wants to join me. Therapy is good, but I won't deny how much it takes out of me. I forgot to bring up my recent nightmares, but I'll make a note of it for next week.

6
the big, red dog

Greyson

Manhattan, NY | September 9, 2023

IT'S BEEN a week since my run-in with my new neighbor, Selah. She wasn't kidding when she said she doesn't leave the house much. It's not like I've been waiting, hoping to run into her, but let's just say that Cliff and I have gone on walks more frequently than usual. Not that he's complaining. We're on our way back from the neighborhood dog park. We're enjoying these last few days of summer before the leaves start to change and the nights get shorter.

I finished the book she was reading the other night and prepared an elevator pitch for when I saw her again. I know she was being shy and didn't believe that I would read it. I need to let her know that I not only read it, but I enjoyed it. Lilith Keene is a genius, and I hope that she's finished reading it already because I need to talk about this with somebody. I'm not expecting us to have a book club, but I've never read romance before and was pleasantly surprised. I'd love another recommendation if she's up for it.

I don't know why I've put so much thought into what to say

when I see her again, but I won't dig too deep into that. I'd be lying if I said that Aileen's comments at the engagement party aren't still ringing in my head. I've toyed with the idea of updating my profile ever since, but I haven't even looked at it until today. While we were at the dog park, I sat while Cliff played and stared at my profile for—I don't even know how long, but I was interrupted when my mom called. We chatted for a while, and I'm glad she didn't ask about my love life. After we disconnected, I thought more about it and decided that updating my profile wasn't a good idea. Neither would be wasting a woman's time who's on my app hoping to find her perfect match.

On the way home, I'm yanked from my thoughts, literally, when Clifford starts pulling on his leash. I look to where he's dragging me, and I notice a woman strolling up the block, her curls whipping in the wind as she approaches my building. We're a good distance, and I'm thankful for his harness, otherwise, he'd knock that woman down. I stop walking, and he gets the idea, slowing down in front of me. I want her to walk freely without being bombarded by my giant dog.

She moves her loose curls out of her face as she greets our doorman with a soft smile. They speak briefly before he lets her inside. Her tank top shows off the tattooed sleeves on her arms, and her ripped jeans reveal peeks of ink on her legs. I've never seen this woman before. We're not far behind her, and once we're in the lobby, he is still dragging me toward her, and I stifle my laughter.

Cliff can be a real handful sometimes. While he's very friendly and loves attention, he'll accept it from anyone, although he prefers it from women. He's a great wingman whenever I've needed him to be, but he doesn't flirt for my benefit. He sees potential friends in anyone he can smell another dog on.

She's waiting near the elevator and rifling through her tote bag as we get closer. I stand a good distance beside her, but Cliff has other plans. He eyes her curiously, and once he sniffs her shoes, he succeeds at getting her attention. She retrieves lip balm from her bag and applies it, smiling down at him.

"Hi, Mister. You're not shy at all."

His tail wags excitedly.

She eyes the leash and looks over to me, asking if she can pet him. I nod assuredly. She bends her short frame to pet his head as we wait for the elevator.

"What's his name?"

I turn toward her, watching their interaction. "Clifford."

She looks to me and quips, "Because he's a big, red dog?"

"Exactly," I say with a smile.

She adds, "Well, I have a Dalmatian named Marshall. So, I ain't judging."

That makes me laugh.

"It's nice to meet another dog owner who doesn't take naming them too seriously."

The elevator dings, and a few of my neighbors get off, greeting me and Cliff as they pass through the lobby. Unfortunately, none of them are Selah.

It would've been nice to run into her again.

She gets on first, and we follow, standing opposite her. I press my floor and quickly check my phone. The doors close, and we ascend. She's looking through her bag again and takes out a book, placing it under her arm as she continues sifting through it. She retrieves her phone and fires a text before slipping it into her pocket. I get a quick peek at the book before she drops it back in her bag. It's the same one Selah was reading and that I just finished.

"You read Lilith Keene?" I ask her.

She wrinkles her face in confusion and asks, "*you* read Lilith Keene?"

"Well, I just read that book you got there. I saw my neighbor reading it and thought I'd check it out. Finished the other day."

She gives me an inquisitive look. "And what were your thoughts?"

I put my hands in my pockets, leaning against the wall as I answer. "It was a lot funnier than I'd expected a romance novel to be. I expected banter and angst, so I was happy it had plenty. The characters were lovable, and it was well-written. This book made me more interested in the romance genre, and I'm excited to read more from this author in the future."

"And what about the spice?"

"I enjoyed it more than I thought I would. I was hoping I'd run into my neighbor again so I could talk to her about it, but we seem to keep missing each other."

"Hmm. This neighbor of yours, does she have long, curly hair? Not much of a talker? Always has an e-reader in her hand?"

I tap my chin. "You forgot captivating, but yeah, that's her."

She gasps dramatically. "How could I forget to mention she's a fucking baddie? I should've led with that."

"I would've caught on sooner if you had."

She chuckles. "I'm about to see her at book club. Anything I should pass along?"

"If you could let her know that I read the book and I'd like another recommendation, that'd be cool."

The elevator dings, and the doors open.

She says, "I can do that. And who should I say this message is from?"

"Grey," I say, holding the doors open.

"It was nice meeting you. I'm Daya."

"It was nice meeting you, too."

"And it was nice meeting *you*," she says to Cliff with a quick head rub as she exits the car. She waves and proceeds down the hall.

The doors close, and I say to Cliff, "good boy. You're getting another treat."

He stares lovingly while I rub his ears.

Clifford's been a pretty good wingman today, and what were the odds of that?

Now she'll be looking for me, and I won't be hard to find.

See you soon, Selah.

7
the hapless in love book club

Selah

Manhattan, NY | September 9, 2023

FOR ME TO BE SUCH A HOMEBODY, I secretly love hosting gatherings. Since I've settled into my new place and made it my own, this will be my second time hosting a book club meeting. I found some new recipes on Pinterest and got some ideas to go with the theme for our book of the month. I've put together a drink menu based on the main characters and recreated a recipe that they made in the book.

I jotted down some good questions for discussion and I'm really looking forward to hearing what everyone else felt while reading this book. We sent memes and gif reactions in the group chat as we read along but agreed to save our notes for our next club meeting. I stocked up on tissues just in case. Oftentimes, tears can flow once we start unpacking whatever stood out to us or anything that made us feel seen. I came prepared with this book because the representation was unlike anything I'd ever read before.

Chess is usually first to arrive, so I was surprised when I answered the door to see her with Eric and Audrey. I open the door wider to let them in, and when they pass me, I notice that Chess isn't holding her motorcycle helmet. If she isn't at her salon or with family, she's on that motorcycle *anytime* the weather permits. I admire her for being the definition of work hard, play hard.

"You didn't ride here? It's a nice day out."

"I know," she pouts and settles in. "After the week I had, I needed to drink." She draws out the word while wrapping her arms around me in a hug.

"We're gonna take her home," Eric mentions, making it a group hug as he squishes us together.

"Let me know when you're done hogging Selah," Audrey says with a chuckle.

When we pull apart, everyone helps me set up the food spreads and make the cocktails. I made mocktails for Eric, per his request. He said designated drivers should be able to have complicated drinks, too. Chess made focaccia, and Audrey brought freshly baked cookies, which I am practically salivating over. Daya is on her way with this popcorn that I'm obsessed with.

I think back to my first few meetings with the girls. I won't lie, I was skeptical at first. Figured the girls would be stuffy and mean, but it was the exact opposite. The food was the main selling point, then I met everyone and was taken aback by how welcoming they were. It also helped that the monthly picks were absolute bangers. So, I kept coming back and started attending outings with them because hanging out once a month didn't suffice. For the first time in my life, I felt like I made friends who genuinely saw me. Not the shell of a person I became to survive, but who I was beneath it all. Books brought me to them.

Books and IKEA.

No one will ever believe that, but it's the truth. A soft knock releases me from my thoughts. I turn around to see Daya coming through the door.

"I've arrived, and I have the *dulce de leche* popcorn," she says as she removes the large bowl from her oversized tote bag and settles in. How she can find anything in that big ass bag is beyond me. She could carry a small dog around in there. Hell, Audrey's small enough to fit in there.

Eric makes his way to her in quick strides. "Just the woman I wanted to see."

"Oh sureee. I missed you too, big boy," she says in a sultry voice.

When she hands him the bowl, he turns on his heels. "You know if you start being nice to me…you better watch it," he says with a chuckle as he walks into the kitchen.

She rolls her eyes behind his back and sets down her bag. She heads over to give me a big hug with an extra squeeze. When we separate, she wears a devious grin.

"I just had an interesting conversation. I met this fine ass man in the lobby. I mean *fine* and I'm pretty sure he read this month's club pick just to talk to you. He's got the cutest dog, too."

I recall the elevator encounter. He said he'd read it, and we'd discuss it whenever he saw me again.

He actually read it.

I haven't seen him with a dog, but she couldn't be talking about anyone else.

"Are you talking about Greyson?"

"Oh, Greyson. You're so formal. He likes you," she says in a singsong voice.

I wave my hand and grab my drink.

"Girl, please. I met him a week ago in the elevator. That man hardly knows me."

"He described her as captivating," she says to Chess and her eyebrows shoot up. "We're going to circle back to what happened in this elevator momentarily. The man read a romance novel just to talk to you. He's interested. Even said he's a fan of Lilith Keene and can't wait for her next book."

"I think I like him already," Chess adds.

Audrey blurts, "Meeting a fine man in an elevator was not mentioned in the group chat this week. Why not?"

"There was nothing to tell."

The girls all collectively give me a look that screams *bullshit*.

"Who is this fucking guy? I need to do a background check on him," Eric says.

"I just said it's nothing and relax. You don't do background checks on any of my *SoulBlend* dates."

He begins humming as he walks backward, still facing me when he asks, "Audrey, what guy lives here that you'd consider attractive that has a dog?"

She takes a break from setting up the charcuterie board to wash her hands. She looks up for a moment. "Hell, if I know. I just own the building. Avery's more involved with this property than I am, but the property manager's name is Harlan."

"Does he live on site? Let's pay him a visit. Surely there's some records on this guy with the dog, and you have a key to the office."

"He does live here, but we're not bothering him. We're going to talk about books tonight, and you are *off duty* anyway." She whips her head around and flings her wet hands at him before grabbing a towel. "Go find something else to do. You're stressing me out."

"Fine." He scoffs, grabbing a handful of food from the board she's preparing, and stuffs his mouth full. When he swallows, he says, "This book was fucking nasty. I was hard as a *building* reading it."

We all burst into laughter.

"See what I gotta deal with?" Audrey says, shaking her head as she resumes plating the snacks.

Eric is nothing like what he seems at first glance. He presents himself as a grumpy and quiet person professionally, but he really lets loose when he's comfortable, like me. I've found him to be a real wildcard, like Chess. You also can never predict what he's going to say next, like Audrey. A bad idea often sounds good, like Daya. He can always cheer you up with a laugh, a good time and is fiercely protective, which sums up the whole group. It makes perfect sense why he fits right in.

"I'm excited for us to talk about this book," Audrey says, bringing over the charcuterie board she's been working on in the kitchen. Eric is close behind with more snacks and spreads to set on my coffee table. Chess and Daya come in with their drinks while Audrey sets up the slideshow. We are *that* kind of book club, and we all contribute. We have somehow managed to make slideshows both entertaining and educational while talking about smut.

It's a talent, really.

"Is Rome coming?" I ask Audrey.

"He'll be here. We read this one together. Well, he read it me with the narrator voice," she adds, blushing.

Audrey's long-time boyfriend, Rome, is a hot-shot criminal defense lawyer. One of the best in the country. When he's not working, he's busy being a book boyfriend, another role he enjoys very much. That's why he secretly loves playing narrator and insists on reading her books to her as often as he can.

He does have the voice for it.

Like Eric, he's an honorary member of the 'Hapless In Love Book Club.' As much as he pretends not to care, he hates missing meetings when he's stuck working on cases. He doesn't have a bunch of time to read our monthly picks, so he opts for the audiobooks while working and commuting. I can't imagine him doing either while maintaining a straight face. Eric sure as hell can't and reads in public, often at the office with Audrey, adjusting himself, turning red and everything. It's hilarious, and he'll just keep on reading.

A knock on the door sounds, I look up and it's Rome letting himself in.

"Sorry, I'm late. I had a meeting with the partners at the firm. Did I miss anything?"

"Not yet. We just started eating and setting up the slides."

"Good shit," he says as he gets settled, grabbing a seat on the sectional beside Audrey. He greets her with a peck and rests his hand on her thigh.

Eric dims the lights and the slideshow starts. Lilith Keene's name flashes across the screen with a photo of the book cover.

Audrey kicks it off. "Welcome, Hapless Lovers. Thank you all for coming. Tonight, we'll be going over our club pick for August. Lilith Keene's debut and new favorite of mine. Last month, we dove into enemies-to-lovers territory with this workplace romance. Let's see what you rated it."

She flips through everyone's star ratings; I'm not surprised to see five stars from the whole club for this book. We usually start off serious, then get into the spice before crying. Currently, the memes in the slideshow have us laughing uncontrollably at the best dirty quotes. 'The Hapless In Love Book Club' slogan is: ***If it ain't got spice, no dice.***

I fucking love this book club and everyone in this room.

8
daylight

Greyson

Manhattan, NY | September 17, 2023

IT'S BEEN three weeks since I met Selah, and we only see each other in passing. I've been fortunate to run into her a few times while she picks up her mail or comes home. I've managed to get two more book recommendations from her since her friend, Daya, spread the word. I'm grateful because I've been traveling recently and had plenty of reading material.

I had a few gaps in my schedule this weekend, so I was able to catch two back-to-back weddings for my *SoulBlend* users in Jersey and Philly. I'm glad I brought my camera because there was some incredible scenery and I'd been itching to take some photos lately.

I used to find it awkward whenever I'd show up and they'd ask me to make a speech for the couple, but I come prepared now. I started keeping a few on deck in my notes app, so I fire away once they pass me the mic. My assistant, Hazel, had the idea for couples to include a note featuring their love story with their wedding invitations, which was absolutely genius.

Alex picked me up from the airport and we rode back to my apartment with Clifford. He always watches him when I go out of town. 'Uncle duties,' as he likes to call it. I can't wait to get home and take a nap because I've had my wedding fix for the fall. I crammed four weddings into two weekends. I took a few days off to recover, which I rarely do, but I'm hoping to find more reading material for the time being.

He parks on the street, and when I grab my bag from his trunk, I notice a familiar head of curly hair walking towards our building. My vision is blurred to everything around us and locked on her. She throws her head back with a boisterous laugh and smacks the shoulder of someone in front of her. That's when I see she's walking with someone. A man of tall stature and messy blond hair is carrying bags and walking into the lobby with her. She said she was dating, and I assume one of those dates went well.

My thoughts are interrupted by Alex calling me. I come around and he's waiting while Clifford sits beside him. His brows wrinkle in concern and I shake my head. I use my exhaustion as an excuse, which he seems to buy, but he may still grill me in private. We head towards my building and greet David on the way in, who always has a treat for Cliff. On the elevator ride up, Selah crosses my mind again. I quickly shrug off any assumptions since I hardly know her and shouldn't be concerned with her love life.

She's my neighbor and that's it.

My beautiful neighbor that I think about often.

My beautiful neighbor that I think about often seems to have a boyfriend.

My beautiful neighbor that I think about often seems to have a boyfriend, and is off limits now.

That's it.

9
coffee envy

Greyson

Manhattan, NY | September 26, 2023

LIKE CLOCKWORK, my mom calls right as I'm heading out the door. She insists on talking to me during my morning commute. It's a highlight of my day. She's so excited about the upcoming holiday because Henry and I will be visiting. Chuseok is Korean Thanksgiving, and we celebrate it in September or October, which is based on the lunar calendar. I'm looking forward to seeing my parents, though Dad and I aren't as close. I don't visit home as often now that things have really picked up at *SoulBlend* and my parents remind me every chance they get. I stop to grab a coffee before work. My favorite coffee shop, *Artie's*, is around the corner from the office, so I park there and walk over. I'm prepared to wait because the morning rush is no joke. There's no telling how long this may take, but it's all good. I've got time and I'm in no hurry.

When I step inside, it isn't any busier than normal. Everyone is coming and going for the most part. I usually don't bother looking around, but while I'm standing in line, I scan the shop—peeking to see what new baked goods they've got on display as I wait. I search over my shoulder at the cafe side, which is pretty empty aside from a few patrons.

I do a double take when I notice a very familiar head of dark curly hair seated with a laptop, presumably working. As I pay closer attention, I recognize the gold rings catching the light as she scrolls with her mouse. I don't get a good look at her face because her back is to me, but she's facing the window, and I hope that I can catch her reflection. Right when I think I'll get a good shot, she's leaning over on the opposite side to retrieve something from her bag beside her. I follow the movement, in the slouchy cropped sweater and jeans that hug her generous curves. That's when I observe her leg bouncing nervously under the table. She pulls AirPods from her bag and puts them in. Now facing forward, I see her reflection for a brief moment, and it's *her*.

What's she doing here?

I order my usual and a box of donut holes for us to share, since I've suddenly decided that having donuts and coffee with my neighbor is more important than getting to work on time. I've had the pleasure of having a few run-ins with her since we met. I check my calendar after, and I see that I don't have any meetings until after eleven. I didn't plan on being late today, but I feel like I should at least say something to her.

I don't even know if she's going to want to eat with me or even wants company. She seems to be working. I probably shouldn't.

I grab my order and swallow the urge to turn around and bolt as I trek toward her table. She doesn't notice me at first, as she is occupied with her work and is probably listening to something. When she glances up and locks eyes with me, her look of surprise shifts into a shy smile. We greet each other at the same time and nervously chuckle.

"I was just grabbing some coffee on my way into the office when I saw you. I wanted to say good morning and see if you had eaten already. I got some extra donut holes." I lower the container onto her table.

"Good morning, Greyson. That was nice of you. I'd love some."

She takes a donut and bites into it. The soft moan that escapes her tells me I made a good choice. She freezes, covering her mouth shyly, and I stifle a laugh.

"May I?" I ask, motioning to the seat beside her.

"Of course, sorry," she says while removing her AirPods.

"Don't be sorry. I said I had somewhere to be. What brings you here?"

"Oh, I'm working. I usually work from home, but I'm going to work in public once a week since my therapist is encouraging me to do 'immersion therapy.'"

"I can't say I've heard of that. I'd love to know more. If you don't mind telling me about it."

She shakes her head, waiting until she's finished chewing to answer.

"I don't mind. I'm inserting myself in situations that make me anxious and uncomfortable. As much as I've grown accustomed to working from home and away from people, I know it's not healthy to shut the world out. I do leave the house for dates and outings and I prefer working from home over the office. My therapist would like me to get acquainted with being around people who aren't my friends, family, and cat."

She looks down and titters, "Sorry, you didn't ask for all that."

I wrinkle my brow in confusion. I don't ever want her to feel uncomfortable around me. I run my thumb over her knuckles to comfort her. The touch feels like I grazed a hot coal. She looks up and her face softens.

I wonder if she feels this too.

"That makes sense. If it makes you feel any better, this is my favorite coffee shop and the sweets are fantastic."

She offers me a soft smile. "That does make me feel better. I'm going to do this for the first half of my day and head home for the rest."

"Sounds like a plan. You mind if I join you for a bit?"

"Not at all," she says, taking a sip of her tea.

I quickly text my assistant to inform her I'll be a little late and silence my phone. We talk about the morning traffic and how she's been since I last saw her. I decide not to ask about any dates she may have gone on or the guy I saw her with last week. That is none of my business.

When I share that I finished the books she recommended, she seems surprised. Then she quizzes me a bit to prove that I read it, and I pass with flying colors. She couldn't stop giggling through her questions, and her shyness is so cute. I ask for another recommendation, and she gives me one, warning me it's a 'spicy' one. Then she explains that means it's nasty.

"I know you're a nasty girl, but your secret is safe with me," I tease.

She rolls her eyes in response and chuckles to herself.

"I'm not deterred by anything 'nasty,' if anything, I'm more intrigued."

I lock eyes with her, and she quickly averts her gaze back to her screen, failing to hide her shy smile.

12

She dives back into her work and I respond to emails, occasionally stopping to indulge in my coffee as I try not to disturb her much. I don't mind the silence between us, it feels familiar. I watch her hands type loudly as I zero in on the tattoo on her right thumb. *Happier than ever.* It's as if my silence is bothersome when she stops abruptly as her hands hover over the keyboard. I see her glancing over at me in my peripheral when she quips, "were you ever taught that it's not polite to stare?"

I return her gaze. "I was just observing something."

"What were you observing?"

"Your tattoo."

Her eyes travel to it instantly.

"Oh." She lets out a breathy laugh and continues, "I feel like you're always eyeing this one. The others don't get much love."

"I noticed. I'll give them all my attention. Trust me."

She raises a brow. "That's a weird promise."

She directs her attention back to her screen.

"Is it? *Happier Than Ever*. What does that mean to you?"

She smiles softly. "Well, I am happier than ever, but it's actually a Billie Eilish song. Have you ever heard it?"

"I don't think so, but I'll check it out."

I sip my coffee, growing comfortable with the busy sounds of the cafe and her loud typing. I notice how she keeps trying to pretend I'm not here, but whenever I'm silent for too long, it makes her uncomfortable, and she makes conversation with me. This is the most I've heard her speak in weeks, and I'm enjoying it.

I'm not quite ready for this moment to end.

Who knows when I'll get another?

As if she could hear my thoughts, she reminds, "I thought you had somewhere to be."

When she reaches in the box for another donut hole, I purposely brush my hand over hers when I grab one. I keep my eyes locked on hers when I pop the donut in my mouth and chew slowly. Her gaze roams and stills on my lips, following my throat as I swallow.

So, she's bashful yet watches me eat as if she imagines something else on my tongue.

"It can wait," I respond with a shrug.

"Y-Your job can wait? For what exactly? You're just sitting here watching me."

"I'll let you think that's what I'm doing." I sip my coffee. "Yes, they can wait for me to get there. The day will go on."

She wears a questionable expression and goes right back to

typing. I don't miss the smile she's trying to hide as she keeps busy.

"Am I distracting you, Selah?"

She shakes her head as she scrolls her mouse.

"The other tattoos on your fingers, what do they mean? I noticed the one with your name, but the other one?"

She lifts her right ring finger to give me a closer look. "This is one of my newer tattoos. *Ctrl,* my favorite SZA album. It's been a soundtrack for navigating my twenties as a Black woman."

I listen intently as she explains. I love the way she lights up while talking about her tattoos. I'll ask until I've learned the story behind each one of them.

She brings her left index closer, which reads *Selah.*

"It's my name, but it's also a song by Emeli Sandé that I love. If you've caught on by now, all my tattoos are inspired by music."

"Noted." I nod with a smile that she returns before focusing on her tasks.

Whenever I've shown interest in something that's important to Selah, she's always so shocked. It's as if she has no idea how fascinating she really is. Something tells me there's a lot to learn from the songs behind these tales scribed on her skin. I pull out my phone to make a quick note for myself.

Happier Than Ever.

Ctrl.

Selah.

Listen to these immediately.

I look at the time and can't help but notice the messages from Hazel. She hasn't been blowing me up, but she's concerned because it's not like me to show up late. I respond, assuring her that I am fine and will be in shortly. I decide that I've avoided work long enough and should leave Selah to hers.

I enjoy the view of her scrunched brows as she concentrates, loudly typing and chewing on her lip while she reads along. My coffee is envious as I drink her in. I savor this moment and commit her to memory in case there isn't another opportunity to admire her this closely again. I reluctantly clear my throat to gain her attention, to which she peers up with those big brown eyes and in this moment, I don't want to leave.

"I should probably get going."

"Yeah. Probably. It's good to be employed," she says sarcastically. I chuckle and rise from my seat, grabbing my coffee cup. We do that thing again where we're both speaking at the same time. I'm saying goodbye, and I think she's talking about therapy.

I need to shut up and listen.

"I'm sorry," we say in unison before laughing awkwardly. I do a zip motion over my lips to give her the floor and she laughs silently.

"I was saying that I want my therapist to know I'm making an effort. I've been coming here every Tuesday morning. So, I might see you again."

"You will. Next week," I respond eagerly.

She nods. "Have a good day, Greyson. I hope you don't get in too much trouble for being late."

"I'll be fine. I hope you have an even better day. See you around," I say with a smile.

I shift on my heels, stopping at the counter to order a refill before I head out the door. When I look back on my way out, she waves.

My day is more than good. It may be too early to say that, but I don't care.

I pull up my notes for the music she mentioned. I open the *Kiwi Music App* and add the songs to a new playlist before heading into the office.

Next Tuesday.

10
glasses

Selah

Manhattan, NY | October 3, 2023

I'VE BEEN DOING this whole immersion therapy experiment for the past month, and it's been challenging. It wasn't so bad last week, though my handsome neighbor had something to do with that. He wasn't as annoying as I thought he'd be when he sat down. He was good company and calmed my nerves a lot. I breezed through the rest of my shift here, and the time flew by. I know he said he'd be back again today, but I won't get my hopes up. He seems like a busy guy, and I can't expect him to set aside time to sit with me in a cafe just because I have anxiety and it's a Tuesday.

I'm sure he has better things to do.

I brought him up in therapy again this week. Dr. Garnett was intrigued, to say the least. Everyone keeps making a big deal about this guy. He's just friendly and very attractive. Correction: he's *the* most attractive man I've ever seen in my life, but that doesn't mean I should pursue him. He's also my neighbor. Why doesn't anyone else think it's a bad idea?

I grab some tea and my headphones to set up my workspace

in the cafe for the morning, queuing up a playlist for when my anxiety is high before logging on for the day. I remind myself this is temporary, and I just need to endure a few hours before I can return home. I've done this three times before today and can do it again. Eventually, it'll get easier.

I carefully sip my hot tea and review my agenda for the day. As I sift through my morning to-dos and my music starts to calm me, I check the clock on the screen and consider that a lot can happen in a week. If he needed to bail or reschedule, it's not like he had my number to give me a heads-up.

Should I have given him my number?

I tell myself it's okay and that even my therapist would agree that it's not healthy to get attached to someone to avoid expressing your emotions. I am fully capable of coping on my own and working here without having an anxiety attack, whether my neighbor shows up or not.

Twenty minutes pass and I accept he got busy or forgot. The more I think about it, the more I feel silly for suggesting this man should come and sit with me in the morning when he should be at work. He was already late last week, and I worry that he may have gotten in trouble for it even though he was all nonchalant like he owned the place.

What if he got fired?

What if he lost his job because he sat here with me?

Oh my God.

A shadow looms in front of my table. I peer up slowly, and it's none other than Greyson. I bite my lip to prevent from grinning like an idiot, but he doesn't.

"Excuse me, Miss? Are you expecting someone?" he asks.

He has his coffee and donuts just like last time, with a smile that doesn't waver. Next thing I know, I'm smiling back.

"I am, actually."

"What a shame. I guess I'll have to share these donuts with another beautiful neighbor of mine." He makes a show of looking around and frowns. "I'm afraid I don't have any others and your date seems to have stood you up. I think we should save each other the embarrassment and sit together. What do you think?"

We stare each other down and I'm the first to break. His gaze is too intense for whatever is happening right now. I look down and cover my face with my hand.

"Don't be shy now," he teases.

I chuckle. "Fine. You can join me. You're better looking than the guy I was expecting anyway. And I won't tell Estelle you said you don't have other beautiful neighbors."

He makes a show of wiping his forehead and sits beside me.

"I owe you one for Estelle. She'd kick my ass." He pauses and raises his brow. "So, I look better than the other guy? Good to know," he adds with a wink. I quickly take a bite of a donut and hide my smile behind it.

"Are you unemployed?" I blurt and cover my mouth with the half-bitten donut.

So much for not embarrassing myself.

He gives a quizzical look, and says, "quite the opposite. Why would you ask?"

"I was worried you got in trouble for being late last week."

He leans back in his seat and crosses his arms.

"You were worried about me? I didn't get in trouble. I promise."

I observe him when he's not looking and quickly wave my mouse to make edits to my draft, finishing the donut with my free hand. I notice him moving, and I peer over to see him pull an oval case from his pocket and slip on a pair of black-framed glasses. I didn't know it was possible for this man to look even more sexy but fuck.

I need a water hose to drink from right now since this tea just isn't doing it for me.

I clear my throat to grab his attention.

"Would you excuse me for a moment?"

He nods, and I practically fly out of my chair, quickly shuffling my feet toward the counter to get some ice water.

When the barista hands me the cup, I immediately thank her and resist the urge to dump it over my head and ask for a refill.

I take slow, deep breaths on the trip back to the table and when I pass Greyson, his scent hits me and I want to scream. I feel like I'm ovulating right now and it's not a good time. I hate that I'm even considering this, but the crippling anxiety sounds a lot better than being aggressively horny in public.

I take my seat and sip my water so I don't choke because that would be embarrassing. He points at my cup and tells me he would've taken care of it. I argue, of course, because that's what I do. I'm taken aback when he assures me that if I need *anything,* I can call on him. I'd say he meant it in a literal sense when he pulls out his phone and suggests we exchange numbers but then repeats himself and puts extra emphasis on *'anything.'* I'm pretty sure I just felt my leg shake in response to that. I offer a shy smile and save his contact under *Smell Good Man.* Acts of service is my love language, and I think he should shut up.

He should shut up right now.

Shut up, Greyson.

As if he can hear my thoughts, he gets quiet and starts typing something on his phone. I take a break from my draft and send a quick message to my team via chat before I resume working. I open a message from Skye, my work bestie, and can't help but chuckle. She sent a funny meme before Greyson joined me. She always knows when I could use a laugh, a snack, or a distraction. She lives in Houston, and I don't know what I'd do without her. Black women need other Black women in their lives, especially in corporate America. If nobody here understands me, she does, and I couldn't be more grateful for our friendship.

I send a laugh reaction and slyly inform her of who's beside me. When I mentioned last week's run-in, she was curious if we'd have another.

ME

GIRL.

You remember that neighbor I told you about?

SKYE

The man who's been reading romance novels to impress you?

I've been waiting on an update.

ME

That's the one.

He just showed up at the cafe.

SKYE

He came?? OOH.

Would you look at the time?

I gotta go, Charlotte! The exterminator is here!

While the girls call me Cobweb Queen, she calls me Charlotte for that same reason. I exhale a laugh. I swear if she ever met the book club, she'd fit right in. While I don't love our regular off-site events for work, I will say being able to hang out with her in person is the best part.

ME

LOL I cannot stand you.

I close our chat and remember to add a few topics to the agenda for this afternoon's meeting. Greyson's been quiet, but he's busy with something on his phone, so I won't bother him. He looks really fucking good today and fighting the urge to stare is becoming unbearable. He's wearing a black form-fitting turtleneck and his sinewy muscles have sidetracked me enough. I avert my eyes, but I fear he caught me when he breaks the silence.

"Do you have a 'work husband?'"

I snort and shake my head. "Hell no."

"Boyfriend?"

"No," I respond with a head shake, purposely avoiding eye contact.

I wonder why he asked that.

I'm responding to a message from a teammate when I'm enveloped by his scent. A soft 'hmm' follows that sounds awfully close. I spy him peering at my screen.

"No sexy spreadsheets today?" he asks.

"What?"

"I've seen you do things to spreadsheets that make my pants tight."

I burst out laughing.

"Sir, please."

"Sir?" he asks in a gravelly tone and peers at me over his glasses.

I cannot take this.

He attempts another stare down with me, but he's looking over those damn glasses and I won't make it. I will try though. I fail again while smiling at his handsome face.

Once he wins the stare-down, he changes the subject, telling me how he had done some traveling recently and that he was able to get a lot of reading done while he was away. We discussed the books I recommended to him and what stood out. I love that he reads my book suggestions and unpacks his theories with me. I gave him two more recommendations to start on and warned him that they were spicier than what he's been reading. To which he said, 'Game on.'

I smile at my screen as I keep typing. I can feel him staring at me, and I don't mind it. His gaze feels like the warm sun on my skin on a spring morning. I want nothing more than to bask in it. When I return his gaze, he doesn't shy away. He studies my body language like his desire is to become fluent.

Just to make sure he's really attentive, I grab a hair tie from my wrist and pull my curls back into a high ponytail. I resume working and wait for it. It doesn't take long before he notices.

"The sunflower. What song inspired it?"

I bite my lip to hide my smile.

"Sunflower Vol. 6 by Harry Styles."

I think back to what he said last week and I believe it now.

I'll give them all my attention. Trust me.

11
"i'll fix that."

Greyson

Manhattan, NY | October 17, 2023

I'VE ALWAYS LOOKED FORWARD to Fridays, but now it's Tuesdays. We don't spend more than thirty to forty-five minutes together at the coffee shop, but I enjoy it. It's refreshing how I always learn something new about her. She's gotten me to open up a bit since I don't share as often as I ask questions.

I got to the coffee shop early today and told Hazel I'll be working from home for the first half of the day and to move my meetings after lunch. I claim her favorite table before someone else does, and I set up my laptop and iPad for the time being. I know her preference by now, so I proceed to the counter to place our regular orders when the 'donut of the day' catches my eye. It's a maple-long john with bacon crumbles. I smile to myself as I recall her mentioning her favorite donut shop in St. Louis sells them. I order half a dozen to make her smile and get started on my to-do list as I wait for her.

She arrives twenty minutes later with a surprised expression when she spots me working at her favorite table. She eyes me suspiciously as she settles in. Then, she notices the box of donuts, and once she sees what I picked out, she smiles.

"Just like home," she says softly, meeting my gaze as she tucks her curls behind her ear before reaching for a donut. "Thank you."

"No problem. I hope you like them."

She takes a bite and her eyes shut. A soft moan escapes her as she savors it.

My brows shoot up at her, and she places her hand over her mouth with a giggle.

"Anyways, what are you up to over there?" she asks.

"I thought I'd bring my work and keep you company longer than usual."

"I don't mind the company. Are you sure you're not only doing this to prove you have a job?" she teases.

"That may have crossed my mind. Do you come across men that are unemployed often?"

"Unfortunately, yes. I've met quite a few on *SoulBlend* dates."

"Tell me more about that."

"I've met more that I wasn't compatible with than I was. If you ask me, I don't understand the hype around all these people finding their perfect match. I haven't even found a person I wanted to go on a second date with who was a *match* for me, so I think that app is trash, or maybe that's just my luck." She frowns as she unpacks her laptop.

I listen intently. I've never had the pleasure of hearing anyone's brutally honest opinions about the app.

She continues, "If there wasn't an end goal to me going on these damn dates, I would've deleted it. It's still an option, but I'm not great at talking to men in person either."

"But you find it's easier to talk to them on the app?"

"Well, yeah, but there's something wrong with it right now. Like if a guy sends me a voice message, it doesn't play and my inbox shows I have unread matches when I don't. So that's annoying."

I hope she doesn't think I'm disinterested. I'm listening and taking notes of what she mentioned so I can investigate further.

It sounds like a bug, and I wasn't notified of it, which irritates me that my team hasn't mentioned this.

"I'll fix that," I say absentmindedly.

"What?" she asks. "I was talking about the *SoulBlend App*."

Shit. It's a wonder she didn't find out anyway.

I glance up and her brows are wrinkled in confusion.

"Fun fact. I created the app and founded the company. I don't just have a job, but I'm an employer. Ain't that some shit?" I add with a smile.

Her jaw drops and she's speechless so I just have to mess with her once more.

If she had looked me up, she wouldn't be surprised right now.

"Am I the best *SoulBlend* date, yet? This is date number four. *If* you're counting," I add playfully.

"Oh my God. I just talked so much shit." She winces and covers her face with her hand.

I reach across the table and rub my thumb over her knuckles on her free hand. "I didn't think you were talking shit. It's client feedback. I can't fix it if I don't know what's wrong."

She stares at my hand on hers curiously and says, "I'm really sorry."

"Don't apologize for speaking your mind. Ever. I appreciate your honesty. I don't get feedback like that often, especially not to my face."

"Would you be okay with me looking at your profile? I may be able to narrow down why you're attracting these matches."

She hands her phone to me with her profile on display. I'm taken aback by her profile picture for a moment because she is just so damn beautiful. I clear my throat and get back to the task at hand. I review her profile thoroughly, and I'm seeing a lot of things that are not adding up to the woman I've come to know recently.

"Hmm."

"What's that mean?" she asks apprehensively.

"Do you want my honest opinion?"

She nods.

"For starters, this isn't *you*. The person you're promoting yourself as isn't who's in front of me right now. Why is that?"

She looks down and lets out a defeated sigh. I immediately regret what I said. *I should've worded that differently. Shit.*

"I'm not looking for a life partner and I figured if I made my profile more appealing to what I assume men are looking for, I'd have better hits."

I raise my brow and lean back in my chair.

"How's that been working out for you?"

"Not well, as you can see."

"I think you should update your profile," I say, placing the phone back in her hand. "Answer the questionnaire *honestly*. Don't give answers based on what you think men will like. Your profile should reflect you. Share your interests and only fill out the prompts you relate to. Show us who you are and we'll set you up with people that compliment you."

"So, you're saying it's my fault I've been on all these bad dates?"

"Not entirely. I'm going to investigate what you said and see what I can fix. As far as matching goes, if you're lying on your profile and are getting a bunch of losers, that part is on you since you're not using the app for its intended purpose. Do you want better dates? Show them who Selah is—the app will do the rest of the work for you."

"Since you made the app, I suppose you know best. I've got to know though. Who's your perfect match?"

"Don't have one," I say without looking up from my screen.

When I catch her staring at me, she shifts her focus back to her screen and gets back to her work. I make a note of her feedback before sending it to my team for us to review and discuss further. I'd like for us to see where we can look for fixes to rollout in the next update and keep at it until we've made the necessary improvements.

Some people would be upset to hear their product ripped

apart in that way, but I'm motivated by it. It's possible that has something to do with the fact that Selah was the one delivering the blow. I admire how whenever comfortable; she is the opposite of how she presents herself to be. It only intrigues me to uncover more layers of her. The fact that she hates my app and continues to use it for reasons other than finding a life partner—it sounds to me like she's looking for something casual and if that's the case, we could help each other out. I won't be the one suggesting it though. She's going to have to ask me. I'd say yes, but I'm placing the ball in her court.

Let's see how Selah plays.

12
pole dancing

Selah

Manhattan, NY | October 20, 2023

I CHECKED *Pole dancing* off my list when Daya started attending classes with me earlier this year. I always wanted to try it, but since my body didn't meet society's beauty standards, I convinced myself I needed to lose weight before starting a class. That's what kept me away from it, but I was wrong. Any body type can work a pole. I've never felt sexier or more confident about my curves than when I'm dancing. Plus, it's another thing to get me out of the house, so my therapist is on board with it too.

I throw a few extra thick hair ties in my duffle bag and text Daya to let her know I'm leaving. We always meet at this shop around the corner from the dance studio to grab smoothies and catch up before class. It's much needed since we're too busy sweating and don't get much time to talk in between routines.

I take the elevator to the garage and I think about my recent coffee shop visits with Greyson. I've been doing that experiment for a month, and it's been excruciating, at least until he popped up. I can't explain it, either. His presence soothed any qualms I had. Once he approaches me, my only thoughts are not to embarrass myself in front of him, which I'm certain I do every time we have an interaction. I find that I'm not as anxious because I don't notice anyone else once he joins me.

Greyson's visits can't be more than forty-five minutes, but they feel like so much longer. I've been prepping for an upcoming sprint cycle and couldn't give him much attention, but he didn't seem to mind. He keeps me company and makes an effort to get to know me. I'd say that makes the experiment successful.

He caught me off guard when he first approached my table. All those people in that café and amid it all, he found *me.* I now know that he's a detail-oriented man. He asks about my tattoos, and I'm not used to men noticing anything about me. These tattoos are my battle scars. An everlasting montage of music etched into my skin. I've gone on twelve dates this year, and not one of them asked about my tattoos. Greyson noticed three and promised to *give them all his attention.* I'm not sure what he meant by that, but I'll admit I like the sound of it.

Daya is going to love these updates about the 'hot neighbor,' as she calls him. She's more confident with men, and I'm hoping she can give me some advice on how not to embarrass myself whenever I'm around him. He's appeared in a few of my dreams since we met, that's all I'll say about that. It's a reprieve from my regular nightmares, so I'm not complaining, but he makes me flustered. He is the exact opposite of my *SoulBlend* matches. I think if I went out with him, I'd enjoy myself for once. I could check some spicy tasks off my list. All of them if there's any validity to his recent comments.

I hope to hear you calling me Grey soon.

I'm not deterred by anything 'nasty.' If anything, I'm more intrigued.

A part of me believes that I shouldn't complicate things with Greyson because if something goes wrong, I still have to see him. On the other hand, he's a beautiful, tolerable man who may be able to satisfy my needs...and I am running out of time to complete the list by my birthday.

Nope.

He's my neighbor and that's it.

My hot neighbor whose big arms I've dreamt about.

My hot neighbor whose big arms I've dreamt about picking me up and fu—that's enough.

greyson

We're leaving the dog park and walking through the neighborhood when my stomach starts rumbling. As we stroll down the street, Cliff starts sniffing the air excitedly. I let his nose lead the way, hoping there's a food truck close by. To our surprise, there is. A smile stretches across my face when I spot the familiar logo, *Aguilar's*—our favorite. I know the owners well, one being my best friend Elena, and her cousin, Marco. They love Clifford so much, they added a '*puppy meal*' of mini tacos on the menu, just for him. I ignore my rumbling stomach as I place our usual order. Elena overhears my voice and peeks out the window with a wide grin.

"Gris[1]! You have my boy?" she asks with raised eyebrows.

She hardly ever calls me Grey.

"I do," I say with a chuckle.

As soon as he hears Elena's voice, he whips his tail around excitedly.

"I'll be out in a sec," she says and holds one finger up.

She whispers something to her cousin Marco, who's taking my order. I grab my wallet to pay, counting the bills and handing them through the window when he shakes his head.

He says, "We go through this every time you eat here. You are family and we don't want your money."

1. Grey

"How am I to support a small business if you refuse to let me pay?"

He clears his throat and discreetly points to the tip jar.

Marco is a smart man.

I stash the bills in the tip jar while Elena has her back turned, and he gives me a thumbs up.

She steps out of the truck and exclaims, "My boys!"

Of course, Cliff gets to her first, enjoying chin scratches and baby talk. Then she walks over and folds her arms around me, holding me in an embrace for a moment. She rubs her hand up and down my shoulder blade in a soothing way as if she knew I needed that.

She pulls back and looks me up and down, holding on to both of my shoulders. She's so short that she's craning her neck to get a good look at me.

"How are you feeling, Gris?"

"Good. Just out with Cliff to get some fresh air. He smelled *you,* so we came straight here, and I'm starving," I whine, throwing my head back and rubbing my stomach.

"I can help with that. You're going to stay out for a bit? I can take my break with you."

"I'd like that."

I grab my order, and we sit with Elena at a nearby table. I'm facing the street and Cliff sits beside me, patiently waiting for his food. I unclip the water bottle bowl that hangs from his leash and fill it up, placing his food and water in front of him. He looks at me, waiting for my cue so he can dig in.

"You can eat, Bud."

He digs in and drinks some water.

While we eat, Elena is catching me up on what's new with *Aguilar's* and their upcoming catering gigs. I told her that I met my beautiful new neighbor the last time we had brunch, but I haven't given an update since. When she asks about her, I mention I ran into her at the coffee shop a few weeks back and we now have a standing meeting. I wouldn't call that a date, but it's a step up from our run-ins.

"I think you should ask her out. You said it yourself, she's dating and you caught her eye fucking you in the elevator." She cackles.

"You know I don't want anything serious."

"Oh, I'm aware. She could be on the same page, you know? Whenever *I* go out, I'm just trying to have a little fun. You do realize that you can date without the intent to marry, right? It's 2023, Gris."

She's got me there.

"You're right. I shouldn't assume. I'll ask her."

"The worst thing she can say is no and I doubt she will," she adds with a warm smile.

Cliff whines and when I look down at him, his face is soaked from the water bowl. He stares expectantly at me, waiting for more food. I always get him fresh fruit, and he can smell the watermelon at the table. I chuckle and add some cubes to a bowl for him. He scarfs it down, of course.

When I look up, I recognize two women walking on the other side of the street. It's as if we talked her up because I'm looking right at Selah as she walks beside her friend, Daya. My breath catches as I stare. I try to play it cool so as not to bring Elena's attention her way. I've already agreed to ask her out, but if she sees her, she'll encourage me to do it now. They don't seem to catch sight of Cliff and me before they disappear into a pole dancing studio.

Wait. Selah pole dances?

The thought sends blood rushing straight to my dick. I stiffen.

Down boy. We're in public.

I can actually see her from here.

I'm just having dinner with my best friend and my dog while I watch my gorgeous neighbor slide down a pole across the street.

Man. That sounds bad.

I'm going to do it anyway.

We discuss my concerns about dating as someone who's accustomed to casual relationships. She offers some advice as a fellow workaholic who occasionally makes time for hookups and dates.

"I know you don't forgive yourself for the divorce, and you're scared to hurt someone else. It was seven years ago, and you were kids. The man in front of me wouldn't make that mistake again."

"You really think so? Not just because you're my best friend?"

She stares at me deadpan. "You're reading romance just to make conversation. You *like* her. Get to know each other. There's no harm in that. Ask her on a *real* date. I'll help you plan it. What's she into?"

"Music and books," I say without hesitation.

"Ooh! Take her to that romance bookstore in Brooklyn. I'm sure she'll love that."

"What else?"

"Grab food and just talk."

"I could do that."

"See? Now, you just gotta ask," she says with a hopeful smile. "Keep me posted and let me know when you get back home. I love you guys."

She hugs me goodbye, and Clifford enjoys some head rubs before she heads back to the truck.

I look up in time to see the instructor teaching a move. She climbs the pole and twirls a few times before extending her leg. My eyes find Selah, who watches closely before repeating that same move with grace. I'm enamored by her. I feel my pants getting tighter at the sight of her.

To distract myself, I call Henry to check in on him. He picks up on the second ring. I hope I'm not bothering him, but he lets me know he could use the break. He fills me in on college and his latest dilemma because there always is one. He even asks about Selah, and I tell him I don't have much of an update. He asks about our parents and we talk about them for a bit. I don't visit much outside of the holidays, but he stays with them in the summer and has time off from school. I get up from the table and toss our trash as we start our walk back home.

I tell my brother I love him and that I'll let him get back to studying. He stops me when I go to hang up to thank me for calling and admits he's been homesick. Mom sends him back to school every semester with a supply of food that should last, but he's already gone through half of it. He mentions how he's tried to ration the food on campus, but it doesn't compare to Mom's cooking. Hen goes to NYU, so he isn't too far from me or our parents in Brooklyn, but I remember that feeling all too well. I ask if he's free tomorrow for lunch and decide to send him back with more meals.

"We can't have you homesick *and* hungry. Don't even mention that to Mom. She'll move into your dorm."

He chuckles. "That sounds good. I'll see you tomorrow. I love you. Goodnight."

"Night, kid. Love you, too."

12

We greet David at the door and he gives Clifford a treat. We're halfway through the lobby when I hear someone enter behind us, making me glance over my shoulder before I freeze.

It's Her. Selah.

We lock eyes and she gives me a soft smile. "Wait up?" she asks.

As if I would do anything other than wait for her.

She moves the handle of her bag higher up on her shoulder before quickening her pace across the lobby floor, headed toward me. Her breasts are swaying with each step, and I'm trying my hardest not to look down at them.

I'm really being challenged tonight.

What have I done to deserve this torture?

She stops in front of us while she catches her breath. She stares up at me and her eyes glimmer. Clifford's tail wags rapidly at her presence. She bends down to greet him and scratch his head. He leans into her touch and licks her hand, which makes her laugh and it's my new favorite song. A melody I hope I never get out of my head.

Speaking of my head, I see her mouth moving.

She's obviously speaking to me and I have no idea what she said.

Get it together.

"I-I'm so sorry. I zoned out for a sec. What did you say?"

"No worries. I asked where did you two come from? He smells like watermelons."

She scratches his chin with one hand and rubs his back with the other, and he relishes the attention. I remind myself to give him a big treat when we get home and buy him a new squeaky toy for being such a good boy.

My friends have officially been fired as wingmen.

"Oh. We took a walk, and then we stopped at *Aguilar's* for dinner. If I have him with me, I grab him their puppy meal and fresh fruit."

She smiles and I swear it could light up Times Square.

"What a great Dog Daddy you are."

I stiffen, and my throat bobs at the word 'Daddy' coming from her lips.

Is she flirting with me? God, I hope so.

She nervously chuckles and averts her eyes when the elevator stops at our floor. "Whew," she says. Pretending to wipe sweat from her brow. "Saved by the bell."

I howl. I don't mean to laugh as loud as I do and it startles her, but she recovers and giggles alongside me. We smile and wave at our neighbors who flood out into the lobby. Selah steps into the elevator, and I follow, motioning for Clifford to join us in the car and sit down beside me. After pressing the buttons for our floors, I scratch his head and tell him what a good boy he's been today. I look up and see her smiling softly. She has her e-reader in hand, as always, but she's not reading. She admires Clifford and me as if she likes us.

Only one way to find out.

I clear my throat and break the silence.

"So, where were you coming from? The gym?"

"Oh, um. I was at a dance class."

She takes her time with each word and blushes as she gets it all out.

"I didn't know you dance."

"I do now." She giggles and pauses. "It was a pole dancing class. I go every week."

My eyebrows shoot up. I can't help myself.

"Pole dancing? Are you any good at it?"

I lean back and scan her frame, swiping my tongue across my lip. There's a glimmer in her eye. She recognizes the challenge and serves it back.

"Wouldn't you like to know?" she asks with a smirk.

Good girl. I'll bite.

"I would, actually."

Her gaze holds a simmering flame.

"We all want things we can't have," she quips with a flirty smile.

Game on. She has no idea what she just started.

I open my mouth to respond when the elevator stops at her floor. She walks over to rub Cliff's head and tell him goodbye. She smiles up at me before she steps out of the elevator. I grip the side of the door to keep it open a few moments more, just to drink her in before I call it a night.

She turns around to face me and says, "Saved by the bell once again. Goodnight, Greyson."

"Wait," I say, stepping off the elevator with Clifford as my heart races. She stops and eyes me curiously. I take a deep breath and tell myself to get on with it.

Here goes nothing.

"Would you like to go on a date this weekend?"

She smiles softly. "I would. Where are we going?"

"There's a romance bookstore in Brooklyn. I'd like to take you there and grab lunch, of course."

She raises her brow and squints at me. "You want to buy me smut books?"

"Yes."

"Paperback or hardcover?"

"Anything you fucking want."

She's eyeing me suspiciously and chewing her lip. I worry she's going to change her mind.

"It's a date. Don't forget your wallet. Books aren't cheap."

"Oh, I'm aware," I chime.

"Still on for Tuesday?" she asks.

"I wouldn't dare miss it. Goodnight, Selah."

"Night," she says and saunters down the hallway.

This woman is something else.

We press the button and wait for the elevator. I pull out my phone and send a text to the **Fools In NY** group chat with Alex and Elena to tell them the news.

I look at Clifford and say, "I'm going on a date with Selah."

He wags his tail in response.

Looks like we're both excited.

13
first date, kinda nervous

Selah

Brooklyn, NY | October 21, 2023

I LOOK myself over in the mirror and hold my breath as I spritz perfume on my chest and neck. My doorbell rings, and my eyes widen.

He's here.

As I step into the hallway, I do another quick spritz in my hair and fan myself. Smoothing my hands over my dress, I approach the door, exhaling deeply before I answer it. He stands there drinking me in before he speaks and I suddenly feel hot.

"Hi."

"Hey, you look amazing."

"Thank you."

He smiles wide and fishes his wallet from his pocket, waving it at me.

"I didn't forget."

I raise my brows and do a clapping motion.

He guffaws. "Selah, I'd like to prove that I have a paycheck since you think I'm unemployed."

"Are you trying to seduce me?"

"Is it working?"

"No. Ask me at the end of the date."

"Fair enough. Are you ready?"

I nod, shutting the door behind me.

The car ride to Brooklyn is unique. He opened my door and buckled my seatbelt for me. I worry he may have heard my heart beating out my chest, but he didn't acknowledge it. We locked eyes for a moment when he pulled back to close the door, and I smiled softly. He rolled up his sleeves, revealing veiny arms and a few tattoos of his own that are usually hidden. He even *drives* sexy, with one hand on the wheel and the other resting on the center console. At one point, he throws his arm in front of me when he hits his brakes.

How will I survive the date if everything he's doing has me ready to bite a pillow and scream?

His music selections are great, but we talk the entire time, which is odd for me because I'm not much of a talker. I take Daya's advice and guide him into conversations by asking questions. This will give me time to consider my answers, so I'm less likely to blurt shit out and embarrass myself. So far, it's working.

He takes me to a pizzeria for lunch and I couldn't be happier. I was nervous when he didn't ask beforehand what I liked, but he did good. He asks if I had any 'fun facts' about myself, which I thought was cute. He mentioned he loves attending weddings. I share that I collect vinyl, and he lights up like he got an idea. He shared that there's a record store near here if I don't grow tired of him after the bookstore. Of course I'd like that. Why would I get sick of him? He's doing amazing, and no strikes so far.

Knock on wood.

He shares that he was born and raised here in Brooklyn, and this restaurant was a childhood favorite. I love that he brought me somewhere meaningful to him. He asks me about growing up in St. Louis, my job, how long I've been in New York and how I'm liking it here. The *'Fuck It List'* comes up when he asks more about the pole dancing, which I should've been prepared for. I give a quick summary of what it is and that I'm trying to complete thirty tasks by my thirtieth birthday.

"What inspired your '*Fuck It List*?'" he asks.

"I feel like I wasted my twenties with a partner that dimmed my light. I missed a lot of opportunities because I prioritized him and once I left, I had no clue how to be alone. I've spent the last two years learning who I am through taking risks and forcing myself out of my comfort zone," I sigh. The '*Fuck It List*' encouraged me to stop making excuses and just go for it. I've learned that nothing is too big or small if it truly matters to me."

I notice a tattoo peeking through his neckline, and I ask about it, deciding to ask about them gradually like he does mine. He has flowers that he taught me to pronounce as *mugunghwa* 무궁화[1] on his right shoulder and bicep. He informs me it is the national flower of South Korea and can symbolize either eternity or inexhaustible abundance. The conversation flows and we stay far longer than we expected to, but we're enjoying this time together.

When we head to the bookstore, I am enamored by how pink and adorable this shop is. Greyson is right behind me, holding all the books I want and asking questions as we make our way through the store. He is such a good sport and doesn't get annoyed by me pointing at every book I've read just to tell him that I've read it. Instead, he's fascinated.

He surprised me when he suggested we find a book to read together for the first time, so I made it a mission to find a book with our favorite tropes and a blurb that gave us chills. By the time we ring up our haul, the clerk tells us we picked great selections. I take a few steps away and check my phone when she rings up the final books so that I don't have to see that total. He wasn't lying when he said I could have any book I fucking wanted in that store.

He loads the books into his SUV truck and asks if I'm sick of

1. hibiscus syriacus

him yet. I'm not, so he takes me to the record store in the neighborhood and we managed to come out with a few gems for a good price too. I argued with him that I wanted to buy my own vinyl, but he refused. Still no strikes.

We take a walk on the Brooklyn Bridge in time for sunset and it's incredible. I share another fun fact about myself: I love a starry sky and beautiful sunset. Though, since I moved to New York, I don't have the pleasure of seeing the stars like I did back home.

The ride home is smooth, just like the day had been. It's even more intense because we had an incredible date, and Greyson is effortlessly sexy. It's crossed my mind that we should go back to my place and check a thing or two off my list, but I'm perplexed since this is the best date I've ever been on and he's my neighbor. I also wouldn't mind going out with him again.

We step onto the sixth floor and he's carrying bags from our shopping hauls in one hand. He's done that all night, kept a hand free. I figured it was because he wanted to hold my hand, but he hasn't tried to.

I would let him.

He insisted on walking me to my door, and I'm biting my lip to hide my smile. I've been grinning all night, and my cheeks hurt. It's a vast comparison to any date I've ever been on. We walk side-by-side when I look over and find him eyeing me curiously.

"What's something on the list that you need a partner for? There's gotta be something 'safe for work' on there."

Oh my god.

"Experience an earth-shattering kiss," I mumble.

"You know I didn't hear that. Can you be a little louder or at least whisper in my ear this time?"

We stop in front of my door, and I focus on unlocking it while I gain the courage to repeat myself.

"Experience an earth-shattering kiss," I say louder. I nearly tumble into my apartment when the door swings open, and he wraps his free hand around my waist, catching me.

Always embarrassing myself in front of him.

He clears his throat and sets me down, dropping the bags in the entryway.

He continues our conversation. "I knew you had something on there that wasn't nasty. You know nasty doesn't bother me," he adds with a wink. "All those dates you've been on and not even one kiss, huh?"

I shake my head reluctantly.

"Do you want help with that one?" He licks his lips.

I stare at him incredulously.

"Uh, I was just answering your question."

"So, you don't want *me* to help with that goal?"

I giggle nervously. "I didn't say that."

"Tell me what you want, Selah," he says in a gravelly tone.

Oh My God.

"Um. I want you to kiss me, Greyson," I whisper hoarsely.

He leans forward, staring at my lips, tilting my chin towards him. His mouth closes over mine with a demanding kiss. His tongue swipes at the seam of my lips, and I grant him entry, savoring his flavor. He indulges, pressing his hard body against me and I melt into him. He tapers off the kiss with gentle nips as he returns to his height. Our chests rise and fall as we catch our breaths.

He rubs his thumb over my bottom lip, holding my gaze. I feel my legs quivering.

"Is it working?" he asks.

"What?"

"You said to ask at the end of the date."

Oh. The seducing me thing.

"Yeah," I say breathily.

"Remember, I'm a call away if you need *anything,*" he says, flashing a smile as he walks backward.

He's diabolical.

"Goodnight, Selah. See you Tuesday?"

I stand in the doorway reeling as I take him in once more.

"Of course. Good night, Greyson."

14
the haunt

Selah

Brooklyn, NY | October 24, 2023

MY EX IS the topic of discussion since my nightmares have become more prevalent, so I'm irritated during this session. I hate talking about him. I hate thinking about him. He quite literally haunts me, and while I understand life isn't fair, I shouldn't be the one suffering. I got my freedom, but I don't *feel* free. Still. I may be to blame for that. Forgiving and forgetting isn't easy, nor is that something I wish to do. He's not worthy of either.

You know how we're taught as little girls that when a boy is mean to you, he likes you? Well, that's dangerous for many reasons because we aren't teaching them to be kind, and us girls learn to accept whatever crumbs they give us. We're easily impressed by the bare minimum, and them being mean isn't a dealbreaker if you're conditioned like many of us are. However, it leads us to find a man like I did. I didn't even like Jourdan on our first date, but I gave him a chance as if I owed him something.

I didn't.

If only the strike system existed for me back then.

I attended a well-executed pity party with a fog machine and house of mirrors. During my time there, he learned all my ins and outs for his benefit. Emotional manipulation was his favorite game to play and I lost every time. You'd think he'd be satisfied with his wins, but he never was.

His bruising victory laps made me a sore loser. Still, I'd forfeit and cry for mercy. He loved me, at least that's what he'd say during timeout, but he refused. Even claimed there was no way out, not even a fire exit.

It doesn't escape me that after just one date with Greyson, I already feel more safe and secure with him than I had during the entirety of my relationship with Jourdan.

Greyson is interested in me for *me* and not for what he can gain from our relationship. He shares things, personal things, about himself that I'm certain no one knows. He makes me feel *good*. Like when he's speaking to me, I'm truly the only one holding his attention. When I was with Jourdan, I had to not only learn the game we were playing, but *defeat* him.

I called his bluff, learned his tells, and studied him for *my* benefit. I eventually escaped Jourdan's house of mirrors and never looked back. He handled the breakup as expected, victimizing himself and making me the bad guy. I ignored him, though he was creative, using threats he didn't act on. I haven't heard from him in over a year, or any of his aliases either. Although, I swear I saw his face on a missing person poster once, I figured my mind was playing tricks on me, so I just let it go.

Today, Dr. Garnett and I discussed my nightmares and my date with Greyson. I preferred to start with the bad and then work on the good things. I pull up recent entries from my dream log. The nightmares have been more violent lately. Jourdan has been present in them a bit more often, but usually, it's a faceless individual trying to harm me in some capacity. Mostly chasing me down with weapons or breaking into my home. Then there's the original one, which is back home flashbacks with my ex.

I go through my dream log with her and we try to decipher any common patterns or situations that occur. I'm not taking any sleep medications because I can sleep, but she's going to have me do more sleep studies to see what's needed here. I'm not getting as much sleep as I'd like, but I use that time to be productive in other areas. It helps me get a head start on a lot of projects but the issue with that is, I'm exhausted all the time.

The vivid nightmares started after I left Jourdan two years ago. They started out as flashback reels, and it was a very trying time for me. I was reliving attacks and arguments. Me waking up to him standing over me was a frequent one. I can't figure out a way through them or to curb them.

Doc suggested we try imagery rehearsal therapy, where I explain my nightmares in extreme detail and we rewrite the story with a different ending—reframing regular nightmares into something that's no longer scary. I'm open to trying it. We'll start it next week, and I'll keep updating my dream logs.

Moving on to more positive things, I finally had a pleasant date with a man I didn't meet online. My date with Greyson was amazing, and we had the best time, not to mention that kiss. We've been texting since we've exchanged numbers, and he's been busy these past few weekends, traveling for work.

I've been going on dates in the meantime, but they do not compare, I'll say that. First, there was the married guy who said he had a roommate that was really his wife. He revealed that after several shots. Then there was another guy, and our date didn't happen because he got arrested for DUI on the way. My most recent match insisted on a day date, brought his kid along, and didn't give me a heads-up either. I am proud to say that I've been using the strike system and have left when it felt right. Sometimes, before they hit a third strike. They've been awful dates, but at least Greyson was a palette cleanser.

My homework for the next week is to keep logging my nightmares so that we can try out IRT therapy, keep setting boundaries, and try a new nighttime routine to compare the sleep and dreams you have with a routine *and* without.

15
when life gives you pot, make brownies

Selah

SoHo, NY | November 11, 2023

CHESS, Daya, and I are currently getting a front-row seat to a baking lesson from Audrey. Baking is one of her favorite things besides planning, and anytime she can indulge, she's more than happy to do it. Tonight, she's assisting me with completing two tasks from my *'Fuck It List:' Learn to Bake* and *Make Pot Brownies.* I'll forget everything she is teaching us right now, but I'm following along and helping with everything I can. I always have the best time in her massive kitchen, and I'm certain I'd never stop cooking if I had a kitchen like this.

She puts me on duty to melt the canna butter because I have the most patience, and after my egg incident a few months ago, she thought it was best that I don't handle the wet ingredients. I think that's fair. Once we've got everything mixed in the pan, she starts pouring a separate batch that is 'pot-free' in a pink pan for us to enjoy after the high sets in. That's a good idea. How will we know the difference? This batch is salted caramel; the other is chocolate chip in a blue pan.

While they're baking in her convection ovens, we're keeping busy by cleaning up and talking about what we want to order in for dinner tonight. Audrey has the idea to queue our food deliveries to arrive within the next two hours. We couldn't decide on one thing, so orders from a few of our favorite restaurants will be here shortly.

Once the brownies are done, we let them cool and prepare for the fun tonight. Chess and Daya are making mocktails, cutting up fruits, and mixing up drinks while I am deciding on a good movie lineup. I think I've included at least one of everyone's favorites, and before I start to overthink it, I set down the remote to go help Audrey. She's currently making a pillow fort with little success because her playful chocolate lab, Ghost, is very interested in dismantling every part of it. He's quickly distracted by a squeak and when we look up, it's Chess holding one of his toys. He dashes to her and grabs it, running off to go play elsewhere, leaving us to finish the fort.

Now, we have cooled brownies cut into perfect squares. Audrey is more experienced with edibles, considering she does these with her younger brothers from time to time. She bites into hers without a care, but the rest of us look at each other nervously before taking a bite.

She draws a marijuana leaf on the lid of the pot brownie container and writes 'safe' on the lid with the caramel ones—keeping them accessible for us.

"Take your time, ladies. Remember, start with a small bite. Wait a while before taking another one," Audrey advises over her shoulder as she goes to hide the leftover brownie stash safely away from her pup.

I take a small bite and close my eyes, savoring it. This is the best brownie I've ever had and it doesn't taste any different than a regular one. I'm highly anticipating my next bite.

"Fuck," Daya blurts, and a gasp from Chess follows.

I open my eyes, whipping my head between the two of them and Daya's eyes widen. I look down at her hand and see the teeth marks in her brownie. She quickly wipes the crumbs from her mouth. Chess places her face in her hands.

"She took a big ass bite, didn't she?" Audrey asks without turning around.

"Y-Yes," Daya squeaks.

"What do we do?" I ask nervously.

Audrey sighs. "Just let me think for a second."

The house is so silent you could hear a pin drop until faint squeaking from a dog toy cuts through it and we start laughing.

After we settle down, she comes back to the island and sits with us, her palm resting on her forehead, still thinking of a plan.

"Well, I'm not letting her go down by herself," Chess states as she takes an even bigger bite.

Audrey snorts and stares at me deadpan.

"I already know you're next up, so go ahead." She waves her hand.

I do want another bite, but I'm a bit nervous about getting too high. Then again, we'll be together. I remind myself that this is for my list and its purpose is to encourage me to live a life for all the years I spent wishing I could.

"Fuck it," I say, taking a bigger bite than last time.

She chuckles and takes another bite.

She mentions when she walks away, "If one of us is fucked over, we all are. Food will be here by the time these hit. I'm texting Rome. We should be supervised and he'll be home soon."

A while later, we're all cozy in the pillow fort with Ghost, watching a movie. The blankets are warm and I still feel normal. I look over at the girls and they look the same. I'm not sure what to expect from an edible high, but from what I've heard, I'm nervous.

"Do y'all feel anything?" I ask.

"Nope," Chess and Daya say in unison.

"You will," Audrey warns with a chuckle. "We are *not* eating more."

"Okay," I resign.

6

This movie is getting wild and I just can't look away. Chess is snuggled up to me while we lay on the fort, enraptured in the movie. I've seen it before, but maybe this is a director's cut because they've got my undivided attention. I'm startled by a strange jingling sound and start holding my breath while I listen harder for it. I try not to alarm Chess as I carefully listen for the sound again. I hear it once more, with footsteps approaching.

Someone is in the house with us.

What do we do?

I look around for something to protect us with, but we're in the dark with only the projector to light up the room. I lock eyes with the remote and clutch it. I've never heard of anyone being bludgeoned with a remote, but I'll do my best to protect my friends. My heartbeat quickens as the footsteps come closer to the couch. I hear a man's voice grumbling and the jingle again. The light flicks on and I hear Rome's voice, so I drop the remote with a thud. I can't make out what he's saying, but the sound brings him straight to me.

I'm surprised to see him upside down. I wonder how he got that way.

He's carrying a pizza box and a bunch of bags. I'm curious as to how they're not floating with him.

Weird.

He continues walking upside down as he enters the room and I watch in awe.

He stops for a moment and asks, "Why are you watching a movie in Portuguese?"

I stare in confusion. "It's in French, Rome," I say matter-of-factly.

"No, it's not. You and Chess don't even speak French, Audrey does." He pauses and looks around the room. "And I don't see her anywhere. So, you going to tell me what's going on?"

I look at Chess and whisper, "Do you know how to speak French?"

"Yeah. I just learned today," she says loudly.

He lets out a deep sigh and walks off to the kitchen, setting down everything before he returns to the living room.

"Why are you on the floor? We have couches."

"Why are *you* upside down?"

"What? I am not—you're all high right now, aren't you?"

I wrinkle my brow and think about his question.

Wait. What did he ask? Oh well.

He continues, "That's why you asked for all this damn food. You're high. Well, did you know you also ordered a bunch of food? It was waiting outside the door for you!"

Chess and I burst into laughter and she sits up slowly. *I wonder if she has tingly fingers too. I think that means I should be doing jazz hands right now.*

"I'm hungry," Chess says as she stretches and enters the kitchen. I observe as she opens the container for another brownie. Rome makes his way over in quick strides and snatches it from her hand. He pulls it back and holds it above his head so she can't reach. Chess stands on her tiptoes and wiggles her fingers, trying to steal the brownies from his grip and is unsuccessful.

Rome is still upside down.

I wonder if he's always been capable of this.

"Hell no. You don't need any more of this shit. I know exactly who made these. Where's your ringleader?"

I look around and didn't even notice Audrey wasn't sitting with us anymore.

We hear a loud crashing noise coming from downstairs that causes me to jump, and we're all looking around in confusion. Rome lets out a huff before he helps me off the floor and asks us to come with him.

I'm very surprised to find him no longer defying gravity.

"Ghost! Come here boy!" he coos.

He makes kissing sounds to lure him out, but he doesn't come.

We navigate the house, following where the crash came from when more noises sound from the basement. Rome quickens his pace and I look around to find that Chess has disappeared. I whisper-yell for her and she soon appears beside me, sliding across the marble floors on her white socks holding a wrapper for chocolate buttercups. One cup is stuffed in her mouth and she shoves the other in mine.

"I was hungry," she says with her mouth full.

We're toppling over in a fit of giggles and Rome is sighing as he waits for us to remember what we're doing.

"We're looking for my girl and my dog, remember? I really hope he didn't eat any of that shit you're tripping on. Babysitting four of you is enough. I don't need a sick pup to worry about, too."

When he reaches the basement door, we hear muffled music, and he stands in front of us before opening it, ushering us behind him.

Rome takes careful steps making sure we're close behind and don't slip.

When we get to the bottom of the stairs, we find her and Daya jumping up and down in the ball pit, rapping the lyrics to Wu-Tang Clan's *Method Man*. Ghost has gotta be down here somewhere playing. They don't notice us over the music. He stands off to the side for a moment, admiring her.

"I love that woman," he says to me with a smile.

He is so gone for her. I love to see it.

I've never asked why she has ball pits in her basement, but

she insisted on having them, and I think the dog loves them more than she does.

One is a drained indoor pool that has a trampoline floor filled with plastic balls. Ghost has his own ball pit; it's an above-ground pool that he can get in and out of easily. Whenever he sees Rome, he runs over to him and is greeted with head scratches before jumping back into his pit.

Chess runs in front of us and uses the diving board to launch herself into the pit. She wears a look of surprise when she bounces off the floor, assuming she forgot about the trampoline underneath. Rome stands beside the pit, looking stressed, and shakes his head. Audrey is hyping her up and starts jumping with her, striking poses mid-air.

I climb down the steps on the other side and stand in the pit, swimming through the balls until I meet Daya in the middle. We join hands and jump around when the song changes to Lil' Kim's *The Jump Off*.

"Chess is going to throw up and I'm going to have to clean it," Rome says as he rounds the pool and tries not to laugh at us. I notice him rapping along before he finds Audrey's phone to turn down the music. Seeing serious Rome let himself have a little fun makes me smile. He squats beside the pool in front of Audrey and reaches his hand out for her.

Audrey grabs his hand and says, "Come in. The water's fine."

He chuckles. "I think you should take a break from swimming to eat and sober up. You can get back in the pool later, baby. Come on."

She rolls her eyes but treks over toward the steps to leave the pit. We follow behind because food sounds good right about now. He makes sure we all get out safely before he walks over to Audrey, assessing her. He picks her up and carries her over his shoulder. Starting off towards the stairs, he whistles for Ghost, who follows behind.

"Let's get you all fed and see if the neighbors are hungry since Audrey ordered enough for the whole block to eat."

"Don't underestimate my appetite. Watch me," she argues.

He goes into dad mode, seating us at the dining table as he sets up our various orders as a spread in the middle of the table with Ghost on his heels, hoping that he drops something on the floor for him.

"You should let loose every once in a while," Daya suggests to Rome.

"I am a lawyer, not a stoner. I missed that train. Didn't have time to party in college. I was trying to pass the bar."

"That's why you're so grumpy now. You don't know how to have fun and you hate parties."

"How potent did you make those brownies, babe?" he asks, looking at Audrey.

She glances over at him, and before taking a bite of her burger, she says, "Not very potent."

He wears a knowing look. "You've all been acting like you're eight years old tonight."

"You say that like it's a bad thing. My childhood sucked," Audrey argues with her mouth full.

The table is silent at her admission, looking around at each other for a subject change. Rome chews his lip hesitantly while she seems unfazed and focused on her food.

I take a stab at breaking the quiet spell.

I clear my throat and exclaim, "we're healing our inner child!"

She looks up at me with a soft smile.

"To healing our inner child!" Chess agrees.

I hold out my burger and the girls join me, doing a cheers motion with our cheeseburgers.

Rome shakes his head in response, chuckling at us. "You know, as much as I complain, I love you *little instigators,* I just love this one more," he says as he pulls Audrey in close, placing a kiss on the top of her head.

"You getting sappy on us, *Romeo*?" Chess asks.

"Will I ever lose that name?"

"Never," we sing in unison.

"We love you too, *Romeo*. You're a good babysitter," I add.

"Thanks."

"Eric is a better one, though," Daya says.

"That's fair."

16
worth a shot

Greyson

Queens, NY | November 12, 2023

I HAVEN'T SEEN Selah since I got back home from Miami. I attended two *SoulBlend* users' weddings over the weekend. We text every day and still have our standing coffee date on Tuesdays.

The other night, she FaceTimed me while wearing this little pajama set. She propped up her iPad while she was making dinner, and I witnessed her being herself where she was most comfortable, at home. I didn't take that for granted, knowing how much she values her alone time and was happy to be a part of it. It was like a long-distance date, even though she lives downstairs.

I got a suggestive text from her late last night and I didn't show up at her door, but I played along. The following day, she woke up apologizing profusely and explained she had an edible. It amused me, but she felt embarrassed. It didn't change how I viewed her. I'd gladly do everything she mentioned in that text. She just needs to ask for it sober.

Some nights, Selah texts me late and says that she is having a hard time sleeping, and I'll stay up and talk to her and try to help her ease whatever is on her mind so she can get some rest. I don't worry about missing out on sleep because I can come in late whenever I need to. I just wish I knew what was keeping her up so often. She doesn't really say, and I don't want to scare her off if I pry.

I'm currently taking some pictures of Elena and Marco while they're doing a catering gig for an event in Queens. They hired me to take some new photos for their website and social media. I told her since she doesn't accept my money for food, I'd do it for free, but she refused, of course. It brings me back to when I met her years ago and she catered that party with her aunt. We were just kids, but now, she and Marco have a growing restaurant. I couldn't be prouder of my best friend. Plus, I haven't felt inspired to photograph much of anything lately, so when she asked, I was more than happy to help.

I respected the fact that it was an event and not a normal trip to *Aguilar's*, so I didn't eat a bunch. I'm heading home to relax for the night. It's been a week, and I want nothing more than to chill. As I get closer to our building, Selah crosses my mind as usual, and I hope that she's having a good night.

I'll text her when I get settled in at home.

I wonder if she'd like to come by and have takeout with me?

Or not? It's worth a shot, I guess.

17
crave

Greyson

Manhattan, NY | November 12, 2023

ME

Are you home?

SELAH

I'm always at home lol

What're you up to?

ME

Have you eaten? I just got home and was about to order dinner, but I thought of you.

SELAH

You stopped ordering dinner because you thought of me? Are you saying you want me or something edible? Lol

WITH A CHUCKLE, I ponder on how to respond. It's refreshing to see a glimpse of her bolder side, and I'm enjoying it. I remember her kiss and how her lips tasted. I've craved her ever since.

ME

Trust me, you are edible. I was talking about food though, dirty girl. ;)

Would you like to have dinner at my place? I know it's short notice.

SELAH

Sure you were lol

I'd like that. What are we watching?

ME

Anything you want. I'm ordering Chinese food.

Any requests?

SELAH

Chicken fried rice and fried wontons.

With egg, please?

I think I'm ready for eggs again.

I've been avoiding them for a few weeks.

ME

What have eggs done to you?

SELAH

Unspeakable things.

I take a moment to put in our order. It will be here in thirty minutes, allowing me time to mentally prepare for her visit. I can't believe she agreed to have dinner with me. It was worth the shot.

ME

Well, now I'm intrigued.

Apt 12D

Be here in 20.

SELAH

See you in a few. :)

Scanning my apartment, I quickly grab a vacuum to tidy up. I wince. I've been traveling a lot, and my place has seen better days. It's important that I impress her and I hope that a clean apartment and a candle is a good start. I hastily clean until my doorbell rings. As much as I'd love to see her on the other side of it, my smile falters when I open the door and see the food delivery driver instead.

Moments after, the doorbell chimes and my stomach drops, knowing Selah is on the other side of it. I answer the door with an exhale, and there she stands. Dark, long curls frame her face, and a shy smile graces her full lips.

"Hi," she says nervously.

"Hey," I say as I lean on the doorframe, taking her in.

She's in a hoodie and jeans, staring up at me. I regain my focus when she clears her throat. "Are you going to let me in?"

"Only if you promise to tell me about your phobia of eggs," I tease.

She chuckles. "Fine. I'll tell you."

My smile widens as I invite her in, closing the door behind us. Clifford excitedly jumps off the couch to greet our guest. She crouches down to give him her full attention, and he basks in it. I can't help but smile at them.

"Could you take off your shoes?" I ask.

"Of course," she says, taking a seat on the stool in my entryway.

She unzips her boots and meets me in the kitchen wearing socks with pink polka dots, grabbing a seat at the island. I ask what she'd like to drink, and she'd like water. She's quiet while her coffee brown eyes study me as I prepare her plate. I'm enveloped in her alluring scent when I approach, setting the bowl of rice and a glass of ice water in front of her. She thanks me with a soft smile, and I invite her to join me on the couch for a movie.

"Don't mind if I do," she sings, following me to the living room.

She sits at a respectful distance, grabs a coaster for her glass and relaxes on the sofa. I turn on the TV, and when I hand over the remote, she doesn't take it. I glance over to find her eyes searching the room and halt on my record player. I watch as she observes my displayed vinyl, lips parting as if she spotted something she likes.

"Hmm. I'm impressed by your collection over there," she says.

"When we finish eating, I'll show you just how good that collection is. If you set your food down, Clifford will inhale it in three seconds." He lifts his head at the sound of his name. "I can guarantee you'll want to dance with me."

"Hmm. You sound confident, Greyson."

"Is that a problem?"

She cackles and leans in close, enveloping me in her alluring scent. I bite my lip, returning her gaze, and curiosity lingers in her stare.

"Pick the right song, and I will," she adds playfully.

"Challenge accepted."

Laughter and easy conversation fill the rest of the night. After washing my hands, I forgot to roll my sleeves down, and her eyes light up at the sight of the tattoo sleeve on my right arm. It's realism work, adorned with various flowers, cameras, and film. I share the inspiration behind it, leaving out how I got it after Aileen and I split. I didn't ask for much in the divorce, but I wanted our wedding camera. We couldn't afford a photographer when we eloped, so she found a vintage camera at the thrift store for us to take turns snapping pictures throughout the day. I fell in love with the fact that a memory lives forever if you photograph it. Whether there's a good or bad memory behind it, someone can capture the moment with a photo and pass it on for generations. I started collecting cameras and photography eventually became a hobby.

We exchange stories, and what she refers to as the egg incident comes up. As embarrassing as it was, she couldn't stop laughing while trying to tell the story. Then there's two of us laughing uncontrollably. She's moved closer to me on the couch since we started watching a show centered on people bringing their partners to the States to get married. I've never seen it before now, but I'm intrigued. When the show ends, I look at my watch, and it's getting late.

"I know we've got work in the morning," I say reluctantly.

She shrugs her shoulders and says, "I don't get a lot of sleep, so I don't mind. Plus, aren't you supposed to find a song to convince me to dance with you? You guaranteed it. I'm waiting."

I nod. "You are right. Let me get to work."

I stride over to my record player and shuffle through my vinyl, seeking the perfect song to get her to dance with me. After a few moments, a purple cover catches my eye, and I smile to myself as I retrieve it from the storage rack. I keep it from her line of sight, hoping to surprise her. I remove Smokey Robinson's *Where There's Smoke...*record and set it on the slip mat—carefully moving the needle to play *Crusin*, a sure-fire track to get her to dance with me before she heads home.

I turn the player on and grin at the crackling before the song starts. I let the intro fill the space before I face her, an amused look on her face. Aware of my obvious victory, I reach my hand out for her to join me. She chuckles as she stands, taking my hand and I lead her to my kitchen, where we slow dance. She avoids eye contact and can't stop blushing. Her beauty is remarkable, and I can't take my eyes off her. It's intoxicating when she eventually meets my gaze, but it doesn't last long because she shifts her focus to my lips.

"Selah?"

"Hmm?" she asks, not taking her eyes off my mouth.

"I really want to kiss you."

"Then do it," she breathes.

I stifle a laugh, in fear of ruining the moment.

You don't have to tell me twice.

I take her lips in a gentle kiss that grows more desperate by the second. She parts her lips, granting me entry, and I devour her. Soft moans escape her, encouraging me to continue, and I do. Kissing her is dangerous and addictive. I forget to breathe, eager to indulge in all that is her. She sucks on my lip, and I groan in response. If she asked, I would gladly take her to my room. I slow the kiss down to take a breath, and that's enough time for clarity to sink in. I part my lips to speak, and she beats me to it.

"I-I should get home. You know, work in the morning," she pants.

She walks over to the entryway to grab her boots. I take a second to process what she said as she sits on the stool to slip them on. I nod, understandably.

"Uh-yeah. I'll walk you."

"I'll be fine. It's just an elevator ride," she says with a nervous chuckle as she stands.

"I'm not letting my date walk home alone. Even if you live downstairs," I say, grabbing my keys.

"Alright. If you say so, but no seducing," she adds with a pointed finger, biting back her smile.

"I'll be on my best behavior," I assure as I open the door and we step into the hall. I kept my word and walked her home. Once I get back to my place, I'm getting ready for bed when my phone chimes with a text. It's from Selah.

SELAH

Smokey? Really?

You knew exactly what you were doing.

Well played lol

ME

Don't be like that.

You challenged me.

I was simply proving you wrong.

SELAH

Men aren't supposed to be right.

Didn't you know?

ME

It's my first time being right.

Go easy on me.

Goodnight, Selah. ;)

SELAH

Just this once.

Goodnight. :)

I've read a few romances she's recommended, and I think this is what they call a slow burn. I can wait. The fire will be rewarding.

18
mama takes manhattan

Selah

Manhattan, NY | November 24, 2023

MY MAMA HAS BEEN in town for Thanksgiving, and it's been amazing to see her. It's her first time visiting since I moved to New York, and I'm so proud to show her what I've done for myself in these past two years. We had a small dinner yesterday, just the two of us, and it reminded me of old times. I hadn't been able to spend a lot of one-on-one time with my mom over the years because of how isolated I was living in West Chester with my ex. I'm determined to make up for it as much as I can now that I have a better job that allows me to travel. I've visited St. Louis a few times, mostly to surprise her, and I'm grateful I can do things like that now. I'll cry in the airport when she flies home on Sunday. Thankfully, she'll be back in a few weeks for Christmas, so I won't go too long without seeing her.

We're at Audrey and Rome's house for Friendsgiving saying our goodbyes to everyone. As she and Rome walk us to our car, I take in Audrey's beautiful fall decor one last time because when I come over next, she'll have this place all decked out for Christmas.

Growing up as an only child, I'm very accustomed to it being just my mom and I. Something I've loved about how my friends celebrate the holidays makes me feel like I'm experiencing what it's like to have a big family for once. Having my mom here to be a part of it is the icing on the cake. She just jumped in, welcoming everyone with open arms. I noticed her bonding with Chess and Audrey, and I appreciated that. I can't imagine how difficult the holidays must be without a parent.

My dad and I were never close. He and Mom split up when I was a baby, and he wanted no part in raising me. He started over with a family he loves very much and while I always wished I knew my siblings; my mom did a damn good job with me. I'd be a lot more social if I had a sibling or two, but I wouldn't change it for the world. Plus, I really cherish what I have with the girls now. We're just missing Eric, who's spending the holiday with his family in Atlanta. He sent a bunch of pics and gave us a call when we all sat down for dinner, so it felt like he was here anyway.

It's around midnight when we hit the road and if we were in St. Louis right now, the streets would be bare, but it's the complete opposite here. Mama's manning the playlist for the drive home, which has been a vibe so far. She hasn't gotten over the fact that I work for *Kiwi Music,* which is the cutest thing in the world. She'll tell anyone who'll listen about how proud she is of her daughter with the cool job. I knew I had nothing to worry about when it came to Mom's music taste because I got mine from somewhere. She started us off with some Whitney and Mary J, then turned on Bey's *Homecoming* album, so we're having a full-on concert by the time I pull into the parking garage. I remember I haven't checked my mail in a few days, so we enter through the lobby. Rome bagged up our leftovers, so they were easy for us to carry inside.

As expected, I've got quite a bit of mail waiting for me. All I thought about this week was 'my mom is coming to town' and couldn't care less about anything else. I made sure my house was spotless, and the guest room was up to par. I created the illusion that no one lives there by hiding all the unsightly crap in closets and under the beds like normal people do. Now, it looks like I live in a staged apartment and my mom is under the assumption that I'm an adult who has their shit together.

I tuck the envelopes and mailers under my arm to free a hand to lock the mailbox. I look up and see Greyson greet Gino, our night door attendant, as he enters with Clifford. My heart starts racing at the sight of him. I've seen him since *the kiss*, and we've maintained our Tuesday coffee dates, but he makes me more nervous now. That kiss altered my brain chemistry. I also forgot to tell my mom about our date. Oops. He strides across the lobby before he notices me and stops in his tracks. Clifford's tail wags excitedly. We lock eyes, and he flashes a smile that's impossible not to return. As he approaches, I am enveloped in his scent, and I feel heat pooling between my thighs.

Fuck.

What cologne does he wear?

It should be illegal.

"I didn't think I'd be seeing you again 'til next week," he says.

"We just got back from dinner with friends."

"Same here," he says, signaling the leash in his hand. "I'm not allowed to go anywhere without him."

"Hi, handsome," I say directly to Cliff.

His tail wags speed up and I bend down to scratch his chin.

I return to my height as Mama inches closer to me and looks between us with an intrigued expression, clearly waiting to be introduced.

"Um, sorry. Mama, this is my neighbor, Greyson."

"It's a pleasure to meet you, Ms. Bailey."

He extends a hand to her and wraps the other around his wrist, she joins him in a handshake.

"Oh please, call me Elise," she says in a flirty tone.

I try to stifle my laughter because I have never heard her use that voice before. We board the elevator, and it's awkward for the first time since we've met because my mom is here. He doesn't take his eyes off me for the remainder of the ride. I don't have to look at my mom to know she's watching suspiciously and will be grilling me about this interaction as soon as I get off this elevator.

I should start going over my answers now.

When the ding sounds and the doors open, she steps out first and I follow, saying goodbye to them both.

"See you Tuesday?" he asks hopefully.

"See you Tuesday."

The relieved smile he wears before the doors close is enough for my mom to whisper-yell my name behind me, regaining my focus.

I whip my head around and ask, "What?"

She walks beside me bumping her shoulder into me as we start for my apartment.

"Now, who is *that?* And what did he mean he didn't think he was going to see you 'til next week? What do you do with that man on *Tuesdays*, Selah?"

What we actually do is harmless, but I'm going to lie anyway.

"If you must know," I say in a hushed voice. "We play in pinochle tournaments, and they can get pretty *heated*."

She stops in her tracks and makes an incredulous face.

"Bullshit." She breaks out into a fit of laughter. When she settles down, she asks, "Are you hittin' that?"

"No, mama." I chuckle and keep walking.

"Shit. Well, you should be. He smells really good, too," she adds as she follows behind me.

"Doesn't he?" I ask, letting us into my apartment.

"I knew it. You little liar," she whispers.

"I'll tell you if you help me put away all this damn food."

She quickly settles in and darts over to unload the leftovers into my fridge. I follow behind to help and I shriek a laugh at her impressive speed.

"I'm not sleeping with him. You remember the experiment I

told you about for therapy where I work from the coffee shop on Tuesdays? He's been keeping me company, so I don't have a panic attack when I have to do it. That's all."

She sighs, "Well, that was pretty underwhelming, but neighborly." She leans in close like she's got a secret. "That man wants *you,* and not just on *Tuesdays.*"

"Mom, stop. He's just a good neighbor."

"Oh, I'm sure he's *really good,*" she teases.

Alright, now. I've had enough of you."

"You could never." She grabs my broom and sings into it.

"You got that right. I've teased you enough. We've gone on two dates. Nothing more."

"Last month? You haven't even mentioned his name to me. Why is that?"

"Probably because the girls are really invested in him and you'll be too. I don't want to be in a relationship again. You're bound to trip and fall into a relationship with a guy like him. He's great."

I brief her on my interactions with Greyson over the months since we met. From him reading romance novels just to talk to me to our perfect date where I smiled so much my cheeks hurt. Her face when I told her about the books and the vinyl was hilarious. When I tell her that he kissed the life out of me at the end of the night and went home, her salt and pepper eyebrows are in her hairline.

"Mama, say something. Did I break you?"

She exhales deeply and palms her face.

"Listen, baby. We both need to get second jobs."

"Why?"

"So that we can afford to hire Audrey whenever you marry this guy."

"Mama, please."

I roll my eyes in response, and she gives me a knowing look. Once we've squeezed the last container in the fridge and close it without any trouble, we change into our pajamas and retire to the couch for a movie. Before we press play, she sits up like she's got an idea. She turns towards me and her face lights up.

"How about this? Whenever you find out just how *good* of a neighbor he is, give me a call and say 'pinochle.' Repeat it three times if he's good and once if he's not. Then hang up and I'll call you back for the dirty details."

I snort out loud. I've never seen her act like this.

"Mama, you can't be serious."

She pins me with a stare, so I know she is.

"We got a deal?"

"Deal."

We shake on this ridiculous agreement, only because I'd like this conversation to be over as soon as possible.

Pinochle once equals bad.

Pinochle three times equals good.

That's easy to remember.

Not that I'll be finding out just how good of a neighbor Greyson is anyway.

I've dreamt about it a time or two though.

19
elena's on soulblend

Greyson

Manhattan, NY | December 12, 2023

I HAD coffee and donuts with Selah this morning, so I'm in a great mood. The week before the holiday break is usually quiet, which is great because it gives me more time to wrap up a few projects before I'm off for the next two weeks. Though, it's very likely that I will still find some work that needs to be done. Selah mentioned her job also gives her team the rest of December off, so no coffee for us, at least until January.

It's a chill day at work when my phone dings. I flip it over and see two attachments from Elena in the **Fools in NY** group chat we share with Alex. I open the chat to view them and it's two pictures of her posing in a white dress. I remember this look. It's from her recent spread in *A Bite of Brooklyn Magazine*. They covered her and Marco for their food truck issue, and if these are outtakes, they're damn good.

Fools in NY

ELENA

which one should I use for my dating profile?

ALEX

Very funny.

ELENA

I'm serious!

ME

Which app?

She responds with a screenshot of the *SoulBlend* sign-up page.

"Shit," I say out loud, looking around my office.

My thumb hovers over the like reaction to the pictures when Alex's name flashes across my screen with an incoming call.

I answer, and before I can say anything, he demands, "delete her account."

I scoff. "What? No."

"Why not? You made the app. You can do whatever you want."

"I can't just do that. She'd have to violate our terms of service to be removed from the app or deactivate it herself."

"Then I'll get her phone so I can make sure she deactivates."

"You can't be serious."

"Alright, I'm not going to do that, but I need your help, man. Please?" he asks in a pained voice.

There's gotta be a statute of limitations on my vow of silence. The man is hurting, for Christ's sake. Alex is the most confident person I know, but when it comes to Elena, he is just as nervous and afraid as the rest of us.

"Why don't you just make a profile too?" I suggest.

"The app only works for people you match with," he grumbles.

"I'm aware. I did create it. I'm saying that you should make an account to see if you match with her. If you do, it'll be undeniable."

I've never told Alex this, but as someone who analyzes people who are perfect matches for each other daily, the two of them are extremely compatible and have a high chance of matching on the app.

I was inspired by them when I designed the *SoulBlend* prototype. If you could find a way to make two people who are very obviously meant to be together, see it with their own eyes? And how would you prove it with data? If I could get these two to create profiles, they'd likely match so fucking quickly. It could be just what they need to stop bullshitting.

"I don't know, man," he says hesitantly.

"You do realize that if you don't want her to go out with other guys, you could just ask her out?"

"I can't ask Elena out. She'll think I'm joking."

"You don't know that. Plus, if she's looking for dates, now may be the best time to ask her. You wouldn't want her to consider anybody but you if she went back into the pool."

"If I download the app, can't you just go in there and force us to match?"

"I suppose I could, but that defeats the purpose."

"C'mon, Grey. Name your price."

I chuckle. "Are you thinking about what you'd even say to her if you matched? Or how you'd ask her on a date like a normal person?"

"Of course not. I haven't gotten that far yet," he admits.

"I'm sorry, man." I break out into a fit of chuckles. "You have asked me not to intervene for the past decade, but now you'd like me to? I still think it'd be easier if you just had a conversation."

"Maybe I will download the app just to prove you wrong. When I match with a bunch of women that are not Elena, I'll have some choice words for you."

"Alright. That's fair. I gotta get back to work. Help her decide on a picture and consider signing up."

"Okay," he says, sounding defeated, but I just need him to trust me. "Love you, man."

"I love you too," I say as I hang up. Moments later, my phone dings with a text from the group chat.

Fools in NY

ALEX

The first one

ELENA

I knew you'd pick that one! Grey?

ME

The first one

ELENA

I am officially on the dating scene!

She sends a screenshot of her profile to the group chat. I wait for Alex to respond, and he doesn't. My phone dings again, and it's a text from Alex in a separate thread.

Alex

ALEX

I'm on the damn app. You happy now?

I start my stopwatch and wait to hear from them. I'm just curious if my predictions were right.

ME

Very happy. *J. Cole voice* lol

Got any matches yet?

ALEX

No

Now we wait. Should be any minute now. I tap my feet in

anticipation. My phone dings twice. Two separate threads from them both.

Elena

ELENA

Um, Grey? You there?

Alex

ALEX

You motherfucker.

Looks like they've matched. Have fun, kids.

20
happy new year

Greyson

Manhattan, NY | January 1, 2024

I BROUGHT in the new year with Alex, who hasn't mentioned a word about the whole *SoulBlend* thing since. I'm going to assume they're still ignoring the obvious. Elena would've loved to hang out with us, but New Year's Eve is one of the busiest nights of the year for her and Marco. *Aguilar's* has special hours for the holidays, and they stay open till two in the morning. I hope they had a good turnout, and I know they're happy that the holidays are over. She'll sleep all day today, and we'll link up later in the week. The older we've gotten, it's always surprising to see if we can even stay awake for the ball to drop, but we managed to this year. Later, Alex retired to my guest room for the night, and I've been up watching movies. I pick up my phone to find the time, and it's a little after three in the morning. I'll go to bed once I know Elena made it home safely.

My phone chimes with a text from her shortly after, and it's not exactly what I was expecting. She wants me to come outside and get some leftovers. Well, that's a way to get me off the couch and fast. Once I'm outside, I see her food truck illegally parked down the street. Elena doesn't give a fuck, but I still quicken my pace toward her. When she notices me, she hops out with the bag of food and greets me with a hug. Marco's in the passenger seat, and I wave to him before she climbs back into the truck. They wish me a Happy New Year before they take off down the street.

On my short walk back to my building, I'm nearly blinded by a beacon of light as I notice movement coming from a black SUV, and I'm transfixed. My view is obstructed when they toss on a dress coat, but they leave it open as they stride in my direction. They're a good distance and the closer they become, I recognize those curves. A body I've dreamt about having my hands all over more times than I'd like to admit. A beaded gold gown clings to her perfect body that gleams in the light, a metaphor for who she is when she's comfortable. I love seeing her dressed like this, commanding the attention she rightfully deserves.

I realize that I've been standing here on the damn sidewalk with this bag of tacos staring at this woman. Thankfully, my feet remember to work, and I'm able to move again. Only a few steps forward before I consider the time of night and that I don't wish to scare her out here by stopping her on the street.

I greet our night door attendant, Gino, as I enter the lobby. I stand near the elevator, inconspicuously scrolling my phone as I wait for her to get closer before I press the up button. When she appears beside me, I'm engrossed in her seductive scent.

"Greyson? What are you doing up? It's late."

I peer over my shoulder to take her in up close, and she's a vision. I haven't had the pleasure of seeing her around much due to the holidays, but this makes up for it.

"I'm waiting for you to get home. Isn't that obvious?" I ask sarcastically.

"Shut up." She chuckles.

The elevator dings, and I absentmindedly guide my hand to the small of her back as we walk in together. She gasps softly at my touch, and before I remove my hand, she leans into it, breaking away from me once we're inside, and stands off in her usual corner. I press the buttons for our floors and resume my place beside her. I try not to stare, but I can't help it.

Her straightened hair is pulled back into an updo with long layers framing her face. Golden eyeshadow compliments those doe eyes, and shimmers dance across her skin under the light. Reminiscent of a shooting star, but I won't dare shut my eyes to make a wish for fear of missing this moment.

"How was your Christmas?" she asks with a smile.

"It was really nice. I hope you had a good one as well with Elise."

She looks up at me with a bemused expression before responding.

"We did. You remembered her name."

"Of course I did. I remember everything about you."

She hums to herself and puts her hand in her coat pocket as she watches the screen go up a floor. Her habit of watching the numbers ascend is always a painful reminder that our time is limited. I decide to fill the space with conversation, but she surprises me with a question.

"Did you get a midnight kiss?"

I shake my head in disbelief.

"No. Are *you* offering?" I ask, turning to face her.

She looks in the opposite direction, attempting to hide her smile, but the mirrored reflection on the wall reveals it anyway.

"Have you been drinking, Selah?"

She pinches her fingers together and says, "A little."

"I thought so. You're not acting like yourself."

She clicks her tongue and looks away, mumbling under her breath.

"What was that?"

She just looks up at me innocently with those big eyes and shakes her head.

It sounded like she called me smell good man.

If so, I'm not mad at that.

"Did you have a good night?"

"I did. I got to wear this pretty dress. I feel like a princess." She beams.

"You look radiant, and you *are* a princess. Always up in that tower," I joke.

She snorts as the elevator stops at her floor, but she doesn't make her usual run for it. Instead, her feet are planted, and she eyes me curiously.

"What's on your mind, Princess?" I ask, testing the new nickname on my tongue.

"Will you walk me to my door?" she asks shyly.

I raise my brow and hold out my arm for her to grab onto. She lets out a weary sigh as we step out of the elevator. She asks me about my uneventful night and listens intently. I summarize the events of our superhero movie marathon paired with Hennessy shots, Alex turning in after the ball dropped, and these tacos that randomly appeared. I consider that it's far too much food to eat alone and hand her a few tacos.

By the time we reach her door, she's still sorting through her keys until she picks the right one.

She unlocks the door but doesn't open it. Instead, she turns to face me.

"Thanks," she says, peering up at me.

I shake my head in response.

"You don't need to thank me. I do have a question for you though."

"Shoot," she says with a flirty smile.

"Did *you* get a midnight kiss?"

Her eyebrows shoot up. "No. I've never had one of those."

"Hmm. Were you hoping to get one tonight?"

"Yeah. I hoped I'd meet someone at the party, but I didn't."

Her shoulders sink, and she looks down at her feet.

I regain her attention, and we lock eyes; there's desire in her gaze. I want to kiss her so badly, but we've both been drinking. My cravings began with our first date, and it's been torturous to go without the taste of her. I've replayed that moment in my mind far too much to be a drunken regret. I want her to remember and tell me exactly what she wants when the opportunity presents itself again.

So, I lean in and kiss her cheek instead. She shuts her eyes and beams. When I pull back, I'm grinning like an idiot. She lets herself in but gives me one last look before heading inside.

"Happy New Year, Selah."

"Happy New Year, Greyson," she says with a giggle.

She shuts the door behind her, and the locks click as I make my way down the hall. I get back on the elevator with a New Year's resolution in mind.

I'm going to find out exactly what Selah wants from me and give it to her.

21
elevator pitch

Selah

Manhattan, NY | January 2, 2024

I JUST WOKE up from an interesting dream. Another one about my neighbor, Greyson. It's a pleasant reprieve from the nightmares that I'm used to. I sigh and look over at the clock. 8:38 am. It's a Tuesday, and I'm still on holiday break. I have a new toy I have yet to try. I reach into my nightstand to grab the silk drawstring bag. It's lilac and palm-sized.

I press the on button and another to start the functions. This one is intense and there's a strong vibration happening in my hand. This must be for when it's inserted. As I fiddle with the settings, vibrating sounds fill the room, and a startled Peach jumps up from the foot of my bed and nearly takes the blankets with her as she darts out of my room. I chuckle. They're hardly ever as quiet as advertised. I press the off button and select a different function. The clit stimulator starts with the lowest setting.

I can work with this.

I set the toy on my clit and feel the suction instantly. It's intense but bearable. I take deep breaths and focus.

I close my eyes and envision Grey cornering me in the elevator. He leans in, peppering kisses from my neck to shoulder. He grabs my waist to pull me in close and whispers in my ear.

"I think you can come on my fingers before this elevator stops. You want to prove me, right?"

I nod. My breath hitches as his hands lift the hem of my dress. He looks at me with the skirt of my dress balled in his fists.

"Hold this, Princess."

I forget how to speak. I grab the dress, holding it up as his hands dip lower.

His fingers find the pool of wetness through the lace, pulling them to the side.

"So perfect."

He slides a finger between my slick folds before pressing his thumb to my clit and rubbing in soft circles. I whimper at his touch. His intense gaze remains while he showers me with praise and increases the rhythm.

His free moves toward my face.

"Open," he orders, placing two fingers in my mouth.

I take his fingers, swirling my tongue around them while keeping eye contact.

"Good girl," he says before removing the fingers and placing one inside me.

I gleam from the praise and shudder at the fullness. He draws steady circles on my clit while pumping in and out of me. The sounds of my wetness fill the space.

He lowers his head to suck on my hard peaks through my dress, and I wail in response. I've never done that before. As if he can read my mind, something ignites in his eyes. He sucks harder, granting them both attention, but the rhythm of his hands doesn't falter. He adds another finger, pumping in and out of me at a faster pace. I feel my legs tremble beneath me, and my breath quickens.

"You're so fucking beautiful."

He pumps harder, and my head rolls back.

"Eyes on me. Almost there, baby."

I feel the pressure building and grip onto his arms for leverage. My moans echo through the elevator, and he stares in amazement.

"You're going to come for me?"

I cannot speak.

"Use your words."

"Y-Yes. I'm going to come."

I gasp between each word.

"Let go," he says.

The sensitivity in my core is overwhelming as I teeter off the cliff. I increase the suction of my toy and fall back to the pillows, clawing at the sheets as my climax builds. I let out a loud moan, and the doorbell rings in response.

Not the bell I needed rung.

You've gotta be fucking kidding me.

I glance over at the clock and see the time. 8:49 a.m.

Who would be here this early? The girls would've texted first. I open up my doorbell app to see who's out there.

Shit. It's him.

What is he doing here?

He's holding a box and a drink carrier. Pacing outside my door. He rings again.

Did he bring me breakfast?

Without thinking further, I click the mic button on the app and speak.

"Hey. Um, I'm not decent. If you could give me a moment, I'll be right there."

"Yeah, no-no problem."

I now notice the loud buzzing from my toy—which I forgot to turn off.

Fuck. Can he hear that?

"Is everything okay? What's that noise?"

Shit. I scramble to turn it off. Pressing each button but to no avail, I accidentally increase the setting.

Fuck, that feels good.

I stifle a whimper. The toy is so slippery from my arousal that I can't grip the buttons.

"It's—ummm, my toothbrush! I'll be right there!"

After I click the mic off, I press every button simultaneously and hold them until finally it shuts off. *Whew.*

I clean myself up, then dash around my room to get dressed while *actually* brushing my teeth.

I rush towards the door, yelling out, "just a minute!"

I check myself in the mirror and realize I still have my fucking bonnet on. I yank it off, toss it over my shoulder, and give my curls a good shake. Now, I'm out of breath.

So sexy, Selah. Great job.

I open the door, and there he stands with a smile, taking me in as if nothing else exists.

A man has never looked at me like that in the morning.

"Good morning."

"Morning," I say shyly.

"I was out grabbing coffee and when I came across this shop that makes tiny donuts, I thought of you and figured we could try them together?"

"Since we haven't had our coffee dates during the holiday break, I figured I'd bring the date to you."

Because we eat donuts together on Tuesdays.

This man is precious. Wow.

He's so sweet and I'm so awkward.

He wants to come into my house and eat?

Deep breaths.

This is what romance novels are made of.

I'm going to let this man into my house and hope he doesn't kill me.

I open the door wider and invite him in.

He steps through the door, and I head over to the kitchen island when he slips out of his shoes and sets them on the doormat.

That was hot.

That's a number one house rule for me and I forgot to mention it.

I lean over the counter, grab my phone from my pocket, and shoot off a text to Daya, letting her know the hot neighbor is here, and silence my phone before placing it face down on the counter.

He rounds the island, and I'm screaming internally from his proximity. His cologne surrounds me, and I want to bathe in it. He pushes up his sleeves, exposing his tattoos that are usually concealed, and I feel my face warming. I stare at them and swallow.

He interrupts my gaze by asking, "do you mind if I…?"

He aims his head toward the sink and makes a hand-washing motion. I nod. He washes his hands while I stare at him.

He removed his shoes AND washed his hands upon settling in.

Pro: He may be the perfect houseguest.

Con: I think he's trying to steal my heart.

Alert the proper authorities.

After drying off his hands and rolling his sleeves back down. He takes a seat on a barstool and takes a sip of coffee.

"I've never seen you drink coffee, but I took a wild guess at what tea you'd like. Please tell me if you hate it. Wait. You're not allergic to anything, are you?"

He looks panicked, and it's the cutest thing.

"Thank you. Not that I know of. It's hard to ruin tea. If it's sweet, I'm sure I'll love it."

"I figured I couldn't go wrong with peach tea."

I take a sip, and I moan.

I stiffen and avoid eye contact, but I feel his eyes on me

One day, I won't embarrass myself in front of this man.

I gather the courage to look at him, and he raises his eyebrow.

"I'll take that as a positive review, hoping you don't make noises like that when something is bad."

He looks at me expectantly.

"It's perfect. Thank you for thinking of me."

He takes a sip of his coffee.

"I always—shit."

He erupts into a fit of coughs, choking on his coffee. I run over to pat his back and rub it as he settles down.

What was he going to say?

"Sorry. Wrong pipe," he chuckles nervously.

"I'm glad you're alright."

My phone buzzes on the counter. I pick it up and see that Daya texted back. I point to my phone and tell him I need to respond.

"No worries."

DAYA

Dios Mio.

You let the HOT neighbor in?

ME

We haven't had our standing coffee time during the holiday break.

He brought coffee and donuts.

Said he was bringing the date to me.

DAYA

Sounds like he was written by a woman.

Keep me posted.

Make sure he cleans all those cobwebs out!

ME

OMG

BYE

I stifle my laughter and look up at Grey. He's on his phone as well. I apologize for the interruption, and he waves it off. He opens the donut box, taking one out that's covered in powdered sugar. My mouth waters. When he bites into it, his face tells it all.

It's as good as it looks. I've got to try it. I grab napkins from a drawer and set them beside him.

He slides the box across the counter for me to take my pick. I choose a glazed one with sprinkles and grab a napkin to set it on. A comfortable silence floats through the kitchen as I bite into the donut and moan again subconsciously.

Girl.

He looks up at me with a glimmer in his eye.

Am I always like this?

Get it together, Sis.

As if he senses my embarrassment, he averts his eyes. They dance around my apartment and halt. I'm not sure what he's looking at until he gets up and moves towards my fridge.

The list. Shit!

He's reading it.

WWAD?

She'd own it.

I'll own it now and throw up later.

He raises an eyebrow and continues reading.

"So, this is the infamous *Fuck It List*. I'm impressed."

I breathe deeply to myself, waiting for this moment to end.

"I'm so embarrassed."

"Don't be. I know you didn't mean for me to see it, but I don't mind. You don't take yourself too seriously and you're having fun. You may need to give me the backstory behind these, though."

He smiles and I chuckle, covering my mouth.

"Look at all you've accomplished so far! These are difficult feats. I'm proud of you. My family always had high expectations of me as the oldest. My parents planned out my entire life before it began. While I was the first to go to college and use my degree, a dating app didn't exactly fit in with their plan, but I launched it anyway. I guess you could say that was a 'fuck it' moment. It was a stressful time, and I had panic attacks often, but I'm glad I stayed the course," he says, returning to his seat.

"I can relate. I had a few starting out and I still do from time to time."

"How do you manage?"

"Honestly? My friend Audrey, she's absolutely fearless and I think of her every time I'm afraid of something. I picture how she would handle the exact scenario, and I go with that. It works."

"Whenever that doesn't work, a joint does. Though I sometimes forget what I was afraid of."

I shrug my shoulders, and he sniggers to himself.

"I like that. I need to find more fearless friends and a dispensary," he chuckles.

"Well, if you ever meet her and she decides she likes you, she won't let you leave until you are friends. I love that about her."

I smile to myself.

"What about if she doesn't like me?"

"You'll leave in a stretcher. There's no in-between with her."

I break out in a fit of laughter, and he joins me.

"I can't wait to meet her. She sounds like a good time."

I lean over the counter, facing him as I sip my tea.

"So, you took a moment to answer. Were you resting or did I interrupt something?" he asks with a knowing look.

"N-No. I was just in bed."

"But you said you were using your toothbrush. Do you always brush your teeth in bed? That sounds a little strange." He crosses his arms and leans back.

"Are you judging me, Greyson?"

He raises his hands in surrender.

"Of course not. I'm just trying to get the positioning in my head, that's all."

I see he will not let this go, so I'll play along.

"Maybe I was distracted by something."

"Hmm. Are you sure you finished brushing your teeth? If you didn't, I'm certain I could provide some assistance."

He does air quotes around brushing your teeth and gives me a knowing look.

The nerve of this man.

This must be about the damn list.

"I suppose I didn't completely finish, since the doorbell rudely interrupted me," I say, crossing my arms over my chest.

That's it.

He scoffs, placing his hand over his chest, pretending to be wounded.

"I came bearing gifts and truthfully, if I knew that's what you were doing on the other side of this door...it sounds to me like you summoned the right man for the job."

He pushes up his sleeves and leans towards the counter, waiting for my response. I swallow and feel heat pooling low in my belly.

Relax.

He's just a man.

Tell that to my body.

"I never took you for cocky."

He sits up straight, looking amused.

"I'm not cocky. I am confident in my abilities to please a woman. If you're interested in learning more about my capabilities—and before you disagree—it seems you're in the market for them," he adds with a nod to the list.

Who is this and what happened to the golden retriever?

My breath catches as heat pools between my legs. An idea pops into my mind that may be able to help us both. I fear his boldness is contagious because I'm not only considering it, but I start repeating it out loud.

"So, uh, about the list. I'd like to propose something and please stop me if this is ridiculous."

He quirks an eyebrow and leans in, resting a hand on his knee. I take a deep breath, and he studies me.

"I'm listening."

You can do this.

If you need anything, you can call me. His words.

"I have until May to cross everything off. My thirtieth birthday is approaching, and I need to complete it. This would be mutually beneficial for us, and I'd like you to name your price or, in this case, a favor. Would you be open to helping me out? I mean, since you're 'the right man for the job' and all?"

He perks up, crossing his arms and he eyes me curiously.

"You're serious. Do I at least get an interview?"

I chuckle nervously. "Um, if that's what you want?"

"I know you're dating, and there may be other worthy candidates. I'd like to request a trial run or…a *taste test* to prove myself?"

It's safe to say the golden retriever has left the building.

He stares expectantly, and I nod assuredly.

"When can I have a taste, Selah?"

He chuckles darkly and wetness pools between my legs at the sound. His eyes turn ember, a flame stokes within them. My breath hitches at the sight. I'm so lost in them I forget to respond.

I desperately need relief right now, and I was thinking of him, anyway.

What comes out of my mouth next surprises me.

"Right now."

His gaze erupts with fire, and he is on me. His hand envelops my back, and the other gives my nape a gentle squeeze. He leans in closer, eyes locked on mine.

"Are you sure about this? I know what I said, but we can stop. Say the word, and I'll stop at any time."

If he's anything like he was in my dream, I need to know.

"I don't want to stop."

"I was hoping you'd say that."

22
opening statement

Selah

Manhattan, NY | January 2, 2024

KISSING GREYSON RIVALS ALL OTHERS. Weeks have passed without his taste, and I am in need. He commands my mouth, gently coaxing the seam of my lips with soft licks. I welcome him, returning each swipe and twist. The bitter coffee and sugar dance across our tongues as the kiss deepens.

I stand on the tips of my toes as I grip the back of his neck, inching him closer to me. Desperate for more, my grip on his nape tightens, half-moons pressing his skin. He growls in response, greedily taking my offering. My senses heighten and my core drips in anticipation.

He tapers off for a breath, peppering kisses around my mouth. His lips trail my neck, hovering over my ear. Goosebumps dance in unison throughout my body.

He whispers, "I'm going to tease you before I give you what you want. I'll need to hear you beg for it. Do you understand?"

I nod.

"I need to hear you say it, Selah."

"Yes."

"Good girl."

He licks my neck, relishing the taste of my skin. A desperate whimper escapes me. I've never been this turned on in my life.

I want him.

I hastily curl my fingers beneath the hem of my top. He stops me, placing his hand over mine.

"I didn't say you could take off your clothes. Did I?"

I sigh. "No."

With a raised brow and an incredulous look, it's clear he'd like to be the one to strip me. He seeks approval in my gaze, and I assure him.

Yes. Yes. Touch me.

He delicately lifts my shirt and bra with a toss over his shoulder, staring admiringly at my full breasts and soft stomach. It hits me that this is the first time I have been naked in front of a man since my ex, and I stiffen. Insecurities creep in, causing me to hug my waist, covering myself.

Greyson examines me, pulling my arms apart.

"You are perfect, Selah." He says in between gentle kisses on my chest and shoulders. Stepping back to take me in, he says, "Fuuuccck. Just look at you. Incredible."

There's adoration in his eyes, but he could just be saying that.

I'm not used to men complimenting my body. This is different.

Instead of embracing his attention, I want to assure him he doesn't have to say all this.

"I'm not per—" I'm silenced with a kiss, tender and demanding before pulling away.

"I'm going to strip you bare and grant your body the attention it deserves. I'm going to worship you, because it's what you deserve, Princess."

When I part my lips to protest, he acknowledges his hard length straining in his pants and my breath hitches.

"Before you argue, this is what you do to me. I'm starving for you, Selah."

Stoked flames erupt in his irises. My eyes widen, insecure thoughts dissipate, and I am enraptured in him.

He leans in closely, lips hovering over my ear. "Let me feast."

I shudder at his words.

I grip his neck and slant my mouth over his, tasting him once again. He grips my hips, guiding me backward. My back meets the island, and we break the kiss. Chests rising and falling, lips red and swollen. The heat of his gaze is searing. Tugging at my sweatpants, he guides me out of the fabric as I steady myself on the counter. He kicks them aside, directing his attention to me. His gaze is drunk with desire when he picks me up effortlessly and sets me on the island.

Shit.

Add that to my list of firsts as well.

Once I am seated, he kneels before me, and a devious grin spreads across his face.

I am internally screaming.

I fear that Greyson may have ruined me for other men and he hasn't even touched me yet.

He sinks to his knees and peers up at me. He wraps his hand around my ankle, pressing a kiss to the top of my foot. He continues to mark me, trailing soft kisses toward my center. Massaging my calves and thighs in between, I whimper at his concentration on appeasing me, but I'm growing impatient.

I spread my legs and reach down to rub my clit. I'm so sensitive that I quiver at the contact. He stares in awe before he rises and stops me.

"I didn't say you could touch yourself. Did I?"

I roll my eyes in frustration.

"No, but–"

"Taste yourself," he interjects.

When I obey, his eyes darken. I relax my jaw and suck my fingers clean, moaning around them.

"It's a shame you haven't behaved enough to taste me. Now if you don't mind, I haven't finished adoring you."

I feign surprise. "Be my guest."

"I *am* your guest. Be a good *host*. I know you have a tendency to be rude, but now is not the time."

My jaw drops, before I can respond he says, "I'm starting to believe interrupting me is a kink of yours."

"Are you kidding me?"

I cover my mouth as I giggle.

"Quiet, baby. I'll tell you when you can be loud."

He leans down, tongue grazing my nipple before he gently sucks while pinching the other. He hums around my breast and my eyes roll back. It sends a bolt straight to my core. I could come from this alone.

That'll shut me up for now.

He adores my other breast, smiling around my aching peak, biting down. "Fuck! Greyson, please," I whine.

He stops abruptly.

"Please what, baby? Tell me what you want."

The word baby on his lips sounds illegal. I hope to hear it again.

"Fuck me. Please?" I sob.

"Who do you want to fuck you?" he asks, pressing his hand against my wetness.

"You," I sob.

He curls a finger in the waistband of my panties and I'm on fire.

"What's my name?" He stares expectantly.

"Greyson."

He looks amused. "Is that your final answer?"

"Yes."

He frowns. "Wrong answer, baby. I'll give you another round to make things right. For now, I need to see how soaked you are for me." He reaches inside my panties, finding my clit. He presses his thumb against it, and I weep at his touch. "You're so wet and needy." He bites his lip. "Promise you'll behave?"

"Yes. Fuck," I beg.

"Then you'll be rewarded."

He unravels the waistband on my panties, crouching down,

and time slows as the lace descends. He slips the fabric into his pocket and glances up at me with an audacious grin.

I am screaming internally.

Greyson draws careful circles around my clit, gazing at me with a raging inferno. Taking mental notes of how I react to his skill. He swipes through my wetness, slipping a finger inside of me as his mouth lingers over mine.

"Finally," I exhale, he chuckles against my lips.

I lean forward to meet him in a passionate kiss. Our tongues in step, following his lead, our neighborly dance. He pulls back for air and maintains his rhythm while silently affirming me.

I'm convinced he's specially trained in torture.

It's too much and not enough at the same time.

I'm questioning if he could hear my thoughts when he says, "I think you can take another finger."

He adds another and I adjust to the fullness as he envelopes me, wrapping his free arm around my waist to steady me. Cradling his face in my neck as he generously pumps his fingers into me. I arch into his touch, yearning for more, tossing my head back in pleasure.

"Right there. Please—Oh God," I manage through mumbles and shaky breaths.

I feel the pressure growing, using him and the countertop for leverage.

"You feel so fucking good on my fingers. Do you need to come?"

I nod vigorously, avoiding eye contact when he takes his free hand under my jaw, forcing me to return his gaze.

"Ask me if you can come, Selah."

Boy bye.

He must be joking.

I roll my eyes, bucking against him as I chase my pleasure, and he stills his hand.

I was so fucking close.

I huff, narrowing my eyes at him while his eyes carry a mild flame.

He asks, "are you angry with me?"

Like he isn't a fucking menace.

He is infuriating and so fucking sexy right now, I could kiss him.

"I thought you were a good girl, but you're acting like a brat. Are you a brat?"

"Maybe I am."

"Yes or no, love?"

"Yes." I hiss.

He leans forward and nips at my lip, pulling away and holding eye contact. His fingers move inside me, just enough to make me whine.

"Ask me."

"Make me come," I say through gritted teeth.

He raises an eyebrow and freezes his hand again.

"Where are your manners?"

I take a deep breath, asking in a softer tone, "can I please come?"

Greyson seems pleased with my cooperation and resumes swirling my sensitive nub while I grind on his fingers. He grins at the sight, leaning in closely to adorn my neck with kisses. He pumps harder, enjoying the show as I wriggle beneath his gaze. My pleasure builds again as he drives me up the peak, and he urges me with praises.

"Let go."

As I near the edge, an impending fall that I'm certain he'll guide me through, I take the plunge and melt around his fingers. My release drips down his hand and he smiles. If I crumble beneath his touch, I can't imagine what a mess I'll be when he's inside me.

He continues thrusting, prolonging the ecstasy as I ease down from my climax. He retrieves his fingers slowly, licking my arousal off his glistening hand. The sight ignites me, and I grab him in a demanding kiss, eager to taste myself. He grips the nape of my neck, pulling me in closer and we're lost in each other once again. We break away and I need to taste him so badly, I shift off the counter and he grabs me, picks me up and sets me on the floor. I start to kneel, and he stops me.

"You've been a good girl, but you didn't earn it."

I frown. "But I begged like you asked me to."

"You still refuse to call me Grey and until you admit that you're a dirty fucking girl. *My* dirty fucking girl, you won't."

I try to ignore how good "my dirty fucking girl" sounds on his lips.

As I return to my height he says, "You think that sample of you would fulfill a man like *me*? I need more. Bend over that counter for me, baby."

Oh my God.

I bend over the island; I arch my back giving him a better view.

"Look at you."

He rubs my cheek before I feel a hard smack to my ass, I drip in response.

"That's a good girl."

He repeats on the other cheek before leaving a soft kiss to soothe the sting. Lowering himself behind me, he inches closer to my core and blows on my pussy. With one long swipe between my folds, he uses his tongue to part my lips and twirl around the sensitive bud. I cry out instantly.

He grips my thighs, holding me in place as he devours me. He laps at my core, moaning in pleasure while he uses me to appease his appetite.

"You're so fucking good at that," I sob.

He accepts my praise, flicking his tongue in various motions, seeking a rhythm to make me scream. Pressure builds within me and my legs tremble. He's attentive enough to know my body needs release and I hate it. I'm convinced he can read my mind once he removes his mouth, placing soft pecks on the back of my thighs. He slips his thumb between my folds, gathering wetness, while the other hand gently rubs my ass cheeks. He spreads them apart and begins circling my other hole. I shudder in response as the unfamiliar feeling overwhelms me.

"How does this feel?"

"Good," I manage through sharp breaths.

"You know, if you want to come, all you need to do is ask." He flattens his tongue and resumes eating me from behind, his thumb still teasing my ass. The intensity builds and I find myself clawing my countertop.

"I-I need to come. Please?" I fight to get the words out.

He sucks even harder on my clit, and I wail. He appreciates and toys with my body. His moans of gratitude are music to my ears. My orgasm rushes through and sets my body on fire, he holds my sensitive nub tightly between his lips, prolonging my pleasure with gentle sucks. I'm exhausted and get the feeling that he isn't quite finished with me yet. He stops then moments later, his warm tongue glides up and down my inner thighs, collecting arousal as it runs down my legs.

He rises to his full height, pressing his firm erection into me as I remain bent over the counter.

"You look so fucking good when you're at my mercy," he growls.

He helps me sit up and when we lock eyes, his gaze is full of desire. I grip his shirt, bringing him to eye level as our lips meet in a needy kiss. Nothing exists beyond it. We pull apart and I kneel before him with hopeful eyes, eager to please him. Instead, he helps me to my feet, and I grumble.

"Bring me your toy."

"My toy?"

"Oh, I forgot. You named it *toothbrush.*"

He does air quotes around the word *toothbrush,* and I stifle a laugh.

"I know what I heard through the doorbell, and I want you to bring it to me."

Shit.

23
play date

Greyson

Manhattan, NY | January 2, 2024

HER EYEBROWS SHOOT up and she stares incredulously.

"Where are your manners, Greyson?"

I close the distance, angling my face up,

"Forgive me. Can you please bring me your toy? I'm not done playing with you."

She gulps audibly and freezes.

"Now," I urge.

I smack her ass, pulling her from her thoughts.

She darts toward her room, and I don't miss the cute giggle she lets out.

I'm going to have fun with her.

When she returns, I hand her a water bottle encouraging her to drink. She hands me a purple vibrator and I examine it. She shows me its functions and what her favorites are. I stare adoringly before picking her up and setting her back on the counter. I adorn her neck and collarbone with kisses, turning it on the lowest setting, as I ease onto her swollen clit. I take note of her body and how she reacts to me. Her back arches and I turn up the setting, a silent challenge I hope she accepts.

"More," she begs.

I'm happy to oblige, turning the setting up two more notches. I grip her thigh to steady her as she bucks against the vibrator. I swipe my tongue across my bottom lip and dip my head, slipping her nipple into my mouth. She's getting close when she digs her nails into my arm. I switch, twirling my tongue around her breast as I tease the other.

"Fuck," she cries out and I smile against her.

I kiss along her chest and neck, indulging in the taste of her skin. Waiting for her to ask nicely.

She whines, "can I please come?"

"I don't know. Can you?" I chuckle against my ear.

She bucks against the toy, chasing her climax.

"Come for me."

An order, a statement and an offering. She surrenders with my name on her lips, and I'm grateful to witness it. The vibrations continue, and she rides them out as she comes down.

"Fuck," she breathes with a chuckle.

"You did so good."

She beams under my praise.

"Would you like to pick up where we left off with breakfast? Or are you itching to dismiss me?" With a raised brow, I wait for her reply.

She sighs, looking down at herself and says, "I am naked in my kitchen, but I'm still hungry. You had more to *eat* than I did."

I laugh through my nose. "That *is* true. I'd like to fix that *and* get you cleaned up if you'll let me."

"Why wouldn't I?"

"Well, I'm not sure if you've noticed but you tend to be a bit snippy when you're anxious and I could expect you to kick me out any minute now, once the post orgasm clarity sets in."

She drops her jaw in shock and scoffs.

"Greyson, I am *always* nice to you, but I can be snippy when I'm anxious. I'll admit that."

I stare at her deadpan and argue, "You're only nice when I'm on my knees for you."

She covers her laugh with her hand. "What can I say? I love when you succumb to me."

"I don't think you could handle any more of me today."

I hand her the water bottle, instructing her to take big gulps and not small sips like she had been.

I disappear down the hall, coming back with a towel and washcloth.

"Excuse me. Why don't we take a tour?" Her tone is laced with sarcasm.

"I have the same apartment upstairs; I know the layout. You should come over sometime."

I run the cloth under warm water and wring it out, surprisingly she lets me clean her up without protest. She's quiet again, observing me. I wonder what she's thinking. I help her off the counter and hand her the rag to finish up. I tidy up the kitchen while she cleans up and pass her a towel when she's done.

I step into her bathroom to process what just happened. I really did just plan on us having coffee and donuts. I hadn't expected things to escalate in that way, but I am so happy they did. Selah is incredible. She's better than any fantasy or dream I've had. I stare down at the very visible erection through my sweats and shake my head.

I should take care of this and give her space.

Once she's settled, I'll see myself out.

I enter the kitchen and she's dressed again, seated on a barstool eating a donut."

"Trying to seduce me?" I ask behind her. "Because it's working."

She swivels on the stool to look me up and down, and she squeezes her thighs together in response.

"What about you?" she asks, motioning to my dick with her donut.

"I'd love to fill you, but you didn't behave."

She sighs frustratedly.

"I'll give you some time to think about your decision. Surely, you'll regret it."

I press a soft kiss to her forehead and when I pull away, I nearly shiver from the distance. I round the island to rip a note from the fridge, scribble on it, and flip it over. She watches with a wrinkled brow.

"Now, you know where to find me when you change your mind."

And I'm certain she will change her mind.

24
closing statement

Selah

Manhattan, NY | January 2, 2024

"WELL, you're fed, hydrated and satiated. Looks like my work here is done. I have closing questions prepared."

I let out a guffaw.

This man.

"Sure."

"Were you satisfied with my service today, Selah?" He mimics holding a clipboard, pretending to read from it.

"Yes."

He nods, mimicking a drawn checkmark.

"Was I the most qualified candidate for the job?"

I pretend to think hard about his question.

"You certainly impressed me."

His lips tick up on one side, and he swipes his tongue over his lip, considering something.

"The tattoo on your hip. What does it mean?"

"It's from a song called *Woman* by Harry Styles."

"It's beautiful. You can imagine my surprise when I asked to feast on you and saw that very word etched into your skin. Would you call that a coincidence?"

I hum. "I'm not sure, but it surprised me."

"Do you like surprises?"

"Here's a fun fact about me. I hate surprises."

"You seemed to enjoy this one," he counters with a smile.

He is something else.

"Will you think of me the next time you brush your teeth?" He asks and I snort.

"I'm strongly considering it."

"I'm grateful for the opportunity to interview with you today. You've given me a clear overview of the position, and I think my experience can provide value. Do you have a time frame of when you'll reach out to candidates?"

I stifle my laugh and keep playing along.

"Sometime within the next week or two."

He nods understandably, still in character.

"There'll be no further questions. Thank you for your time, Selah." He motions toward the door, grabbing his shoes and putting them on.

"I'll be seeing you, Greyson."

"Oh, you will?" he challenges.

"Bye." I give him a flirty wave as he stands in my doorway.

"Bye, Selah," he says softly, closing the door behind him.

I let out a squeal of excitement and call for Peach. I know she's been hiding in fear of a stranger being in the house. I zero in on the note he left and flip it over.

I hope to hear you calling me Grey sometime soon. ;)

He is really determined about that nickname.

This reminds me of the deal I made with my mama. She is going to *love* this.

Whenever you find out just how good of a neighbor he is, give me a call and say 'pinochle.' Repeat it three times if he's good and once if he's not.

She's at work right now, but I call anyway, and it goes to voicemail. I'm holding in my giggles at how ridiculous this is while waiting for the beep.

I say, "pinochle, pinochle, pinochle," and hang up.

25
teatime

Selah

Manhattan, NY | January 2, 2024

ME

TEATIME!!!

CHESS

What's the temperature?

Daya responds with eye emojis.
Audrey responds with a tea-sipping GIF.

DAYA

Does this have anything to do with the HOT neighbor?

CHESS

Wait. How HOT is this neighbor?

AUDREY

One question at a time!

I'm on the edge of my seat here!

ME

Yes.

The temperature is scalding.

DAYA

Dios Mio!

Do we need to pull up?

ME

Yes, Please!

I'd like to see your faces for this one.

CHESS

Holy shit. Please tell me you were a slut.

You deserve this.

I'll be done with my last client around 3.

ME

Since this is going to be a tea party, I'll tell you when I see you!

AUDREY

OMG! I'm already on my way!

Meetings have been canceled!

Order pizza! I'll bring the wine!

CHESS

The suspense is killing me.

DAYA

Uno night?

I'll be by once I wrap up with my clients too.

See you soon!

ME

Of course!

@Audrey, Tell Rome he's welcome to join!

AUDREY

He's on a work trip this week but asked us to call him when you spill!

ME

I love Rome.

AUDREY

Somebody has to! lol

26
shower thoughts

Greyson

Manhattan, NY | January 2, 2024

AS I SHUT the door behind me, I take a moment in the hall to process what just happened before I head upstairs. My dick is so hard it's painful, and I am trying to calm myself down a bit before any of our neighbors see me like this.

Wait. Did I see a dance pole in her living room, or was I imagining that?

Fuck.

Now is not the time.

I shake my head and take a few deep breaths, encouraging myself to think the most unsexy thoughts for the short walk home. I slip my hands into my pockets, hoping to look normal while I make my way to the elevator. The jingle of keys sounds on one side, and the feeling of soft lace greets me on the other.

Her panties.

I forgot that I took these.

Surely, she won't mind.

After the walk to the elevator that felt like a mile long, I was fortunate to have made it back to my place without anyone joining me or running into any neighbors as I managed to disguise the hardest erection I've ever had. Clifford bounces around in excitement at my arrival, and I greet him with head rubs and settle in before I continue down the hall. I hear the faint squeak of his toy and the creak of the couch when he jumps on it. Once I close my bedroom door and enter the en-suite, I twist the knob to start the shower, testing the temperature before I step out to undress.

I remove my shirt and unfasten my belt and pants in a hurry. I'm desperately in need of relief. I remove my boxers, and when my dick springs free, I mildly regret not allowing her to taste me. The pleading in her eyes and the grumbles when I denied her were so cute, but this was about her pleasure. However, I think I underestimated Selah's effect on me because witnessing my timid neighbor unravel before me was more satisfying than she'll ever know.

I step into the shower and let the water run down my face and neck. My entire body is buzzing with need. I palm my dick and pump once, and beads of precum drip as I imagine Selah on her knees before me—those pretty brown eyes enticing, her mouth open wide and eager to lick up every drop. Ready and willing to please me.

She parts those plump lips to welcome my aching dick, flattening her tongue to take more of me. The warmth of her mouth overtakes me, and I throw my head back at the contact, pressing my hand against the tiles for leverage as I pump faster. I bite my lip and relish the taste of her on my tongue. Her moans play on a loop in my head, and what a sweet song they are.

Her hands fist my dick, spitting on it before taking me in deeper, all while she keeps her gaze locked on me. I thrust it into her mouth, and she takes it, watching her eyes well up as she gags but doesn't waver. She sucks harder in response, moaning around me when I notice her free hand moving down to touch herself, even though I didn't say she could. In this fantasy, I'll allow it. She slides those delicate panties to the side and slips a finger inside herself, her brows scrunching as she concentrates on our mutual pleasure, not missing a beat. She grinds into her palm while she hums with a full mouth.

"Fuck," I groan out.

I can hardly hear the shower as I am lost in this vision of her riding her fingers while she sucks my dick.

"Such a good girl. Make yourself come for me."

Her chest is rising and falling as I watch her perform, a show for my eyes only. Digging her free hand into my hip, she urges me to find a rhythm as I fuck her pretty mouth. I am mesmerized by my beautiful neighbor and her eagerness to please. My desperate release tears through me, shortening my breath as I spill down her throat. She greedily accepts my offering with hunger in her stare. Her hips grind faster against her hand as she chases her orgasm.

Selah removes her mouth to cry out my name, throwing her head back, and I watch in awe as she comes undone. She slips her shiny fingers in my mouth, willing me to indulge in her sweet arousal. I savor every drop of her, and it stays with me as I come to.

Steam envelops me as I rinse the ropes of cum from my abs. I quickly resume my shower before the water gets cold. I remind myself what happened this morning in Selah's kitchen was *not* a dream, and I'll do anything to make it happen again.

27
draw four

Selah

Manhattan, NY | January 2, 2024

"I KNOW your ass didn't just throw down a draw four and then change the subject. That's low down and dirty," I say with a head shake.

We're gathered around my dining table playing Uno, and it's been a bit of a stalemate. Daya has been getting a hold of draw cards and throwing multiples on us every chance she gets. Then Audrey, who's our natural competitor, has been doing the same out of spite. We're all sitting here with full decks and have been talking shit to each other so bad you'd think we weren't best friends.

This is a regular game night for us, no matter what. However, this card game is my favorite. I haven't lost yet with this group, but tonight, it looks like there'll be no winner. I get up from my seat to refill my wine glass, tucking my cards in my pants pocket. I glance around the table at any empty glasses, and anyone who'd like more gives me a nod or a shake. I grab the bottle and head back over to fill their glasses. Audrey is expressing her frustration over not being able to get rid of all the red cards in her hand, and Daya is snickering about it.

Aud points at me. "Anyway, now, back to you. Start from the beginning."

I explain how my morning went with Greyson, leading with the sex dream and the toy that I couldn't shut off that he indeed heard through my doorbell microphone. When I mentioned I lied about the toothbrush and he called me out on it, they erupted into laughter. I know that I will never hear the end of this.

They were so surprised to hear that I let him in and didn't make him sit in the hallway while I called one of them to freak out first. I keep blushing while telling them how easy he was to talk to and that it felt like whenever he could sense my anxiety rising, he would douse it in cold water and bring me back. They insist I explain the sex in vivid detail, so I try to summarize it since a lot happened that led to those three orgasms. Once I mention that, the looks on their faces are full of shock and amusement.

Daya raises her hand like a student, so I call on her like a teacher.

"Does he have a brother? I'm so serious."

I chuckle. "He does, but he's a bit young for you. Twenty, studying med at NYU."

She looks impressed. "So, he knows the female anatomy. I could wait. Probably won't meet a man before he graduates who knows where my clit is anyway."

We're screeching with laughter.

6

After I say goodbye to the girls, I'm packing for my upcoming trip to Portland and I'm not looking forward to it. I love my job, but my anxiety is put to the test whenever I work in person. While we're a solid team, as their leader, I am the face of this group, which means I do a great deal of public speaking in this role. At least when I work from home and get anxious or overstimulated, I can decompress easier than I can in the office. I've scheduled a session with Dr. Garnett tomorrow and will fly there Saturday to hang out with Skye before the summit on Monday. While I am excited to see her, I'm still anxious about my presentations this week, but Greyson helped, oddly enough.

When I suggested he help me with the list, I didn't expect him to be so eager to please. No man has ever done anything like that to me and I'm still grappling with it. He was being truthful when he said he was the right man for the job, but I'm even more curious about him now. I've told myself not to text him, but visions of his eyes piercing me as he laps at my core flood my mind. I shudder at the thought and grab my vibrator to toy with myself. When my lids shut, our film reel plays on repeat. I imagine him unraveling as pleasure jolts through me. I cry his name into the dark and wonder if he's doing the same.

28
sweet tooth

Greyson

Manhattan, NY | January 8, 2024

AFTER DROPPING Cliff off at home, I hop on the elevator, press the sixth floor, and wait anxiously as I descend. It's been four days, and I haven't heard a peep from Selah, so I've decided to take matters into my own hands.

I take a deep breath before I exit the elevator. As I get closer, my nerves get the best of me, but I bite the bullet and force my feet to keep shuffling closer 'til I reach her door. I press her doorbell, clutching the box hard enough that I could crush it. I take a step back, psyching myself up as I wait and hope she answers the door for me. It's been about thirty seconds, but it feels like thirty minutes. I hear heels clacking on the other side of the door. I really hope she's not going on another damn date. The knob turns softly, and my thoughts subside when I see a petite shapely woman answer Selah's door. I freeze, and we stare at each other for a moment before I decide to speak up.

She looks so familiar.

She parts her lips to speak. "So, we meet again. You look so different when your ex isn't draining the life out of you."

As her distinctive jazzy tone fills the space, I recall where I last heard it.

This woman is the wedding planner.

Aileen's fucking wedding planner.

At a loss for words, I stand there processing and panicking. She goes silent and sizes me up. Her glare hasn't wavered, and she stands firm in the doorway.

This is such an odd interaction.

What is she doing here, and where is Selah?

Does Selah know Aileen?

My stomach turns at the thought of them being friends.

She breaks the silence and holds eye contact.

"And people keep telling me to stop playing God. This," she says, pointing between us. "This is why I won't stop. I put the bug in your ear, and you managed to find her."

"Excuse me. What is it you're talking about? I'm lost here."

"When we met at the engagement party, I tried to set you up with a friend of mine, but I had to take a call. When I got back to the bar, you were gone. Remember?"

I think back to that conversation.

Radiant like a field of sunflowers.

Holy shit. Selah is 'sunflower girl.'

"When did you meet her?" she asks, yanking me from my thoughts.

"That same night. I live in this building."

She hums a response and doesn't falter.

I remember the reason I'm here and ask, "Um. Is Selah here by chance?"

"Selah isn't here. She left for Portland on Saturday. Business trip. I'm house sitting and babysitting Peach. We never did introductions, but by the looks of you—I'll call you big sexy." She states, leaning against the doorframe and crossing her feet.

"Excuse me?"

"You heard me. Mr. *Call me Grey if you're nasty.* I am nasty, but I think big sexy is more fitting. Is that a problem?" she asks, but I get the idea that she couldn't care less what I have to say about it. It clicks for me, then.

The fearless one.

If you ever meet her and she decides she likes you, she won't let you leave until you are friends.

If she doesn't like you, you'll leave on a stretcher.

This must be Audrey.

Selah's best friend is planning my ex-wife's wedding.

I fix my stance and respond.

"I don't mind that at all. You must be Audrey."

I stretch my lips into a smile, reaching out my hand to greet her with a shake.

"As I live and breathe," she says with a soft smile.

She shakes my hand firmly, maintaining eye contact.

This handshake plans weddings?

"What've you got there? Something for me?"

She peeks around me with a squint to get a better look at what I'm carrying.

"Well, it was for Selah, but since she's not here, would you like to have it? It's iced coffee and cinnamon rolls."

She perks up. "Don't mind if I do," she exclaims.

I hand her the box, and she says, "would you like to come in and eat with me?" She opens the door wider.

"Umm."

"Oh. Come on. I don't bite. Well, I do, but I wouldn't bite you," she cackles.

I contemplate for a moment, and she chides, "I'll put in a good word with Selah."

As if that was all it takes, I find my feet moving as I cross the threshold into Selah's humble abode.

I'm removing my shoes as she shuts the door behind her and says, "Just so you know, coffee and sweets won't get you the same result with me."

I snort.

"I can assure you what happened the other day wasn't

planned. It just happened and I'm grateful it did." I open the curtains to let the sun in before I stride over to the island for a seat. She stands across from me, watching me closely.

I'm finding it hard to focus being back here without Selah. I fight off images from the other day as I stare at all the surfaces I satisfied her on. I shake my head to free the thoughts before it becomes obvious what I'm imagining.

"Grateful, huh?" She looks at me as if she's reading my mind.

I head over to the sink and wash my hands as she gathers small plates. Each time I've met her, she's brought an odd sense of ease. I imagine she makes Selah feel the same.

I glance up as I'm drying my hands, and she rips off a piece of the cinnamon bun and places it into her mouth, squeezing her eyes shut in satisfaction.

Audrey likes sweets. Noted.

"By the way, I see you strolling down memory lane. All I ask is you keep yourself covered," she says, pointing at my pants. "I know those gray sweats were meant for different eyes to see."

"Ah. Sorry."

She hums her response, visibly enjoying the cinnamon bun and coffee.

I'm starting to get the allure of Audrey. She is an interesting character.

"How'd you get into wedding planning?" I ask.

"Good question. I don't just plan weddings. I guess some of it is in my blood, but events? My family wasn't doing enough in that market beyond the hotels, so I took it upon myself to create something there."

"Hotels?"

"Oh, honey, I thought you were just being charming. The venue of the engagement party, I own the place."

"No, the greenhouse was at the hotel. The *Woodward* Hotel."

She waves her hand, urging me to keep thinking. "You're getting warmer."

"You own *the* Woodward Hotel in Manhattan?"

"Well, not just one. I own them all."

My eyes widen with the revelation, and she nods.

Holy shit.

We proceed with the conversation, and I learn that the woman standing before me isn't just anybody—she's Audrey fucking Wood. No wonder she's so tough; she is the only woman running the Wood empire. Of course, she's firm and fearless.

"You know, I'm embarrassed to admit this, but I haven't heard from her since we—you know. That's why I stopped by."

"Interesting." She pulls out her phone and begins typing.

"Now, Grey, before I start meddling, I should probably ask if you shared that with me because you wanted my help *or* if you needed to get that off your chest?"

"I would like your help with her. I know you don't know me well, and your loyalty lies with her, but was she okay after the other day?"

"Oh. She was more than okay." She cackles. "I'm so glad you asked for my help. Now I don't have to feel bad about doing this." She rounds the island, holding up her phone in a selfie stance.

"Doing what?"

"We're going to take a picture for Selah and I'm going to send it to her. Once she sees you're here, she'll remember to use your number. How's that sound, Big Sexy?"

"I'm down," I agree.

Posing for the selfie, she insists we take three. Two with a smile and another with a silly face. I oblige, and she shows me the results as we choose the perfect one to send her.

Audrey grills me, as I expected, but nothing I don't feel comfortable answering. She asks about my marriage to Aileen and why it ended, and I answer truthfully hoping that doesn't change her opinion of me. She listens intently and seems understanding. She assures me that we were young and that everybody makes mistakes. She tells me that she's never married and has been in a long-term relationship with a man named Rome for the past five years. When I ask if marriage was in the plans, our phones ding at the same time. She smiles wide before retrieving her phone to glance at it.

"I told you it would work!"

SELAH

What the hell are you doing in my house?

How did you get Audrey to let you in?

I got her. My sunflower.

I then decide to change her name in my phone to 'Sunflower.'

ME

I needed to borrow a toothbrush.

SUNFLOWER

You are a little shit. Get out of there.

I can't believe you had her bully me into texting you.

ME

Are you bothered, or is that a part of your charm?

SUNFLOWER

Both. :)

ME

I missed you too.

Keep talking shit, and I will be leaving with that toothbrush. :)

SUNFLOWER

You wouldn't dare.

ME

I would dare.

SUNFLOWER

I think you might be jealous of my toothbrush.

I am *not* jealous of toys. I'm not an insecure man, and I recognize that toys are partners in pleasure. I used it on her for that reason. She's just trying to get a rise out of me. While I contemplate how to respond, typing and deleting repeatedly, she sends another text.

SUNFLOWER

Cat got your tongue now?

Now I know how to respond to this. Let's play, Princess.

ME

I know a cat that has my tongue. ;)

SUNFLOWER

SIR.

ME

Good girl.

She takes a moment to respond as I watch the three bubbles dance along the screen. I decide to be more intentional with my approach because it's possible she'll disappear again if I play along with her.

ME

When can I see you again?

SUNFLOWER

Depends.

ME

On what?

SUNFLOWER

When you get the hell out of my house, I'll consider it.

ME

I need to buy you a toothbrush for my place. ;)

SUNFLOWER

Greyson "I don't know your middle name" Park!

ME

It's Dae-Hyun, after my dad.

SUNFLOWER

Greyson Dae-Hyun Park!

ME

I love it when you call out my name. :)

I see the three bubbles appear and disappear, then reappear again before they stop for a moment. I wonder if I came on too strong and scared her off again. I set my phone down and look around the apartment. I notice Audrey reading on the couch with Peach snuggled on her lap. Chimes fill the air, causing me to turn around and panic when I see exactly who's calling me.

29
incoming call: sunflower

Greyson

Manhattan, NY | January 8, 2024

INCOMING: **Video Call from Sunflower**

"Shit. She's calling."

She stares at me deadpan and says, "pick it up and talk to her. You've got this, Grey."

I take a deep breath and exhale, saying thanks as I swipe to answer the call. Selah appears on the screen.

There she is.

Beautiful as ever.

Annoyance is her expression, but there's a hint of playfulness as she takes me in.

She can be so shy sometimes, and it is so interesting to me.

"Did you just call to stare at me or do you have something you wanted to say?"

"You think you're cute, don't you?"

"I'm not bad. Audrey called me 'Big Sexy.' I could get used to that," I quip.

Audrey yells out, "I didn't lie! Talk your shit, Grey!"

Selah chuckles, "Seriously, what are you doing there?"

"I came to have breakfast with you, but someone neglected to tell me she was skipping town. I thought we had a good time, did we not?"

She offers a nervous smile and takes a deep breath, calming herself.

"Yes, we had a good time."

"Good?"

"I'm just repeating what you said."

"Oh, so *now* you want to be a good girl?"

She chuckles to herself, visibly embarrassed. It's the cutest thing I've seen in my life.

Changing the subject, she asks, "Where's Audrey?"

"Right here, honey!"

I turn around, aiming the phone towards her, and she waves at Selah with her e-reader in hand.

"That better not be Lilith Keene's new book! I saw she was choosing people to send early copies to. Of course you got one!"

"Since you asked me to lie to you, it's *not* her new billionaire romance novel and I *didn't* get an advanced copy."

"Dammit, Audrey!"

"I love you! I suddenly can't hear you, so I'll just keep reading over here."

Selah erupts in laughter, and I revel in the sight. Audrey giggles to herself, getting back to her book.

"When will you be home?" I ask, shifting her focus back to me.

"You ask like there's someone waiting for me there."

"I mean, I literally am waiting for you to come home right now."

I motion to the space around me, reminding her.

A faint smile adorns her face as she looks at me through the screen.

"I'll be back Tuesday."

"I'll pick you up from the airport. Carpooling is good for the economy."

She laughs and argues, "You will not be picking me up. Audrey is."

"That can be rearranged. I'm pretty sure she's *my* best friend now. Isn't that right?"

She guffaws, "He's a charmer, babe! You might want to give him some ass again. It's just a suggestion."

"Audrey!"

I stifle a laugh. "She gives excellent advice. I think you should listen to her."

"Anyways, please get out of my house. Stop cozying up to my friend and I'll see you when I see you. Bye."

"I'll consider it. See you around, Sunflower," I respond, biting my lip.

Her lips part in awe and I disconnect the call, leaving her to marinate on her new nickname. I take a moment to recount this interaction, hoping I'm in a better place now than I once was with her.

"Sunflower. It's good. I like it. You stole it from me, but I'll allow it," Audrey blurts out, slicing through the silence.

"You inspired it."

"I suppose. Grab a seat."

She motions for me to join her on the couch. I sit on the opposite side of the terracotta sectional. It's very soft but firm. I sink into it and I'm sure I'd fall asleep if I sat here long enough. I fully understand why the cat has claimed this couch. Audrey leans back, stretching her legs in front of her, careful not to disturb Peach, who's sleeping soundly on a throw pillow behind her.

"I've decided that I would like to help you with Selah. Also, I'm not very good at minding my own business and she doesn't always know what's good for her. I've had a feeling about you from the beginning and if you prove me wrong, I'll just make you disappear, so I'm not too worried about that either."

"Disappear?"

I caught that word.

She waves her hand and continues, "Moving on. Come back

tomorrow and I will find something for you to do around here. Selah's love language is acts of service. So, you're going to need to prove that you're capable of doing something other than running that pretty mouth. You hear me?"

"Yes, Audrey."

"Good boy. Now get out of her house. You heard the woman."

She aims her head towards the door.

I freeze, not sure how to feel about being called a *good boy*.

She stares expectantly, and I give a nod before heading towards the door to retrieve my shoes.

As I put them on and open the door, she says, "Oh, and Big Sexy?"

"Yes?"

"Bring food tomorrow. Preferably sweets."

"You got it, Ms. Wood."

30
late night talking

Selah

Portland, OR | January 8, 2024

DOWNTOWN PORTLAND IS the backdrop as I unwind in my hotel room. I'm on my second glass of wine and am currently reading a romance that just got to the spice. I let out a gasp, tapping the screen to annotate the page, when I come across a position I was recently in with *him*. Shivers greet me as my thoughts flit back to my time with Greyson at my place.

I've never been touched like that, and while I may be overthinking per usual, I'm freaking out. I've only read about sex like *that* in books. I'll admit I'm a bit inexperienced and curious about some of the things he did to me. I also feel silly for not knowing everything about sex. I'm an adult, for fuck's sake.

Then again, I haven't had many partners, and if sex is supposed to be anything like what Greyson did to me, then I'm convinced I haven't fucked *anyone* before him, and I'd like to be compensated for my wasted time.

Not to mention, he did that solely with his hands and tongue. Sure, the man made me come three times on my kitchen counter before lunchtime, then went on about his day, and I can't stop thinking about it. Of course I didn't send him a fucking text message. What the hell was I going to say?

I grab my phone to look at the time; it's 11:25 p.m. I contemplate sending a paragraph to Greyson and decide against it. Simply because I don't know what to say just yet. The arrangement conversation is still looming in my mind, but I still have an upcoming *SoulBlend* date that I've been chatting with for about two weeks now. He's good looking and takes a lot of pictures at the gym. I'm not easily impressed by that, but I'm keeping my word and will see how we vibe in person before giving Greyson a final answer. I'm really burnt out on dates after all the flops, but I could go for one more.

I opt for sending a simple text to Greyson and toss my phone across the king-sized bed immediately after hitting send to avoid chickening out. It lands near the foot of it when I pick up my e-reader. I dive back into my latest novel, looking for a distraction from my anxious thoughts.

ME

Hi. Are you awake?

A few minutes pass, and I assume he's sleeping, so I start wondering what the hell I'm going to say in the morning when he wakes up to that text. Why didn't I just wait until I got back into town? He's probably going to think I was just hor—

That thought is interrupted by a ding. I jump up and hesitate as if he can see me.

I crawl across the bed to retrieve my phone and see that Greyson responded.

SMELL GOOD MAN

Yes. What are you doing up?

ME

I could ask you the same thing. I can't sleep. I've just been thinking.

SMELL GOOD MAN

So, you're up thinking about me? I'm flattered.

Of course, but I won't confirm or deny that. Lifting my glass, I gulp down more liquid courage to guide me through this conversation.

ME

I have a few questions. If you feel like answering.

SMELL GOOD MAN

Ask away.

ME

What happened in the kitchen last week...

I take a moment...hesitant of what I'd like to say before I just go for it. Maybe it's the wine in my system, but I am feeling bolder as my blood warms.

ME

When you wouldn't let me come. Why did you do that?

And why did it feel better once I did?

SMELL GOOD MAN

Oh, that. Edging. That's the whole point, baby.

Delaying your orgasm to intensify it once you came for me.

I felt how your body responded, but how did it make you feel?

ME

I've never heard of that. It freaked me out. It was nerve-wracking, but overall, it felt amazing.

Why did you want to use my toy on me?

SMELL GOOD MAN

Is that why you skipped town on me?

Couldn't even say goodbye. :(

I used your toy because it's fucking sexy.

I would've loved for you to show me how you like to use it, but I get the feeling you are still too shy to perform in front of an audience.

ME

I am not shy. You don't know me, sir.

I scoff. He's not entirely wrong, but he doesn't know me.

SMELL GOOD MAN

I'd like to get to know you. If I haven't made that clear, let me know.

I'm sure you open up once you're comfortable. Do I make you feel comfortable, Selah?

I'm not sure that I should answer that truthfully, but I don't want to be dishonest with him. I run through different responses in my head until I settle on one that I feel is good enough.

ME

I think you've made yourself clear. Something about you brings me comfort, Greyson.

SMELL GOOD MAN

As long as I can make you feel good. ;)

Have you ever touched yourself in front of someone?

ME

I have not. I've never been asked.

Have you?

SMELL GOOD MAN

Yes. Uh oh. She's coming out of her shell. lol

That's a damn shame.

I'd love to know exactly how you make yourself come when you're alone.

I drop my phone on the bed with a gasp. I didn't expect that response. I pour myself more wine, needing the courage to guide me as this heats up. I take a big sip when my phone trills. Mid-swallow, I make the mistake of picking up the phone, and *Smell Good Man* flashes on the screen, causing me to choke.

Shit.

I'm trying to get my coughing under control and end up missing the call.

(1) Missed Call

My life is a comedy hour because it rings again as I am chugging the leftover wine in my glass to get my bearings. I take a deep breath and swipe to answer as I wipe the dribbles from my lip with the back of my hand.

Be sexy.

"Hey."

My voice is hoarse. I hoped it would sound jazzy and sensual like Audrey, but I'm sure it sounds like I inhaled a carton of cigarettes instead.

"Hey. Are you okay?" His voice is laced with concern.

I clear my throat. "I'm fine! I just...choked...on my drink," I squeak out.

There's amusement in his voice when he asks, "Selah, have you been drinking?"

I roll my eyes dramatically when I respond. "If you must know, yes."

"I knew something was different about you tonight. Truth serum."

I change the subject. "Anyway, we seem to have gotten a little sidetracked. The orgasms? Three. I've never had that many."

"Not really a question, but I think I understand what you mean. I'm a pleasure dom. I focus on my partner's pleasure, often to the point of exhaustion. That gets me off."

"And I thought I was a people pleaser."

He chuckles softly. "I suppose I am."

Oh my God. I clasp my hand over my mouth. I said that out loud. It's safe to say that all this wine wasn't a good idea.

"Sorry."

"Nothing to be sorry about. What is sex usually like for you, Selah?"

"Usually, I just go with whatever my partner wants. I suppose my people pleasing occurs in the bedroom too, but it's nothing groundbreaking or passionate."

"Hmm. And your partners, do they make sure that you're pleased in return?"

"No. I'm embarrassed to say that."

"I don't want you to be embarrassed. We're just talking. I can assure you that sex isn't supposed to be like that. That's not even how it works in the books you read. Everyone involved should be enjoying themselves."

"I also understand that I'm reading fiction books. I didn't believe anyone was really having experiences like that until…" I trail off.

"Until what?"

"You."

"Selah, are you calling me a book boyfriend? That's a hell of a compliment."

"Well, I won't be saying it now. I'd hate to make you even more annoying."

He snickers. "What are you doing up?"

"You texted me."

"It's two in the morning there. Did I wake you?"

He ignores that question, responding with one of his own.

"Have you had an orgasm with a partner before?"

I snort. "Geez. Buy me dinner first."

He counters, "I have. Breakfast too."

I start cracking up, and he joins me.

After catching his breath, he says, "Seriously, if you're not comfortable answering, I will stop."

"It's okay. You've already seen me naked." I sigh. "It doesn't happen often with a partner, mostly by myself, whenever I can get out of my own head. And with you, the other day."

"What do you mean by 'get out of your own head?'"

"I have a hard time focusing. When my brain is bored with something, it seeks ways to entertain itself at any time. I focus better when my mind feels challenged, but when it doesn't, I struggle. I could be driving, working, having sex and—"

He cuts me off. "If you can't focus, you can't finish. Like ADHD?"

He finishes my sentence for me, and I gasp.

"Do you have it?"

"No, but my brother does, and he's going to be a doctor, so he's laid it out pretty good for me." He takes a breath. "Why do you think you were able to focus with me?"

"I'm not sure why," I nearly whisper. "Also, I'm starting to think maybe *you're* the one with the praise kink."

"Call me a 'good girl,' and I'll tell you how it makes me feel," he challenges.

I cackle. *This man.*

"I'm just making sure I follow you. I won't say it doesn't feel good to hear that I was able to help because it does. Got any more questions for me?"

I shake my head as if he can see my face.

"Nope."

"Well, I hope this helped clear your head. You should try to get some sleep."

"You too. Goodnight, Greyson. Thanks for staying up with me."

"Anytime, Sunflower. Goodnight."

31
candor over cake

Greyson

Manhattan, NY | January 9, 2024

I WOKE up recounting yesterday's events where I met Audrey and decide to stop by this Korean bakery to bring her chocolate croissants and fresh cream cake. She's intense, but I know how much she means to Selah. I'd really like to impress her, so I figure these pastries are a good way to do that.

Once I return to my building, hop on the elevator, tapping button number six, and I feel a bit of anxiety about this. It's not that I don't think I'd be good for Selah because I know I could be. I'm just nervous that I scared her off. I fear that I was intense and should've waited a while to show her that side of me. I've become unapologetic about my sexual preferences since my divorce.

Aileen wasn't open to kink and preferred to keep things simple, both in and out of the bedroom. I pushed it down to go along with what made her most comfortable but, it stifled me. I'll admit that I took to working more because I didn't feel safe expressing myself sexually with my wife at the time. I didn't enjoy making her uncomfortable, but she didn't compromise on anything with me when it came to intimacy. I attribute it to the fact that we were young and didn't know ourselves. I don't fault her anymore nor do I feel ashamed for wanting to be in control.

The elevator dings and I exit down the hall. I spot Selah's neighbor, Estelle King, as she leaves her apartment, locking the door behind her. She's lived in this building for a few years and she's quite the character. I can't tell her age, but I'm sure she was a heartbreaker back in her day and still is. Estelle is a flirt and known to give you a confidence boost because she's not shy in the slightest. If she likes what she sees, she will not hold her tongue about it.

She recently stopped coloring her roots and is embracing the gray. Her long hair is styled in loose curls that frame her face, and her makeup is light while drawing attention to her eyes. She dons a cream-colored pantsuit with gold accent jewelry. It compliments her brown skin beautifully. Always dressed to kill and full of sass.

"Good morning, Mrs. King," I say.

"Morning, Greyson. And we've talked about this, call me Estelle."

I nod in understanding.

"Where are you off to this morning?"

"Brunch with my girlfriends."

"Well, I hope you have a great time. You look lovely."

"I always do, but thanks. You can take me out another time," she adds with a wink.

I can't help but smile at her.

"I'd be delighted, but I'm kind of seeing someone."

She gives me a knowing look.

"I've suspected that. Let the girl get some damn rest," she chuckles.

"I will. See you around, Estelle."

"Have a good one."

I ring the doorbell and moments later, Audrey emerges. She's fresh-faced, wearing sweatpants and an oversized tee. Her long, curly hair is pulled back into a low ponytail. She leans against the doorframe with coffee in hand. With raised brows, she says, "I could've sworn I'd run you off yesterday. Good to see you being persistent."

I chuckle and hold out the bag so she can see if I brought sweets. She peers down and sighs contentedly.

"I love a man who follows my orders. A *good boy* indeed. Come on in," she advises, opening the door wider.

Here she goes with that again. I don't know how to feel about being called a good boy.

I usually am the praiser, but I don't hate it?

I follow her into the apartment and settle in. She asks me if I'd like anything to drink and I let her know that coffee is fine. She pours me a cup and places it in front of me. The mug has the phrase *'thanks for coming, now leave,'* and I can't help but laugh. This screams Selah.

"Hand over the treats, I'm starving."

I slide the bag across the counter, and she helps herself. I wash my hands and when I'm drying them off, the deep rumble of a man's voice startles me. A large man enters from the hallway looking as if he just woke up. He musses his blond hair and scrunches his face in frustration. I've seen him before with Selah. I had believed that he was her boyfriend before she went out with me.

His tone is laced with irritation when he asks, "Audrey, what have I told you about not looping me in on your new 'friends?'" He makes air quotes around the word *friends*. "Everyone needs to be vetted prior to being alone with you and this isn't a new conversation."

"Oh, stop it. I have already vetted this man. He lives in the building and passed a background check. He's harmless," she assures.

"Background check?"

"I own this building, honey. I investigated you after our little visit yesterday." She pauses to sip her coffee. "However, he's *also* the one who was bending Selah over this island last week, so your concerns are valid." She adds, pointing to the countertop.

"*This* is the guy?" His brows shoot up as he motions to me, speaking as if I'm not even there. "Alright, Selah." They both nod at each other in agreement.

I'm not sure what I should say, so I opt for just watching this play out instead.

He approaches with piercing green eyes that appear to look through me. I reach out my hand to greet him in a shake, and he stares at it as he crosses his arms over his chest instead. Then starts littering me with questions about myself. I part my lips to answer when she interjects.

"Don't interrogate him," she orders while taking a bite of a chocolate croissant. Her eyes close as she savors it. "He brought me breakfast," she exclaims with her mouth full.

He glares at me with a raised brow and asks, "How do you know about the sweets?"

"I came by yesterday with cinnamon rolls and she asked me to come back here with more treats. So here I am. Can't say I recall you being here. I would've remembered that."

His glare is unwavering, but he reaches out his hand for me to shake, introducing himself.

"I'm Audrey's bodyguard, Eric. I'll admit I'm not always this rude. That's Audrey's job."

She snorts while eating.

"I'm not rude, I prefer the term assertive."

He grabs a croissant, eyes widening when he takes a bite.

"Shit," he says, stunned. "How were those rolls yesterday? Good?"

She nods assuredly and takes a sip of her coffee.

"I think we gotta keep this guy around. He's spoiling us."

"If you had stayed asleep, we could have enjoyed these without having to share."

I reach into the bag and remove a small box, lifting the top to reveal a slice of fresh cream cake.

"Whoa," they say in unison, causing me to glance up.

Eric opens a drawer; I hear clanking and he returns to his spot with three forks. He gives a suggestive look, to which I nod and they quickly move towards me, dispersing the forks. They each carve into the slice, shove it into their mouths and assess. I glance over at them and he inhales deeply, relaxing his grumpy face and Audrey wears a smile.

"Is there more?"

"Of course," I say.

Eric damn near knocks her over as he rushes to the other side of the island to retrieve the box.

"You're sharing with me," he says to her, leaving no room for argument.

She huffs in response. They dig their forks into a slide of their own.

"I'm glad you are enjoying it. It's called fresh cream cake. I got them from a Korean bakery on West 32nd St."

"Cake is my favorite thing in the world. Do you know how to make these by chance? I'd love to learn. Baking keeps me from —" she trails off. "Baking keeps me from harming people."

Eric starts to laugh and breaks out into a fit of coughs. She reaches for his back and he raises his hand to signal he's okay, coughing a bit more before grabbing a sip from Audrey's mug.

"Stubborn ass."

"I was going to say *bullshit* before I started choking there."

"Don't embarrass me in front of company," she advises.

"I'm certain you threatened him. Am I right?" He looks expectantly at me.

"Well," I draw out the word. "Yes."

"And you still came back? Maybe you *are* good for Selah. You don't scare easily."

"Mmhmm," she adds.

Operation impress Audrey, and now Eric, is going well.

"Thank you for that. As for the cake, I absolutely can show you how to make one."

She pulls out her phone and asks, "Are you free to show me now? What do we need? I can order groceries."

"I am. You may have everything here already. I can take a look and let you know." I rise up and head over to the pantry, scouring for ingredients.

A loud meow comes from the bedroom and Peach struts into the main area.

The cat rubs against Eric's leg on her way over to her food and water bowls.

I finish my rummage through the pantry and inform her of what ingredients she's missing for the recipes. She's placing a grocery delivery and asks if there's anything else we need without looking up.

"Selah never has any Oreos or *real* milk here. Always that weird oat or almond shit. It's not very accommodating for her houseguests," he pipes up.

She laughs softly. "Well, it's a good thing you're *not* the house sitter, isn't it? She stocked everything I liked."

"Everyone knows that I go wherever you go. So, I *will* be expecting Oreos and two percent milk the next time she's out of town."

"Sure. Drop it in the suggestion box," she says sarcastically, aiming her head towards the trash can. "I'll order your damn milk and cookies, relax."

He sighs in relief, and I chuckle to myself.

These two are quite a pair.

12

"Oh shit," she blurts, her tone laced with frustration.

"What now?" Eric asks beside me.

She places her hand on her head and says, "Brian is getting

our groceries. A fucking *man* is doing our delivery. Prepare for the order to be wrong."

"Dammit," he huffs.

"Am I missing something here?" I inquire, genuinely curious why that's a problem.

"Men aren't always the best grocery shoppers. At least not in our experience. They're lazy and just grab anything to get out of the store." She looks to Eric, "Your cookies will be broken or even worse…they'll be golden Oreos," she teases.

"Take that back," he says through gritted teeth. "He *better* bring me Doublestuf Oreos or I'm going to lose it. And that milk *better* be two percent."

The fact that he is serious makes me hold in a laugh. Audrey, on the other hand, erupts in laughter and he's unamused.

I change the subject and ask, "When is Selah's birthday, if you don't mind me asking?"

"I'll only tell you if you let me in on the plans. You've only messed around one time, but you seem very interested in her. Am I wrong?"

"Well, I don't suppose I haven't thought that far into it, but I think I may be interested in more? Selah challenges me in a way that I've never experienced before. Sure, you've met my ex-wife, so you know I'm capable of committing to someone."

"Her birthday is May seventh. As for your ex…" She pauses and starts humming as she loads the dishwasher.

Eric joins her and they're both humming a melody I'm unfamiliar with. I'm not sure what it is with them, but he is just as odd as Audrey is. Odd, but good company.

"What were you going to say about Aileen?" I interrupt.

She grows silent and turns to face me, opening her mouth to speak when Eric blurts, "Why did he mention Aileen? Are *you* her ex-husband?"

"What did you think I was humming for? You joined me!" she exclaims.

"I just like that song; I didn't know you were doing it intentionally."

"Please explain the humming and then tell me what you were going to say about her."

Eric says, "Audrey has a habit of humming when she doesn't have anything nice to say."

"Well, you wouldn't be the first person that had something unkind to say about her. My friends have their opinions as well," I admit.

"Are you sure you want to hear my take? You two seem cordial."

"Go for it," I urge.

"This is better than any reality show," he adds, placing his head on his chin and waits for her to share.

"Remember what you asked for. Last chance before I open the floodgates." She looks to me for permission and I grant it with a nod.

"I've worked with a lot of brides in my career, so I've seen it all, but Aileen, she's one for the books," she says with a scoff. "The past eight months working on her wedding have been interesting to say the least. She's manipulative and there's a motive for *everything* she does. Even if it doesn't make sense to question her actions, you should. I'm not sure how she was when you were married because she said you were young, but if she behaved anything like she does now, I'm not surprised that you're divorced.

I haven't had the pleasure of working with Daniel often, but I've seen enough to wonder why he's marrying her. He loves her, without a doubt. I just don't think he really *knows* her."

She sips her coffee before asking, "Would you like for me to continue?"

"Absolutely," I say, crossing my arms in front of me.

I'd love to take a bite of cake, but I fear she may say something that'll cause me to choke, so I'll wait.

"In this industry people tend to show their ass in ways you

wouldn't imagine in preparation for a wedding. I get paid an awful lot to oversee things, mostly bullshit. All they need to do is show up, say their vows and get on with their lives. However, she insists on tagging along for meetings, as if she doesn't trust me to honor her wishes. Most brides hand it off to me because they've got better things to do.

I assumed she was just needy or lonely with Daniel working in the UK currently, but she likes to show me off to her friends like a show pony. Even makes posts on her socials about me being her new *'bestie.'*"

Eric is vibrating with excitement, and I am still along for the ride.

"This woman has also had the balls to ask me if she can stay at one of my family's resorts for *free*. As if her *billionaire* fiancée can't afford it. When I asked her why she would expect something like that from me, her response was 'I thought we were friends.' I informed her that I've been hired to do a job and have a strict policy against mixing my business life with my personal life. She didn't love that, but she backed off."

Pausing to sip her coffee again, she says, "Last chance before I go for the jugular. You can opt out now."

I grab a bite of cake and shake my head as I swallow. "I can handle it."

"Finish her," Eric chimes.

We break out into a fit of laughs, before settling down.

She continues, "I'm not going to say I've never had a bride that I've wanted to drag outside and fight in the street before, because that would be a lie. I will say that your ex-wife is one of my top three brides I'd love to get in the gloves with *or* go bare knuckles. I'm not sorry," she adds with a shrug. "Oh, and I think you should bring Selah to the wedding so she can see how much better you can do. Any questions?"

Well, fuck.

She really went for it.

Am I surprised to hear these things about her? Not really.

"I have a few, actually. Though I'd like to process everything you just said."

"Understandable," she says.

I look to Eric and ask, "was that entertaining enough for you?"

"Sure was. I hear a lot about her on the rides home from the office, but I've sat in on a few meetings and can confirm everything she said is true. Now that I know *you're* her ex, I fully support you moving in on Selah. Hell, I'll even help."

"That's what *I'm* doing," she says.

"Even better. This is in my job description, you know?"

"Meddling is *not* in your contract," she argues with a laugh.

I like the idea of bringing Selah, but it could also be awkward for her. I need to know if she is interested in the arrangement first. I know she mentioned the arrangement should benefit us both. That could work, but it could also scare her off and that's the last thing I want to do. I also don't mind showing up without a date.

"I'd like to think about the wedding date. I don't want to move too fast with her."

She gives me an incredulous look. "You had that woman spread on this very countertop and you're concerned you're moving too fast by asking her to be your date to a wedding? Honey, y'all are *way* past that."

She isn't wrong.

The doorbell rings and Eric rushes to answer it. Greeting the delivery person and retrieving the bags. He shuts the door behind him and peeks to make sure his order is in there. Picking up the Oreos and shaking them near his ear.

He unloads the bags and she cross-checks every item and confirms it is indeed correct.

"It better have been," he grumbles.

"Anyways," she changes the subject. "Let's get to baking and talking about Selah!"

I perk up at the sound of her name.

"Sounds like a plan to me."

32
business trip

Selah

Portland, OR | January 10, 2024

DAY FIVE IN PORTLAND. As someone who prefers to work from home, it's been an adjustment, but at least I could check *Fly First Class* off my *Fuck It List*. Plus, the view from my hotel is amazing. Once meetings are done for the day, I'll be back in my room with a book. You don't realize how lonely working from home is until you have a meet-up. in person with your coworkers who you don't know personally. We're all oddly aligned and comfortable with each other from regular debriefings, but it isn't the same as being around each other every day. The company tries to recreate social experiences virtually, which I don't mind, but they're still awkward. Birthday parties, break rooms, office gossip, smoke breaks, food runs, they're all nonexistent in virtual spaces and don't get me wrong, I am not complaining. I prefer this to going into the office every day, but the constant meetings will deplete you.

The highlights of work-from-home meetings include pets walking by, cute kids and their greetings, someone forgetting to mute themselves while talking shit, or their camera is on and their face is speaking loud and clear. These are things you cannot get in the office, and for that, I wouldn't trade the experience.

I am always nervous to lead a meeting, even virtually. I make sure I'm as prepared as possible, so nothing trips me up. My anxiety is really put to the test here as a product manager. I'm leading many meetings with our stakeholders to discuss our recent developments with the *Kiwi Music* App and the new features we'll be rolling out this spring. This is the biggest project I've been a part of since joining the company a year ago, and it has been such an honor to lead our team through the rebranding. The *Kiwi Music* App is getting a whole new look. I'm in love with the prototypes I've seen, and I hope our listeners enjoy the new features while finding them to be even more user friendly.

Collaborative playlists, updates to users' "play profiles" to fit their personalities, and even a follow feature to stay connected. We've improved our recommendations feature to provide more accurate playlists for our users, and a weekly playlist will be released every Saturday morning with a breakdown of their listening preferences ahead of the annual playlist that ranks how they enjoyed music for that year.

Being able to work around music every day while helping people discover new artists and giving them a platform to connect so they can express themselves with soundtracks for their daily lives. is an absolute dream come true. I had never loved a job before this, and I hadn't felt like I belonged in any role, but here? I know my shit when it comes to tech and when it comes to the perfect playlist, I'm your girl. Something that the team has bonded over is that we all love music and enjoy curating playlists for our personal profiles in the app, often sharing our creations with each other. I may not be much of a talker outside of work, but I engage with the playlists they send and keep up with their recommendations.

It's simple, really, if you want me to talk, bring up music or romance books.

When my presentation is over, I'm certain my underarms are sweating, but it's alright. I knew the possibility, and that's why I packed dark clothes for this trip. Once I'm seated and marketing is up next to present, I feel like I can finally breathe for the first time since I entered the room.

It's exhausting pretending to be neurotypical in public settings, but masking is a part of my daily routine at this point. At home, it's a different story. I'm not ashamed of my ADHD, but it's nobody's business at work, and I find the quieter I am, the fewer questions people ask. I'm ready for the meetings to end so I can head back to my hotel room and decompress.

However, Skye, a software engineer on my team who seems to always sense whenever I'm overstimulated, offers a knowing look from across the boardroom table. Skye can get me to talk about more than just books and music. She always shares treats from her snack hauls with me on these trips and it helps. Often a cookie or a cupcake and she refuses to share with anyone else, so I've gotten creative with my lies about where they come from.

My ass.

A food truck.

The vending machine.

A raccoon by the dumpster.

It may be the sweets that calm me or the fact that someone can pick me out of the crowd no matter how well I think I'm masking, but it never makes me feel judged. It feels like when you were a kid playing by yourself on the playground then another kid walked up randomly and started playing with you. They might not have said much at first, but they chose *you* and from that day on you never had to play alone.

We used to make friends that way. Some of us still do. I know I still do.

I often wonder if Skye is neurodivergent too or someone close to her is. Either way, it's nice to have someone who creates a safe space for me when I come on these business trips. Otherwise, they'd really fucking suck. When my day is done, I'll need to curl up in my room with a book to recover and mentally prepare to do this all over again tomorrow. I'm not a social person. Do I sympathize with social people? No, because they don't sympathize with us. Audrey gets a pass because her entire life is events and hospitality, but even she has a social battery that needs recharging just like the rest of us. I sink back into my chair and wiggle my feet as I wait for this meeting to end.

When the meeting ends, Skye and I work alongside each other. Our desks sit in front of the floor-to-ceiling windows that overlook downtown Portland. We settle in and she sets a warm chocolate chunk cookie on my desk with a napkin. I smile up at her and she scrunches her nose in response, biting into the gooey cookie.

I pity anyone that doesn't have a Skye in their lives.

33
acts of service

Greyson

Manhattan, NY | January 10, 2024

WHILE I'VE BEEN SHOWING Audrey how to make fresh cream cake from scratch, Eric has been sitting at the island acting as if he's a spectator attending a live cooking show. After we place the cake pans in the oven, I remind them the exchange was to be learning more about Selah.

"I've got some more shit for you to do around here if you've got the time."

I nod. "I've got nothing but time. I'll just need to take my dog out a few times today."

She stares at me incredulously and asks, "You cleared your schedule to run errands for Selah?"

"You said you were putting me to work, so yes."

Her brows raise in surprise as she faces me and gently slaps Eric on the shoulder.

"What a good boy," she praises.

"I still don't know how to feel about being called that."

Eric guffaws, "you'll get used to it."

12

After we've iced the cake and everyone's had a slice, we've finished eating when Audrey breaks the silence.

"You know, Selah has a bunch of boxes tucked away in her guest room and she thinks I don't know about it."

She gestures for me to follow her to the guest room and I see the boxes she's talking about. Mostly unassembled furniture and I don't mind putting it together for her. I'm sure it'll make things easier for her, so I just asked Audrey to show me where Selah would want these things set up before I get started. That's when she takes me across the hall to her office and I am surprised to see her book collection displayed in few tall stacks on the hardwood floors, rather than on shelves. Especially the books I bought her. As enthusiastic as she is about reading, I don't like seeing her space like this, but I don't want to upset her by moving her things around in a way she isn't comfortable with. I step out of her office and back into the guest room in hopes that some of these boxes are for bookcases and if not, I'm running out to get some today. I know how important her books are to her and I just can't ignore this now that I've seen it. Thankfully three of these large boxes are for bookcases, so I ask Audrey and Eric to help by carefully removing her books while I get measurements to make sure everything will fit in her office. I take on the project of adding a reading nook to a free wall of her home office.

The wide bookcases are mounted to the wall, an oversized sofa chair sits in front of them, and an end table too. Audrey found a lamp that matched the theme for everything else in her office so she placed it on the table. She helped us organize the books in a way she'd prefer before we placed them on the shelves to avoid the possibility of her rearranging them when she returned home. While my focus was on the nook in her office, I discovered an unboxed full-length mirror and mounted that in her room. I call Audrey in to get a good look at it after I've vacuumed the mess from drilling into the wall, which scared Peach into hiding.

"If she gives you a hard time about this, you can tell her I said she should be able to see how incredible she looks every day."

Her lips part in awe as she assesses the room and my comment.

"I think that'll shut her up. You did good."

I decide to write a little note for Selah to find in her office when she gets back as I take one last look at my project for the day.

I really hope she likes it.

34
i hate surprises

Selah

Portland, OR | January 10, 2024

Audrey

AUDREY

So, about Big Sexy…

ME

What about him?

AUDREY

He came back today to hang out with me and Eric.

Shared a recipe with me for fresh cream cake.

Stayed and made it with us too. It was amazing btw.

We like him.

ME

Eric hates everyone but us.

What's in it for him?

AUDREY

Eric liked that Grey doesn't scare easily and he brought us sweets from a Korean Bakery.

Oh! I put him to work. Just a little surprise for when you get back. Thank me later or now, whatever works best for you. As always, sweets are an acceptable payment method.

Eric also hates that you never have Oreos or cow milk for him. His words.

ME

Lol. Get Eric some damn cookies and milk.

I don't even know what he did, so I'll thank you later!

You know how I feel about surprises, Aud.

AUDREY

I did! lol

I promise you won't hate this one. I know you're already nervous, but rest assured, you'll enjoy it.

ME

That doesn't help at all, but I trust you.

AUDREY

You're gonna love it! I'm excited!

I miss you and can't wait for you to come home!

ME

I miss you too! I'm ready to be back and I'm off the rest of the week.

AUDREY

Even better! I love you!

Goodnight! I'll pick you up tomorrow!

ME

I love you too. Goodnight!

35
collateral

Selah

Manhattan, NY | January 11, 2024

AUDREY AND ERIC pick me up from the airport and I'm anxious the entire ride back because of this 'surprise' that's waiting for me. I practically jump out of the SUV when we park. They catch up to me as I'm stuck waiting for the elevator. I'm holding my breath as I survey my apartment. When I reach my office door, I brace myself as I turn the knob. I'm very meticulous about my things. Everything has a home and a reason it exists where it does. I beeline for my desk to scan it thoroughly, and once I discover it's been untouched, I sigh in relief. Audrey leans against the doorframe as if she's waiting for me to finish up here.

"I'm offended that you think I'd let anyone touch your desk. Now that you're done, are you going to look around this damn room and notice what's different?"

I look to my left and begin surveying the room, my eyes bouncing high and low in search of anything new, when my eyes land on a series of tall bookshelves on my far right, filled with my books that were previously stacked in piles on the floor in that exact spot. Organized alphabetically by author in order by series—that was Audrey's doing. I sigh in disbelief at the chair, side table and reading lamp beside it. It's the perfect addition to my office.

The little reading nook I've put off setting up stares back at me and my heart swells with joy. I am itching to curl up with Peach, a blanket and a book to get lost in. That will be the perfect way to wind down for the night. Traveling drains me and I don't do it often. While I read on the trip and the plane, it's not the same as the comfort of your own home. I blink back the burning tears that are eager to escape from the thoughtfulness of my best friend and my neighbor who pulled this off for me in my absence because I would've fought them on it the entire way if I were here.

I wince at the fact that Greyson did this and has now seen exactly what I read. He's gotten a glimpse and has read a few recommendations, but not *everything*. Not that I am ashamed, but damn. I feel like he knows my darkest secrets, but something tells me he has his own.

My friends have offered to help with this project since I moved in, I kept telling them I'd get around to doing it eventually, but I kept forgetting honestly and while I kept buying books, I got used to stacking them and going about my day. I love my e-reader and use it daily, but it didn't prevent me from buying more physical books. Hence the overflowing collection that was desperately in need of order. I turn around and Audrey is smiling.

"That's not all, babe."

"You're kidding."

She shakes her head. "Follow me"

We walk into my bedroom and a large full-length mirror I bought when I got my place is now mounted and placed exactly where I imagined it to be.

"He was a little frustrated about this mirror not being unboxed. Said that you should be able to see how incredible you look every day."

I roll my eyes, but it doesn't hide my smile because Audrey gives me a knowing look.

"I'm annoyed with you for having that man all in my house acting like a husband or something."

The look she gives is incredulous and she snorts. "Girl, please. He was just here last week, pleasing you like a husband or something. Bossing men around is my favorite thing on Earth, and this was for a good cause. I think the words you're looking for are 'thank' and 'you.' I'll wait."

She stands with her arms crossed over her chest, her eyes closed, and face turned up while she waits for a response. I chuckle at her because, as usual, she's right. "Thank you. I really do appreciate this."

"You're welcome, honey. She opens her arms and wraps me in a hug. You wouldn't let us help, so I thought I'd get creative while still doing it behind your back. Now you got something to talk to him about."

When she releases me, she reminds me, "Don't forget to thank Greyson, he's expecting to hear from you. I had to talk him out of going to the airport to pick you up."

"Oh God. He was serious." I cover my face with my hand.

"He was, but I told him I had you and I'd have you check in once you got home safe. Can you at least do that? Or he might show up at your door again with food."

"That wouldn't be the worst thing, but I will thank him. I promise."

"You better. With words please? He didn't let me do anything but organize those books. I told him where to place things, but he did the work. Thank him, please." She gives me a stern look as she stands beside Eric, who's waiting in the entryway. She adjusts her purse on her forearm and shuffles towards the door. She halts as if she forgot something, pointing toward my kitchen, she informs, "oh and there's leftover cake in the fridge, Grey made it with me. I had to fight Eric off to make sure he saved you a slice."

"That was nice of you. Eric, too," I chuckle. "Thanks again. I love you, Aud. I appreciate you so much."

"I love you too. Don't mention it." She adds a soft smile and follows Eric out the door.

I stand in my living room for a moment. I had anxiety about coming home to a surprise, but I never expected *this*. I'm so grateful and want to relish it for as long as I can.

I go to my office and admire my bookshelves for a moment, I run my fingers through the assortment of books and examine the shelves. Determined to spot the new homes of my favorite reads. Until I notice an empty space. My stomach sinks when I realize one of my books is missing. I look closely and see a tiny sheet of paper in its place. I carefully remove the note and read it.

Consider this collateral.
I'll be hearing from you soon, Sunflower. :)

That little shit.

I huff as I pull out my phone, firing off a text to a certain infuriatingly sexy man.

ME

Thank you. I got your little note. I was going to tell you when I made it home. Can I have my book back?

I stew in my bedroom and wait for a response. I force myself to unpack my suitcase now, or else it won't get done. Once I'm finished, I hop in the shower and throw on some comfy clothes to relax. My growling tummy starts to roar, and I head to the kitchen to scour the fridge for something quick. That's when I notice the leftover cake Audrey mentioned. I grab a fork and dig in.

Damn, that's good.

My phone dings back-to-back. I pull it from my pocket and see **(2) Text Messages from Greyson.**

GREYSON

That's it?

Where are your manners, Princess?

ME

Thank you for setting up the reading nook and the mirror.

It was really kind of you and you shouldn't have.

Can I have my book back, please?

GREYSON

You're welcome and no.

ME

Why the hell not? I'll just come upstairs and get it.

GREYSON

I'm not finished reading it, that's why.

And be my guest, you know where I live.

You're always welcome to come. ;)

I snort to myself and take a deep breath as I try to push away thoughts of how good he is at making me come. Before I respond, he sends another text.

GREYSON

Actually, while you're here, I have a question for you. These colored tabs and highlighted quotes, what is the purpose of it?

Fuck. I didn't even think of the annotations in that book. Mostly filthy and unhinged notes, but anything that hit close to home and had me sobbing is acknowledged in there as well. I'd say it was equal parts spicy and sweet.

ME

Those are things that stood out to me. They're called annotations.

Like a note to self, or something you want to be able to reread later.

Please ignore them.

GREYSON

Interesting. I'll be paying close attention to what stood out to you. I know you're upset, but I just needed to know what makes this your favorite book.

ME

You could've just asked me what I liked about it.

GREYSON

Where's the fun in that? This way I can see it for myself and thanks to these little notes, I get a peek inside your thoughts while I read along.

I can't even argue with that, but I don't even know how to respond. So, I sit there staring at the screen for a few moments, mindlessly eating until my fork is scraping the plastic container.

ME

I'm not as upset as I was since you actually want to read it, but you have to discuss it with me AND give it back. Deal?

GREYSON

Deal. Are your other books annotated like this?

ME

A lot of them are, yeah.

GREYSON

I'd like to check one out from you next time instead of stealing it. That's If you don't mind.

ME

I don't mind one bit.

It's the least I can do since I now have a special place to read at home. Thank you, Greyson.

Also, the cake you and Audrey made is astounding.

GREYSON

You're welcome, Sunflower.

I'm surprised there was any left, but I'm happy that you liked it.

I try to ignore the way my stomach flips when he calls me *Sunflower*.

ME

Well, I'll stop interrupting your reading.

I'm about to go do the same.

GREYSON

Will you be in the nook?

I smile at that question.

ME

Yes, I will.

GREYSON

Send me a picture when you get settled. I'd like to see you enjoying the fruits of my labor.

I get nervous and start running through excuses in my head.

ME

I just got off a plane and I'm not all done up.

GREYSON

Selah, you are the most beautiful woman I've ever seen. Send the picture. I'll be waiting.

That shut me up for sure. I take a look in the mirror and I look fine. I grab my blanket and my e-reader, calling out for Peach to join me as I leave my office door open. I get cozy in my chair and melt into the cushions, pulling up my most recent read. I grab my phone and angle it to take a picture of myself with the nook in the background. I don't do anything silly; I opt for flirty facial expressions and once I settle on two I like, I send them to Greyson and quickly shove my phone face down.

I pick up where I left off on my reader and moments later, I hear a few repeated dings that make my heart race. I don't know why I'm afraid to look at his response.

GREYSON

Good girl. Like I said, the most beautiful woman I've ever seen.

Have a great night, Sunflower.

ME

Goodnight, Greyson.

Thanks again.

GREYSON

Anytime :)

36
that dreaded 'c-word'

Selah

Manhattan NY | January 17, 2024

MY SESSION with Dr. Garnett today was vastly different than usual. We had a lot to discuss, and I prepared her by being honest about what's changed since our last session. I neglected to mention the hookup since I was anxious about my trip. I felt it was best to not start with the elephant in the room, so I led with Portland before explaining the recent developments with Greyson.

We discussed my recent nightmares and the common themes I've noticed, which were rough. They usually involve me reliving an experience with Jourdan. Often a negative one that I'd rather forget. Sometimes I see him, a faceless person, or I'm stuck in a dangerous situation with no way out. She recommended I keep a dream log, so I have. I document them in my notes app and we unpack them in my sessions. I don't enjoy it, but I also know that uncomfortable conversations are necessary for healing.

Saving the best for last, I tell her about how things have escalated with Greyson, and that I checked off a task from my list. I cannot stop thinking about the sex, and while we've been texting and talking on the phone, I'm not ready to see him in person. I don't think I can act like it didn't happen.

He's easy to talk to even though he makes me nervous. I wouldn't say I have a crush on him, but he's a very attractive man. He's kind and quick-witted, really making it a challenge to stay in a bad mood when he's around. I appreciate what a safe space he's been and that when I opened up to him about my lack of sexual experience, he didn't make me feel uncomfortable. I'd be lying if I said my curiosity hadn't piqued after that phone call, but I'm also a bit concerned. I fear that a man touching and worshipping my body like that could blur the lines for me.

WWAD? She'd enjoy herself and deal with the consequences later.

"Do you want to sleep with him again?" Dr. Garnett asks through the screen, regaining my focus.

I think about it for a moment before answering. I start to lie but decide to answer truthfully. Lying won't make me feel any better.

"I would, but I don't want it to be another situation where I just accepted the first man that gave me attention. I'd like to keep dating. While I've come to not even look forward to it, I know that if I'm at least trying, I'm not settling. That alone is progress for me. I believe that if I remain open-minded without that, I'll trust my judgment better for the next man I let into my bed and my…" I pause.

"Finish that thought?"

"My heart."

"I see. Greyson makes you think about your heart. Is that why you're avoiding him right now?"

"Well, I wasn't thinking about my heart until he started keeping his word and paying attention to details about me. Honestly, he's done that since day one. Then he built me a reading nook while I was in Portland and he's reading my favorite book right now because he wants to? I just don't understand him." I cover my face with my hands.

She snorts. "I'm sorry. I'm going to give you a moment to sit with what you just said."

"I must sound ridiculous and ungrateful, huh?"

She shakes her head. "What exactly are you hoping to understand about him? His intentions?"

"I don't know. He hasn't done anything that makes me think he isn't genuine. In fact, he's awfully pleasant for a man who fucks like that. It's hard to believe he'd be interested in something casual like I am," I sigh.

"I think we're getting somewhere." She shifts in her seat and takes notes for a moment. "He made sure you were comfortable before he left and you weren't upset. Sounds like you're on the same page. Now, about him building things for you, that'll require a conversation. I know you'd much rather decipher it on your own than talk about it, but if you want an answer, you know what you need to do. That dreaded 'C word.'"

"Ugh. Communication. You know I'm not much of a talker, Doc."

"I'm aware. That's why I'm employed," she chuckles. "Greyson seems like a reasonable man. I'm going to encourage you to have a real conversation before our next session."

The timer sounds and our session is over. I let out a sigh of relief.

"Let's recap. What's your homework for over the next week?

"Try a regular sleep routine—go to bed earlier and try to unwind by the end of the day. Make note of how a regular routine affects my dreams. Start up my coffee shop experiment again. Stop avoiding Greyson and communicate."

"Alright now. Looking forward to seeing your progress. I'll see you next week, same time. Take Care, Selah."

"You too, Doc."

The screen darkens and that's a wrap. I made it through another session and I'm exhausted. It's nothing a nap and some cuddles with Peach won't fix.

37
sweat & silk

Selah

Manhattan, NY | January 19, 2024

THE ELEVATOR DINGS and I step off, trying to breathe through the usual nerves that come with first dates. I'm mentally preparing myself in case something odd happens. I hope the food is great and he's at least decent company. Though I am still leaning towards deleting the app, and how this night goes will be a determining factor.

My thoughts halt when Greyson enters the lobby. It's the first time I've seen him since I got back from Portland. I'll admit, I didn't reach out right away because making him sweat was intentional. However, I hadn't expected him to involve Audrey or assemble a damn reading nook in my absence like he did.

We've texted since and things have been tame. He asks me to send him a daily song for his morning commute, and he still requests them on the weekends. Even if he doesn't listen to them, I think it's cute and don't mind the consistency. He's charming, makes me laugh 'til I cry and is so easy to talk to. He is currently reading my favorite book and sending me his reactions as he reads along. It's nice that he takes interest in things that matter to me.

Greyson Park is a beautiful enigma. I've never encountered anyone like him beyond a book page. Though there's a strong possibility that he could just be a *good neighbor.* When he finally spots me, my entire body heats beneath his gaze. I take careful breaths as I move through the lobby. He stays rooted and waits for me to get closer. His hands rest on the bulky camera hanging from his neck and I wonder what he photographed today. I'd ask him to show me if I wasn't on my way out. Admiration is apparent in his stare as he drinks me in. This lobby is packed, and it feels like we're alone here. I lose my resolve and crack a smile when I stop in front of him.

"The princess leaves her tower. Where are you headed tonight? You are absolutely captivating."

He bites his lip as he glances at my dress once again.

For a moment, I recall what those teeth felt like on my neck and by the look on his face, I think he can read my thoughts.

"Thank you." I smile, tucking a curl behind my ear. I freeze, but manage to get the words out, nervousness in my tone. "I'm going on a date."

He frowns for a moment and quickly regains his composure when he asks, "Oh really? Anywhere special? That dress is… wow. Fucking amazing."

His praise washes over me and my nerves subside.

"Thank you. We're going to dinner at *Doce* in Brooklyn. Have you ever been?"

"I have. You'll love the food." He pauses and furrows his brow. "If you get the black truffle burger, try it with Brie. And if you can handle dessert, the molten *dulce de leche* cake is incredible."

I'm practically drooling.

"Oh. All that sounds like heaven. I'll try it and let you know what I think. I should get going."

I nod politely and take off in the opposite direction. I'm a few feet away when Greyson stops me.

"Selah."

"Yes?"

I turn to face him, slightly startled at his closeness. He steps back, giving me space before he continues speaking.

"Let me know when you've made it home safely. Please?"

"Sure, *Daddy,*" I joke.

He leans in, his tone gravelly. "Call me 'Daddy' again and I'll make sure you scream it all night."

He returns to his height with darkened eyes, swiping his lip with his tongue. I peer at him curiously, and the hunger in his eyes could swallow me whole.

Shit. Somebody has a Daddy kink.

My mouth grows dry. I swallow audibly as his gaze trails up and down, drinking me in from head to toe. I feel ten degrees warmer as liquid heat pools between my thighs.

I'm equal parts horny and terrified.

"I'm sorry, I–" I stutter.

"Do not apologize. What have I said about that?"

"I take it back. I don't apologize."

He lifts my chin with his index finger and rubs his thumb faintly across my cheek. Careful not to ruin my makeup.

"Good girl."

I stifle a whimper, feeling my cheeks heat up.

I hope I'm not sweating; everyone will see it in this dress. It's silk. Fuck.

Where has this man been in my text messages?

I don't have time to decipher this.

"I have to go now," I manage through a strained voice.

They must've turned the thermostat up in the lobby. I need fresh air NOW.

"Have fun on your date."

He winks and I swivel on my feet to head outside. It isn't until I hear the doors shut behind me that I exhale. I don't bother turning around because I know he'll watch me until I disappear from his view. He thinks I don't know he does that, but I do. I smile to myself thinking about it. I check my phone to see the wait time on my Uber: two minutes.

38
woman

Greyson

Manhattan | January 19, 2024

I STAND in the lobby watching her hips sway in that dress as she leaves. I bite my lip and admire her until she's no longer in my line of sight. Missing her the moment she escapes me, an unfamiliar feeling sets in. I'm not proud of the thought that crosses my mind. It's not like me and if I were in my right mind, I wouldn't do it. However, Selah inhabits my mind and has done so since that first night in the elevator. I force my feet to make the trip back to my apartment and am warring between doing the right thing and the stupid thing. Wish me luck.

The right thing would be enjoying a quiet evening at home with my dog and hoping Selah has a nice time on her date. The stupid thing would be to go down there and cause a scene because she should be with me. See what I mean? Absolutely fucking stupid and nothing like me.

I have been reading too many of her romance books and the lines between reality and fiction have obviously been crossed. I recline back on my couch and settle on a show to binge for the night. I am very capable of doing the right thing.

I don't make it very long into the show before I start thinking about her. I'm not mad she's going on a date, but I won't deny that my stomach dropped when she said those words. I've never been a jealous person, so it caught me by surprise. I hope I didn't come off as upset.

The last thing I'd want is for her to think I'm being possessive over her when we've only had sex one time, and I'd hardly call it that. I pleased her once and it was an honor. I just thought it affected her. At least that's what it seemed like based off that call last week. I know she surely affected me. I wasn't prepared for it either, but here we are.

I can't be alone in this because she intentionally riled me up. It was wrong to send her off with wet panties, but she shouldn't be on a date anyway. If she wants a date, she should be on one with me. It's been a while since I actually asked her out, so I accept responsibility for that. She said one to two weeks to decide on the final decision on the arrangement. She should know what she wants after this date she's currently on. That's it.

I'm not mad at her for going on a date, I'm mad at myself for not asking her. At least if I did, I'd have more clarity. I leave the ball in her court. She may dribble or make a shot, which is normal. Sometimes, she'll kick the ball or walk out with it under her arm. What did she do tonight? Walk off with the fucking ball. It's still her ball, yet I'm sitting here working on a defensive play.

I'm distracted by my growling stomach and that reminds me I need to decide on dinner. I remember the restaurant that Selah is going to tonight and that sounds very appetizing.

The idea has reentered my mind. The stupid one.

I should not be craving a meal from the same restaurant Selah is currently on a date at.

I should not place an order at that restaurant for pickup.

I should not be entering my card information in for enough food to feed a small family.

I hover my thumb over the submit button before I decide to cancel my order entirely and exit the app.

That's it. I will not do this.

I can have dinner anywhere in Manhattan.

She's a grown woman and can do whatever she wants.

If she's interested, she'll come to me.

The ball is still in her court, and I have no choice but to accept that.

I will do the right thing.

I should do the right thing.

39
date or delete

Seylah

Brooklyn, NY | January 19, 2024

I SCREAM INTERNALLY the entire Uber ride. By the time I arrive I don't even remember the name of the man I'm supposed to meet. I pull up his profile to jog my memory before entering the restaurant. His name is Aaron. I'm greeted by the hostess and share the name on the reservation. She smiles brightly and leads me to the table where my date awaits.

He looks nothing like his profile photo. He's not unattractive, but he surely isn't the man in the pictures. Which makes me very uneasy.

Strike One.

I'm tempted to go back the way I came until he spots me. His brows raise and he flashes a smile.

"Sup," he says, greeting me with a fist bump before I seat myself. I do not hide how unimpressed I am as I take my seat. I observe his eyes track the hostess' ass as she pads toward the front of the house. He reeks of vodka and I assume he hit the bar first. Seriously, he smells like he washed his ass with rubbing alcohol. I hold my breath and try not to vomit at the table. My stomach turns instantly. *Strike two.*

He can't pronounce my name, nor does he try to. *Sea-luhh* is as good as it gets, I guess. He barely speaks, so I carry the conversation for a bit before I use my dinner as an excuse to be quiet. Thankfully, the food is amazing, so it's a distraction. He starts giving his undivided attention to his phone, grinning and chuckling while clutching onto it.

He chews with his mouth open, and the sound is both infuriating and disgusting. He eventually remembers I'm present and starts asking me questions about myself.

"So, what do you do?" he asks with a mouthful of ribs, barbecue sauce on his face.

He looks like a child. Smacking his lips, talking with his mouth full, and wearing his meal. The third strike is impending, and a part of me is curious how he'll earn it.

"I'll wait until you're done chewing," I say with a polite smile.

His expression shifts to annoyance. I don't give a fuck.

If he thinks he can be ruder than me, he's sorely mistaken.

He eventually sets his phone on the table to get wipes for his hands. I excuse myself to the restroom and take a glance as I pass by. It's open to the *SoulBlend* app. He's *literally* talking to a match right now, but I choose silence over violence. Instead, I fire off a text to the group chat, asking one of them to call me with an emergency in the next ten minutes. They send thumbs up reactions and I return to my seat.

He's still engrossed in that phone and I take a few more bites of my food as I wait for the 'emergency call.' Another hell date for the books.

I won't say that Greyson is in my head, though I can't help but think about his first date and how unique it was. It was easy and natural, giving me just enough of himself to pique my interest. He set a goal to captivate me before even seeing my face.

Should I have gone out with him instead?

I could have if I weren't avoiding him and keeping things short since our last encounter.

Our last attempt at a 'date' ended with him dining between my legs. His fingers and tongue explored me. He praised me in ways I never knew I craved. I recall how good he looked on his knees for *me,* committing me to memory. It was a fleeting moment, a fantasy, a wish come true. Like it never happened, *but it did.*

It could happen again if you'd give him your answer.

Aaron pulls me from my thoughts, asking me if I'm alright. I assure him that everything's fine and reengage with him, tossing thoughts of my hot neighbor aside. That is until I notice a man with a familiar build step through the doors of the restaurant. It's Greyson, in the flesh, as if I conjured him with my mind. He walks up to the hostess and says something before his eyes search the room. My heartbeat thumps in my ears and my pulse quickens.

He couldn't be here for me.

If this is how I react at the sight of him, then I'm out with the wrong guy.

We'll unpack that later.

When our eyes meet, a wide smile stretches across his face. He places his hand over his chest with a sigh of relief. He pulls out his phone and starts typing. I then feel my phone buzz in my clutch. He continues typing and I retrieve it. I glance down and see three texts from Greyson.

SMELL GOOD MAN

Do you need saving?

Tuck your hair behind your ear if Yes.

Rub the back of your neck if No.

I ponder on this before deciding to tuck a lock of my hair behind my right ear. I glance up at him and he smiles.

SMELL GOOD MAN

Let me grab my cape and I'll be right there.

I stifle a laugh.

This man.

He walks over and everything surrounding us is a blur. He moves with such grace, and his scent envelops me when he approaches.

God.

Why does he smell so fucking good?

How is he planning to get me out of this?

He stops once he reaches our table. He looks me up and down before saying, "Fancy seeing you here. And who might this be?" He glares at Aaron.

Who takes a moment to acknowledge him, when he does, his eyes bounce between Greyson and I.

"Do you always go out with married women?"

"Excuse me?"

"You're on a date with my wife. There's nothing more to say. Come along, babe."

He motions for me to follow him before turning on his heel, going still as he waits for me.

"Wife? You're married?"

I wince and respond, thinking quick on my feet.

"Separated, actually. It's a long story. If you'll excuse me."

I rise from the table, trailing behind Greyson and pretending to argue.

Once we're out of earshot, I ask, "What are you doing here?"

"Grabbing dinner. You know I'm always up for a bite," he adds playfully.

"That's not what I meant by saving me. What the hell was that?"

"I read it in one of your books and thought you'd appreciate it."

I cover my laughter with my hand.

"You're incorrigible."

"Hey, I made you smile and that's all that matters to me."

I roll my eyes, but I know it does nothing to hide his effect on me.

"Are you coming home with me, *wife*? Or do you want to stay?"

I try to ignore the somersaults in my stomach from him calling me *wife*.

We take a moment to look back at my date, who is seemingly agitated as he glares at us. "The damage seems irreparable."

"What am I going to do with you?"

"Anything you'd like, as long as you ask nicely."

I bite the inside of my cheek to stop myself from flirting while my date is twenty feet away. *Though he's done it in front of me all night.*

I look down, taking a deep breath, dreading this awkward interaction. I think of Audrey's ferocity and channel a sliver of it to push through this.

"Give me a second to grab my coat and let him down easy."

I pat his shoulder and turn around when he grabs my arm, holding me in place.

He whispers in my ear, "don't apologize," and plants a soft kiss on my cheek.

That's exactly what I planned to do.

How did he know that?

When he releases me, I saunter back towards our table. When Aaron sees me, he stands. I start, trying not to apologize. "Listen. This has been an odd night. I will take care of the bill. You're a nice guy, but my husband over there–"

He interrupts, "Look. I don't want anything to do with this. I'm not interested in a threesome or being a third. So, if you all are into that shit, I'm not judging but that's not me. I'm getting the fuck out of here." He points a thumb towards the door.

I nod understandably. *I'd rather him think that because I had no idea what I was going to say.* "I didn't mean for him to crash our date. He's not handling our separation well."

"I can't believe this shit."

He stands up and slips on his coat, grumbling to himself the whole way out of the restaurant. He breezes past Greyson and exits. He must've picked up his dinner order in the meantime because he's now holding two bags. I gather my things and when I approach him, he informs me he already took care of the bill. He refuses to let me put my coat on myself, even though his hands are full.

Such a gentleman.

He sets his food bags on an unoccupied table, standing behind me as I slip one arm into each side of the coat. He follows me out of the restaurant with his food, holding the door as I step outside. We walk side-by-side in comfortable silence until we reach his SUV. He stands beside the car, grabbing his keys, and he stills as if he forgot something.

He turns to me. "Did you take an Uber or drive?"

"I Ubered in case I drank."

"Well, now that I'm here, you won't need one to get home."

"That's not necessary," I protest.

"Don't argue with me on this, Selah. It's not safe. I don't want you riding with a stranger when I'm right here. Please, let me take you home. We're going to the same place. Please?" he asks with pleading eyes.

He's done enough for me tonight, and it's just a ride home. He's being neighborly. That's all.

"Okay, big boy. Take me home."

40
tinted windows

Greyson

Manhattan, NY | January 19, 2024

I OPEN HER DOOR, biting the inside of my cheek to hide my smile. As she gets settled in, I reach over and buckle her seat. I hear her breath hitch, and I turn my head toward the sound. Her proximity intoxicates me. I want to kiss her right now.

I want to kiss her and bring her home with me. I don't think she'd go for that, though.

We stay like this for a moment. I move in closer, lips hovering over hers—waiting for her to give me something, anything to let me know that this is okay. Her eyes glitter, her chest rising and falling heavily. "Sel—" I'm interrupted by her grabbing the back of my neck and her lips colliding with mine.

This kiss feels like the northern lights breathing life into me I never knew. I feel reborn. I've kissed before, but it's never been like this. I'm hungry for her, and I've been starving for weeks, desperate for her taste and attention, willing to take anything she'll offer.

This feels different from the kiss in her apartment. This one holds promise. She lets out a moan, and I swallow it, taking everything she's comfortable giving me right now. Her hands start moving over me, and that's when I realize that I am standing on the curb leaning over this woman who's kissing the life out of me, and my dick is straining in my pants.

I need to get her home NOW.

I come up for air and say, "I want to keep this going with you, but I think it'd be best if we were alone. Would you be okay with that?"

"Yes," she says, catching her breath, her lips swollen and red. "I'm so—" I interrupt her unnecessary apology with another kiss, twisting my tongue around hers and nipping her lip as I pull away.

"Stop apologizing, Sunflower. You don't need to do that anymore. With me or anyone else."

"Okay."

I kiss her forehead before closing the door and rounding the car to my side.

I settle in, warm up the car, and pull my phone out of my pocket. I open the *Kiwi Music* app and hand my phone to her. She doesn't take it and looks at me incredulously. "Tell me how you're feeling right now with a song."

"Just one?"

"As many songs as you need to express yourself. I think this is the best way for you to share what really goes on in that beautiful head of yours when words don't seem like enough." Her face softens, and she accepts my phone, ignoring the shock that occurs whenever our hands touch. She ponders for a moment before typing away, and she is making a playlist. It's not lost on me how much her face lights up at the action.

Uh oh, we have something that brings joy to the great Selah Bailey.

I pull out of the parking spot and start the drive home, working overtime to contain my excitement that she would like to go home with me. Of course, she could shy away again and change her mind, which will crush me, but I'll respect it. She's leading the way with this, and I won't press her.

She breaks the silence after a few moments. "You ready?" she says, holding up my phone.

"I'm all ears."

She presses play, and I keep my eyes on the road, but can see her anxiously awaiting my reaction in my peripheral. The song has a funky beat, and the singer's voice has a unique rasp. I've never heard it before, but I love it, and then I hear the line she must've been waiting for me to react to. It's about desire and how eager you are to get that person alone. My eyebrows shoot up, and peer over at her. She returns my gaze with a simmering heat, as if she, too, is trying to contain herself. I notice her shift in her seat and squeeze her thighs together, seeking friction.

I feel her pain, and if she keeps it up, we may not even make it home before I pull over and bury myself deep inside of her. I reach over and grip her thigh, hoping my touch puts her at ease.

We're about fifteen minutes out.

Another song comes on. I don't know this one either, but it's another funky beat, and the vocals are smooth. I like it. It's about taking your time to please your partner, planning for it to take all night long. Good to know she and I are on the same page because she won't be tapping out until I allow it. She moves my hand before squirming around in her seat. My eyes are on the road, but I turn the music down and ask her if she's alright.

"I'm fine," she says while visibly shifting around still. I notice her leaning forward and picking something up off the floor. She giggles, placing something in my lap. We finally get to a stoplight, and I glance down, doing a double take. It's panties. Her panties. I'm shocked.

She took her panties off in my car and put them in my lap.

Fuck.

This woman drives me wild.

I look over at her, and she's biting her lip, a simmering flame burning bright in her irises.

I grab the sopping panties, balling them in my hands before sniffing them, keeping our gazes locked. Her breath hitches.

The light changes, and I drop the panties in my lap, setting my foot on the gas. I reach over to rest my hand on her thigh once again, this time slipping my hand beneath the hem of her dress. She lets out a soft moan at my touch. Goosebumps erupt over her body, and I smile to myself.

Another song stands out to me on this playlist she made. I turn the music up to listen closely, and I hear the line loud and clear. The song is about wanting your partner to choke you during sex.

She surprises me again.

My kinky little sunflower. I love this side of her.

"There'll be plenty of that tonight, Princess. Don't you worry."

She gasps and covers her mouth as if that could hide her blushing.

She moves my hand toward her aching center.

Ten minutes out.

I angle my head toward the panties resting in my lap. "I should gag you with these for teasing me while I'm driving. I'd like to get you home in one piece *before* you fall apart."

She parts her lips, and I stop her before she speaks.

"Don't you dare apologize to me," I say firmly.

I pat her thigh. "Spread them."

Opening up for me, her thighs part, granting me access. I glide through her lips, gathering arousal on my fingers. I take my hand away, and she shudders at the distance. I suck her juices off my hand, letting out a loud pop.

She whimpers, eyes pleading for me. "So needy." I grant her the attention she needs by slipping a digit inside, and she clenches around it in response.

Fuck.

"You're so wet for me."

Throwing her head back in pleasure, her moans fill the car. It's better than any song she could play for me. Eyes locked on the road and one hand pumping in and out of her sweet pussy, I can't think of a better way to have ended my night.

Thank God for tinted windows.

Focusing on getting us home safely while she's using me for pleasure isn't an easy feat. She deserves my undivided attention, and she will receive it once we get home. "That's it, baby. Ride my fingers. Show me how you'll take my dick."

She shudders at my words as she becomes even wetter if that is possible. She grinds faster, the sounds of her wetness filling the car. I don't even hear the music at this point. If it stopped, I couldn't tell.

She digs her nails into my forearm as she bucks against my hand. She's close.

Three minutes out.

"Come for me, Princess," I urge, curling my fingers until I hit her sweet spot, building her pleasure to earn *my* reward. She detonates gracefully, crying out my name amongst other unintelligible words. I only caught a glimpse of it. I've seen monuments, masterpieces, and the seven wonders of the world, and they are *nothing* compared to her.

One minute out.

She rides out the aftershocks of her orgasm on me, rubbing softly over the half-moons she dug into my arm to soothe the sting. *A silent apology*. I won't give her shit for it this time. I pull into the parking garage and park before I retrieve my hand, teasing it over her lips. "Suck." She obeys, twirling her tongue until she licks my fingers clean.

Fuck.

Eager to taste her climax, I reach over to swipe through her lips, collecting arousal, placing each finger in my mouth, indulging in her. Our eyes lock, and a raging fire burns in hers, chest rising and falling with each pant. I can't wait to see her shatter for me again and again.

I lean in close. "You're so fucking beautiful when you come. Ready to do that again?"

She grabs my face as her lips take mine.

I capture her moans as quickly as they escape, my hands tangled in her curls. Our tongues tango, battling for power, and I succumb, savoring her flavors and meeting each stroke of her tongue.

I've never cared much for kissing before, and I'm convinced that's because it wasn't with *her*.

Clawing at my shirt, she tries to undress me. I stop her hand and place soft kisses on her palms.

I help her adjust her dress, making sure she has her clutch before we exit the car. While pocketing her panties, I tell her to stay put as I grab the bags and come around to let her out. She grabs my hand, which catches me off guard, and holds it as we make our way to the elevator in the garage. Pressing the button with my other hand, we wait for the elevator to arrive at our level.

I lean in close and whisper in her ear, "I know you're ready for me to take you home. If you'll be a good girl for the elevator ride, you'll be rewarded with my tongue. How's that sound?"

She draws in a breath and responds with a hum.

"Tell me you'll be a good girl for me."

She exhales in annoyance from me teasing her out in the open, but I can't help it.

"I'll be a good girl only *if* you stop teasing me."

"Well, that isn't going to happen," I say in a playful tone. She grumbles to herself while crossing her arms over her chest as we wait.

I chuckle to myself and put my hands in my pockets, toying with her panties, smiling to myself because she's about to find out how badly I want her.

The elevator dings, and she looks up at me curiously before strutting inside, her ass swaying with each step. Her curves in that dress have me biting my lip as I follow behind, standing beside her. She steals another glance over her shoulder, but this one is full of hunger and anticipation.

Once the doors shut, my lips are on hers. This kiss is rough and unrelenting as we fight for dominance, but I don't let up. I coax her mouth open with gentle licks, desperate to taste her again. She moans and lets me in as I grip the back of her neck with my free hand.

She presses herself against me, feeling my strained dick through my pants, and I hiss in response. She stands on the tips of her toes, trying to reach me, grabbing my clothes to bring me closer. I'm certain we aren't close enough. I need to be *inside* her.

The elevator stops suddenly on the sixth floor, and the doors open. We're caught with none other than Estelle standing there, all dolled up.

We scramble at the sight of her to resume standing side by side when she wears a look of amusement as she assesses us. "Well, don't stop on my behalf. You two go ahead. I'll wait for the next one." She steps back and gives us a wave before the doors shut.

"She's going to want to talk about this tomorrow."

"You think?"

"I feel like I should give you something to brag about then."

She peers up at me with an intrigued look. "For once, I *won't* argue with you."

"I'll be sure to enjoy it while it lasts."

She snorts before staring at the numbers ascending on the screen, assuming she's nervous about the possibility of another interruption from a neighbor who won't be as understanding as Estelle is.

I place my hand on the small of her back in an attempt to soothe her, and she nestles into me. I smile at the contact as my hand travels up her back and settles on her arm, giving it a gentle squeeze. I lean down to press a soft kiss on the top of her head, and she sighs contentedly.

Selah is coming home with me tonight.

41
back home

Greyson

Manhattan, NY | January 19, 2024

THE ELEVATOR DINGS as the doors slide open and instead of quickly rushing out, she waits for me. We exit hand in hand as I lead her to my door. She waits by my side shyly. I remind myself of the panties in my pocket and shake my head.

My little sunflower is far from shy.

I turn the key into the lock and glance at her as I open the door. She looks nervous and I am too. I reach out for her hand to enter together. I hear Clifford on the other end of the door, his tag jingling, and once I open it, he's standing and wagging his tail anxiously. He perks up at the sight of me, but once he sees Selah, he charges to her.

"He loves company," I say, shutting the door behind us.

She gives him head scratches and he loves it. I remove my shoes and enter the kitchen to settle in, asking her to do the same. I watch them interact and my heart swells. He lights up at the sight of her.

Like father, like son.

She catches me staring and smiles sweetly. Peeling back the mask and giving me a glimpse of that radiance she hides from the world. I yearn for her familiarity and I don't care who knows it. In fact, if she'd let me, I'd take her out in public every chance I get to prove exactly how grateful I am to know her. How much I cherish every moment of her precious time. For now, I will worship her with action, not words. I don't wish to scare her off, but I plan to draw this out and make the best out of every single second I've been granted.

She removes her shoes when Cliff settles down. He grabs himself a plush animal from his toy bucket and curls up with it in his bed. Once he's distracted, she joins me in the kitchen.

She slips in behind me to wash her hands while I start unloading the food bags. I turn around too quickly to grab bowls and we collide. Instinctively, I grab her, wrapping an arm around her waist and I press her into me. I look down at her and her body is tense before she eases into my touch.

She stares at my shirt with raised brows and says, "Good reflexes, sir."

"Why, thank you. I can't have you falling for me just yet. I've grown accustomed to you giving me a hard time."

Selah blinks up at me with those big brown eyes and says, "I'm easily impressed by fictional men. Real ones must work much harder for my time."

"Don't I know it?"

She chuckles to herself.

"What do we have here?"

She peers over my shoulder towards the island. I let her go and instantly miss the warmth of her touch.

"Well, I wasn't planning on sharing, but I think you're cute enough that I'll allow it this time."

"So, you think I'm cute?" she challenges, mischief in her stare.

I poke her nose and add, "Plus I saw your plate at the restaurant and you didn't eat hardly enough to sustain what I'd like to do to you. Come sit."

I point to the stools across the island and she climbs up,

keeping her eyes on me. I grab utensils then bowls from a nearby cabinet and start opening the containers, listing off what each dish is and asking her what she'd like to try. Once she makes her choices, I fill up a bowl and add a fork before I slide it gently across the counter. I do the same for myself and eat standing up. She takes her first bite, unable to hold back the moan of approval.

I look forward to hearing more of that from her tonight.

"Is it good?"

"Are you used to hearing women moan when they aren't enjoying themselves?" she asks, her tone laced with sarcasm.

I take a moment to entertain her, rubbing my chin to appear in deep thought.

"I can't say I'm used to that. However, I am curious to hear all the sounds *you're* capable of making."

I return her gaze and she covers her mouth, hiding the grin across her face before waving me off as she continues eating. We enjoy a comfortable silence while taking turns catching each other staring.

I can't help it. She is so fucking beautiful.

"So, there's still a lot that I don't know about you, but I came here tonight with the intention of sleeping with you."

I feign surprise.

"I don't think you came here to sleep, baby," I tease.

"Fine. I came here with the intention of *fucking* you." She draws out the word while holding eye contact.

There she is. My dirty girl.

"That's more like it. Good to see you being honest about what you want. Ask away, Princess. A question for a question. How's that sound?"

"I can do that," she agrees.

The first round of this game is off to a hilarious start because on Selah's first turn she asks two questions and one pertains to my birthday. I share that I'm thirty-one and a Pisces, hoping that'll suffice. I refuse to share the date, but I'm honest and tell her that I hate my birthday. I didn't consider that being her next question, but she surprised me. I remind her it's my turn, when she finds another question from my statement about disliking my birthday. She rolls her eyes and apologizes.

I tsk. "We've been through this. Take it back."

"Fine. I am *not* sorry."

"Good girl," I say with a wink and she avoids eye contact when she blushes.

I decide to use this game to my advantage and ask her questions I desperately want answers to. She can play small if she wants to, but I'm not. I ask if I make her nervous because I want to know the reason she runs off and has been avoiding meeting me. She shares that she finds me attractive and that she isn't the most experienced with men like *me.* I'm not sure what to make of that, which prompts me to ask what kind of man she thinks I am. She taunts that it's her turn and I give her the floor. *I'll save that one for last.*

"I'm curious every time I see you with a camera around your neck. Could I see your photos?"

"Of course. I'll grab my portfolio," I say before heading to my office. I return with the thick book for her to flip through. There are a couple hundred pictures in here. This one isn't for gigs, it's for me. Whenever I get *the perfect shot,* the one that captures my vision, it goes in this book. She flips through the pages, examining every detail and stops when she reaches my vacation photos. Her eyes light up at my nature photography.

"This island, where is it? With these tortoises?"

"Seychelles. It's in Africa. I went with my best friends to a wedding there a few years ago. Pictures don't do it justice, honestly."

"I'd love to go there someday. I've never even been out of the country," she says reluctantly.

"Well, sounds to me like you're just going to have to make a new *fuck it list,*" I add with a smile.

She peers up at me. "That's not a bad idea."

I nod in agreement and use my next turn to ask if she's ever been in love. She argues about keeping things simple by asking about birthdays and ages. I inform her that I have no interest in asking things I already know the answer to. Her birthday is May seventh, she's twenty-nine years old, and she's a Taurus. When she gives me a shocked look, I blame Audrey, which grants me a chuckle. She reluctantly answers that she was in love once, but it wasn't reciprocated. Then, she uses her turn to ask the same. I share that I too was in love once and that I'm not sure I could do it again. I consider what to ask for my next turn and decide to keep going for the answers I *really* want.

"Have you ever been married?"

"You're just going for it. Aren't you?" She shakes her head and takes a deep breath. "I've never been married, but I was engaged once." She discloses in a low voice. "I broke it off two years ago. We wouldn't have made it to the altar. He was–" she trails off, deciding on a word. "He was awful." Her playful demeanor has dissipated as she holds her waist, staying focused on the countertop.

Shit.

You dived into a sore subject.

She adds, "I've enjoyed being alone since and these dates I've been going on are recent. I tried putting myself out there when I made the *SoulBlend* profile and you know that has been an interesting experience."

"I'm sorry, I wouldn't have brought it up if I had known."

"The whole point of this game is to get to know each other. I'm not upset and there's no need to apologize. If I'm not allowed to say sorry, neither are you."

I nod understandably.

"What about you?"

"Yes. I got married fresh out of college. We lasted almost three years before we called it quits and I haven't had another serious relationship since," I admit. "Actually, Audrey is planning her wedding."

Her brows raise in surprise at her best friend being mentioned. She makes a comment about how my ex must be rich because Wood weddings aren't affordable. I simply shrug, hoping that deters her because I'd rather not speak about her any more than I need to. She picks up on my signal and informs me this will be the last round of the question game.

"Do you have any kids?" she asks nervously.

"No, just that big one that barks."

I don't want to say his name and get him started. I peer into the living room and he's not in any of his usual spots, so I assume he's in the guest bedroom. We must've been talking too much for him. I decide to circle back to my earlier question, even though it's possible her being brutally honest may either boost or bruise my ego. I'll handle whatever she throws at me and go for it.

"You mentioned that you're not experienced with men like me. I'd like to know what kind of man you think I am?"

"You're a man who knows exactly what he wants. You can back up the shit you talk. You're intentional. Then there's the whole pleasure dom thing." She looks down as she blushes.

"Did you look it up?" I ask as I lean back against the counter, crossing my arms.

"I did and it only made me more curious." She lets out a resigned sigh and continues. "I can't believe I'm telling you this, but I've been celibate for the past two years. Well I was before you came over."

My brows raise in surprise. "Why didn't you say anything?"

"What was there to say? Go easy on me?" She chuckles.

"I think that would've been a good start. Selah, if I had known—I—"

She puts her hand up to stop me. "Don't. I needed that, and I can't stop thinking about it."

"Me either."

I watch her closely and when she doesn't respond, I'm unsure of how to interpret her silence. I enjoy her company and her comfort is most important to me. While I ache for another taste, I'll savor what lingers on my tongue.

"I know what happened in the car, and I don't want you to feel pressured tonight. We don't need to do anything else."

"What if I want to do everything?"

My eyes widen as she rises from her seat and struts towards me with a slow, seductive sway of her hips. Her pebbled nipples are nearly cutting through her silk dress. *Fuck.* The flames in her irises engulf me, setting fire to the remains of my resolve. I pick her up, setting her on the counter as I pepper wet kisses along her neck and collarbone. Desperate to taste her skin.

I drag my tongue up her neck and order, "Define *everything,* Sunflower. Tell me everything you want."

"I want you to show me all the ways you can make me come. I want to feel your tongue on me. I want…to be a good girl fo-"

I cut her off with a devouring kiss. She grips my shirt to pull me closer as she moans in my mouth. She can have anything she fucking wants. If she asked me to obey her every word, I would. I break away to nip at her neck and her breath picks up as my hands travel down her legs to spread them open further.

I kneel before her and she's dripping for me. I am salivating for this woman. I hover my mouth over her entrance and maintain eye contact.

"If you take your eyes off me, I'll stop. Do you understand?"

She nods in response.

"I know you're excited, but I need you to use your words."

"I…understand."

"Good."

I am so close to tasting her when I remember something she said earlier.

"You were being a brat and called me 'Daddy' before you went on a date with another man. Is that something you feel comfortable calling me?"

"Yes."

"Yes, what?" I ask.

I hold my hand to my ear, needing to hear her say it.

"Yes, Daddy."

"Good fucking girl."

42
fine line

Selah

Manhattan, NY | January 19, 2024

I'M REWARDED with a swipe of his tongue, and when I throw my head back to cry out, he stops as promised.

Eyes on me, or I'll stop.

I beg for him to continue, and he does once my eyes are back on him. Greyson on his knees, focusing on my pleasure, is the hottest thing I've ever seen. I'm certain I could come just from this view. My legs tremble and squeeze around his face, but his tongue doesn't falter. He stares at me with daring eyes when he pulls my legs apart and holds them open. He delves his tongue inside my channel, fucking it in and out of me as I whimper.

When he stops teasing me, he swirls his tongue around my clit and flicks until I beg and sob. He slips his fingers inside of me and curls them, and I grip his hair as I buck against him.

His moans vibrate through my core as he latches on my sensitive clit, urging me to come. I scream out his name, and he laps up every drop as I ride out my orgasm.

He stands before me, and I gawk at the glistening arousal on his face.

"You listened so well and kept your eyes on me. That's my good girl. You want to come again?"

"Yes, please."

I don't care how eager I sound. I need him.

I wrap my arms around his neck when he grips my thighs to carry me to the couch. He seats me on his lap, and I straddle him.

"Show me how needy you are for my dick. Grind on my thigh."

I stare down at his thigh nervously as I lift my dress, lowering myself on it. I've never done this before, and I'm nervous. I focus on my rhythm, rocking against his thigh. It feels so fucking good, and I bite my lip, returning his gaze.

"That's it. You're doing so good."

I grind harder at his praise, eager for more. I lean into him to lick his neck and moan in his ear. He groans and palms his bulging erection through his pants.

"Use my thigh, baby."

I grind faster, arching into him, and he trails his tongue around my nipples, sucking as I feel my pleasure building. I wail his name when I reach my climax.

"Fuck, yes," he urges.

He grips my hips as I ride his thigh.

"Grey, oh god," I pant.

He's entranced by me as I come down.

"You called me Grey. It was a matter of time, nasty girl."

"Shut up," I chuckle. "You're annoying."

I slump against him, and he carries me to the bedroom. I take his lips tenderly, moaning into his mouth.

He flicks on the lights when we get to his room and sets me on the bed. I argue for him to turn them off, but he refuses. Claims he wants to see all of me but agrees to dim the lights as a compromise if it makes me more comfortable.

He laughs at my feet dangling off the edge of his tall bed while he undresses. I'm practically salivating as I drink him in.

His physique is remarkable with sinewy muscles and veiny arms. He has a few more tattoos he's revealing to me and my curiosity is piqued. I squeeze my thighs together as I admire this beautiful man before me. He keeps his boxers on then grabs a condom from the nightstand, and I take that as a cue to undress myself. I've barely slipped out of my minidress when I catch him standing in front of me.

"I didn't ask you to undress, did I?"

I freeze and hold my hands out in surrender, though my eyes are still on his boxers and the hard dick I've fantasized about for months.

"You didn't," I say slowly.

"Are you eager for me, Princess?"

"Yes, Daddy."

"Well, if you're so eager, let me help," he suggests, pulling down the zipper with too much force, and it rips.

"Shit," he says with a wince.

I gasp, assessing the ripped seam.

I really liked this dress.

"Dammit, Greyson," I whine.

"I'm sorry, baby. I'll buy you one in every color."

He kneels before me and presses a kiss to the tattoo on my ankle. My frustration dissipates as he kisses me all over my body, paying extra attention to my tattoos.

"I'm going to kiss these tattoos and you're going to tell me what inspired them. I understand you're excited, but you won't get what you want until I get answers," he orders.

I can hardly focus on what he said as he drives me wild, toying with my nipples in between kisses. I whimper in response as he kisses below my bra line, patiently waiting for me to name the song that inspired that tattoo.

"Fine Line," I whisper.

He drags his mouth further down, peppering kisses along my ribs where an open birdcage rests.

"Gone Girl," I say in between breaths.

"We're almost done. You're doing great."

He gently kisses the flying bluebird with a honey dipper alongside the cage.

"Last one, baby," he urges with a pinch to my nipple.

"Daylight," I whine.

"That wasn't so hard, was it?" he teases.

He's a fucking menace.

He rises to drop his boxers, and I watch in awe as he rips open the condom and rolls it onto his dick.

"Lie back for me."

I oblige quickly, spreading my legs for him as he kneels on the bed to assess me. Being exposed like this before him should make me feel uncomfortable, but it doesn't.

I'm also glad I got a wax.

I hold my legs back as he rubs his dick against my aching pussy until I beg. I'm so fucking wet and pleading for him. Finally, he sinks into me and I gasp.

He pushes in slowly, allowing me to adjust to his size.

"You feel amazing. Fuck." His fingers dig into my hips as he pulls out all the way to the crown. "You have plans tomorrow, Selah?"

I shake my head, unsure of why he's asking that now.

"Good. 'Cause you're about to be up all night."

My eyes widen as he ruts into me. Hard.

Oh god.

I moan and shut my eyes, and he halts his movements.

"Same rule applies. Eyes on me, or I'll stop. Do you understand?"

I look up at him and gulp.

"Yes, Daddy."

He thrusts deeper into me, and I hold his gaze, only looking away to occasionally watch him slide in and out of me. I reach down to dust my fingers over my clit and he raises a brow before fucking me harder.

"That's it, Princess. Rub that pretty pussy until you come."

I take his punishing thrusts, keeping my hand on my sensitive nub as I writhe beneath him and grip the sheet with my free hand.

Our moans fill the room and I plead for more, begging him not to stop. His thrusts are unrelenting as I convulse beneath him, crying out his name. He follows behind with my name on his lips, and it's the sexiest thing I've ever seen. He collapses beside me and I roll onto my side with a devious grin as I suck my arousal off my fingers, holding eye contact. He rips my hand away and places it in his mouth.

He's so fucking sexy. Shit.

I follow him into the bathroom, and he cleans us up. He mentions he's surprised that I didn't argue and just let him take care of me. I take a moment to myself before joining him in the bedroom and process what just happened. Mama will love to hear that he's a *very* good neighbor. I'll tell her tomorrow.

Women get fucked like this in books, and men only talk like that in them. What woman wrote Grey? I'd like to thank her for her service.

I enter his bedroom and toss his shirt over my head before lying beside him and nestling into his chest. To my surprise, he lets me rest against him.

"I'll send you those songs in the morning since you tortured me over them," I giggle.

"Don't act like you didn't enjoy yourself," he teases.

I hum, nestling further into his chest, as I trace the one-frame tattoo on his right forearm with two cranes. I sit up and press a soft kiss to the tattoo before resting back on his chest, listening to his heartbeat. After a moment, I break the silence.

"What does this one mean?" I ask softly.

"The cranes in my culture represent longevity, purity, and peace. I got it during a time when I really needed hope."

"Did you ever find it?"

"I did."

"Good," I say sleepily.

43
breakfast & entering

Greyson

Manhattan, NY | January 20, 2024

I WAKE up from the best night's sleep I've had in a long time with Selah in my arms. Last night was unreal. She came alive for me and undone in more ways than one. I am still in awe of her. She is remarkable. I haven't shared my bed in a long time. It's been me and occasionally Clifford wanting to snuggle, but I won't deny that I like the way this feels. Her lush curls are splayed across the pillow, and they smell of cherries.

I realize that she came here in that little dress, and I want her to feel comfortable here, so I decide to do something I shouldn't. I consider she might not like this, but I want her to stay, at least for the morning. She should have her necessities, and her cat needs to be fed, so I'm going to go downstairs and let myself into her apartment, but just to grab a bag of things she'd need to freshen up and lounge around with me. I also don't want her to have to do the walk of shame back to her place in what's left of that dress. I didn't mean to rip it. I'll buy her a few more.

I ease my arm from under her, careful not to wake her. It's possible that she may not see this as a kind gesture so I should start thinking of a way to make it up to her if she gets pissed with me. I manage to get dressed and quietly exit the room without so much as a stir from her. She should be exhausted, so I'll pat myself on the back for that later. I find her bag and retrieve her key ring. I freeze when Cliff lifts his head, he notices me, and I know with one bark this whole operation is over. I remain still, watching him and he is not ready to get up for the day. As expected, he grunts softly, drops his head back down and I wait a moment more before I slip out the door.

The elevator ride is fine, and I don't encounter anyone. I feel guilty the whole way because I am doing something wrong even if I have a good reason for it. I rifle through her keys until I find the right one that grants me access to her place and when I open the door, I remember where Peach's food is from when I saw Audrey feeding her. I settle in and swap out her water bowl. She starts meowing from a distance once she hears her food pinging against the bowl. Her cries grow closer, and I step back waiting for her to emerge. Once I come into her view, she gives me a look of indifference. I introduce myself and to my surprise she walks up to sniff me for a bit and rubs herself against my leg.

I head to Selah's room and look for some kind of bag to fill up. I am reminding myself that while it looks and feels like I'm a thief right now, I am not. I find a tote bag hanging off her closet handle and I search her drawers for a change of clothes, I find something simple and move on to the bathroom. I opt for the toiletries that are lined up on her counter, assuming those are her favorites, adding them to the bag. I remember to grab a shower cap, and I notice her bonnet laying on her bed, so I pick that up too. Next time, I'd love it if she'd pack a bag beforehand. Well, that is if she'd like to do this again. I have a bit of a stare down with her e-reader and decide against it. I know she doesn't go anywhere without it, but I could be declaring war if I touch that thing, so it stays put.

I'm out of her apartment quickly and leave the place as neat as I found it. I underestimated how much more nerve wracking the walk home would be with her things, hoping she isn't awake when I get there because this will be very awkward to explain. I slowly turn the knob as I tiptoe back into my apartment, it's silent when I return, but Clifford isn't in his bed.

Now, I'm nervous.

I pad toward the hallway, and I see my bedroom door opened wider than when I left it. I peek in and to my surprise, Selah is still sleeping soundly, an arm draped over Clifford as he snuggles up beside her. My heart warms at the sight. It's been just us for so long that it's nice to see Cliff enjoying her presence as much as I do. I'd like to grab my camera, but it'll make too much noise, so I silence my phone and snap a few pics of their cuteness from the hallway. *Just for me.*

I write her a little note explaining what I did and why with an apology on the back of it. I leave it on the pillow beside her and I hope it makes her laugh when she wakes up. I leave the bag in the bathroom for her, and I start tidying up the kitchen so I can make us breakfast since cooking calms me down when I overthink. She tends to stress clean, and I suppose you could say that I stress cook. Last night was the best night I've had in a long time, but I learned that I have a jealous streak when it comes to Selah. I don't like the idea of her entertaining other people. I'd like a shot at giving her what she needs and I need to figure out how to have this conversation. I haven't had a crush since college, and I don't remember feeling this way.

Shit, I've been *married* and it didn't feel this way.

44
make a u-turn

Greyson

Manhattan, NY | January 20, 2024

BACON SIZZLES ON THE STOVE, and I avoid the grease popping when I feel my phone vibrating in my pocket. It's a Sunday morning, and I assume it's my mom, but when Aileen's name flashes across the screen, I wince. I'm aware that I don't have to answer, and this isn't a good time for her to be calling. I'd also hate for her to call again when Selah wakes up, so I'll see what's going on with her now.

"Good morning," I say with a stiff smile.

"Morning, Greyson! It's so good to hear your voice. You haven't reached out in a while, and you had me a bit worried. I wanted to catch up."

I just had the best night in years, and there's an incredible woman in my bed I'd love to get back to.

I don't want to deal with this right now.

Let's keep it short and sweet.

"I'm doing good. I've just been tied up with work. That's all. No need to worry about me."

"Ugh. Everything with the wedding has been so hectic, but

it's coming together. Planning it without Daniel here has taken a toll. You know he's often in London running the Kline distillery. It sucks, but we'll make it work."

"Do you have plans to move to the UK? Or him to the US?"

Keep it short and sweet, remember?

Asking questions is not short and sweet.

"Why would I do that?"

Nope.

Let me make a U-turn.

This is none of my business.

"Forget I asked."

Short, but not sweet.

"Are you sure you're okay?"

"I'm fine," I say flatly.

"Oh," she exclaims as if she just remembered something. "Have you been dating since the engagement party? Given it any thought? It'd be so nice to see you with someone."

I'm grumbling under my breath as I think of a safe way out of this conversation.

"Come to think of it, I met a sweet woman at the bake shop that I could set you up with. She is single. If you're interested, of course."

Absolutely not.

Annoyance bubbles at the surface.

I don't understand why she cares so much about this.

She's literally getting married.

"Actually, I've been seeing someone, and she'll be my plus one," I blurt.

What the hell am I doing?

We just slept together, and I just promised she'd come to my ex's wedding.

I quietly slap my palm to my forehead.

She practically screams in my ear with glee.

"Oh really? I'm thrilled! Can't wait to meet her! Is it serious?"

Thinking about how I'm about to ask her to stop going on dates AND exclusively sleep with me, I'd very well like to think it's somewhat serious.

I mean, she's in my bed cuddling my dog right now.

There is always a possibility that she could say no, but what if she doesn't?

Keep it short and sweet.

"It is."

I've officially lost it. It's finally happened. Jesus Christ.

"I'm so happy to hear that."

Now we're having two conversations that could absolutely scare her off.

Just when she was starting to like me, I fucked this up.

I can't even blame Aileen because this one is on me.

"Well, I hate to rush you off, but I'd like to wake her up with breakfast."

I wait for her response, and she's silent as if she's processing before she chimes, "Yeah! Sorry to interrupt. I wish you would've told me sooner. Have a great day, Greyson. Love you!"

I hate that she still says this at the end of calls and texts. I stopped saying it back years ago because we're not in love. Sure, we'll always care for each other, but boundaries are necessary, and that's one of mine. I won't say something I don't mean to appease anybody else. Especially not "love."

With an eye roll, I add, "Have a good one. I hope everything runs smoothly with the wedding plans. Take care."

I take a deep breath and let it roll off my shoulders, clinging to positive thoughts about this conversation with Selah to convince myself that the outcome may not end disastrously.

I'm finishing up the bacon on the stove when I think I hear her shuffling around. I smile to myself, blissfully ignoring the impending sense of dread currently filling my stomach. It's threatening to steal my appetite despite how hard I've worked on this meal.

Everything is going to be fine. I've asked a woman to flat out marry me once, surely, I can ask Selah to be my date to a wedding. I have asked women out before, and I don't know what it is about Selah that makes me second-guess myself, but shit. I psych myself up until I hear her footsteps approaching.

I can do this. She may say no, but at least I tried.

45
the morning after

Selah

Manhattan | January 20, 2024

I WAKE up in Greyson's bed, surrounded by his scent and missing his warmth. However, Clifford is snuggled up against me. For such a large dog, he's a big baby. I listen closely and hear the sizzling of pans in the distance. I smell breakfast cooking and smile to myself. I roll over to see a small yellow note resting on his pillow. It reads:

> *Sunflower,*
>
> *- I took your keys and entered your apartment, BUT I didn't want to wake you & had a reason.*
>
> *- I fed Peach*
>
> *- I grabbed what I thought you'd need & locked up*
>
> *- Everything is on the bathroom counter*
>
> *- I wanted you to feel at home*

There's an arrow on the bottom of the page instructing me to flip the note over. It reads:

Would you accept my tongue as a proper apology?
Yes, or no?
Circle one

This man is truly something else. My laughter wakes up Clifford, who stretches beside me.

"Your dad is silly." His tail flops around in response.

I head to the bathroom to check the bag, and he did a good job. Greyson himself has a great skincare routine, so he knew exactly what to look for. With hair and body products, he seemed to have panicked and picked up many different things, but the basics are all here.

There are pajamas and a change of clothes so I wouldn't have to do the walk of shame from his place in my ripped dress from last night. He even set out a new toothbrush for me. I'm surprised to see my shower cap *and* bonnet, too. He must be hoping to get another night out of me.

I wanted you to feel at home.

I freshen up and grab a pen off the nightstand, remembering to circle an answer on the note he left me before I follow the smell of bacon, hoping to find him at the source. When I enter the kitchen, his back is to me—he's shirtless, and I try not to drool as I admire the muscles in his back. I'm certain I stand there gawking like a creep for who knows how long when he looks over his shoulder and winks at me.

He turns to face me with a wide smile, and I make note of how happy he is every time he sees me. His eyes rake over me, and he bites his lip before he speaks.

"Good morning, Sunflower."

"Breaking and entering with a side of breakfast? You're so good to me."

He places his hand over his heart like I wounded him.

"I had my reasons. Peach was at the top of that list," he reminds me.

"You're right. Thanks for taking care of her."

"Anytime."

He wraps me up in a hug, and I nuzzle into his chest, sighing in contentment, breathing in his scent. He rests his chin on my head for a moment, kissing the top of my head as we pull apart. I glance over at the spread and he perks up.

He clears his throat and gestures toward the counter. "Uh, I made bacon, egg and cheese croissants, kimchi jeon 김치전[1] and kongnamul guk 콩나물국[2]. I have cereal and donuts too, if none of this sounds good to you."

He seems nervous, and I'm not used to this side of him. It's cute.

"Are you kidding? I appreciate that you cooked, and I'm going to try it all."

"Really?"

His face lights up, and we're just cheesing at each other. After a moment, he breaks the spell with a shake of his head.

"Sorry. Let me get your food."

"That's okay. I can get it."

He tuts, blocking me from entering the kitchen further. He wears a worried expression. "There's a bug going around that prevents you from lifting a finger. It's serious, and I'm afraid there's no cure." He shakes his head in concern. "You've been showing symptoms, so I'm just going to have to take care of you."

I throw my head back in laughter.

This man.

I sit at the island and look around the kitchen as my body heats with memories of last night. He unleashed something in me that I never knew existed, and I am already counting down the minutes until I can experience it again. The woman I became was unlike me in every way. I was led by pleasure, attuned to

---

1. Kimchi pancake
2. Soybean sprouts

my body's needs and desires. Hell, I even felt safe enough to submit to him. He was so encouraging and open. Even when he gave up control, he obeyed my every word. I need to be careful because I could get addicted to that kind of freedom. I'm not sure what we're even doing, but last night shifted things. I, for one, am not interested in any more *SoulBlend* dates—not when Grey is right here and is so skilled at making me feel like *that*.

He releases me from my thoughts when he asks, "So, you remember when we discussed that arrangement and I gave you a taste of my qualifications?"

"Yeah."

"Well, it's been two weeks and I wanted to know if you're any closer to making an offer."

Without giving it any further thought, I say, "If you are still interested, the offer still stands for us to have a neighbors-with-benefits arrangement."

"Really?"

The sigh of relief he lets out is adorable.

"Yes, really," I assure him with a locked gaze.

"You've made an excellent choice, Ms. Bailey. I knew you were a good businesswoman."

Once I've finished my meal, I get up to put my dishes in the sink, and he takes them out of my hand.

"You forgot about the bug that fast? Forgetfulness is a symptom, you know," he adds, his tone laced with concern.

I can't help but laugh as I let him take over the dishes, too. I don't think it's fair, but I won't argue about it in his house. He walks over to me with a soft smile.

"I wanted to talk more about our arrangement. Why don't we take a seat?"

He gestures to the couch that I rode his thigh on hours ago. He takes a seat, and I sit beside him nervously.

As if he can read my mind, he says, "You can sit here," and guides me to straddle his lap. Being in this position with him fully clothed still sends liquid heat to my core, and the grip on my hips doesn't help my excitement either.

"I don't know how to say this without sounding like a possessive asshole, but I'm going to try. I like the time we spend together, and I didn't like seeing you on that date. Let me know if I'm being ridiculous, but I feel like we understand each other, and the sex is...phenomenal." His cheeks heat. "I'm not saying commit to me, but I'd like to know if you'd be okay with us exclusively doing whatever this is. No dates and no sleepovers with anyone else."

That doesn't require much thought from me because it's been in my mind since I woke up in his bed.

"I don't need to go on more dates if you're willing to provide what I need."

"Selah, I've shown you just how willing I am to cater to your needs and anything else on that list." He nips at my neck, and I giggle in response. I sit back on his lap and stare down at him playfully. He grips my waist possessively, and I bite my lip to fight the urge to moan under his touch.

"You know what I think? I think you like me. Might even be obsessed with me," I tease.

His eyes carry the hunger of a man starved and I can't look away.

"I thought that was obvious. What are *you* going to do about it?"

He asks, following with a smack to my ass that makes me cry out in pleasure.

He chuckles darkly. "You know what I think? I think you like me too. And if I took off your panties right now, your pussy would be dripping for me."

Oh my god.

His brows raise as if he thought of something. "What was your answer to that note? Yes, or no?"

He stares up at me expectantly as I reach in my pocket to retrieve the tiny yellow sheet of paper and place it in his hands.

He looks it over, and the hunger in his eyes intensifies.
"Well, allow me to apologize properly."
And in case you're wondering, Greyson is excellent at apologizing.

46
nwb

Selah

Manhattan, NY | February 8, 2024

IT'S BEEN a few weeks since Greyson and I made an arrangement to be neighbors with benefits. We discussed all the things I assumed you should with someone you're entering into a casual relationship with. Thankfully for me, Greyson is more experienced with this sort of thing, so he was able to fill in the blanks. We both get tested regularly and even though I've been celibate, I still do it for peace of mind. We use protection, and I have an IUD should we ever have a mishap. We've discussed every possible outcome, so now we're just having fun. After my conversation with Dr. Garnett, as soon as I let him know I agreed to it, I thought it'd be best to set some ground rules.

No sleepovers
Be honest
Don't fall in love
Respect each other's boundaries
Practice safe sex

He agreed with all of my terms and only had one thing to add. We've been following the rules, and I think the only one that's been a bit tricky to stick with is the *No Sleepovers* rule. If I fall asleep at his place, I'll sneak out and vice versa. It sucks since Greyson likes to cuddle, and I actually don't mind it. Unfortunately, I broke that rule before I created it, and slept over that first night. While he kept me up late, I slept amazingly, and I didn't have any nightmares. I know that's important, but I shouldn't be relying on a single person to soothe me. I'm in therapy and doing the work for a reason. The last thing I need is to get wrapped up in someone else because they're a balm over everything I'm afraid of. So, I have to sleep alone and endure some nightmares in order to maintain boundaries.

The girls have been grilling me for details about Greyson and how the arrangement is going, but there's not much to tell when things are going smoothly. We're just having otherworldly sex, getting to know each other, and being productive, that's all. They're starting to get the heart eyes over Greyson like we do when Audrey talks about Rome, and that's concerning because we're not heading towards anything more.

This arrangement is already working so well for us. It couldn't be more perfect, and I'm happy to have found someone who's on the same page as me. This past month is proof of that. I am having the best sex of my life with a man whose right upstairs, and I can call on him whenever I'd like. In fact, that's what we do. It may be the best perk of sleeping with my neighbor, and I'm honestly annoyed that I was so against this in the beginning.

Greyson Park is attractive. Attractive isn't even the proper word for a man like *him*, but he also makes me feel safe. I'm not used to feeling that way around a man, and I'm enjoying that. He worships my body, and my mind is free of insecurities whenever his eyes are on me. There needs to be a study done on the effect of this man, and how you can just forget everything you don't like about yourself under his gaze.

greyson

It's been a few weeks since Selah and I have arranged to be neighbors-with-benefits. While this isn't my first time having a casual relationship, having one with a neighbor is new to me. Selah mentioned that she's been more of a relationship kind of girl and that concerned me until she shared her ground rules which I assumed she googled, but I was impressed either way. I agreed with all her terms and had just one of my own.

Be my fake girlfriend for my ex-wife's wedding

I expected some pushback, but she agreed. I feel better about the lie now that I have a willing accomplice. Out of all the rules, the one I dislike most is the *No Sleepovers* rule. I hate having to sneak out of her apartment or wake up to see her side of the bed empty. She doesn't know this, but I've had quite a few casual flings over the years, and not one of them has slept in my bed. That's always been a boundary of mine. However, the first night with her, I wanted her to sleep in my bed. There was no doubt in my mind about it. When I woke up beside her, I had no regrets.

So, while I know that's a common rule in arrangements like these, it took me off guard when she expressed it. I mean, she was cozy like she owned the place. She was even snuggling with Clifford, and I got photo evidence. I just don't get it, but I respect her wishes, and that's why this works.

I don't mind when she does fall asleep beside me afterward, and sometimes I secretly hope she'll break her own rule, even by accident. It was nice having her there that morning and making breakfast. As much as I've grown accustomed to doing things by myself, I'll admit that I enjoyed taking care of someone else again. I'm not going to overanalyze what that means because I'm sure it'll only make the least uncomplicated relationship a complicated one, and Selah doesn't deserve that.

In fact, she's made it very clear she's not interested in

anything serious with anyone, and it's not like I can't relate to that. Both Selah and I have been hurt in the past, and while neither of us has opened up much about it, arrangements like these work to protect ourselves. I wouldn't be doing a good job of protecting myself or her if I started unpacking shit in hopes of eventually making things more serious than they are.

Usually, I'm doing pretty good around this time of year, and thanks to my vow to maintain casual relationships, I've never had to complicate things any further. However, with Selah, I fear that we've unintentionally complicated things. We get along *too well,* enjoy each other's company, and spend a lot of time together. Making time was an issue in my marriage. I was always working and took on every project imaginable. Of course, it's different now that I own a company and have a team I can delegate tasks to, but I'm *actually* relinquishing control so that I can simply make time for her. My casual relationships have always had an amicable end and a mutual understanding. However, I'm dreading when that day comes with Selah.

As much as she's resistant to love, someone is going to come along, and she won't want to do this shit forever. I'm going to enjoy this for as long as it lasts, but of course I have my concerns about when it comes to an end. I have a big one: Clifford. He adores her.

We're on the same page, but we don't always behave like two people who regularly meet up for sex. I wonder what her friends say about us. Alex and Elena think I'm lying to myself and that I am bound to want more. They've said I wasn't even this happy with Aileen, and I just shrugged it off. I've assured them that I've got this handled, and I plan to ride this out as long as she's willing.

47
wednesday pt. 1

Greyson

Manhattan NY | February 8, 2024

Sunflower

SUNFLOWER

Do you have any plans for Wednesday?

ME

On Valentine's Day? No.

I do have to head home for lunar new year on the 10th, but aside from that, I'm free.

SUNFLOWER

Would you like to do something with me?

ME

Is this your way of asking me to be your valentine?

SUNFLOWER

IF I was asking, what would your answer be?

ME

My answer is yes IF you're asking.

SUNFLOWER

Good. My place @ 7pm on Wed. Come hungry and don't be late.

ME

I'm always hungry for you and I'll be there at 6:55pm.

She sends an eye roll emoji.

SUNFLOWER

That's not on the menu. Sorry.

FOLLOWED by a picture of her laying in bed wearing my shirt with toothbrush emojis.

She drives me fucking wild.

ME

Watch it, Princess.

SUNFLOWER

What are you going to do, Daddy?

Spank me through the phone? LOL

I chuckle to myself.

This girl is something else.

The luxury of having a bratty neighbor with benefits? It doesn't take me long to get to her when she's running her mouth. I punch the sixth floor on the elevator and descend.

When she answers the door, the look on her face is priceless.

"What are you doing here?"

"I can't spank you through the phone, so here I am," I add playfully.

When she lets me in, I pin her against the door and run my nose up the side of her neck, hovering at her ear until she's whining.

"Four spanks over my knee and you're going to count them.

Then you can grind your needy pussy on my thigh until you come. Understand?"

"Yes, Daddy," she says breathily.

"Good girl."

48
wednesday pt. 2

Greyson

Manhattan, NY | February 14th, 2024

I SHIFT the large bouquet to my other arm as I ring her doorbell and take a step back. I glance at my watch to check the time; 6:55 p.m. like I promised. When she answers the door, my words are stuck in my throat. Her usual curls are straightened and she's wearing a dark red dress that hugs her curves so well it looks painted on. I hand her the bouquet of pink peonies and she smiles at me. I chuckle nervously. *Why am I nervous? It's just a date.*

"Like what you see, sir?" she says in a flirty tone and bites her lip.

I swallow and think of a response.

All I manage to say is, "I was on time."

She looks impressed. "You did. Are you hungry?"

"For you? Always."

"I meant for dinner," she chuckles.

"As long as I get to have you for dessert."

"That can be arranged," she says, opening the door wider, and I follow her inside.

I settle in while she grabs a vase for the flowers. Her dining table has a spread of various dishes of Chinese food and everything smells incredible. I refuse to let her make my plate and suggest she take a seat while I take care of her. She argues only for a moment and gets comfortable while she waits for me to join her. She assesses me with curiosity as I learn my way around her kitchen.

"The other day you mentioned you were visiting home for Lunar New Year. Can you tell me more about that?"

"Mhm. Seollal 설날[1]. We celebrate with our families, so my brother Henry and I went to visit our parents in Brooklyn to spend the day together. We dress up in our hanboks, eat, play games and bring in the Lunar New Year together. I have leftovers at my place if you want to try anything.

She perks up. "I didn't make anything for dessert."

12

By the time we're done eating, we've played an unconventional version of the question game. A few rounds were random rapid-fire questions like 'who's your favorite superhero' and 'what was the last movie you saw.' Then they became more suggestive as the night progressed, so I fed off her energy and asked about some tasks on her *Fuck It List*. She was surprisingly open and we dove deeper into her curiosity about kink. So, I recommend books for her to read on the subject. I'm happy to fulfill her fantasies, but she should be well-informed beforehand.

She surprises me when she jumps up and says, "I haven't forgotten about our last dance."

"Funny because I haven't forgotten either."

"Good," she says simply and I watch as her hips sway over

1. Korean Lunar New Year

to her record player. She squats down and starts sifting through her collection of vinyl, brows wrinkling in concentration and I stifle a laugh. Moments later, she exclaims, "Awe shit!"

She returns to her height and after moments of crackling, Nina Simone's *I Put A Spell On You* croons through the speakers. My brows shoot up and she turns to me, mouthing the words. I stand and pull her to me when she breaks out into a fit of giggles. She interlaces her hand in mine and we lock eyes as we glide across the hardwood floor until the song fades.

"I never took you as possessive, Selah Bailey."

She scoffs, "I'm not. It's just a song."

"Sure, it is," I say, leaning in close to nip her ear. "You won this round."

"What's that?" she asks, holding her hand up to her ear. "I'm going to need you to repeat that, Grey."

"I said you won this round."

She mumbles something that sounded a lot like '*good boy.*'

I start to ask her what she said, when she blurts out, "I have a fun fact for you."

Well played. Knowing I can't resist them.

"Let's hear it."

She leans in close, standing on her tiptoes to whisper in my ear.

"I'm not wearing any panties."

I wrap my arms around her and hold her plush to me.

"Prove it," I challenge.

"Gladly. Would you unzip me, please?" she asks, and I release her.

She stands before me and I unzip the snug dress, dropping it at her feet and holding her hand as she slips out of it.

"Happy Valentine's Day, Selah."

"Happy *Wednesday*, Grey."

"Hmm, it's about to be a very happy *hump* day for the both of us."

She bursts into laughter as I hoist her over my shoulder and carry her to the bedroom. Unaware of how exhausted she's going to be in the morning.

Happy Wednesday, indeed.

49
galentine's day

Selah

Manhattan, NY | February 17th, 2024

"WHAT DID you and Rome do for Valentine's Day?" Daya asks Audrey.

She just took a big gulp of her cocktail and raised her finger to ask for a moment to swallow her drink.

"We had sex—on my jet, so we joined the mile-high club. It had never occurred to me that, after all this time, we hadn't done that. Then again, y'all know how I am about planes. So, he tried a different approach to calm my nerves and it worked," she adds, wiggling her brows.

"That's it?" we ask collectively.

"Oh, y'all wanted romance. Why didn't you say so? He took me to a lodge in the Poconos and we had more sex. Y'all know how I feel about seclusion. That's the best gift for me. It was *so* beautiful and quiet. I even got to take naps and we had the best view. He planned it well because I didn't suspect a thing."

We're all heart-eyed listening to her gush about her literal book boyfriend in real life. It's so special to see your friends being loved out loud and properly. I knew Rome wouldn't disappoint on Valentine's Day. He never does. He makes us all believe there's hope out there for the rest of us hapless in love ladies.

"What about you?" Chess asks, shifting everyone's focus to me.

"I know this'll be hard to believe but I, Selah Bailey, asked a man on a date."

"I'm sure it was very indirect and you talked about it like it was a business meeting instead," Audrey chides.

"Damn it. I hate that you know me so well," I chuckle. "We had an indoor picnic at my place. I wanted to try my hand at doing something romantic while checking something off my list. I ordered takeout from a new spot because Grey is a foodie and I wanted to keep challenging myself to be adventurous with food. We loved it." I pause to sip my wine and they all stare expectantly.

"We played the question game, as we often do and got more personal with each other. He even asked me about the sex tasks on my list about kink and recreating scenes from books. He let me discuss it freely with him and I appreciated that. He recommended reading material on kink and BDSM. He wants me to be well informed before he agrees to act out any of my fantasies."

The girls are staring at each other knowingly and that worries me a bit. They're going to start up again about how they think Greyson is the one for me, but I told them we're just having a good time.

Chess pipes up, "Oh, he's a good dom. I just felt myself start to drool a little bit. I'm sorry. You mentioned he's got a brother. Just one? What about that friend of his?"

"Alex? He's *really* good looking and single. I don't know about him being anything like Grey though."

"Keep an eye out and let me know what you do find," she suggests.

I give her a nod.

"So, I know y'all talked about it, but did you get some?" Audrey asks.

"I did," I say proudly. "Then he held me until I fell asleep in his arms. He respected my '*no sleepovers*' rule though and didn't stay the night. Though I'll admit when I woke up and he wasn't there, I missed his warmth. What does that mean?"

She sits closer and holds me to her side. "Girl, it means you like him. More than you're telling yourself you do. That man isn't just 'neighborly' as you keep saying and *you* know it."

Maybe she's right. It was the first night I've had a man in my bed since I left my ex and I felt safe with him there. I didn't have any trouble sleeping either, but I don't think it's a good idea to get attached to him in that way. This is why rules are a good idea. Without them, things can get confusing.

Chess changes the subject, releasing me from my thoughts. "Now, Daya, did you have an orgasm on Valentine's?"

"I had a great night with my audio erotica boyfriends. Does that count?"

"It sure fucking does, babe. Let's hear about it."

50
unfriendly reminder

Greyson

Manhattan NY, | March 8, 2024

I'LL BE thirty-two on Monday. It's not that I mind getting older because I don't, it's just what that day has come to represent. What was once a day I celebrated became a day I dread. An unfriendly reminder of the worst day of my life. I've done the exact same thing on my birthday for the past seven years. Isolate myself from everyone, turn off my phone, order pizza, and watch a basketball game if I don't sleep the rest of the day away. I know it sounds sad, but at least Clifford's here.

I have to find out how to maintain my usual plans without telling a lie to Selah. I just have a feeling she wouldn't take well to hearing about how I spend my birthday alone like a sad sack. If anything could make her disinterested in me, it would be this. While I'm over Aileen, this behavior would give anyone the impression that I'm not. I'd prefer that she didn't know about it, so that I don't have to bother explaining or worry about turning her off.

I know that I like spending time with her, and I'd really hate to blow this. Selah truly is a kind and understanding person, but I can't guarantee that she will have the reaction I'd hope for, so why bother? If I want to keep her in my life for the time being, I just need to keep myself busy for the next seventy-two hours. Once my birthday passes, everything will be fine, until this time next year.

March 9, 2024

I failed at 'keeping myself busy.' I didn't even last a full day. We're currently laying on the couch together. She's reading and I'm watching sports highlights while she lays in my lap. I don't know what I was thinking. This is *Selah,* not just anyone. It's possible I'm going to get hurt when this inevitably ends. Plus, if she finds out about my birthday bullshit, she'll think I'm still in love with my ex and will surely be gone. There will be no explaining myself with that. Sure, my friends understand my reasons, but they knew me before I got married.

This is why I've found it easier to just not get involved in anything potentially serious and then I never have to wait for the other shoe to drop. When I keep my focus solely on work, I don't have to worry about anything but running a business. I'm not a guy worth staying for and I'm sure she knows this already. We have all these rules in place for a reason. We're just enjoying the ride until we get off on the last stop. If that happens on Monday, at least I've been through it once before.

51
daydreaming

Greyson

Manhattan, NY | March 11, 2024

I WAKE up facing the sun, and I hear light snoring behind me. I laugh silently at the sound and the realization.

She stayed.

I did keep her up very late, so of course, she fell asleep and didn't sneak out.

I had a large appetite that only she could satisfy. I'm quickly learning that when it comes to Selah, I'm always starved and desperate for more.

I glance over my shoulder, and as always, I'm astounded by her. I rake over her luscious frame and the way my shirt clings to it. Her long curls are spread across the pillows, and I stare in awe. I know she will be upset when she realizes she didn't cover up her hair last night.

Note to self: Order silk pillowcases and a bonnet for her to keep here.

I roll over carefully and wrap her in my arms. I don't wish to disturb her…I just need to be closer. She stirs and settles into me; her hair is now in my face, and I don't mind one bit. I inhale deeply and am welcomed by the scent of cherries. My dick stirs in my boxers at her proximity. I don't wake her and get comfortable, eventually falling back asleep.

I'm later awakened by her back arching into me. I reach under her shirt and pinch her nipples, and she squeaks in response, pressing her bare ass against me.

"On your back, now," I order.

She giggles and rolls onto her back while I grab a condom from my bedside drawer. I'm on top of her instantly, gripping her thick thighs and scattering kisses along her stomach and inner thighs. Soft whimpers escape her throat the closer I get to her dripping center.

"What's that, baby? You don't like being teased?" I taunt as my mouth hovers over her glistening pussy. Her doe eyes are pinned on me as I blow on her pussy. The sheets are in her grip when she begs for me to taste her.

"Please, Grey. I need—"

"What do you need?"

"I-I need to come."

"That's my girl."

My girl.

I smile against her before swiping my flat tongue along her dripping pussy. She focuses on me while I dine on her, swirling and flicking my tongue at her sensitive bud. I am a flower in need, leaning toward her light and quenching my thirst with her juices. Feasting my eyes on her beauty, I am a grateful witness to how her body responds to me.

Her hands are in my hair, craving more as I sink my fingers into her, curling until I reach the spot that makes her scream. I wrap my lips around her clit and suck in tandem with my fingers pumping into her tight pussy. She grinds against my face as her orgasm builds, crying out my name as she comes for me.

I remove my fingers and crawl up the bed. She opens her mouth for me like the good girl she is and sucks my fingers clean, moaning around them. When I retrieve my hand, she eyes me closely.

"I love seeing my cum on your face."

The groan that escapes me is animalistic. "I need to fuck you. Now."

"Then fuck me," she challenges.

I chuckle. "Bend over, brat. And keep the shirt on. It looks better on you."

Usually, I prefer her naked but seeing her in my shirt makes me feel like she is mine. I could get used to it.

"Yes, Daddy."

She quickly bends over and arches her back for me, that plump ass in the air and her face in a pillow.

"Good girl."

I roll the condom on my dick and smack her ass, and she moans loudly in response. I nudge her entrance before sliding into her, easing in until I bottom out. I dig my hands into her hips, her ass smacking against me as I thrust into her. Her muffled screams in the pillow and the sounds of our skin slapping fill the room. I feel her stroke her clit as her fingers slip and graze the base of my dick.

"Fuck. Keep rubbing that clit, Princess. I need to feel you come on my dick."

Selah tosses her head back, releasing screams and whimpers of pleasure as I piston into her.

"I'm coming!" she shouts as her pussy clenches around me. I fuck her through her orgasm, my own isn't far behind. I come hard and collapse beside her, pulling her close to me and pressing soft kisses on her back and neck.

"You took me so well."

She sighs contentedly, nestling into me, her hair in my face again. We lie in a comfortable silence for a while, and she says, "You're really nasty in the morning."

"That's what you get when you wake up next to me."

"Hmm. I think I may need to do that more often."

"I'd like that."

I'd really like that.

52
meet the parents

Greyson

Manhattan, NY | March 11, 2024

I'M STILL REELING from Selah's accidental sleepover and she's still here. I convinced her to call in sick and enjoy a very late breakfast with me. We're playing another round of the question game when I hear voices outside my door, followed by jingling keys.

"Were you expecting anybody?" Selah asks.

"No," I respond with a shake of my head.

I focus on the doorknob as it's being unlocked, assuming it's either Alex or Elena trying to surprise me. My parents stroll through the door instead. This isn't unusual behavior for them, but it couldn't have come at a worse time. Dad's holding a bag of groceries, and Mom stands in front of him empty-handed. I had no idea they were coming, but I know exactly why they're here.

"Happy Birthday, Greyson!" they say in unison.

Shit.

I hear a spoon drop behind me and Selah blurts out, "It's your birthday?"

Shit.

I whip my head towards her and offer an apologetic nod. I search her gaze for any sign of anger and find sadness instead.

Dammit.

"Where's Clifford?" my dad asks in a playful voice.

Clifford barrels down the hallway at the sound of his voice. He sits and wags his tail excitedly beside me. Once my mom spots Selah, she perks up and I see the wheels turning in her head. I take a deep breath to mentally prepare for this impromptu visit and think of an explanation for why I hadn't mentioned it was my birthday.

I don't need this today.

"Eomma![1] appa![2] 엄마, 아빠." I shout, jumping up from my seat.

I meet them in the entryway, and Mom practically knocks me down when she launches herself into my arms. My dad chuckles softly as I scoop her up into a hug.

"You look good son," he adds gruffly.

"Thanks. You too."

She pecks my cheek and whisper-yells, "She's pretty! You haven't mentioned her!"

I set her back on her feet, placing my hands on each of her shoulders and giving her a look of warning. Her mischievous grin challenges me and I know I've lost this battle before it's even begun.

I just wanted to be alone with her today.

I step back and my mother breezes right past me, beelining for Selah. Whose anxiety is apparent because her back is to me and she's busying herself washing dishes.

Please don't scare her off.

"And who might you be?" Mom asks playfully and grabs a towel to help Selah.

I know she means to be welcoming, but she's already

1. Mom
2. Dad

anxious. I'm already dreading this interaction and it just started. You don't usually meet the parents at whatever fucking stage we're at.

"Um, I'm Selah. Grey's…neighbor."

I watch this encounter and raise a brow at her response.

Neighbor?

Well, she didn't lie, but I don't like the sound of it.

What we did this morning was far from neighborly.

"It's nice to meet you, Selah. I'm Greyson's mom. Excuse my excitement, I just haven't seen my son with a woman in a while," she says with a warm smile.

"It's nice to meet you, Mrs. Park," she says nervously and shakes her hand, wrapping her left hand around her wrist.

I wrinkle my brow at her doing the handshake properly and as if she can read my mind, Mom whips her head toward me with an astonished look.

I recall shaking Selah mom's hand the same way when we met, and I guess she remembered. Surely, if I knew they were coming I could've prepared her, but she's doing great.

Selah looks over her shoulder with an apologetic stare and I shake my head in response. She chews on her bottom lip and resumes her conversation with my mom. My dad clears his throat, regaining my focus. He wears a knowing look while petting Clifford's head.

"You could've told me you were coming." He pats my shoulder. "Adeul 아들[3], we haven't seen you since Lunar New Year and you haven't been calling as much. I couldn't risk calling and you disappearing. This was our best chance. Your mom missed you. *We* miss you."

"I miss you too, appa 아빠."

"It doesn't seem like it. Take these groceries. I want to sit down," he grumbles.

I take the bags from him and step towards the kitchen. He

3. Son

strides halfway to the living room then changes direction, nearly running into me as he heads toward Selah. I roll my eyes and take a deep breath.

Please don't embarrass me in front of her.

My mom whips her head around and grins.

"Yeobo 여보[4], This is Greyson's *neighbor*, Selah. Isn't she lovely?"

I don't miss the emphasis she puts on neighbor. It's subtle, but intentional.

"She is. It's nice to meet you," he says and bows his head and gives her a handshake.

"Nice to meet you too," she says with a bright smile.

She seems a bit more relaxed than before. I assume the speed cleaning helped. Her gaze is assuring, causing me to feel better already. My shy father retires to the couch after his quick introduction. I eavesdrop on my mom and Selah's conversation while I put away the groceries and they're hitting it off. Mom has been reading spicy romances, so they're bonding over that. I quickly vacate because I've read some of those books and I'd rather not hear my mom recount her favorites.

I try to hide my smile when I round the corner and see Clifford laying beside him, resting his head on his leg. Dad absentmindedly scratches his head while he flips through channels. I find it interesting because I always wanted a dog and my parents wouldn't let me have one, but these two look like the best of friends. I let out a sigh as I plop down. I predict we'll sit in silence because he's not much of a talker.

As expected, he doesn't say much other than asking me about how business is and what's new in my life. I keep my updates short and all about work. I bite back the urge to mention Selah because I'm unsure of what to say and she's not even twenty feet away. Though she wouldn't hear me over the giggle

4. Honey

fits coming from the kitchen. I'm glad to hear they are having some fun.

When I ask him how he's been, he keeps it short as usual. Then goes into his usual spiel about how I should visit more than just the holidays. I would, but he and I don't get along very well. My parents not supporting my marriage caused a rift. My mom and I have since worked it out, but my dad is just too stubborn.

"I'm happy you were home, Greyson. I know it's not a good day for *you* and you're not too happy with us showing up unannounced, but it was my idea."

He scoots closer to me and pats my shoulder.

"So, be mad at me. I was only hoping to cheer her up. It may be your birthday, but it's also the day we became your parents. We only see one of you often and you're a half hour away.

"Is eomma okay?" I ask with concern; my stomach drops at the thought.

"She's fine, aduel. So am I. She's just been a little down and has been missing her sons. The phone calls help, but it's not the same as sharing a meal or being able to hug you."

"I understand."

We peer over the couch at her and Selah in the kitchen and she is teaching her how to prep Wanja Jorim[5]. If mom is cooking, she'll always make your favorite meals. Always. I saw the groceries she bought, and she must have plans to make a Korean buffet tonight. I won't complain about them crashing since mom's cooking. I only wish Henry could be here. Every chance he gets he mentions how homesick he is.

My mom makes a few meatballs by hand, then tells Selah to try. Her brows are wrinkled in concentration as she tries to mimic my mom's actions and it's the cutest thing I've ever seen. I smile to myself.

When I look back at my dad, he's wearing that knowing

5. Korean meatballs

expression again. I shrug it off and face the TV. Moments later, he excuses himself and I relax on the couch, getting cozy with Cliff.

My dad returns to his seat and surprises me again by asking, "Would you like to get out of the house? It's a nice day. We could go to a dog park and get ice cream."

"Who are you and what have you done with my appa?"

He chuckles and says, "I'm sure your neighbor will be just fine. Your mother won't bite her."

I don't feel great about leaving her alone, but it seems like they're having a good time. I can't remember the last time my dad and I did something just for us. It had been when I was in high school, but since he invited Clifford, I'm in. It's impossible to have a bad day when he's around.

"Sure, I'd just like to say goodbye to her before we go."

I rise from the couch, making my way to the kitchen where my mom and Selah are making quite the mess.

"I'm sorry to interrupt, but I need to borrow her for a sec."

"Don't keep her too long. We're having fun," Mom exclaims.

Selah follows me and we take off far enough down the hallway from prying eyes.

"Are you mad at me?" I ask nervously.

"No. Why would I be?"

I lean in close. "Give me a kiss if you're not mad."

She smiles against my lips and grants me a soft kiss.

When we separate, I stare adoringly.

"I promise I won't be gone long."

"It's fine. Your eomma has good taste in books, by the way."

"Don't tell me about that. I beg of you."

She giggles and I take her lips in a hurried kiss.

"I need to teach you more Korean. It's sexy," I say, licking my lips.

She covers her face with her hand as if she's embarrassed.

My shy little sunflower.

"You should get out of here and have some fun."

"Not before I teach you some new words. Hae-ba-la-gi 해바라기[6]."

She repeats after me, lighting up when she gets it right.

"It means sunflower."

"One more. Sella 셀라[7]."

She repeats after me and says with a curious smile, "that sounds like my name. It's beautiful."

"Just like you." I nod, pressing a kiss to her forehead before I head back down the hallway, and I lock eyes with none other than my mom, who's peeking around her corner, watching in amusement.

By the time Selah turns around and returns to the kitchen, my mom resumes cooking as if she wasn't just being nosy. I walk over to her and squeeze her in a hug, hoping to distract her from making any comments about what she just saw.

"So, in America, neighbors do borrow sugar," she says with a raised brow.

"Eomma, please," I plead.

"Calm down. I like her." She smacks my arm with a dish towel. "We'll talk later. Have fun with your appa and be nice."

"I love you," I say, wrapping her in another hug.

"I love you too, adeul."

---

6. Sunflower
7. Selah

53
like father, like son

Greyson

Manhattan, NY | March 11, 2024

FROM THE MOMENT we got in the car, my dad's been chatty and it's very strange. He asked if he could put on some music for the ride, which was also odd and based on his selections, I can tell he's been taking recommendations from Henry. He insists we take the scenic routes and while I'd like nothing more than to get back home, I'm enjoying this side of my dad, so I agree we can take our time.

"I wanted to talk to you about something, aduel."

I inhale deeply to prepare myself and shake my head.

"I knew something was wrong with eomma."

"I told you there's nothing wrong with either of us. I meant that. We're in good health."

"Then what do you want to talk about?"

My dad and I don't have tough conversations. We're avoidant, whereas Henry is the complete opposite and lets nothing linger.

"Aileen."

I grip the steering wheel tighter and sigh. I'd like to be

respectful, but I'd much rather pull over and walk away because this feels like a trap.

"I'd rather not, especially not today," I respond, my tone firm.

"I've been quiet enough. I need you to listen."

"Fine."

I glance at Cliff in the rearview mirror, who's sticking his head out the window and making the best of this beautiful weather today.

I'd love to stick my head out of the window right now, too, Bud.

"I know our relationship shifted once I expressed how strongly I was against you marrying Aileen. Your mother agreed with me and while you forgave her, things between us were never the same. I'd like to fix that, and we'll need to talk about it. You're a lot like me when it comes to talking about the hard stuff, we choose not to because it's easier."

I'm annoyed that he made that comparison, even more so that it's accurate. No matter how much we say we don't want to end up like our parents, we often do. If this conversation gives me a chance to avert that, then I'm game.

"Okay, let's talk about it. Why were you so against me marrying her?"

"We never supported you marrying Aileen because we knew what a marriage looked like with two people who were willing to fight for it to work against all odds. There was only one person in that relationship willing to put in that effort and it was you. That's how we raised you. You're not a quitter and you'll learn everything you can about something to achieve it. Just like when you were a kid, taking computers apart and putting them back together," he chuckles to himself.

I don't know what I expected him to say, but it wasn't that. I'm not sure how to respond so I keep my focus on the road and nod my head.

When he doesn't continue, I glance over at him, and he's staring out the window.

"Appa?"

He sighs, "Your eomma and I faced so many challenges, but we fought hard because we both wanted this. You should know we struggled with fertility for a long time, between you and Henry. We had a few miscarriages when you were little and they really affected our marriage. We just wanted a family; it didn't have to be a big one. Your mom and I agreed that you should have a sibling. So, we kept trying and it was really scary, aduel."

I hear the emotion in his voice, I peer over at him and he's taking deep breaths. I've never seen him this way.

"It's okay. You don't have to share anything you don't want to."

He ignores my comment and continues, "I wasn't sure how to fight this with her. She became very depressed and every time we weren't successful, I felt like I lost a piece of her. It got to a point where we were desperate for help and met with a bunch of doctors before we found one that agreed to help us. We tried IVF. It took a while before it worked, but we got Henry."

He chokes up and takes a moment to collect himself. I reach out my hand for him and he takes it. I breathe through the emotions building in my throat and keep driving. We're almost to the ice cream shop, which is just what we'll need after this conversation.

"Your mom still struggles with depression and that's what I meant when I said she's been sad lately and I wanted to cheer her up with our visit today. She goes to therapy and is being treated for it now, but it took a lot for her to get here. You know how our culture views mental health. It was difficult for me to understand, but we reached a dead end and I was open to anything. She needed me to fight for her on the days she wasn't strong enough. *That's* what a partner does. You didn't have that type of relationship with Aileen and you know it."

He looks at me expectantly and I nod.

"You're right. She was not a partner, at least not after we got married. As for mom, I never knew."

"She was great at hiding it from you both. I didn't like it. Especially as you grew up, but what she says goes."

I pull into the lot of the ice cream shop and we go through the drive-thru, grabbing milkshakes for us and a vanilla cone for Clifford that he inhales when I give it to him. Dad let me know there's more he wanted to discuss, but the heavier stuff is out of the way now. He hasn't brought up Selah yet, but I'm waiting on it.

"You know, after everything your mother and I endured, we understood there were more important things than our children getting married and having children of their own. So, after you got your diploma and told us you were getting married, it surprised us because you hadn't even lived yet. We really hoped that you would just wait, but you eloped."

I snort, "Well, part of growing up is doing the opposite of what your parents tell you to do."

"I wish we knew that ten years ago."

We're cackling together and it feels like a weight lifted off my shoulders. I can imagine he feels it too. I hate knowing that he's been holding onto that for so long.

"Our parents didn't know about our fertility issues, and we didn't feel comfortable telling them because they would've suggested herbal medicine. We tried that and needed more help. IVF was still new, and we were nervous. Infertility changed your eomma and I, but we got our boys. I know we were hard on you, but we just wanted you and your brother to have a good life. I hope that you're truly happy and don't resent us. Are you happy, Greyson?"

I take a moment to consider before answering.

This is the happiest I've ever been in my life.

"Yeah, I am."

"That's all I ever wanted for you. I love you, aduel."

I can't remember the last time he said that to me, and I cherish it.

"I love you too, Appa."

12

When we get to the dog park, I give Clifford water and once we hit the grass, he takes off to make new friends. Dad and I find a nice place to sit in the shade with our milkshakes and watch him play. Dad shocks me when he suggests he and mom should get a dog, preferably one that doesn't shed. I always assumed they didn't like them because they didn't let us have one growing up. He shares that they love Cliff, and they always loved dogs, but with everything they were facing over the years, it would've been more responsibility. I mention that mom could talk it over in therapy, but an emotional support animal might be good for her. We talk about Clifford and how helpful he was for me, while he isn't an ESA, he saved my life and I'm grateful for him.

We discuss therapy more in depth and I learn a lot about how it's been helpful for my mom and their marriage.

"Do you go to therapy?" he asks.

"No, I should though. I'm considering it after hearing that mom goes."

"Well, I go. That's the only way she'd agree to it," he says with a chortle.

That surprises me, but I'm proud of him. I won't say it out loud because I don't want him to be embarrassed.

"Eomma is clever. I should've known something was up when you started talking. This is by far the most you've spoken to me in thirty-two years."

We burst into laughter.

"So, about that pretty woman in your apartment. She looked awfully cozy to be your *neighbor*." He makes air quotes around the word neighbor.

"Appa, don't start."

He gives me a side eye over his glasses. "I'm starting."

I let out a deep sigh because I knew it was coming.

"Does she know how you feel?"

"No," I sigh.

"I had a feeling. I never stopped looking at your eomma like that."

I'm taken aback by that and I'm not sure where he got that assumption after being around us for a few minutes.

"How do I look at her?"

"Like if you blink, she'll disappear. You look at her like you've found the peace you've been looking for all this time."

My eyes well up and I try to blink the emotion away. I put my face in my hands, trying to avoid crying in front of him.

"It's okay, aduel." He leans forward, patting my back.

"How do you know I've been looking for peace?" My voice cracks.

"Well, you don't talk to me, so I find things out from your eomma."

I scoff, wiping my eyes on my sleeves.

"I should've known nothing stays between us."

He chuckles, "She can keep a secret, but she's always going to tell me. Especially when it involves you and your brother."

"I guess that's fair." I search for Clifford, and I find him running around with a poodle and a pug. My dad speaks and regains my attention.

"Since we're being honest, she said she saw you kissing your neighbor."

I exhale, "When did she say this?"

"She texted me after we left," he says matter-of-factly.

"Of course she did," I chuckle.

12

"Aileen sent us an invitation to her wedding. We're sending money but your mom and I aren't going. Henry is though. Are you?"

"Yeah. Selah's my plus one."

He perks up with a playful grin. "Now I wish I was going."

"Who knew you were a fan of drama?"

"It's your eomma and those novels. Whenever she finishes one, she comes and tells me all about it. Keeps me entertained, it's better than her dramas."

"Why don't you read them with her? I do it with Selah. That's actually how I got her attention."

"I may have to take your advice. You know, I read this article not too long ago that said you are a modern-day matchmaker."

"I'd say that's a stretch, but it sounds good."

"I loved it and got it framed for my office. I'm proud of you, son."

My heart warms at those words I've always wanted to hear from him.

"Thank you."

His phone trills, he picks it up and says, "It's your mom." He holds up a finger and steps away to answer the call. He returns moments later, finishing his milkshake and tossing the empty cup in the nearby trash.

"Are you ready to get back and see what they cooked?"

"Absolutely."

We're on our way back to my place. Clifford is sprawled out along the backseat and will be asleep soon. Dad and I are laughing and talking the whole way home and it feels natural. Henry isn't going to believe me when I tell him about us spending time together without any awkward silence.

I pull into the parking garage, and Dad reminds me, "Don't tell your mother about the ice cream. She won't care that it would've melted by the time we got back. Eating sweets without her is considered betrayal."

"You have my word."

54
surprise

Selah

Manhattan, NY | March 11, 2024

ONCE THE DOOR shuts behind Grey, his mom and I jump into planning mode. She loved my idea about inviting Henry and his friends over for dinner. Thankfully she has everyone's number because I haven't had the pleasure of meeting them yet. They'll be here soon, and I am so relieved. It was weird that he didn't mention it was his birthday when we were together all morning and yesterday, but I remember him telling me he hates his birthday and refusing to tell me when it was. I thought it was strange, but I didn't press it because I figured it would come up sooner or later. Since Grey hates his birthday and I am naturally inclined to do the exact opposite of what he expects, I wanted us to bake him a cake.

When I saw all the groceries his parents brought, I asked his mom if she would teach me how to cook Greyson's favorite foods. She was thrilled and showed me how to make Wanja Jorim, which was messy, but fun. We got started on the fresh cream cake after so it would have time to cool before dinner. I'm learning everything quickly and I'm feeling confident. I'm sure I won't remember all these recipes tomorrow, but I really hope that Grey appreciates the dinner.

We're bonding over romance novels because to my surprise she likes to read them too. The spicier the better, which made for hilarious conversations once it was just us girls. I wonder if she'd be interested in joining our book club. I don't think Greyson would mind, but I'll mention it to him first. He wasn't exactly thrilled at this visit today and I'm curious if it was because of the day or if he'd be like this in general.

When everything is nearly done, I run downstairs to feed Peach and grab another set of clothes for dinner. Grey came down here and fed her this morning, I noticed he cleaned her litter box too. He's sly about sneaking into my apartment to take care of my cat. It's cute and thoughtful. I smile to myself as I fill a tote bag with a few necessities and decide on a dress that will have him tripping over his tongue but is still appropriate for meeting the parents.

I grab a pair of shorts, a tank and my bonnet in case I decide to sleep over...on purpose this time. I didn't have a bonnet last night and was fortunate after everything we did; my hair didn't look a mess. I freshen up my curls and style them, pinning one side out of my face with a cute clip. I apply light makeup that draws attention to my eyes, cheekbones and my signature brown lip. My new earrings are the final touch. I take one last glance at myself in the mirror and I look damn good. I almost feel kind of bad that Grey will be dying to touch my ass in this dress all night.

Oh well. That's what he gets for not telling me the truth.

When I get back to Grey's apartment, his mom hypes me up and loves the dress. I put my apron back on and get to work on the cake icing while we wait for everyone to arrive.

A tall man that looks like a younger Grey arrives first. A wary smile stretches across his face as he approaches the kitchen. He greets me as 'Sunflower Girl,' and I call him 'Baby Hen.' I try to shake his hand, but he refuses and engulfs me in a hug instead.

"I can't believe you got him to leave the house today *and* go somewhere with appa."

"Eomma," he says, striding into the kitchen.

He wraps Mrs. Park in a hug and lifts her off the ground. She shrieks with joy until he puts her down. She gives him a big kiss on the cheek and recommends that he wash up and help before he starts stealing food.

The next to arrive must be Elena. She's short with long wavy hair and is absolutely stunning. When she gets through the door, I notice her hands are full of bags, so I rush over to help her. She hands me a few bags and looks at me with honey eyes. Up close, she looks very familiar. I wonder where I've seen her before. We introduce ourselves and I love her energy. I set the bags on the island and that's when I notice the logo. *Aguilar's.* I ate there one day after pole dancing class with Daya. She locks eyes with Mrs. Park and greets her in the kitchen, wrapping her in a warm embrace. She joins us as we prepare dinner, learning all we can from the chef.

Alex is last to arrive and makes quite an entrance. Grey mentioned he's a successful businessman and he embodies it. He's very handsome, tall and well dressed. His expression is very serious until he settles in. The mask seems to dissolve and his smile comes out to play. His eyes find Elena first and there's something in them I can't quite read, though their embrace seems friendly, it's tender. He smiles at Mrs. Park and envelops her in a kind hug leaving a peck on her cheek. He greets Henry with a wide smile and a hug and they speak for a moment, before he searches for me. When he strides over, his serious expression returns.

Hoping to loosen him up, I speak first. "You must be Alex."

"And you must be Selah. It's nice to finally put a face to the name." A smile peeks out from his lips and I feel successful.

"I was happy to hear from you. I texted him and he didn't respond, which is normal on this day, but I was thinking of him."

"Thanks for coming. He said he hates his birthday and

refused to tell me when it was. His parents came over to surprise him and I hoped he might want to celebrate if everyone was here.

"He usually isolates or immerses himself in work, so I'm not surprised he didn't even tell you when his birthday was." Alex pauses. "You can vouch for this, Elena. Grey used to love his birthday."

She chimes, "Yeah. He wasn't into big parties, but he loved to go to dinner and never got mad at us whenever we told the waiter it was his birthday."

"Man, have you ever met someone who didn't hate the entire restaurant staff singing them the birthday song?" he asks.

"Do you think he's going to be angry with me?"

Alex shakes his head and says, "Nah. I don't think he's going to be upset. This is exactly how he liked to celebrate before. We've all tried to get him out of the house on this day for years, but maybe bringing the party to him is best."

I won't ask, but I wonder what changed everything for him.

Elena adds, "You're learning to cook Korean dishes and brought us together to share a meal. Him getting angry is the least of your worries. I think you've created a recipe for Greyson to fall in love with you."

My eyes widen, and I giggle nervously.

She winces and lowers her voice. "Sorry. I didn't mean to–"

"It's okay," I interrupt.

I excuse myself to dash to the bathroom for a moment alone. *Love,* a word that holds a tremendous amount of weight. A word that makes me want to run far from it. It's different when my friends and family say it to me. That other kind of love though? I've felt for boyfriends in the past, but it's never been reciprocated. After Jourdan, I wondered if I'd ever fall in love again. Or even trust someone to catch me next time. I've grown comfortable with the idea that it just isn't not attainable for me. Though Elena's words replay in my mind as I sit on the side of the tub contemplating.

You've created a recipe for Greyson to fall in love with you.

That's not what I was trying to do. At least, I don't think so. I mean, would it be so bad if Greyson were to fall for me? Yes, because he deserves someone who can love him back. The last time I loved someone, it consumed me. I hyper focused on it, so much that I hadn't even noticed it wasn't mutual. The last time I loved someone, I mistook his attentiveness for adoration. He studied me with a goal to manipulate and abuse. I was nothing but a target. The last time I loved someone, it swallowed me whole. I fear that my heart won't recover from the damage it's endured. I desperately wish that I was someone who could slap a band-aid on my wounds and push forward, but I'm not. I need recovery time.

That's it. I'm overthinking and I need to just relax. Elena meant no harm by her comment and it's not like Grey said it himself. We established rules and falling in love is against them. We have an understanding and everything has been perfect so far. Why would it stop now? If he did break the rule, he'd tell me, right? And if I broke the rule and fell for him, I would know right? Shit. I'm doing it again. I need to get out of my head. We're going to have a great dinner together and Greyson is going to be pleased. I look myself over in the mirror before I head back out there.

I exit the bathroom with slow steps, wringing my hands as I return to the kitchen. Mrs. Park turns around with a warm smile.

"We're almost done, so I'm going to call them," she says, exiting the kitchen.

When she returns, she announces, "They'll be back in thirty minutes."

I can hear my heart beating in my ears and as if Mrs. Park can sense my nerves, she comes up beside me and gives my arm a gentle squeeze. When I meet her gaze, she's holding a bottle of Riesling. A silent offering.

"Yes, please."

55
make a wish

Greyson

Manhattan, NY | March 11, 2024

I TURN the key to my door of my apartment, and darkness welcomes me as I step inside. I'm suddenly brought back to that night eight years ago and my stomach sinks. I consider turning around and leaving, but my dad is on my heels. I take a breath when he squeezes my shoulder, urging me to move forward. When we close the door behind us, Clifford starts sniffing and darts towards the couch. The house is still silent until we hear a thud, followed by a hushed "Dammit" and a fit of familiar giggles.

I flick the light switch and "Surprise" is exclaimed in unison, with Dad joining in. Mom, Selah and my friends come out of hiding with nervous smiles. I'm stunned, I glance over my shoulder at my smiling dad who was in on this. Henry pops up from where Clifford disappeared to. Supposedly, he was smuggling food before dinner, so of course my dog charged him, causing him to topple over. I'm excited to see him and my friends, who I realize have heard a lot about Selah, but haven't met her before now.

I stand there just taking it all in for a moment and I'm grateful. My friends greet me with hugs, and I thank them for coming. Alex brings me a finger of whiskey, I catch up with him and Elena, finding myself glancing at Selah often. She must've gone home to change, and I can't wait to rip this dress off her. I'll admire it for now, but it'll get better acquainted with my floor tonight. That is, if she hasn't had enough of me yet. She's in the kitchen talking to my parents and they are hitting it off. Henry was helping and stealing food, so I assume mom kicked him out since he's setting the table. She finally notices me staring and I urge her to join me. Moments later, she makes her way over with a glass of white wine and my hand is on the small of her back the moment she's in reach.

The north to my south, an undeniable attraction.

She fits right into the conversation, and I can tell off rip that my friends like her. They're very opinionated, Alex especially. He's direct and would've let me know immediately if something seemed off about her. Whereas Elena tends to be more delicate with her delivery.

After a few minutes, I excuse us so we can have a moment to chat alone. There's a worried expression on her face that I want to kiss away.

"I hope you're not upset. It was my idea to invite Henry and your friends. Then they told me that's how you liked to celebrate before—"

I interrupt and take her hand to graze my thumb over her knuckles. "This is perfect. I'm not upset. I'm sorry I didn't tell you this morning. I just don't have—"

"It's okay. We were a bit distracted anyway," she says, looking down at her feet.

"That we were. I won't keep anything from you again. You didn't have to do all this," I wave toward the party. "But I really appreciate it. Thank you."

She meets my gaze and the tension in her shoulders has melted away.

"It gets better than this, you'll see. I wanted to do this for you. Everyone should be celebrated on their birthday."

I'm already picturing what to do for her birthday, even though she hates surprises.

I realize how hesitantly I've been in fear of scaring her off, but what she pulled off last minute is proof that I'm not the only one interested in something more. The day began with her coming on my tongue and ended with her planning a surprise dinner for my birthday. I'm tempted to kiss her in front of everyone right now. How else could I thank her?

The thought is fleeting once my brother whines, "Can we eat, already? I have nibbled enough and Clifford took the last of my stash."

The room bursts into laughter. Henry Park, always ruining the moment.

I should've done it as soon as it crossed my mind. The next time I kiss her I may not come up for air.

My mom comes up and directs me to the spread on my dining table, half of it is full of my favorite Korean dishes. Galbi Jjim[1], algamja jorim[2], hobak bokkeum[3], kimchi bokkeumbap[4], sangchu geotjeori[5], and miyeokguk[6], which is a birthday tradition in our culture. I smile when I notice the Wanja Jorim[7] that my mom was teaching Selah to make earlier. Her taking the time to learn about my culture and prepare this meal with my family is a gift.

The other half of the spread features my favorites from Elena's restaurant, *Aguilar's*. There's a platter to make your own

---

1. Beef short ribs
2. Korean braised potatoes
3. Zucchini stir fry
4. Kimchi fried rice
5. Korean romaine lettuce salad
6. Seaweed soup
7. Korean meatballs

tacos, elotes[8], conchas[9] and flan. My heart swells because I know how busy she is and I'm grateful she's here.

Elena breaks my daze from the table when she announces, "I brought chamangos[10] too! They're in the freezer!"

My eyes light up. "You're spoiling me. Say no more."

I take a seat at the head of the table with Selah beside me. Everyone gets comfortable as we pass along the bowls, filling our plates 'til we're all content. We say '잘 먹겠습니다 jal meokgetseumnida[11],' before eating. It's not a meal with my family without embarrassing stories from my childhood and when Henry laughs a little too hard, I share some of his as well. The college stories are equally embarrassing, and I'll be hoarse later from all this laughing. Selah shines and is engaged in our ridiculous ramblings. I can't tell if it's the wine or my presence that's relaxed her, but I love seeing her bloom publicly.

I can't remember the last time we all had dinner together, maybe when I founded *SoulBlend?* Or when Elena opened *Aguilar's*? Either way, it's been too long and that stops today. I always appreciated how my parents welcomed any kid into the fold growing up. There was always more than enough food and room at the table. Any friend of ours was considered family. I'm overjoyed at Selah experiencing that same sentiment tonight.

I'll admit when I woke up this morning, all I wanted was to be alone with her. I look around this room and everyone I love is here because of her *and* my meddling parents. I honestly can't think of a better way to have spent the day. I'm also regretful for the previous years I've spent this day alone. I didn't have to be alone, and they would've shown up for me. They did show up for me.

Everyone should be celebrated on their birthday.

My dad and I had a much-needed talk and will be closer

8. Corn
9. Mexican sweet bread
10. Mexican frozen mango drink
11. "I'll eat well."

because of it. My mom shared recipes with Selah and she did an amazing job cooking. My parents got to celebrate with both their boys under one roof. Homesick Henry shared a meal with us and there's plenty of leftovers to take back to school with him. Elena took a night off and it felt like old times. Alex is always in good spirits when the trio is together. Clifford got tacos so he's happy no matter what. I introduced my Sunflower to my favorite people, and they made her feel right at home.

I'm released from my thoughts by everyone singing "Happy Birthday." Selah carefully brings the cake to the table, placing it in front of me. It's a fresh cream cake, my favorite, topped with numeric candles that read *32*. It looks delicious and between us all, there'll be none left at the end of the night.

She stands beside me in a lavender dress that accentuates her curves, her curls are down her back with one side pinned above her ear. She's wearing a dangly earring that I study closely and I realize it's a *sunflower.* I hadn't noticed it earlier, she usually wears hoops, I love it. She snaps pictures of the cake with pride etched across her face. When she leans forward with the lighter, her proximity has my dick stirring in my pants and I'm strongly resisting the urge to palm her ass.

Down boy. We have company.

I whisper, "Did you make this with my mom?"

"I did. I hope you like it."

"I already do. Thank you."

I smile up at her as she lights the wicks and backs away, returning to my side. I stare at the cake as the flames sway, overwhelmed with gratitude.

"Make a wish, Grey."

I close my eyes and blow out the candles.

I wish she was mine.

I open my eyes, and she stands before me with a bright smile that illuminates the room as if the candles were still aflame.

"Did you make a good wish?"

"The best one."

"I hope you get everything you wished for."

"Me too," I say softly.

"Let us eat cake!" she exclaims followed by a giggle.

I sit back, admiring her as she slices into the cake and that's when it hits me.

I'm in love with Selah and she doesn't even know it.

56
open up

Greyson

Manhattan, NY | March 11, 2024

BEFORE EVERYONE GOT up from dinner, I asked them to stay put so I could get a picture. Selah offered to take it for us, but I wanted her to be a part of it. This night wouldn't have happened without her. I set up my tripod and took a photo of us all together. I snapped a few of everyone before they left and got some good shots of my parents too. I haven't seen them look that happy since I was a kid. It really was a perfect night. There's a few where I'm looking at her like a lovesick puppy that I didn't want her to see. I'm still worried about scaring her away. More now than ever.

After the last of our guests leave, I ask her if she'll stay the night with me on purpose this time. She agrees with no argument, which actually surprises me, I fully expected her to go back to her *no sleepovers* rule. She mentions that she needs to check on Peach and I suggest that she could start bringing her over here to hang at my place. She had concerns about her and Clifford not getting along, but he gets along with everybody. Plus, if he doesn't, Peach will smack some sense into him, I'm sure. I got her to agree to a 'trial run play date' between the two of them soon and I'm looking forward to bringing them together. If they hit it off, that's even more time we can spend together and Cliff will have a new friend.

12

When we lay on the couch later that night, I'm catching up on sports highlights while she lays beside me cackling every few minutes at her phone. Her feet are draped across my lap and I started to rub them absentmindedly. Once I realized it, I didn't stop because she's been stifling her moans. I love how domesticated this feels. I ask about the Fleetwood Mac tattoo on her left ankle, it's a quote from the song *Landslide*. She tells me that was the first tattoo Daya did for her after they became friends last year.

Now I know the music behind her tattoos and need to listen to them together.

What is the overall story?

Hoping this gets me closer to figuring out the beautiful enigma that is Selah Bailey.

I remind myself of what I wanted to discuss tonight. My thoughts have been extremely heavy today and I am now considering going to therapy and it has a lot to do with the woman in front of me. If I am not willing to confront my past, my fear of failing another person will come true. I understand that now and I think I'm ready to do the right thing for myself this time.

I'm hesitant to ask her about her experience with therapy so far, but I'm not sure what to expect and I'm nervous. As shy as Selah is naturally, mental health is something she's pretty open about. Of course, when I bring it up, she answers every question I have and even offers advice on what I should be looking for in a good therapist. She informs me she's been in therapy for almost two years and was fortunate to have found her perfect therapist right away. She texts me a list of recommendations she got from Audrey when she moved to New York and lets me know that she'll support me through this and that she's proud of me for advocating for myself.

I told her earlier that I wouldn't keep anything from her and I intend to keep that promise. I have a good reason to keep the love thoughts to myself for now, at least until I can learn more about how she's feeling.

I take a deep breath and ready myself for this conversation.

"I told you some about my ex-wife, but I didn't tell you about our divorce."

"Grey, you don't have to," she says while shaking her head.

"We met our freshman year at NYU and dated all throughout college. I proposed a little while after graduation and we were married for three years. We weren't the best communicators and poor communication is something that can't be ignored. Though we really tried. I poured myself into work after many failed attempts of getting her to communicate with me. I soon prioritized my career over everything and things didn't work out.

I had come home early from a trip to surprise her. Well, I walked in on her packing her bags and she wasn't very happy with my surprise visit. She had planned to leave while I was out of town so she wouldn't have to face me. She served me the papers on my birthday. She didn't even remember what day it was. I missed her so badly after a week away and just wanted to see her, but she forgot. I came home and watched her leave."

"I'm sorry, Greyson," she says and places her hand in mine.

"I wanted to make it work and she didn't. To this day, we haven't really talked about everything that went wrong. I blamed myself and felt like if I failed my marriage, I could make up for it with *SoulBlend*. Like, if it wasn't in the cards for me, I could help others."

I pause and rub the back of my neck as I gather my thoughts.

"I haven't celebrated my birthday for the past eight years. I haven't spent it with anyone besides Cliff. Today, I woke up with you in my bed and I was so happy you stayed the night. I originally hoped I could spend the day alone with you."

She frowns and averts her eyes. "I'm sorry I ruined your plans," she whispers, her bottom lip wobbles as she sucks in a breath.

"Hey." I say, and she looks up at me. "Today was the best fucking birthday I've had in a long time. All my favorite people were here, thanks to you."

I lean in to kiss her forehead, then her nose. She giggles in response.

"C'mere." I pat my lap urging her to climb on it. She lifts her dress as she straddles me and we lock eyes.

"What are you plotting?"

"Nothing," she sings as her eyes dance over me. "Just thinking about how your tongue felt this morning."

I raise my brows in response.

Fuck me.

"I've been dying to touch you all day. This fucking dress should be illegal," I growl and grab her waist. "Can I properly thank you for my surprise?"

"I don't know, can you?" she says in a mocking tone, wearing a playful smile.

"Alright, brat. My room n—"

My words are halted when she climbs off my lap and unzips her dress revealing nothing underneath. The fabric melts from her body onto the floor as she heads straight to my room.

I get up and grab the dress, following behind and it's very clear who's running the show tonight.

I wonder if she'll call me a good boy.

Happy Birthday to me.

57
a movie and a show

Greyson

Brooklyn, NY | March 24, 2024

I'VE BEEN in therapy for three weeks now and as excruciating as the stroll down memory lane is, I understand it's necessary to unpack what went wrong with my marriage. It just leaves me feeling nauseous afterwards. I'm determined to do the exact opposite with Selah and that's worth the discomfort. It's wearing on me that still I haven't told her how I feel and I've decided to do it before the wedding. As promised, I'll help with the remaining tasks that require a partner, just in case she's inclined to quit if this doesn't work out after I tell the truth. I'll admit I'm using the list as a distraction to buy myself more time with her. Like she'll be less upset with me if I help her complete the list.

12

We have forty-four days before Selah's turns thirty and a handful of uncompleted tasks on her list. I'm determined to help her cross them all off. Today I've brought her to watch a movie at the park. I'm unloading blankets from the car while she carries the takeout we just picked up. It's a beautiful night out and I really hope she enjoys what I've planned. She thinks we're only here to check one task off her list, but I got an idea. If she's interested, we could accomplish three tonight. *Recreate a spicy scene from a book, have sex in public without getting caught and watch a movie in the park.*

I understand how shy my sunflower is and can already see her face when I suggest it. There's a high chance she'll say 'no' and I'll respect that. This would be bold and risky, but isn't that the reason she made the list in the first place? I know how important it is to her and refuse to let her give up, especially when she's so close. Plus, she's getting orgasms out of it, which is a mutual perk.

Don't you wish your neighbor with benefits was a freak like me?

Once I find the perfect spot for us, we settled in. The perfect spot for Selah is a distance from others with a good view of the screen. Which is perfect for me since we'll need some privacy if she's down for a little adventure. I was surprised when she'd told me what she wanted to see and that it's a favorite of hers. A classic New York gangster film. She never ceases to amaze me. I make sure she's comfortable before it starts so we can stay seated and enjoy the show. After the movie starts, I urge her to sit between my legs and she does. I drape the thick, sizable blanket over us as she rests the back of her head on my shoulder and continues watching the movie.

After a while, I whisper in her ear to remind her about the *'Fuck It List'* and that we aren't finished yet. She argues that we're working on it right now and while she isn't wrong, she seems to have forgotten what's left to do.

"So, there's this book of yours that I read where the couple is watching the Eiffel Tower light show at sunset."

She glances over at me with wide eyes and an incredulous expression.

"Grey, what were you doing reading *that* book and why are you talking about it now?"

I chuckle against her cheek at her shyness. I know how dirty she can be, but she's gotta ease into it.

"Well, I've got some things in common with the guy, don't you think? I mean, I'm *a lot* younger and I too have a beautiful woman wearing a sundress underneath a blanket *in public*."

When I wrap my arm around her to bring her closer, I feel her heart beating against me.

"Baby, you wouldn't."

There she goes calling me baby.

"I fucking would, but only if you want me to. I don't think you could be quiet though," I tease. "Would you stay quiet for Daddy?"

She looks at me and nods in response, spreading her legs slowly. As much as I encourage her to use her words, I'll accept that.

I trail my hand slowly down her soft stomach and casually lift her sundress to reveal herself to me. I dip my hand lower and when I feel her soaked, bare pussy, I stifle a moan of my own.

"No panties in public? Bad girl."

"I'm not apologizing." she retorts.

Fuck. I love this woman.

I reward her with a pressed thumb to her clit and the soft gasp she lets out at the contact ignites me. I hold it, giving another order when she rests her head in my neck.

"Keep your eyes on the movie and stay still."

When she keeps her eyes closed and whines, I tap my thumb against that sensitive bud, and she does as she's told.

"Good girl. Now, let me take care of you."

I draw gentle circles around her clit, slowly increasing the pressure. Taking my time to see how well she can hold her excitement and keep her voice down. Aside from some quickened breaths, soft whimpers and some lip biting, she's doing so good for me. So good that I need to make this more of a challenge.

I take my free hand, carefully brushing my thumb over the stiff peaks through her dress. One at a time, studying her as she watches the movie. She parts her lips, but no sound escapes them. If we were alone, she'd surely let me know how that felt. I continue teasing her clit and nipples, focusing on her breathing and facial expressions.

"More," she breathes into my neck.

I quiet myself with a bite of my lip.

"You want me to fuck your needy pussy with my fingers? In front of all these people?"

"Yes, Daddy."

Oh fuck.

"Fuck, baby. Hold your moans for me."

She nods and shifts her attention back to the movie. Sighing when I gently slip a finger inside, my movements are slow and careful at first. I know this body and how to play with it. I'm in no rush, but when she grows impatient and starts to grumble, I chuckle into her neck. Adding another finger, I pump in and out of her pussy a little faster, but not enough to move the blanket. I guide my free hand down to her aching clit, rubbing to encourage her orgasm as she fights the urge to whimper. I know her tells and when she digs her nails into my leg, I know she's close.

"Nod when you're about to come, baby," I order, keeping my voice low.

Her breath quickens and she nods, keeping her eyes forward. I feel her core clenching around my fingers as she struggles to hold still and bites back her cries.

"Come all over Daddy's hand like a good girl," I urge.

I'm coated in her arousal and resisting the urge to devour it is excruciating. I'm addicted to her taste, but she behaved and so will I. She glances up at me with a soft smile, her chest rising and falling as she comes down.

"You did so well, baby." I kiss the top of her head.

She eventually falls asleep on my chest, and I let her rest as I watch the movie. Her soft snores make me smile and as accomplished as I feel about what we did tonight, we're not even close to being done yet. There are two more tasks, and I'd like to make them memorable for her.

I have an idea, but I'll need some help executing it. My stomach sinks at the thought of this backfiring, but I've gotta try. I slip my phone from my pocket, careful not to wake her and fire off a text. There's only one person who can help me pull off a grand gesture for the woman who hates surprises…and they just responded.

58
love knocks

Selah

Manhattan, NY | March 27, 2024

TODAY HAS BEEN DRAGGING and it doesn't help that I'm anxious. We're currently in the middle of a scrum sprint cycle at work. We do these often, using this time to review short iterations of feedback to evaluate and adapt our workflows. I look forward to sprints, but as the product manager, I'm required to be *very* sociable. That part I dread, mostly because of my anxiety, not because I don't know what the hell I'm talking about.

Though I will say it is difficult navigating through life when it feels as if your mind and body are constantly at war with each other. Thanks to Dr. Garnett, I feel better equipped to manage my panic attacks when I feel them coming on. So, I am holding on for our session tonight. I'm on my lunch break enjoying a turkey sub at my kitchen counter and reading when my phone trills beside me. Mama's name flashing across the screen. I swipe to answer.

"Hey, mama."

"Hey baby." The warmth in her voice makes me feel better already.

"I hope I'm not bothering you. I just missed you and wanted to talk to you about something."

"You're never a bother. I'm just on my lunch break. What's going on?"

"How are you feeling?"

I sigh, "Honestly, tired. I'm resisting the urge to take a nap because I'm afraid I won't come back."

"Nightmares keeping you up?"

"Yeah," I say reluctantly.

Amongst other things.

"And you're still being stubborn about refusing to share a bed with that fine ass man you've been playing pinochle with?"

I snort. "Yes, and you're not the only one who calls me stubborn."

"You got your hard headedness from your daddy. That wasn't my doing."

"Mom, you had a child with him. I'd argue you hold some responsibility here."

"Anyways, if I were you, I'd be lying all over and under that man. I don't understand why you won't sleep over. Are you afraid you're going to fall for him? Is this your way of protecting yourself?"

I remain silent.

States away and reading my mind.

I hate it when she does this.

I can fool everyone but my mother.

"Baby, when you fall in love, you have no control over it. You can lay down a thousand ground rules, but if your heart wants that man, those rules won't stop shit. You hear me, Selah?"

"I hear you, Mama," I nearly whisper as a single tear streams down my cheek.

She continues, "I understand why love feels like a threat to the life you've worked so hard to create for yourself, but it doesn't have to be. Nobody in those books you read is ever prepared for the love that knocks on their door, either. Love doesn't give a damn if you're ready for it. When it knocks, you answer. I just want you to think about that, baby. I didn't mean to upset you."

"It's okay, Mama," I sniffle.

I glance at my clock to see how much time I have left before I need to log back on. Twenty-five minutes. Should be time to not look like I was crying by the time I get back on camera.

"If you're done giving me a hard time, what did you have to tell me? I gotta get back soon."

"I almost forgot. Your Auntie Ruby is dragging me to a speed dating thing tonight. That's why I called."

I jerk my neck back in response.

"How much did she pay you?"

She cackles. "Nothing. I'm just a little lonely these days. Thought I'd give it a try with her. Maybe find myself a pinochle partner. It is going well for you."

"Alright, now. I've had enough of you," I chuckle.

"You could never."

"You got that right. I gotta go, Mama. I love you and good luck tonight."

"I love you too, baby. Thank you."

I sit with her words long after we disconnect the call.

59
here goes nothing

Selah

Manhattan, NY | March 28, 2024

"IT FELT SO REAL. It's not real. He's not here and he isn't coming back. I am safe. I am free." I repeat to myself in a breathless chant. Tears stream down my face while the freshness of the dream still lingers in my mind. Menacing dark eyes staring back at me and a familiar presence that took my breath away. I saw him. He was here, in my apartment walking through my bedroom watching me sleep. Jourdan.

The nightmares have increased lately. It's frustrating because whenever I'm making real progress, I'm pushed ten steps back. Between this and the sleepless nights, I feel as if I'm being punished for getting to know someone new. It's like this is his way of reminding me that I'll never be whole again. It's impossible to be whole when you don't even know who you were before them.

It doesn't matter how much time has passed or how much you have grown, your abuser will always haunt you. A permanent fixture in your mind that you'd do anything to remove. You could keep driving, cross state lines and start a whole new life like I did. Some days are easier than others, but the work is never done. I just wish this never happened to me. I wish I never met Jourdan. I hate that I'm still battling this in his absence. I hate that there's no estimated timeline of when I'll feel better. There's no handbook to healing but if there was, I'd flip to the fucking end pages and find the answer key.

I know because of Jourdan I won't be normal again and I hate it. Sometimes I find myself getting frustrated with Greyson. I don't show it, but I feel it. I get angry because he's just so kind and patient, I don't understand how someone couldn't love him. He explained what caused his marriage to end, but I'm sure he's different now because I see a man very deserving of love. So much so, that it's easy to get caught in his orbit and forget how impossible that is for me.

Sometimes, I wonder what being loved by him feels like, but I don't allow myself to think about it for too long. I understand what we have right now is as good as it gets for me, and I won't ruin that with daydreams of what could be. My therapist is confident that I'll eventually be able to let someone in, maybe even Greyson, if I want to. I don't understand how I can't even enjoy a good night's sleep without being haunted by my past. If I'm not having a nightmare, I'm tossing and turning in fear of having one. There's chaos in my world, I couldn't bring a man like that a sliver of peace. I keep thinking about what Elena said on his birthday.

You've created a recipe for Greyson to fall in love with you.

I got a glimpse of what it would look like if we were together at his birthday dinner, and I realized something. The man is a sorcerer. The thought of him causes my body to betray me, heightening my senses. He's discovered every zone and magical button to drive me wild. I don't need anybody, but when Greyson is present, I need *him*. His good nature can make anyone feel like a main character in his story. His way with words and mindfulness have me convinced he's a figment of my imagination. It's as if he's studied every book I love and emulated the exact man I've desired. That sounds unbelievable, doesn't it? I'm not so lost in fiction that I can't tell the difference. I know this isn't a romance novel. This is my life and I'm not chasing a happily ever after. I know that's not in the cards, but a girl can dream. That's a far better one than I see when my eyes shut.

6

I know I'll regret this later, but I'm breaking my own rule. I grab my phone and call Greyson. My heart races out of my chest with each ring.

He picks up with a groggy voice. "Sunflower, what's wrong?"

"Can I come over? I don't want to be alone."

"What? Of course."

"Will you stay on the phone with me?"

"I will."

As I get out of the bed and start readying myself to leave my apartment. I'm silent, but he can sense my anxiety over the line, like he always does. He keeps me distracted by spewing out random fun facts, some about himself and some not. It's making me smile as I get dressed to leave. I'm working on my breathing as I make my way to the elevator and he remains on the line, as promised. When I watch the numbers ascend, his gravelly voice assures me he's still here and not to be alarmed when the doors open. He warns that there's a really good looking guy waiting outside the elevator for some reason. I chuckle for the first time since I woke up and sure enough when the doors open, there is a really good looking guy waiting outside.

Concern etched across his face as he opens his arms wide to welcome me. I dart over to him, wrapping my arms around his waist as he envelops me into a hug. The familiarity of his scent causes me to nestle into him until I rest my head on his hard chest. I savor his touch and while it's been a few days, I realize how much I've missed it. He leans down to press a kiss to the top of my head and a single tear escapes me. Before I can wipe it away, it soaks through his shirt. He doesn't acknowledge it, only pulls me in tighter and we stay like that for a while. Anyone could walk by, but it's late and we just don't care.

"Let's get you inside. C'mon."

I nod and extend my arms around his neck, so he reaches under my thighs to pick me up, carrying me to the door. He lets us in and removes my shoes. I look over to see Clifford in his bed, too sleepy to react. Grey carefully navigates the dark hallway until we enter his bedroom. He sits me on the bed and climbs in beside me, opening his arms so I snuggle into him. I peel off my sweats, which he tosses onto a nearby chair.

I take a deep breath as my heart pounds. He opened up to me and I should do the same.

"I want to talk to you about something."

"Okay."

"I-I have nightmares. Vivid ones of my ex. I told you we were engaged, that I didn't want to marry him. I was just afraid of how he'd react if I said no."

I pause, gathering my thoughts and he rubs his thumb over my balled-up fist.

Here goes nothing.

"I haven't said this out loud to anyone besides my therapist, but he was abusive. It was mostly emotional and verbal abuse, but he got physical sometimes. I left two years ago and never looked back. It's made it difficult for me to imagine myself in a new relationship, especially when I'm still haunted by my past."

Judging by his breath on my neck, I know he's upset, but he remains silent.

"I have PTSD because of him. I know you've noticed I startle easily, but you never draw attention to it. And when I'm anxious you know how to soothe me. Before I called you, I saw him in my dream. He was in my apartment. In my room. It was just a nightmare, but I didn't want to be alone."

"I'm so sorry, baby," he whispers and presses a kiss to my shoulder. "Has he tried to contact you or come around since you left? You'd tell me if he did?"

I shake my head. "I would tell you, but he hasn't bothered me for a long time now. Almost two years now. He isn't coming back."

I figure if I say that enough times out loud, it may come true.

He could evaporate from my thoughts and never bother me again.

If I could wish for anything it'd probably be that.

"Thank you for trusting me with this. Any man who puts his hands on a woman is a fucking coward and he better hope he never runs into me. I hate to hear that you've been battling this alone."

I shift to face him and nestle into his chest. His pained expression softens as he wraps his arms around me.

"Thanks for being there for me. I know I broke my rule," I admit.

He snorts, "that's exactly what it is, a rule *you* made and keep breaking. I never liked it to begin with."

"And why is that?"

"I think you sleep better in my bed," he states while pulling the covers over us.

I hum to myself.

I do. I don't say that though.

greyson

As the morning light illuminates my room, I smile to myself as I take in every curve and edge of my little Sunflower. She slept soundly through the night, and I made sure to readjust her bonnet anytime it started to slip off. She would not have been happy if she woke up and her curls were set free. Like I said, she sleeps better in my bed. She doesn't have to admit it when it's a proven fact. The most beautiful woman in the world is sleeping in my bed, on my chest, safe and sound. She's exactly where she needs to be.

I couldn't go back to sleep after what she shared, but I'm glad she could get some rest. I'm not upset that she hadn't felt comfortable sharing until now, I'm upset that it happened at all. The thought of that fucking guy harming her infuriates me. The fact that she's been tormented for years makes me sick to my stomach.

When she wakes up, we're throwing out the *no sleepovers* rule. It's her choice if she wants to sleep here or not, and I'll respect it, but the rule itself has to go. She's always welcome here and if she ever wants me to sleep at her place, I certainly don't mind. However, if I can make her feel safe and protected, I will.

I mean, fuck. I love Selah and she just told me what she's afraid of. It makes sense why she is comfortable with this arrangement. She's not stuck with me if things went sideways. Her heart is safer if we keep things the way they are, but mine isn't. I can't be the only one feeling a greater pull between us, but I will be the first to acknowledge it. I plan to tell her sooner than later. She doesn't have to say it back, I'll gladly love her until she catches up. Near or far.

60
ox-eye daisy
Greyson

Manhattan, NY | April 9, 2024

I'VE OFFICIALLY BEEN ATTENDING therapy for a month now. My friends and family are elated that I am finally talking to someone. I like my therapist, Dr. Pierson. I have virtual sessions every Tuesday on my lunch break. She's easy to talk to and holds me accountable. Today we talked about Selah and my fears about prioritizing work over a relationship again. I really don't believe that I can have both and whenever I am forced to choose, I always pick work.

She has suggested that I try co-working at home with Selah one day a week. It's different from how she has to work in the coffee shop to be around people. I am being encouraged to stay home with her and see how that makes me feel about keeping a work/life balance. I'll give it a fair shot because she absolutely loves it, but when I have tried it in the past, I didn't enjoy working from home. I don't think anyone who lives in Manhattan enjoys the commute, but I do love interacting with my staff. I also wouldn't mind spending more time with Selah that isn't on the weekends and in the evenings, so I can manage one day a week just to see how it works for us. We agreed to start next Friday and see how it goes.

12

Peach and Clifford don't hate each other, which is interesting. The trial run went well, and we alternate between my place and hers. Clifford really enjoys playing and napping with his new friend. I love it because it gives Selah a reason to spend more time with us without feeling guilty. She does get annoyed whenever I come over in the daytime because I open her curtains to let the sun in. Peach on the other hand, loves it and sunbathes in the windows all day. So, I don't mind her getting a little snippy with me when Peach is happy. It's just a little sunlight; she's not a vampire and she'll live. Plus, her giving me a hard time is a part of her charm.

Aileen and Daniel's wedding is in two weeks. I am only nervous because Aileen's behavior is unpredictable and while she has pestered me about dating and bringing a plus one, I can't guarantee how she'll react. I'd like to believe she'll be distracted enough by it being her special day that she wouldn't start any drama. However, like I said she's unpredictable and based on what I've heard from Audrey, she has been a Bridezilla. One of the worst of her career.

If she makes Selah uncomfortable at any point, I won't hesitate to leave. I can't imagine how odd this whole situation is going to be for her and I just want her to know I'm not leaving her side. I'll admit as much as I love weddings, I wasn't looking forward to this one until she agreed to come with me. We're attending an Audrey Wood wedding at the Woodward in Manhattan, which is going to be extravagant and we'll be a couple for the night. That's the part I'm really excited about. I want Selah to see what things could be like between us. I hope that could warm her up to the idea of us pursuing more.

12

I'm proud to say our conversation about her *no sleepovers* rule went over well after that night. She's been over my place quite a bit since then and I've slept over at hers. Once she shared that she doesn't have nightmares whenever she sleeps with me; I saw no reason for us to sleep separately, but it wouldn't be Selah without some resistance. We don't share a bed every night, but as often as she allows it, we do. I know it took a lot for her to open up about her ex. I brought it up in therapy because I wanted to know how I can support her through this. I've been advised to keep meeting her where she's at and don't pry. She is becoming more comfortable with me and I'm grateful for that.

Today's therapy session is different than usual because I've decided I'm going to tell Selah how I feel soon. Dr. Pierson was able to fit me in for a session before I have this talk with her so I can be prepared. She's roleplaying the conversation with me based off what I've practiced and is going over what reactions to expect. As much as I'd love to get a positive reaction, I know a negative one could be more likely.

Selah could feel betrayed and while that wasn't my intention, I'm aware of that possibility. Being honest was a rule of this arrangement and the moment things shifted for me, I should've been upfront. She's been through enough bullshit in her life and can't feel safe around someone who's dishonest. I'm probably being too hard on myself, but I love her so much that the thought of hurting her makes me sick. I fear I've really fucked myself this time and I haven't even told her yet.

We discuss what will I do if her reaction is positive and it catches me off guard. I've been so worried about losing her, that I haven't given much consideration to what I'd do if she'd stay. She doesn't have to say it back if she doesn't feel it. If she feels anything for me or believes she someday could, I'll take that. I'd shown her how things could be if she were mine and I meant it.

The voice in my head taunts me as the anticipation builds. I don't remember being this nervous since I proposed all those years ago. If I had an ox-eye daisy right now, the petals would be ripped from it. Hopeful for a game where the odds are in my favor.

She loves me, she loves me not.

She loves me, she loves me not.

She loves me, she loves me not.

What if she loves me?

61
working from home

Greyson

Manhattan | April 19, 2024

TODAY, we're co-working at my place, per my therapist's suggestion. This experiment is to prove that I can have a work/life balance, maintain a relationship, and a successful career. If it goes over well, I'll be proven wrong. Selah has been nothing but supportive of me going to therapy, and when I asked if she'd work from home with me once a week at my place, she was all for it. I was a little surprised she agreed because I know she has a routine that she likes to stick to.

So far, it's been going well because we've both been busy. I have a partner's desk in my home office, so we're facing each other, but we haven't been able to speak much. I must say it's nice to be able to look up and see her face. While she can be distracting, I don't mind. However, she can stay focused on work while I stare at her, but she argues it's because of her ADHD medication.

I quickly realized how easy it is for her to forget to eat when she's in her zone and locked in on a project, so I keep bringing her snacks and water. She works with headphones on, and I have no idea what she's listening to. I've passed by her desk a few times to peek over her shoulder, and all I know is she better send me that playlist. I seriously underestimated what working with someone whose job is all about music would be like. She just vibes all day and types aggressively, which I now suspect is on beat with whatever she is listening to.

Another thing I've noticed about co-working with Selah is she's a chair dancer, and not in the way you think. Though with the pole dancing classes, I'm certain she can do that too. She keeps rolling her hips and twerking in that damn chair. I've never been jealous of an inanimate object before today. I now see how she acts when she's alone working all day. So not only is her beauty distracting, but watching her work and goof around is a turn-on for me. I'm a little concerned about my productivity today, but then I remember she logs off at noon on Fridays, so I'll be alone after that.

The day is halfway through when Selah gets off and hops in the shower. She'll likely curl up in my bed and read 'til I'm off. So, I take advantage of the time apart and dive back into my to-dos before my afternoon meetings.

12

As we're getting closer to Selah's birthday, I've been thinking of the remaining tasks on her list she has yet to complete. We have a little over three weeks left.

She returns in the doorway of my office with her curls pulled back, and she's wearing one of my shirts. It stops mid-thigh, and she isn't wearing a bra. I bite my lip while I take her in because I've had about enough of her unknowingly seducing me today.

"What are you doing in here? You're done for the day."

"Well, when I'm done for the day, I like to blow off some steam."

"What are you saying?" I stare at her expectantly.

"I was going to grab a toy, but you're here. So, I could use you instead." A devious grin spreads across her face.

I love this woman. Don't say that out loud.

I fight the urge to laugh.

"Use me? I don't think so."

She scoffs and scrunches up her face at me.

"You were driving me wild grinding in that damn chair all morning," I say through gritted teeth. "If anybody's getting used, it's *you.*"

She parts her lips in surprise and her eyes light up.

"Why are you smiling? You want to be used? Thinking about your list?"

"Yes, and yes. I'm intrigued."

Fuck it.

"Do you trust me?"

"I do." She tells me with sincerity in her eyes, and I believe her.

"Remember the safe words? I need you to repeat them for me."

"Red means stop. Yellow means slow down or take a break. Green means

keep going."

"You said you want to give up control, right?"

"Yes, but-"

"Get on your knees," I interrupt.

"Excuse me?!" She jerks her neck back, giving me an incredulous look. I'm going to remain firm and hope she trusts me here. I have an idea, and if she'll help me see it through, I think she'll like the outcome.

"I won't repeat myself, Selah."

She freezes, looking me up and down, and I see the war within herself before she surprises me and lowers to her knees, sitting on her feet. Joining her hands and resting them on her thighs, awaiting my next command.

"That's my good girl."

She beams at my praise. I glance down at my watch to look at the time, and I have a meeting in about ten minutes. Looks like I'll have to multitask.

"Crawl to me." My tone leaves no room for suggestion.

She rolls her eyes and makes a face. I try not to chuckle at her expression, I expected resistance, and I will not push her. She knows what to do if she's uncomfortable, and I trust that she'll use the safe words at any time. I know this isn't going to be easy for her, but once she lets go, she'll see what I'm doing for her. We have a stare down before she leans forward and gets on all fours. She slowly crawls across the floor while keeping her eyes locked on me. She sits back on her feet, hungrily awaiting my next command.

"That's my beautiful fucking girl."

She smiles, and it radiates the room.

"Get under my desk and face me."

She gives me a questionable look before obeying. She gets back on all fours and arches her back, making a show of it with each sway of her hips. As she inches closer to my desk, I'm resisting the urge to smack her plump ass. Seeing her let go of that control while maintaining her confidence is making me so hard right now. She crawls and ducks below my desk, turning to face me as she sits back on her feet. I glance down at my watch again. Five minutes.

"Do you know why I have you down here?"

She nods.

"Are you going to obey me?"

She nods again, and her silence is worrying me. I've grown accustomed to a Selah who enjoys a little back and forth beforehand. It's a part of our foreplay at this point.

"Use your words."

"Yes."

"Yes, what?"

"Yes, Daddy."

I growl in response. My dick is straining against my pants. I reach down and undo my belt. I love watching her shudder at the jangle of the buckle. I lean back in my chair to push it backward before sitting up to pull down my slacks. My dick springs free, and she watches in awe, squeezing her thighs together. The tip glistens, and I pump it once. She gasps in response while I sit back in my chair, inching closer to her. I stare down, admiring her beauty. She has no idea how fucking amazing she looks before me. The buzzing on my watch cuts the moment short and reminds me of the meeting I have in one minute.

"I have a meeting and need to be on camera for a bit. Will you be a good girl and suck my dick?"

She answers with a nod and bites her lip.

"I'll tell you if I need to speak to my team, and you'll be quiet for me. If you are not quiet, you will be punished. Do you understand?"

"Yes, Daddy."

I hum in approval and gently grab her chin, directing her gaze to me, flames stirring within those coffee-brown eyes as her eager lips part for me. She settles between my legs and wraps her hand around my thick dick, teasing the crown with her skillful tongue as she licks further down the shaft. She begins stroking the base while her full lips welcomed me, sucking softly as she works her way down my length.

I let out a curse before grabbing my noise-canceling headphones as I prepare for this meeting. I review the agenda to get an idea of what will be discussed and to gauge how long this will last. These usually tend to be an hour, give or take. Judging by the heavy agenda, we have several different teammates needing to take the floor to discuss different projects and updates within the *SoulBlend* app.

Due to it being a monthly rundown meeting, I'm able to take a backseat after intros and covering my topics unless there's anything pressing for me to address during the Q and A at the end. I glance down at my Selah as she engulfs me, shaking my head because her presence may present more of a challenge than usual.

I clear my throat, putting on a calm expression before I join. A ding sounds to indicate my entry to the call. I greet my team with a smile and unmute my mic to say hello and tell them we'll wait a few more minutes before getting started. I mute myself and busy myself with emails, and she becomes louder in her pleasuring me with moans and sucking. Not reacting is more difficult than I expected it to be.

More dings fill the call as more staff members arrive, and once it's five after, I reach down to tap down on her arm to let her know I'm about to speak. I feel her head nod in understanding, and she slows her movements, still following orders but making it easier for me to focus.

"Good girl."

I unmute myself and lead my part of the meeting, covering my agenda items for the first half, and before I wrap up to pass things along to the engineering manager, Angela, of course, my little brat couldn't be a good girl for long. I feel her spit dripping down my crown. I make the mistake of glancing down at her with a furrowed brow, and she's staring back at me with hooded eyes. I blow out a deep breath and ask my team if they have any further questions, thankfully they do not, before I introduce Angela and mute myself hastily. The meeting continues, and I remain on camera, paying attention to the meeting, jotting down notes as I go. Her hand jerks me as her moans get louder and I think of how wet she gets from pleasing me.

I glance to my left and say, "Reach down and touch yourself. I want you to come while you take me in that sweet mouth."

She chuckles around me and I bite my fist. Angry that I can't observe her during this. The project managers take over and brief us on the next few updates in the coming quarters and features that we are discussing with shareholders. During this, I practice restraint when I can hear sounds of her wetness fill the room while she takes me deeper into her throat.

I cough into my fist as my orgasm builds, unsure of what else to do on camera to disguise it. Selah halts her movements, sliding her mouth off my shaft. I inhale deeply, resting my face on my hand to look engaged. She knows my tells and has been edging me this entire time, which I can't be upset at, since I do it to her often. It's not very fun being on the other side of it. I can understand her frustration now. It becomes even harder to focus when I hear her whimpers and pants from below me, a sign she's close. I peer down and see my little sunflower come undone. I'll never tire of it. My name escapes her lips as she rides out her orgasm.

Fuck.

I'm tempted to call this meeting right now and spread her over my desk.

"Don't move that hand," I instruct, finding it harder to train my eyes back to the meeting. I'm hoping the constant sips I take from my water bottle aren't too noticeable, but they're serving as a perfect way to hide my facial expressions while I try to act normal. The woman on her knees before me is the culprit. Another fun fact about me: I've developed an insatiable thirst that can only be quenched by her.

She doesn't move her hand from her pussy and greets me with her warm mouth yet again. I glance at the clock and see we've got about thirty minutes left, so I pull up the agenda to see what still needs to be covered. I've got about fifteen minutes before I'll need to speak again.

Change of plans.

I turn off my camera and type in the chat. "I'm going off cam while I eat my lunch."

My team responds with thumbs up emojis, not missing a beat in the meeting. I double-take my monitor to make sure that my camera and microphone are off before I give her all my attention. I shut off my headphones and put them away, adjusting the meeting audio to speaker when I notice her brows crinkle in confusion as she eyes me closely.

"Can I taste you?"

"I'm busy tasting *you* right now. Aren't you supposed to be working?"

I lean in closer. "You're busy *edging* me and I *am* working. Give me your hand."

She giggles, inserting her glistening fingers into my mouth and I lick them clean one by one. She gapes at me and I open a drawer to retrieve a condom.

I need to have her now.

"Bend over and grab your ankles, baby."

Her eyes widen in surprise as I vacate my seat, holding out my hand to ease her off the floor and in front of me. I force my pants down my legs and roll on the condom.

"Give me a color."

"Green," she coos while bending over, gripping her ankles. I salivate at the sight of her slick thighs and drenched pussy on display for me.

"No panties?"

"You keep stealing them, so what's the point in wearing any?"

"Good answer."

I dig my fingers into her hips, holding her close to me. I align myself with her dripping core, teasing her until she whines. I chuckle before sliding into her. The little gasp that escapes her drives me wild. I sink inside her fully, keeping my hold on her hips when I stop abruptly and pull out. She huffs in response, granting a smack on that perfect ass and she moans like the dirty girl she is.

I glance over at my monitor, ensuring everything is still muted as I left it. My team is still droning on and on, handling things well in my absence. Growing impatient, she shakes her ass on me and I slam back in, filling her to the hilt.

She squeals, gripping her ankles harder as I pound into her relentlessly.

"Right there. Fuck," she orders in quick breaths.

Her palms travel to the floor for leverage when she throws her ass against my hips.

"You take that dick so fucking well. Fuck me back."

She flattens her hands on the floor and slams her ass into my hips repeatedly, meeting my thrusts.

"Are you going to come with me, baby?"

"Y-Yes."

When I feel her pussy tighten around me, I smack her ass, sending her over the edge. I follow, my vision tunnels and I'm roaring her name. I come down with the realization that I am in the middle of a workday and am still in no rush to pull out and get back to work. I peek at my monitor again and everything as it should be. The meeting is still going on and I have a few more minutes before the Q and A starts. I pull up my pants and hold her upright when I slip out of her.

"C'mon, Sunflower," I urge, picking her up and carrying her to the bathroom.

She wraps her legs around me, nestling her head into my neck. I set her on the bathroom counter to clean us both up, peppering kisses on her damp skin. She wraps her arms around my neck and her mouth is on mine while I carry her to bed. She's done with work for the day and I'll be off soon. I want nothing more than to be in this bed holding her. I force myself to break the kiss and lay her down on the bed. She pouts as expected.

"I'll be back as soon as I'm done, baby."

I press a kiss to her forehead, staring admiringly, "you were such a good girl for me."

She purses her lips, pulling over the covers.

"I'm always a good girl. *You've* been a bad boy today. Now, get back to work."

I scrunch up my face. "Always a good girl?"

She snorts and tosses a pillow at me, I duck. "Shut up and go to work."

"Alright. Alright," I chuckle.

I check myself in the mirror on the way back to my desk to

rejoin the meeting. I'm back a bit early. I chug from my water bottle and turn my camera on. Nobody notices a thing and the rest of the meeting runs smoothly. Once I wrap up for the day, I run upstairs to feed Peach and climb in bed with Selah for a nap. Before today, I hardly worked from home but doing it with her felt good and not just because of the sex. I think Dr. Pierson was right. It feels like for once I could have the success *and* the girl. I suppose I could work from home more often. It sure has its perks.

62
deja vu

Greyson

Manhattan, NY | April 20, 2024

I WAKE UP BESIDE HER, and it feels like a normal day. I was on clouds with her yesterday, and I am still reeling. I'm careful not to disturb her when I get up and take Clifford for a quick walk since it's still early. When I get back, I'm making us breakfast, doing the devoted partner thing without the title and I love it. She's sleeping in and I let her while I make a nice spread of her favorites. The oven dings, and I'm taking out some blueberry muffins, which I know she's going to love. I really like taking care of Selah and I'd love to do it for the rest of my life if she'd let me.

I hear the shower turn on, and I'm thinking about telling her today how I feel over breakfast. After yesterday, I can't be the only one that feels something here. I shoot a text to Alex and Elena in the **Fools in NY** group chat for support, and they hype me up, assuring me that everything is going to be fine, and I can do this. Okay. I can do this. Three small words that'll change everything between us once I voice them.

She comes out of the shower in a cute white short set that I can't wait to peel off. Her curls are full and defined from a fresh twist out. She smiles brightly for me, and that fuels me even more to take this leap. She walks around the kitchen with me, finally accustomed to that 'bug' that means she must be waited on hand and foot in my home. She looks and says what she wants while I fill her plate. I sit across from her at the dining table as she eats and moans around her fork and fingers with each bite that features an ingredient that surprises her. I stare admiringly as she indulges in my cooking, a favorite pastime of mine.

She is so beautiful, and I love her fucking so much.

When she finishes her breakfast, I take her plate and set it in the sink. I grab her hand, and she follows me into the bedroom. We sit on the bed facing each other, and I take her hand in mine.

"I wanted to talk to you about something important."

"Sure. Everything okay?" she says, her brows wrinkling with concern.

"Everything is fine. I promise."

She squeezes my hand, and that makes me feel even better about what I'm going to do. Like there's a small chance she may not be upset with me. I shut my eyes and take a deep breath.

Here goes nothing.

"I'm in love with you, Selah."

I breathe a sigh of relief when that sentence finally escapes my lips. I open my eyes, and her face doesn't mirror mine. She doesn't look relieved. She looks upset. She shakes her head as her eyes well up.

"No, you don't, Greyson. That's not possible for me."

No. No. No.

"It's possible for me because *I* am in love with you."

I step closer, her eyes widen, and she takes a step back. I try again, and she backs away like she fears me. She's distancing herself already.

Oh my god.

She starts getting dressed, and I feel my heart cracking with each pound in my chest. Every second that passes is more painful than the last. I wish I could take it back. We were so happy five minutes ago.

"I thought we had an understanding, Greyson. We were having fun together. Falling in love wasn't a part of the plan, and *you* agreed with me."

She's pacing around my bedroom and throwing her toiletries in her overnight bag. "Fuck. I really wish you didn't say that," she chokes. "I *really* like you, but I'm not capable of this shit. I'm not. *You are.* You've been a husband before. *You're* meant to love and be loved. I'm not. I've never been handled with care. I'm not meant to be a girlfriend. I'm nobody's wife. I'm nobody's fiancé. I'm nothing but a fucking flight risk. I stayed so fucking long that I'll bolt before I get stuck somewhere again. Running makes me feel free," she cries.

Tears stream down her face, and I want to kiss them away. Tell her how wrong she is, but I know she won't believe me. She believes these lies about herself instead of the way I see her. I find my voice, and I try with her.

"Yes, I was a husband, and I wasn't good at it. I'm a better man now because I want to be. I haven't loved anyone since my divorce. You might not know what love feels like, but *I do.* I want to love you. I want to give you everything you deserve. You can't believe any of that about yourself. I don't handle you with care? You're going to say that you had no idea I felt more? I love you so fucking much, Selah."

She stares through me, and her lip trembles. She grabs her bag, and I follow her throughout the halls, asking her to stay and talk to me. This scene is all too familiar that my stomach is turning. I hear her sniffling, and I just want to hold her, but she doesn't want that. She's walking around and putting her things in that duffle bag.

"You're leaving now?"

She's not coming back.

She doesn't want me.

I never wanted to go through this shit again, and now look.

Same song and dance, new woman, and it's all my fault. She set her terms and she was clear. I thought I could change her mind. A part of me hoped she loved me too or believed that she might be able to someday.

"I can't love you. I wish I could, but I just...can't," she manages through choked sobs.

"You don't have to love me back today, but you could love me. Can you please stay so we can talk? I love you so much that I will wait for you. I'll fucking wait, Selah. For as long as you need me to. I promise I will. There's no one else in this world for me. It's you."

"Please. Please stop saying that," she begs. "This is why I shouldn't have roped you into this shit with the fucking list. I should've just found someone on the app. That was the plan."

She throws her strap on her shoulder and opens the door. My feet follow her out because I'm not finished with this conversation.

"Maybe you should've. Except you didn't want anyone on the app, did you? You wanted *me*. Do you regret me? Us? Answer me, Selah."

I plead to her back, waiting for her to face me. She turns toward me with red-rimmed eyes, and tears stream down her face. "Don't ask me that," she sniffles.

Clifford walks past me and goes to Selah. He knows something is wrong.

Dammit.

This is exactly what I was worried about. She squats down to his level, rubbing his chin and pressing a kiss to the top of his head.

She says, "I love you, Clifford. Tell your daddy I'm sorry."

The doors open, and I whistle for Cliff. He stays put, watching Selah board the elevator. She lets out a wracked sob as the doors close, and he whines for her. A tear wets my shirt as I call for him again.

"Come on, Bud. She had to leave," I choke.

He stares curiously at me before he walks over with his head hung low. I follow him back into our apartment and shut the door behind us. I sink down to the floor with a defeated sigh as another tear falls. Clifford plops down beside me with a loud exhale.

He loved her, too.

"I know the feeling, Bud. At least we have each other."

She may not love me, but at least she loves Clifford.

63
runaway bride again?

Selah

Manhattan NY | April 20, 2024

THE DOORS open and I step onto the platform. Clifford watches me from the hallway, with a tilted head. He's confused and concerned about Greyson and me.

Me too, sweetie. Me too.

This is why rules were put in place. He was the one that was more experienced with casual relationships. He was the one that shouldn't have fallen in love. He was concerned about me coming from long-term relationships and look at what happened. I'm doing it again. I packed a go bag, and I am running. This fucking elevator cannot close fast enough. I need to get far away from here.

Greyson is in love with me. Why doesn't he understand? I can't trust *anyone* not to hurt me. Loving me simply isn't enough. It doesn't ensure my safety. Manipulation was a familiar friend disguised as love and I was the butt of the joke. I didn't know until the end that Jourdan never loved me. I was simply an easy target. Even after two years of therapy I don't trust myself not to get caught in another spiderweb. The best way to protect myself is to have strict rules and boundaries.

Grey's voice quivers when he calls out for Cliff, but he stands in the hall waiting for me. I never wanted to hurt him. My stomach turns at the cracks in his voice. I never intended to hurt anyone. This was the one time I did something selfish because I thought I deserved it, and I see now that I was wrong. I dragged him into this. We wouldn't even be here right now if I'd stayed away from him like I tried to in the beginning. The doors are closing and Cliff whines.

I'm so sorry.

A wracked sob escapes me before the doors fully shut. I'm certain he heard it. I couldn't hold it any longer. I watch the numbers descend through teary eyes until they stop on my floor. I managed to make it home without running into anyone else. I plop onto my bed and scream into my pillow. Everything was perfect. These past few months have been smooth and peaceful. Every day with him feels like a dream, so I'd be lying if I said it never felt like we were 'more,' or at least heading towards it. Then yesterday was unreal. I can't fault him for riding that high and baring his soul. He could've lied, but he didn't. He promised he wouldn't lie, and I respect it, even if I don't like the truth.

I hate how I reacted at that moment. I really care for Greyson and enjoy his company. We get along well, and this arrangement made sense, at least I thought. I'm just not capable of giving him what he deserves so I won't waste his time. He could find himself a woman that's ready to be loved and appreciate him now. He said he'd wait for me. Why? What good would that do for him? If you're ready to love and be loved, why waste time waiting for someone that isn't to eventually come around? I'm surely not worth all that trouble. I'm not healed enough, and I don't want to damage anyone's heart while mending my own.

I am chaos and Greyson is peace.

6

I don't want to hear anything about 'Stubborn Selah' right now. I need a neutral voice of reason, and that's Eric Callahan. I send off a text to see if he's down for some shenanigans today.

ME

"Do you want to get violently high and go to IKEA?"

ERIC

What's going on?

Questions!

How can I drive if I am violently high?

Also, how violent are we talking?

Cause I got this Alaskan Thunder Fuck that just came fresh from the farm.

ME

Is the Thunder Fuck violent enough to forget how I handled something?

ERIC

Selah, what did you do?

Wait. You didn't do the runaway bride again, did you?

Not with Greyson. What happened?

ME

I did the runaway bride again.

ERIC

Tell me what this man did to make you put the sneaks back on.

ME

He said he's in love with me.

ERIC

Well, fuck.

That'll do it.

It sounds more like you need the violence and adult supervision.

ME

I don't want to talk about it.

I just want to get out of here.

ERIC

Be there in twenty minutes.

Bring Oreos.

Doublestuf ONLY.

ME

Bet.

64
burgers + wine

Selah

Manhattan, NY | April 22, 2024

I FEEL like shit and called out of work today. If I'm not crying, I'm sleeping and Grey is on my mind every minute. Even my bed smells just like him and once I noticed that, I've stayed right here. I'm curled up with Peach under the covers when there's a knock at my door. She pops her head up and looks at me with the same expression.

Who could that be?

I'm nervous that it may be Greyson, but my doorbell app proves me wrong. It's just Estelle with wine and takeout? I press the mic to tell her I'll be right there. When I answer the door, I'm greeted with a smile and her lovely perfume. She wants to know if I'm free for burgers and wine. I'm pretty sure if I was busy, I'd clear my schedule for that.

"Your place or mine?" she asks.

"Mine. I have something I'd like to talk to you about. So, come on in."

She gives me an incredulous look before she enters my apartment. Once I close the door behind her, she starts whispering loudly.

"What's going on with you? You don't look like yourself and where's Greyson? Is he out of town? Finally giving your body a break?" She asks playfully.

She sets the wine bottle and glasses down on my dining table, and I grab a bottle opener to get started pouring because I surely could use it after this week.

"Yeah, he's given me a break, alright. Mostly because he told me he's in love with me, and I panicked. I'm currently avoiding him, and it doesn't help since I'm hiding in my house, and so much reminds me of him—Hold on. You got fries with those burgers?"

"You trying to insult me? Go get some plates and spill. I'll pour the wine."

I glance at my watch and wrinkle my brow in confusion.

"Um-Estelle, it's 10 a.m."

"Hush. I'm retired, and the cheese on the burger pairs nicely with that wine. Now hurry up with those plates, I'm hungry."

"Fair enough," I chuckle.

We get settled at my dining table, and I tell her everything. What's been going on with the whole neighbors-with-benefits arrangement we created a few months back, and how things have escalated in an unexpected way. How much he's helped me with the *Fuck It List*, the reading nook, the dates, and his birthday dinner. I leave the whole 'I love you' fiasco for last, hoping to get some advice from her on how to get through this because I don't know anyone else who's had a successful relationship like Estelle did with her late husband, Robert.

She gives me a knowing look for the duration of the conversation and asks to see these projects he was working on around my place. When I take her to my office and show her the reading nook, she assesses it thoroughly and even sits in my damn chair before she says anything. Then I take her to look at the mirror in my room and her silence is killing me. She walks back into my office and gets cozy in my chair. I follow behind and stand in the doorway, staring expectantly.

"So, what do you think?"

"I think that you know the answer, and you're bullshitting me. That boy loves you *a lot*. He looks at you the way Rob looked at me."

I'm taken aback by how casually she responded to that.

"I really like this chair. Could you send me the link?"

I nod. "When did you know that you were in love with Robert?"

"I trusted Robert instantly, gave it up on the first date. We said 'I love you' after two weeks and were married within a month. We celebrated thirty beautiful years together. I wouldn't change a thing," she says with a smile. "Actually, I would change something about him."

I'm curious as I await her response.

"I wish he wasn't allergic to fucking peanuts. I *love* peanut butter cups. There were so many times I almost took my husband out on accident from eating some damn candy. It was terrible."

"I don't know what I thought you were going to say, but it wasn't that," I cackle.

"I've always been a mess, but that man loved me tenfold," she sighs before pointing out, "Greyson does, too."

"Greyson isn't Robert."

"Tell me why you believe he couldn't be *your* Robert? I hope you know whatever bullshit you try to feed me; I disagree with."

"Damn. It's like that?"

"Sure is. Come sit. I've lived in this building for many years, and I haven't seen him with many women. He's all about his business, friends, and Clifford, but he met you and made room. My husband was the same way with his companies and daughter when we met. He created space for me, and that was all I needed. It's all you need, too.

What I want you to understand is that you can have it all whenever you stop standing in your own damn way. You're in your own way, Selah. Look at everything you've built for yourself. Greyson doesn't want to take anything away from you. He wants to give you more."

I step into my office and sit at my desk, swiveling in my seat to face her.

"How do I get out of my own way?"

"I think that you need to keep your word and go to that wedding. Tell him that you do want to talk about what happened and how you feel because he deserves to know. I haven't seen him around much. I'd assume he's been working from home."

That's not like him.

"Whether you love him or not, don't leave that boy in the wind. It isn't right. I'd put my foot in his ass if he did that to you."

"What's stopping you from doing that to me right now?"

"This damn chair is too comfortable, and send me that link already," she says with an eye roll.

I send her the link, and when her phone dings, she cheers excitedly.

"I'm scared, you know. I want to fix it. Not speaking to him has been torture. I miss him."

"I know. You gotta get out of your own way, girl. Greyson will hear you out, but the 'L word' you're so afraid of will cost you something you don't want to lose."

"I hear that. Thanks, Estelle."

"Of course. Now, avoiding that sweet boy isn't right, and based on what you told me about him, it might earn you some spankings. Sounds to me like you're playing with fire. Unless you like having an ass that hurts to sit on." She raises her hands in surrender. "Now you know I don't judge."

"I do like the spankings. He does follow up with a booty rub and a kiss," I admit with a shrug.

"Well, I would like that too, shit."

We break out in laughter.

I love this woman.

65
the dreaded 's-word'

Greyson

Manhattan, NY | April 23, 2024

MY RECENT SESSIONS with Dr. Pierson have been rough, but I am not giving up. Therapy isn't easy, and I'm proud of myself for finally getting to this point and sticking with it. We talked about Selah today and the upcoming wedding. She recommends I continue letting Selah have her space and of course, if she comes to me for anything, I should meet her wherever she's at.

I unpacked her reaction and keywords she mentioned so we could dig deeper into that. Overall, I'd like to make sure that I am able to love her in every way she needs it and properly. *That's* why I'm here.

Selah and I still aren't speaking to each other. I haven't seen her since she ran out of my apartment over a week ago. I must admit not having her in my daily life has been torture. My house is empty without her laughter filling it. My bed is cold without her warmth. My plants are no longer thriving in her absence. Clifford misses her and Peach. They'd become good friends and then their parents stopped talking to each other. I'm worried about him, and I hope that for all our sakes, she and I can clear the air soon.

I'm not happy she stormed out when I told her how I felt, but when I role-played this—her running away was a scenario that we discussed, so I'd be ready for any reaction. Except nothing could have prepared me for walking out. I just wish she would've stayed and talked to me. I didn't want her to leave, and I hate that she felt she had to. I have so much patience for Selah, and while I am frustrated with her, my feelings remain.

I love her on her best and worst days. She is my sunflower and always will be. Even if she never wants to see me again. Though I've gone a few days without her in my life, it's excruciating and after knowing what it's like to love her, I'll never be the same. Aileen's wedding is this weekend, and it's safe to assume she isn't going to join me. I've hoped we'd at least make up or have a conversation before then.

I don't regret how I handled things with Selah because she deserved to know the truth. I promised that I wouldn't keep anything else from her, and I meant that. Even if there is no chance that she'll love me back. She needs to know that as much as she feels she isn't worthy of love, she *is* loved. Selah doesn't allow herself to be human, and that's all I've asked of her.

I'm maintaining the working-from-home experiment without her, and it's an obvious change when she's not around, but I've made an effort to stick with it. Except I've felt terrible every day and haven't been back to the office since last week. Clifford has been enjoying my time at home, and Selah has even made sure I've been eating. She set a picnic basket outside my door yesterday and today. I'm thankful she has or else I wouldn't have eaten anything. Unfortunately, I can't even thank her since she disappears before I answer the door. Either that or I suspect she had Estelle deliver it. While we're not really speaking, she's been dropping off lunch and sweets. She sends texts to let me know there's food waiting for me, but she never explains why.

Later that day, I receive a text from her and I get

nervous when her name flashes on my screen. I'm secretly hoping it isn't about food, but I'll take what I can get because I miss her. So much. I have my fingers crossed that one day soon, she will want to talk about where we go from here.

SUNFLOWER

Hi.

I don't want you to think I don't intend to talk about what happened. I do.

Did you still want to attend the wedding together?

ME

Of course, I would, but I don't want you to feel like you have to.

SUNFLOWER

I want to.

I also made a promise I intend to keep.

Still fake dating or just friends?

I was not expecting her to say that at all. She's still down for being my fake girlfriend. I'll take it over what we've been doing. Avoiding each other has been fucking hell. If I can have her for another day, I'll never leave her side.

ME

Fake dating, but I won't ask you to do anything you're not comfortable with, Selah.

SUNFLOWER

I'd like to be there, but if you don't feel comfortable,

I understand and will stay home.

ME

I want you to see you. So badly.

Of course I want you to come.

Would you like to ride together or separately?

SUNFLOWER

I'd like to see you too.

I know we need to talk, but I just need a bit more time.

I'd like to ride together, if you can stand me.

ME

It's fine by me.

I'll pick you up at 1 on Saturday.

SUNFLOWER

I'll see you then.

How was your lunch?

I tried a new recipe.

ME

Amazing. Thank you!

It would've been better if you were here with me.

SUNFLOWER

I'm glad you liked it.

Did you give Clifford the treat I put in there?

ME

He loved it. :)

I miss you, Selah.

SUNFLOWER

I miss you too.

I start to text 'I love you,' but decide against it. She said more today than she has been. That's gotta be a good thing. Plus, I'm giving her space, and she asked for more time. I can wait. I will wait.

"Saturday," I repeat to myself. I'm unsure of how we're going to pull this off, but I wasn't going to miss another chance to be around her.

66
that dreaded 'l-word'

Selah

Manhattan, NY | April 24, 2024

TODAY'S SESSION with Dr. Garnett is unique, to say the least. I think she's hoping for a breakthrough today. We're diving into my self-sabotaging and fear of commitment. I understand now that all my efforts to protect myself have done more harm than good. When I mentioned we're still going to the wedding together, she made an interesting face and said we'd unpack that in this session. That only made me more nervous.

"Why aren't you speaking to Greyson? What happened?"

Just diving right into it, huh?

"I'm not speaking to Grey because he told me he loved me. I freaked out and ran."

She jots something down on her notepad.

"Why did you feel the need to run?"

"I don't know-I-I'm not proud of it. I just didn't know how to process anything at that moment, so I removed myself from the situation."

"And what did you do after you left? Did you allow yourself to process what happened, or did you avoid it?"

She fucking knows me. Too well, I fear.

"I got high, and Eric pushed me around in a cart at IKEA."

She writes something else in her notepad and I am growing concerned. I trust Dr. Garnett to be honest with me, but I am nervous to hear what she has to say.

I know she is going to drag me, and I deserve it.

"So, you *were* avoiding your feelings. That's all you had to say." She sits up straighter in her chair and slips her pen over her ear. "How did *you* feel after that? I don't want you to consider anyone else's feelings right now, just your own."

"I felt awful. I wanted to knock on the door and talk to him, but I convinced myself not to. I crawled in bed and stayed there. I called in sick yesterday and slept constantly, tortured with nightmares. At least when I shared a bed with Greyson, I didn't have any. He protected me, even when he hadn't known about them. I miss him. So much," I say as tears soak my shirt.

I grab the tissue box and pat my face dry. Her face softens as she assesses me.

"I know you ran and said some things you didn't mean. I'd like you to place yourself back there with him. If you hadn't run, what would you have shared with him?"

"I'd want him to know that I'm taken aback by what he just said and that I'm not angry with him. I just need a minute to think."

She nods and listens intently.

My voice is shaky with every word. "I'm frustrated because he promised he wouldn't keep anything from me, and he had to have been holding onto that for a while. I wish he had been honest about this sooner, but I imagine it was difficult for him to share, and he was probably afraid. Given everything he's experienced, it makes sense why he didn't tell me right away.

I'd want him to know that I trust him, and I'm scared too. I'm scared of getting hurt and falling for the wrong person again. There are sirens blaring in my head telling me to run, but that's not what I want to do right now."

"You're doing great, Selah," Doc says with a soft smile and encourages me to continue whenever I'm ready.

"I've never been in a healthy relationship and when I thought I loved before, it wasn't reciprocated. So, I've convinced myself that I'm not lovable so that I won't be disappointed if someone can't meet me in the middle again. I've enjoyed the casual arrangement we have because it allows us to avoid the expectations that come along with actually dating someone. Though, I believe that whatever this is that we have together is healthy." I pause and take a sip of water. "He listens and includes me in his life. He's a busy man who makes time for me even when I just want to lie down and read. He'll come over with a book and join me. We can coexist in comfortable silence. I've never had that before," I chuckle as tears fall. "Sorry," I choke, wiping my tears.

"It's okay. Take your time and if that's enough for today, we can stop," she says softly.

I nod understandably, but I'd like to keep going.

"I feel safe around Greyson, I really do. When he said he loved me, there was a part of me that didn't panic. I was excited about the possibility. Like maybe that tiny glimmer of hope could prevail over my fears for once. I've daydreamed about what it would feel like to be loved by him and I realize now that he's always made me feel loved, heard and seen...he's honestly like the men in my books."

Her brows scrunch as she takes more notes. I sip more water and stare at my keyboard.

"Selah?"

"Um. Doc, I-I think I love him too."

Her eyebrows raise and she looks over her glasses at me.

"About time. I've known this for a while, but I had to wait for *you* to get there on your own. I couldn't just give you the answer," she says with a knowing smile.

I scoff. "Well, why the hell not? That could've saved some time and embarrassment."

"As your therapist, I am here to listen and make sure you're equipped with the tools you need to advocate for yourself. I can challenge you and give you a little nudge whenever you're close, but my job is to help you trust yourself to find the answers."

"I suppose that makes sense. It's kind of annoying, though."

She chuckles and I join her.

6

I said out loud that I love him and I felt a weight lifted off my chest.

I do love Greyson. I'm struggling with accepting his love because I don't believe I can maintain it. He asked me to stay and that's what I should've done. I got frustrated and blamed him as if he did this on purpose. I know he didn't. It just fucking happened. I'd be lucky if he'd ever speak to me again. When he said those words, I got scared. My mind went back to all the times Jourdan said it and *never* meant it. 'I love you' is a cause of destruction that was once my lifeline.

Dr. Garnett suggested role playing the conversation so that I can get more comfortable expressing these feelings out loud. She'd like for me to feel confident sharing with him whether it's received positively or not. He opened his heart to me and I abandoned him. Knowing what he's been through, I don't expect him to forgive me because I wouldn't. I know I talk a lot about how I wish I was normal again, but I never was. I don't wish to be the woman I was before I met Jourdan. She wasn't brave, didn't take risks or make her own friends. Though, I'll admit whenever the world feels like too much, I lean into the remnants of her for comfort.

The goal of the *Fuck It List* was to abandon my comfort zone and see what was out there. The woman I've worked so hard to become after I left is a result of that experiment. A piece of fucking paper and some goals I wrote down. The people I've met and the love I've surrounded myself with. That very love I fear from a romantic partner I've accepted platonically. I'd like to acknowledge my 'new normal' because while I survived, I wasn't living until *now*. This may be as close as I get to being normal and Greyson loves me anyway. I know he does. He's never made me question if he'd be good to me. I always thought I wasn't good enough for him because *I'm* imperfect. I have blemishes and scars that I refuse to cover up, I wear some with pride, but not all. He's accepted me, but I haven't accepted myself.

I need to give myself permission to let him love me while I'm still a work in progress. I may never be fully healed, but Greyson meets me where I am and gives me all he's got. Imagine how much more he could do if I let him. Mama said whenever I felt it, I wouldn't be able to stop it no matter how hard I tried. I've read a lot of romance novels and while they are fiction, that part about love they do seem to get right. She wasn't lying about that.

Love doesn't give a damn if you're ready for it. When it knocks you answer.

67
wear the damn dress

Selah

Manhattan, NY | April 27, 2024

CHESS MADE a house call to help me get ready when I called her freaking out last night. I made the mistake of looking up Aileen on social media. I'm not sure what I expected her to look like, but she's fucking perfect. She's petite, thin, and beautiful. There's never a hair out of place and the woman is always ready for a photo opportunity. She's regal and classy. She's marrying a billionaire and looks the part. Like she gets invited to high tea. Greyson was once married to *that* woman. I know they met in college, and she was his first love. It was a long time ago and I understand what they say about comparison being the thief of joy.

I shouldn't even be worried. She's marrying someone else and I'm pretty sure I blew it with him. It's just that she and I couldn't be more opposite. I know I'm overthinking it, but I wonder what Greyson sees in me if that was someone he once loved and hoped to spend the rest of his life with. I consider that if she hadn't walked out all those years ago, they'd still be married. I don't know anything about Aileen other than what I found online and what Greyson has told me. I don't even know if he was happy with her, but I've created this whole situation from nothing.

I'm mentally preparing myself for my most ridiculous plan to date. Even though he professed his love, and I panicked, I promised I'd be his date to the wedding, and I fully intend to keep my word. I don't know what I was thinking texting him and using the wedding as an icebreaker. I was on a high after therapy and once he responded, I shelled up, deciding to keep it simple. I would love to tell him everything if he'd be willing to hear me out.

When I reached out the other day, I was sure he'd leave me on read, but to my surprise he didn't. Greyson is still on board and plans to be my fake boyfriend tonight. I can guarantee he'll do a spectacular job since he already does by default. I'll just need to push down these feelings about our fight and words left unsaid to match his energy and remember that it's a little game we're playing. A secret that only we know. A dream that expires at dawn. We agreed to this, so, I'll enjoy it while it lasts and be the best fake girlfriend ever. It'll be bittersweet to get a taste of what it's like to have him in that way, knowing it's likely that I won't. That's why tonight is so important. If we can get one more day, I'll cherish it forever.

"Close your eyes," Chess orders.

I shut my eyes, and she generously spritzes my face with setting spray. I fan myself until it dries, and when I open my eyes, I'm stunned. I admire my soft, glam makeup in the mirror, and I'm obsessed. Chess takes my pin curls down and applies the product before softly brushing them into soft waves. I hold my breath while she sets the style with hairspray.

Audrey sent over a dress this morning that she described as 'sickening.' It's crimson red and I told her I thought that color was a little over the top for a wedding and would outshine the bride. Then she assured me, there's no such thing as 'over the top' at a black-tie wedding. And as someone who knows the bride personally, she said, "Trust me. Wear the damn dress and walk in there with her ex-husband. Thank me later." I refrain from looking at it as it hangs on the back of my door.

Chess helps me step into the crimson full-length gown. I'm surprised to see the thigh slit, and in that moment, I am very happy I shaved my legs above the knee last night. I pull it up and secure my taped breasts into the corset bodice and she grabs the asymmetrical strap to secure it in the back.

I am so nervous to see how I look. I trust Aud's taste, but I feel like I must look so fucking snatched walking in there beside Greyson. Everyone is going to be looking at him and wondering who he's moved on with. Knowing I'm the person he wants to be with for real and we're pretending to be a couple today, it's important we look damn good together and this dress has to quiet my insecurities about myself.

"We are all secure, doll. Come see how fucking hot you look," Chess advises. "I'm going to call Aud really quick on FaceTime so she can see your final look."

She answers after two rings. "Honey, I couldn't have picked a better dress. It was made for you," she says through the phone. Her voice filled with pride.

I take a deep breath and slowly turn towards the mirror in my bedroom. The one Greyson installed, I smile to myself when I think about that and hold my eyes shut a second longer. When I open them, I'm baffled. If my makeup wasn't already done, I'd be crying. I've never worn a prettier dress in my life.

"That's why I said to thank me later. I love you, honey! I'll see you in a bit. Love you, Chess!" she says.

"Love you too," we say in unison before the call ends.

Chess gives me a moment to really appreciate how I look. I see her reflection eyeing me in the mirror.

"You still think the bride is more beautiful than you?"

I turn toward her, but I'm at a loss for words. I manage a soft smile as I hold back tears and shake my head.

"Good. Between you and me. She *never* was. Even before you got all done up."

"I love you," I say and wrap my arms around her in a hug.

"I love you too. You better not cry and fuck up my hard work," she chuckles. "However, if you do, I'm a professional and can fix it."

We're interrupted when my doorbell rings.

It's him.

Chess goes to let him inside while I make sure I've got everything I need before I go. The butterflies in my stomach are fluttering wildly and I really hope this dress isn't too much. I feel gorgeous and it's not like I would change into anything else, I'm just anxious. Once I hear his voice, my heart starts racing. I take a few deep breaths before I leave my bedroom.

When I emerge from the hallway, he takes me in with parted lips. His eyes say plenty before he does and that makes me smile wide while avoiding his intense eye contact. "Selah, you are perfection. I'm mesmerized right now. Fuck," he chuckles nervously. "I've never seen a dress like that. It's remarkable."

I'm certain I'm blushing.

He looks me over before he wraps me in a tight hug, and we stay like that for a moment and I sink into him.

"I missed you," he says softly.

His head rests upon mine and he rubs the bare skin on my back. He takes a deep breath as we pull apart and he grabs my hand. I smile at the contact because I realize how much I missed it during this time apart.

"You ready?"

I nod and take his hand as he leads me out the door.

His words replay in my head and my earlier insecurities melt away.

I'm mesmerized right now.

You are perfection.

68
meet me in the hallway

Greyson

Manhattan, NY | April 27, 2024

THE CEREMONY SHOULD'VE STARTED twenty minutes ago, but I assume that Aileen wanted to make a grand entrance *or* something wasn't to her liking and she has refused to come out until it has been fixed. I can't imagine what could be wrong as I take in my surroundings once more. This venue is straight out of a fairytale. The infamous ballroom of the Woodward Manhattan Hotel has been transformed with white and gold decor. Elegant floral arrangements of carnations and white roses trim the aisle and archways. On the far end of the room is where we'll gather for the reception. Ivory wisteria flower arrangements cascade from the ceiling. It's stunning.

I don't even want to think about what she may be putting Audrey through today. She's planned the perfect wedding, and I'll be sure to pay her in compliments because I know she is counting the minutes to be done with Aileen as a client. I wonder if they're going to exchange vows, and I'm curious to see what Korean traditions she's included in this wedding. I'll never forget how furious her parents were when they found out we had eloped.

Selah and I are seated in a row, with Henry to my left and Elena and Alex to her right. My thoughts are interrupted when my phone buzzes. I reach for it, and it buzzes again. Everyone who would be texting me is right beside me. I pull it out, and I'm surprised to see it's from the bride. Who *should* be standing before us with Daniel at this very moment.

Unsure of what this message will say, I prepare myself by taking a deep breath as I unlock my phone.

AILEEN

Can we talk for a moment?

I'm in a dressing room.

ME

If you hadn't noticed we're kind of waiting for you to come out here and get married.

It can't wait?

AILEEN

No, it can't.

Please, Grey.

She sends an emoji with pleading eyes, followed by a ping of her exact location.

I frown at my phone and sigh as I slip it into my pocket. I lean into Selah and excuse myself. I stand and try to slip out of the ceremony without attracting attention, which is very hard due to my height. Soon after I stand up, Alex locks eyes with me, concern etched across his face, and I give him a nod. He nudges Elena, and she watches me attentively before she grabs Selah's attention.

I exit the room, not without glares from her family, of course, and poor Daniel looks like he's going to vomit. The door slams behind me and I wince in response, whipping my head back and forth, making sure I'm alone in this hallway before I keep moving. Hoping Audrey is nowhere near because she'll have my head for that disruption. I pull up the **Fools in NY** group chat to tell them Aileen wanted to talk and that I won't be long. I open the thread with the bride and follow her ping until I reach the supposed room she's either stuck or hiding in. I take a deep breath and raise my hand, knocking twice on the door.

"Grey? I'm in here," she says softly.

"Are you alright? What happened?"

She turns the knob revealing a small dressing room, currently being used as an added storage closet. Littered with velvet stools and short benches.

She stands on the other side, peering up at me with red, watery eyes, and I'm surprised to see her makeup intact for the most part. Her petite frame adorns a floor-length pleated gown. Her veil has scattered pearls, and her hair is styled half up, half down, with bangs framing her face and brushed waves flowing to the middle of her back.

"What's going on?" I ask and she tries to speak but bursts into tears instead.

I close the door behind me, giving her a moment to work through these feelings before getting to the root of the issue. She softly sobs into a tissue and pats at her face before calming her breaths.

"I'm scared to fail at this again. We didn't work and we were friends at *first*. How do I know I'm not going to do this again to Dan?"

I grab a nearby stool and set it close to her, taking a seat. "We were just kids fresh out of college without a clue. I honestly think if we had waited like our parents wanted us to, we wouldn't have gotten married at all."

"I-I think so, too."

She pats carefully at her face, trying not to ruin her makeup. It will need to be touched up anyway.

She continues, "I've been thinking a lot about our marriage lately and where I fell short. I didn't give you all of me and I let you take the blame with my friends and family. I didn't have your back and you were my best friend. I told everyone it was your fault because that was easier than admitting my shortcomings. I don't have to question whether you've had my back because that's the kind of man you are. You deserved better than me and I was a coward.

I'm sorry, Greyson. I didn't fight for you. When shit got tough, I cut and ran. While you were a workaholic, you made efforts to keep things alive and I resisted. I just wanted things to be easy and once they weren't, I got scared and gave up. I know I didn't speak up before I filed for divorce. I shouldn't have blindsided you. I find myself feeling like I'm going to run again when things don't exactly go my way and he tries hard to compromise with me. I can be very stubborn at times."

I pretend to be shocked. "That's news to me."

She manages a tearful smile. "I have more I'd like to get off my chest. Please?"

I raise my hands in surrender. "The floor is yours. It is *your* day."

"Daniel's work is extremely demanding, requiring him to be overseas quite often and I don't always get the attention I'd like, but he prioritizes me. He ensures that I never go a moment feeling unloved. Being alone in the States has taken a toll on me and I've decided to split my time here and in London with him, working remotely. I'm going to make sacrifices this time around and stay the course. I don't want to make the same mistakes."

I nod, listening attentively. She places her hand over mine.

"I always knew that you loved me, Grey, but it just didn't feel this way with us. This love fulfills me. It's overwhelming, yet I crave more. I'm not certain I can handle all the love he has for me, but it feels safe and right. You know? I'm sorry, I didn't mean to-"

"It's okay," I assure her. "I know exactly what you're talking about. You and I never had that. Sure, we loved each other, but it wasn't that once-in-a-lifetime love."

"Exactly. Quite literally, I'm afraid I wouldn't be able to live without it and you created something with that beautiful mind of yours that led him to me. *SoulBlend* helped me find my person on the other side of the world. I can't thank you enough for that. Thank you, Grey." She peers up at me and her eyes well up with tears again.

"Hey. It's okay, Aileen."

She sniffs and argues, "No, it's not okay. I shouldn't have left you on your birthday. I had wanted to rip off the band aid so badly that it was all I thought about. I hadn't even known what day it was when we had that conversation, but I'll never forget it.

By the time I remembered, I was already on the ferry halfway to Jersey and wasn't sure how to apologize for what I'd done, so I didn't. It's no excuse. I'm awful and I don't even deserve this second chance right now. I really don't." She waves her hand out signaling the ceremony.

"Once again, my timing is just immaculate," she says sarcastically. "I'm so sorry, Grey. I really hope you can someday forgive me, and we can start over, working towards a new friendship. I hate how much I've hurt you."

"I appreciate that. I'd like to take the time to process everything I heard, and I want you to enjoy your day. I too have been dissecting everything I did wrong in our marriage because I am also afraid of making the same mistakes with someone new. You're not alone with that." I sigh. "Where's all this coming from?"

She sniffles, blowing her nose into a tissue.

"Therapy. Daniel insisted on it. We've been going for a year. Says he doesn't want to pass our trauma onto our future children."

My eyebrows shoot up in surprise. "Daniel's a smart man. Now, in case you've forgotten, you're getting married today, and everyone is waiting."

I grab her hand and help her stand up. She leans forward for a hug, and I wrap her in one. I press a chaste kiss to the top of her head and as we pull apart, I say, "He's the one. Let's get you out of here and in his arms, shall we?"

She smiles, still sniffling, and says, "We shall."

I turn the knob to open the door, and as we exit the closet, she says, "I saw her."

"Selah?"

"She's gorgeous."

"Tell me something I don't know." I say confidently as we walk side by side.

"Does she know that you're in love with her?"

"Yeah, I'm just waiting for her to catch up," I answer with a wry smile.

"You should get back to her. It's not a good look that you ran after your ex-wife and left her sitting alone."

"You're one to talk. It's not a good look that you left your fiancé in there waiting and asked to speak to your ex-husband in the middle of your wedding. Not to mention for a conversation we could've had at any time during the past decade."

Her response is cut off when Audrey spots us in the hallway. The flames within her irises could take the entire building down. I open my mouth to cover for Aileen then I think of how badly this looks and the words die on my tongue. She speaks for me, apologizing profusely and saying that she needed to have an important conversation before going down the aisle.

Audrey stares at her with an intensity that could burn holes through her tiny frame and says nothing. Her silence is frightening. The scene becomes more ominous once she turns up her lip and hums a tune. My heart pounds in my chest as she raises her hand slowly and I brace myself. I fear this may be the moment she opts to drag my ex out into the street for a fight as she once said. *Isn't Eric supposed to be around so things like this don't happen? Where the hell is he?* Then to my surprise, her hand stops moving when she simply presses a button on her headset. Her face is still expressionless and her hums come to an abrupt halt when she finally speaks to answer the phone.

"Still no eyes on the bride. If I do find her, she may need makeup. Can someone pay for hair and makeup to stay longer? I haven't checked the entire venue, but I'm close." She rolls her eyes as if she's annoyed with the conversation. "We won't have another code purple. You have my word," she says, sizing Aileen up while speaking as if she's not in front of her. "This bride is not a runner. If she is, I think she knows better than to run from *me*."

Her lips form a sinister smile.

Audrey in work mode is nightmare-inducing.

She parts her lips, nodding as if the person on the other end of the call can see her. Her eyes scan the hall as if she's looking for something. She nods again before pressing the button on the earpiece to end the call.

She softens her gaze on us.

She asks, "Are we having a wedding today or do I need to go out there and call it off? It wouldn't be the first time I've snuck a bride out. I support you either way because the checks have already been cleared. Your choice, honey."

She looks at me for reassurance and I nod approvingly. *Go to him.*

She inhales deeply and smiles back.

She confidently proclaims, "We're having a wedding today, Audrey. I'd like to marry that incredible man in there." She points her thumb toward the door. "I just needed to apologize to Greyson first."

She angles her head towards me and starts crying again. Audrey searches me for answers, and I simply shrug because I don't have any. Not right now, anyway.

"I'm sorry," she says again, grabbing my hand and squeezing it gently. She lets it go and tells Audrey she's ready.

"Come with me," she orders, taking off in a speed walk, swaying her arms quickly as Aileen follows close behind. I stay rooted to the spot, watching them take off, and Audrey whips her head back at me and pins me with a glare and mouths *we'll talk later.*

I expected that.

Hums fill the hallway as they descend.

"What the fuck was that about?"

Eric's tone catches me by surprise. I stand there for a moment to prepare my answer before turning around because I know it doesn't look good and he will not let up until he gets the truth. He may be Audrey's bodyguard, but he is protective of all the girls in the same way.

"I can explain."

"You fucking better."

69
nobody gets me

Greyson

Manhattan, NY | April 27, 2024

I STEPPED OUTSIDE to talk with Eric and assure him that while walking around with the hiding bride didn't look good, I was innocent. I'd never dream of hurting Selah, and I made that clear. I'm relieved we had the conversation, and it was needed, but the timing was not good. I've been trying to discuss this for a long time, but then I think about my father and how long it took him to share it with me. I know she's been making changes in her life just as I have and that it takes time.

In the middle of our conversation, I'm surprised to see Eric pull a joint from his breast pocket. He mentioned that Audrey was stressing him out and he should be able to relax since it was the weekend, but since there was the possibility of a *code purple,* the chances were slim. I recall her talking about a code purple on her headset earlier.

We won't have another code purple. You have my word.

I learned a code purple is rare and was named that for bruising. At least three times, Audrey has either threatened or incited violence at a wedding or event she hosted. The last time this occurred, it was shortly after he'd been hired. I'm curious to learn more about this, but I gotta get back to Selah. I've been gone long enough. I was able to convince Eric not to smoke before the ceremony so that we didn't smell like it. I encouraged it during the reception instead because there would at least be food, and everyone would be too drunk to notice if we were high. He loved this idea and suggested that we were already at a hotel and didn't have to drive home because his boss owns the place. *Smart man.*

I wonder if Selah wants to stay at the hotel. We could play pretend for the whole weekend instead.

It's worth a shot.

I walk back into the venue, and all eyes are on me as I stride back to my row. I resume my seat between Henry and Selah, who is doing just fine.

I reach for her hand out of habit, but she squeezes it and holds on. I smile at the familiarity, staring at our joined hands.

"Oh, babe. Elena's thinking of joining my book club," she says, regaining my focus.

I'm caught off guard by her calling me babe, but I like it.

I remind myself we're playing our roles, even in front of my friends and Henry, who already know everything.

"I think that's a great idea. You'll love the girls, and it's an excuse to give yourself a night off when there's a meeting," I say to Elena.

"Sounds good to me. I like having a valid excuse to take a night off. It makes me feel less guilty about taking a break," she adds.

That sounds very familiar.

Before I can respond, the band changes songs, and we all stand for the bride. Then, Aileen and her father appear through the doors, and the crowd gasps when they see her in her wedding dress. I instantly recognize the song and smile at the familiarity. *Young And Beautiful* by Lana Del Rey. A thread of the woman from before stitched into this new life. She's all put together again. There's not a hair out of place or a tear in sight.

The floor-length veil is carried behind her as she walks down the aisle on her father's arm.

Daniel cries as she slowly approaches the altar to be given away. I never doubted how much he loved her but seeing that was a reminder that he really *sees* her. The band stops playing when she reaches Daniel, who helps her onto the platform. He lifts her veil, and she wears a soft smile. The officiant begins their opening remarks, and we settle in for the ceremony. I wrap my arm around Selah, bringing her closer to me. She hums at my touch, and Elena's eyes track my movement, giving me a knowing look. She then taps Alex, who glances over at us with a similar expression.

They exchange their heartfelt vows, and I'm surprised to hear Daniel speaking Korean by the end of his. My eyes were dry until then. I squeeze Selah's hand as we sit through the rest of the ceremony and for today, I embrace this fantasy. I can imagine what it'd be like to stand before our loved ones and for her to say yes to me. If only for today, I'll cherish it.

"You may now kiss the bride," the officiant says.

The crowd stands, erupting in cheers and applause as Daniel dips Aileen into a passionate kiss fit for a movie ending. Their photographer quickly captures the moment before it ends, and I can guarantee that's *the* shot that'll be plastered all over the papers next week. It's a damn good one, too.

The recessional begins as the guests stand up to snap pictures and videos of the couple before they head out. They exit down the aisle hand in hand while their photographer is in place at the opposite end to snap the final moments of the ceremony. They really are a beautiful couple, and I'm excited to see these finished photos. They hired one of the best photographers in the country for this wedding, and I'm such a geek about all their equipment.

I look over at Selah, and she's eyeing me closely.

"You're salivating over that camera, aren't you?"

I could kiss her right now just for noticing.

"Is it that obvious?"

"Everything is obvious when you're paying attention," she adds.

I lean down and take her lips in a sweet kiss. She smiles and grabs my hand as we walk across the room to join Henry and my friends at our table for cocktail hour. I could get used to this. Her words replay in my head as I try to remind myself that she's just in character, but no one is in earshot.

Everything is obvious when you're paying attention.

70
in plain sight

Selah

Manhattan, NY | April 27, 2024

THE CEREMONY WAS BEAUTIFUL, and Audrey did such an amazing job with this wedding. I know she's one of the best, but I feel like this one is going to open so many doors for her. There are so many people here. I've seen celebrities and politicians. This is huge for her. I know it's been a stressful year putting it together, but this ballroom looks like heaven on earth.

When Aileen and Daniel arrived at the reception, she had changed into what Greyson had called a hanbok. Hanboks are traditional Korean clothing and are worn for special occasions like weddings, festivals, and funerals. Hanboks are a significant part of the wedding ceremony and can also have symbolic colors and embroidery to represent their wishes for their marriage. He explained to me that Aileen's is a modern take and was made to look more like a traditional wedding dress.

I loved seeing Greyson and Henry light up whenever they spotted something that was a nod to their culture implemented in the wedding. From the speeches to the food and even the table settings were written in both English and Korean. I noticed Grey getting teary when Daniel was speaking Korean during his vows, and I thought it was so sweet. He said he loves weddings, and he wasn't kidding. He leaned over to translate for me while wiping tears, and I thought about what it would be like if we were up there in front of everyone saying, 'I do,' and it didn't make me want to run for the hills.

The thought of having Grey as a husband didn't make me feel uneasy or afraid like before. I glanced at the finger that once held a band of regret and teared up at the possibility that I may not experience that kind of happiness with him because of how recklessly I've handled his heart.

After today, we've fulfilled our ends of the deal that we'd need a partner for and can go back to not speaking. The smoke of 'fake dating' will be cleared, leaving me to face the consequences of my actions. I hate it, but he gave me a chance, and I blew it. 'Don't fall in love' was the number one rule and as angry as I was with him, I'm a hypocrite. I trusted *myself* not to break it and failed. As much as I hate to say it, my mom was right. I'll never tell her that, though.

You can lay down a thousand ground rules, but if your heart wants that man, those rules won't stop shit.

Greyson hasn't taken his eyes off me all night, and it's done wonders for my confidence. I've also noticed he hasn't gone very long without holding my hand tonight, and I don't know what that's about, but I assume it's part of the game we're playing. I like it, but the voice in my head keeps reminding me that it isn't real, even though I'd rather enjoy it while it lasts than not experience it at all.

6

We sit back at the table for a moment with Alex while Henry is on the dance floor, flirting with some girls and having a good time. Alex keeps watching Greyson suspiciously, and I'm not sure what's going on between them, but I'm curious. The DJ has been doing requests for a while, so I don't think anything of it until I hear him say, "This one goes out to Greyson and Selah."

Alex raises his brows and starts chuckling to himself. I realize now *this* is what he was waiting for. Greyson waves him off and asks me to dance as Allen Stone's *Give You Blue* comes on. He takes my hand in his and guides me to the dance floor. I know everyone is watching, but I don't care if he doesn't. Other couples resume dancing, and new ones gather beside us. Even Elena drags Alex from his seat to dance with her, and now *we're* the ones chuckling. He cleverly flips us off out of her view before shifting his focus back on her. Grey holds me close and takes his free hand in mine as he leads me across the floor. I follow his footing and keep a steady rhythm, forgetting about the others around us as we enjoy this moment. Our moment.

His gaze never wavers and sends chills through me. I used to complain about the intensity of his stare. It was unfamiliar. It's jarring to encounter eyes that see you clearly after years of successfully hiding in plain sight. I don't want to go back into hiding. I don't ever want to love someone who can't see me again.

I can't trust myself not to cry, so I nestle my face into his chest. I inhale his scent out of fear that I'm running out of time to enjoy it. The lyrics of this song he dedicated to me are a vow to love someone as much as humanly possible, and I can't decipher that right now. I can't tell what's real or fake. I don't even remember what's part of our arrangement, and I made the fucking rules.

All I know is that I am hopelessly in love with Greyson Park.

I have no idea if he'd give me another chance and it's absolutely terrifying.

When the song ends, and another follows, we mindlessly sway to the music. As if he could sense the impending war in my mind, he whispers my name to free me of my thoughts. I take a deep breath as I peer up at him, meeting his adoring gaze. He dusts his thumb over my knuckles to ease me. A silent reminder that screams, *'you're not alone.'* Our eyes are locked when he leans in to claim my lips. His grip on my lower back ignites me, and I wonder if heat sears his skin with my every touch, too. When we draw back, he parts his lips to speak but is interrupted by the DJ making an announcement about the cake cutting.

6

We shower the newlyweds with flower petals as they exit the venue. The crowd has dwindled by this time of night. Daniel opens the passenger door and helps her in with her fluffy gown. She elegantly waves to everyone from the window as he gets in the driver's side. When they pull away, a *Meet the Kline's* sign decorates the rear of the vintage car. We're walking side by side into the venue, and when I peer over at Greyson, he's observing me with an unreadable expression.

"Do you hate me?" I ask, breaking the silence.

"Quite the opposite, actually."

I take a deep breath and recall everything Dr. Garnett and I discussed. I stop in my tracks and turn towards him.

"Look, I wanted to say I'm s—"

"Not tonight," he cuts me off.

Before I can think of a response, he crowds me, leaning down to press his forehead against mine. He stares into me with hunger and devastation.

"Are you ready for the night to end?"

"No," I whisper.

He hesitates. "Do you want to play pretend a while longer?"

Tears fill my eyes, and I swallow. "Please," I plead.

"Okay. I'll get us a room," he says, kissing my forehead.

He takes my hand while we wait for the elevator. Eager to be alone and play our roles when no one is watching. Desperately clinging to the fantasy that lives within these walls to avoid our harsh reality. The blanket of the moon provides comfort, whereas the exposure of the sun withholds it. We are vulnerable in the light and resilient in the dark.

The sun will rise and shed light on my flaws, demanding accountability. Tomorrow is a day of reckoning, while tonight is make-believe, and we will revel in it. I hope he'll never forget me. I could never forget him. The doors open, and I tighten my grip on his hand.

We're holding on for just a little while longer.

71
body language

Selah

Manhattan, NY | April 30, 2024

IT'S BEEN an awful few days, with the exception of the wedding. When we made it to our room that night, the air was charged. As soon as he locked that door, all bets were off. Everything was in the way, and we couldn't get our clothes off fast enough. When he kissed me, his lips set me on fire. His touch was gentle and lingering, which was another painful reminder of our expiration date. We made love that night. It was yearnful, hungry, and devastating—the kind I've read about in books that makes you sob uncontrollably. I couldn't hide my tears since he wouldn't take his eyes off me. Then held me through the night like if he let go, I'd disappear. I held on for the morning to clear the air.

Sunday wasn't my day of reckoning like I hoped. I tried to tell him how I felt again that morning, but he was firm that he wanted to play pretend until we got home. I didn't blame him for avoiding the conversation because the state of bliss felt far better than baring my soul. The ride was full of excruciating silence, but he didn't let go of my hand until we got back to our building. We held on until the very last second. It was a goodbye that left me nauseous and drained. I got to my apartment, put my phone on DND, and hid under the covers. I cried myself to sleep and only woke up to call in sick before I was out again. I lost track of time and didn't tell my friends I made it back safely. I was awakened by Audrey bursting through the door with Eric, Daya and Chess.

Friendly reminder: If you go MIA, your friends who have a key to your apartment will let themselves in, force you to shower, eat, and take your meds.

6

My thirtieth birthday is next week, and I'm not even looking forward to celebrating. Greyson has become a significant part of my life in so little time, and it's agonizing that he's unaware. He's unaware of how much I miss his smile and laugh. Or the warmth of his hand. He's unaware that he sends my anxiety running with its tail between its legs as if there's no room for that when he's present. He's unaware that my insecurities melt away underneath his gaze. He's unaware that when he's in a room with me, no one else exists. My life without Grey is lackluster, and he doesn't even know it.

In our time apart, anxious thoughts have run rampant, and every time I pick up my phone, I can't follow through. I've done cowardly things like knocking before leaving lunch outside his door and hiding instead of facing him. He's been working from home every day since the last time we did it together.

I know what I need to do, and thanks to Dr. Garnett, I'm more prepared than before. I'm going to tell him today, and he doesn't have to respond but it might be easier if he doesn't.

Greyson is honestly perfect, and it's irritating. This man has my *fuck it list* memorized. That's important since I don't. He read several romance novels to specifically find a scene that could be recreated and paired it with another task we already had planned. Then creatively found more things to tack on to help me complete my list. He's so supportive of me accomplishing my goals, even the silly ones, and that only motivates me more.

I'm such a hypocrite, and it's making me sick to my stomach. It was my rule for us to be honest with each other during this arrangement, and here I am, holding my tongue about being in love when I want to scream about it. I never disliked Greyson. He makes it awfully hard to.

He was himself from day one. His kind eyes, disarming smile, and sheer audacity. I chuckle to myself when a tear escapes me. I'm sure he sensed I didn't want to be bothered that night, but he managed to do it in a way that didn't make me feel bothered at all. Still, I was wary of him and kept our conversations short, which only led to him seeking more things to discuss with me. No matter how unapproachable I made myself, he wasn't deterred.

Then, when he walked up to me in that coffee shop, his familiar face silenced every blaring alarm in my mind. He hadn't known, but my anxiety was high that morning, and his presence calmed me. Then when he came back and turned it into a standing meeting, it made me feel cared for. He's always succeeded at making me feel that way. My thoughts are interrupted when my calendar reminds me that my workday ends in ten minutes.

I start wrapping up when Greyson crosses my mind again. As much as he's handed me his phone with the app open to change a song or introduce him to an artist, I haven't paid much attention to his music taste aside from his record collection. I realized I've never looked at his *Kiwi Music* profile and I'm desperate to feel connected to him in some way.

I don't know what his username is, so I enter his number to locate his account in our system. He appears in the search results under the username *greypark*. His profile photo is a picture of

Clifford as a puppy and my heart squeezes. I tap his profile and scroll through his created playlists, which are standard themes, like shower mix, nineties hip-hop, morning commute, etc. I peek through some of them and I'm impressed.

I keep scrolling through his account when the title of a playlist stands out to me: *Body Language*. I'm hesitant to look through it because I assume it's a sexy playlist filled with songs he's played for other women. I suppose I'd rather hurt my own feelings since my cursor is hovering right over the playlist. Suddenly, my alarm sings as a reminder to log off and startles me, causing me to jump. I should take that as a sign to stop being nosy, but I don't. I take a deep breath and brace myself to see what songs Greyson likes to play in the bedroom. I close my eyes and click on it anyway, nervous about what I may see. I slowly open my eyes, and to my surprise, I couldn't have been more wrong.

My breath catches and I cover my mouth in awe as I take in the songs on this playlist. These songs don't have anything to do with him, but they are *very* familiar to me. So familiar that I have them tattooed on me. And since one is dedicated to an entire album, that's here as well. Tears stream down my face as I sit and stare at the screen. He was asking about them for months and I wondered why. He never mentioned the music after the fact, so I assumed he didn't listen to it. I select the *info* tab to find the date he created this out of curiosity. *September 26, 2023*. I pull out my phone and check my notes app to see if I documented anything from September twenty-sixth last year, and I did.

September 26, 2023

I went to the coffee shop today. Week three. Anxiety was through the roof, and this shit isn't getting easier. I wanted to give up and go back home. I would've, but Greyson walked up to my table and asked to join me. I'm certain he was late for work because he sat with me for about forty-five minutes. He observed me while I worked, and I didn't mind it. I didn't mind him. He noticed my hand tattoos and asked about them. "I'll give them all my attention. Trust me." I went home around lunch, and while I had help today, I did it. He says he'll join me next Tuesday and I really hope he does.

I consider sending him my journal entry on this day to break the ice, but I'm shaking.

WWAD?

She'd speak up no matter what, and that's what I need to do.

Here goes nothing.

72
knock on wood

Selah

Manhattan, NY | April 30, 2024

IT'S BEEN an hour since I discovered the playlist, and I'm stress-cleaning while I hype myself up. Greyson loves me, and I love him. So much. I kneel and swipe under the couch when I come across a toy of Clifford's. I miss that big guy so much. My eyes fill up with tears, and I blink them away as I rise to grab my phone. I need to talk to Greyson, and I need to do it before it's too late. I have no clue what to say, but before I know it, I am copying and pasting that journal entry into the text box. I hover my hand over the send button, count to three, and mash it.

My heartbeat is all over the place as I clutch the phone in my hands—a literal lifeline. Moments later, I watch in anticipation as three dots appear and disappear. I opt for setting my phone face down and walking away before my nerves get the best of me. I start stress cleaning to keep myself busy while I wait. I jump when my phone chimes back-to-back. I'm nervous when I turn my screen over and see his name. I open the thread and find three links to *Kiwi Music* playlists.

He sends the link to the *Body Language* playlist, then another one called *Songs For Selah*. The description states, 'songs to make the coolest woman in the world fall in love with me.' I chuckle, but this is a damn good playlist. If I didn't already love him, I could be persuaded. The last link is for a playlist titled *Morning Commute.* My heart skips as I scroll through each song I've sent him for his daily commute over the past few months. More texts filter in, and my anxiety heightens.

SMELL GOOD MAN

In case you needed more supporting evidence. I love you, Selah, but if you're about to ask to just be friends, I can't. It's hard enough living near you and having to stay away.

I know you don't love me back, but I just hope one day you'll allow yourself to be loved. Because you deserve it just as much as you think I do.

Tears drip onto my shirt as I reread those messages over and over. Unsure of what to say, but he thinks I don't love him, and he couldn't be more wrong. I never needed more supporting evidence. It's evident in every action, touch, and word that he expresses. Greyson cherishes me. Simply knowing him has sent me to unknown heights. He loves me in ways I never thought possible. This love isn't constricting or stifling. Nor have I had to alter myself to appease him.

We're a perfect fit because we don't try to do what everyone else thinks we should. We make our own fucking rules—and break them, but shit happens. I think the lesson here is that rules are overrated, or what Mom said about love knocking unexpectedly. That's it. I have a lot to say that he needs to hear in person. I start typing, chewing my lip in the process.

"I can do this," I say out loud, chanting softly.

ME

Greyson, I believe you and I don't want to be just friends either.

You don't know how I feel and men aren't usually right. Remember?

SMELL GOOD MAN

Of course I remember.

ME

Are you home?

SMELL GOOD MAN

I am.

I leave in a hurry, hit the twelfth floor on the elevator, and study the numbers as they ascend. Something that usually brings me calm turns my stomach.

Seven, eight, nine, ten, eleven, twelve. Ding.

The doors open, and I speed down the hall. My steps falter once his door comes into view. I raise my shaking hand to knock twice on his door. I step back and wait. I hear his feet shuffle against the hardwood floors. He whips the door open and stares at me with concern. He steps out into the hall and closes the door behind him. My heart lurches at the possibility of not seeing Clifford.

"What are you doing here, Selah?" he asks curiously.

"I owe you an apology, and I'd like to talk about us…now."

"Let's hear it," he challenges, crossing his arms and leaning against his door frame.

"Love doesn't give a damn if you're ready for it. When it knocks, you answer," I blurt.

He wrinkles his brows and stays put, hearing me out.

"That was something my mom said, but–uh–stay with me. I said some things I didn't mean, and I'd like to apologize. Before you slam that door in my face, I want you to know that I do love you, Greyson. I wasn't prepared for you. I didn't even get a warning. You actually didn't knock on my door at all. You used a battering ram and brought donuts," I chuckle and sniffle.

"It's impossible not to fall for you, the beautiful man you are. You are the first person to really see me and love me wholly. I've spent most of the time I've known you trying to convince myself that you're just a figment of my imagination. While you've proven to be very real, I could argue that you are a fictional man in real life."

"Tell me something I don't know," he jokes.

"I don't regret you, and I couldn't if I tried. I don't know what it's like to truly be loved by someone, so I panicked. I shouldn't have ran, and I don't expect you to forgive me, but I want you to know that I am sorry. I am so far from perfect, but I at least wanted to be somewhat close before I bothered somebody with my chaos. However, you're a moth to my flame."

"But you didn't burn me. Loving you isn't fatal, Selah. It's worthwhile. *You* are worthwhile. Contrary to what you believe."

I sigh. "I don't know what the hell I'm doing, Greyson. I've never done this…but I want to, with you. If you'll have me."

"We're going to learn together." He pushes off the door frame and makes it to me in two strides. My breath hitches as I peer into his eyes. His large hand angles my chin upward and stares adoringly. "Are you going to let me love you, Selah?"

"Yes. You know, the night we met, that was so rude of you to interrupt me while I was reading. You are so lucky I didn't kic—"

He cuts me off with a carnal kiss. I meet each stroke of his tongue, moaning softly. His hands explore me as he pulls me plush to him and lifts me off the ground. Nothing exists beyond us, and I need him *now*. We eventually come up for air and I remember what I forgot to say. "Wait. I have fun facts for you."

He chuckles against my lips and sets me down on the ground.

"Well, you know I can't resist fun facts."

"Your presence calms me down when I'm anxious. Every

single time."

His eyebrows raise in surprise before he presses a kiss on my forehead.

"I have a few more," I say, holding up a finger. "The coffee shop experiments weren't working until you joined me. Mama Bailey thinks you're meant to be my husband and insists that when we marry, it must be an *Audrey Wood* wedding. Last one. I miss Clifford *and* his Daddy."

He grips my waist and takes my mouth, moaning as we compete for dominance, and I eventually succumb. Heat pools low in my belly, and that's when I realize we're still in the hallway. I nip at his lip as I taper off the kiss, peering into his ravenous gaze. His tone is gravelly and full of desire.

"I know you, and that interrupting kink has something else to say. Tell me, baby," he encourages.

Ugh. I love this man.

"I do. Grey isn't a fitting name for someone who's brought so much color into my life."

He scoffs. "Oh really? What would you prefer, Sunflower?"

I place my finger on my chin and hum softly as I consider. "Smell Good Man," I proclaim.

He vibrates with laughter. "I knew I heard you call me that when you were drunk once." He backs up to his door and turns the knob. "Would you like to come in? Fun fact: I have a big red dog who misses *you* very much. His dad does, too. More than you know."

"I thought you'd never ask."

73
fingers crossed

Greyson

Manhattan NY | May 6, 2024

I'VE BEEN WORKING on Selah's birthday plans with Audrey for a few weeks now, and I'm so nervous. She's assured me that Selah will love it, but I can't help but be worried about something going wrong. Everything must be perfect, and I can't blow this. This is going to be my big grand gesture, and I'm stressed about it. When she told me she loved me back, she made me the happiest man alive, and now she's mine, for real.

I asked her officially if she'd be my girlfriend, and she said yes. I feel like a kid again with her, and I just want to make her happy and reassure her that taking this chance with me was a good decision. I believe how I celebrate her birthday will give her a little glimpse of what this relationship will look like. She needs to know that her heart is safe here and that she will always be a priority to me. I wanted to do something big to prove how much I love her, and I hope everything goes to plan. I made it a goal to make the woman who hates surprises change her mind and adding a little romance should do the trick.

I fire off a text to make sure she's prepared for tonight while resisting the urge to give her any clues. I know the way her mind works so she's going to be trying to figure it out, but she won't. Audrey assured me this plan was perfect, and she wouldn't suspect a thing. If there's anybody who knows Selah best, it's her. I take deep breaths and start the shower, hoping to melt away my stress about tonight. Everything is going to be perfect. It has to be.

74
love of my life

Selah

Manhattan NY | May 6, 2024

GREYSON SENT me a vague text earlier telling me that our date tonight will be split into two parts. I should pack an overnight bag, comfy sneakers for walking, a change of clothes, and my passport. I'm not sure why, but alright. I pack everything he tells me, and I get dressed for the first part of our date. I have no idea what he's planning, and as much as I don't like surprises, I'm oddly excited to see what's in store tonight.

I text him when I'm on my way upstairs and he advises me to let myself in while he finishes getting ready. Greyson gave me a key to his apartment when he had to go out of town a few weeks ago to look after Clifford, but he didn't take it back. I offered it to him, and he said that it was mine now. When I get settled in his apartment, I smell something delicious cooking and follow the scent. I'm very shocked to find a chef instead of Grey in the kitchen. I am practically salivating over how good everything smells. I greet him in the kitchen, and he introduces himself as Marco Aguilar, of *Aguilar's*. I'm excited to see what he makes. I hate surprises but he and Elena sure can cook. I step away and call for Clifford because he didn't charge me when I walked through the door. He's not coming when I call for him either.

Grey appears from the hallway dressed in a navy sports coat, matching slacks, a white silk shirt, and loafers.

He looks as sexy as he did the night we met.

"You're awfully dressed up to be in the house tonight, sir."

He looks at me with a devious grin, scooping me up in an embrace as his lips take mine in a greedy kiss. Before he pulls away, he says in my ear, "Now, Princess, you know I prefer *Daddy* over sir."

His laugh vibrates through me, and I feel heat pooling between my thighs at the sound of *Daddy* on his lips.

"Where's Clifford? He never ignores me." I wrinkle my brows in concern.

"Oh. He's with Alex tonight. I wanted us to have the house to ourselves, and he tends to steal you when you come over. Not that you seem to mind."

"I don't mind at all. I love Clifford."

He places a kiss on my forehead and says, "I'll have him dropped off in the morning so you can spend the day with him." He looks at me expectantly. He wants me to be comfortable, always. I get the feeling that if I wasn't, he'd drop everything to pick him up now if that's what I wanted.

"That'll be perfect. I'll make him mini pancakes."

He tuts. "You are not lifting a finger on your birthday, and we're not going to argue about it. I have breakfast arranged as well."

He strides over to the candlelit dining table, decorated and set to perfection. I notice fresh sunflowers as the centerpiece, and my eyes well up at the sight. I'm not sure what to say and I'm in awe of what he's already done so far. I can't imagine what else he's planned.

"Because I know you're not a fan of surprises, I had Audrey help me with printing menus for tonight's meal so that you can at least have an idea of what I plan to serve you. We made an itinerary, too. It doesn't spoil what I have planned but gives you enough to expect a night of romance. I'd like to ease any anxiety you have and make this a night to remember."

I'm speechless and rooted to this spot. I admire the effort he's put into this date, and it hasn't even begun. Asking Audrey to help, which couldn't have been hard because she loves playing matchmaker and doesn't know what to do with herself if she isn't planning something. Designing an itinerary so that I don't have anxiety over whatever surprise he's got up his sleeve? I've only read books about men who are this kind and attentive.

I may not make it through the night without shedding tears. I appreciate all the effort he's put in, and the night has only begun. He sits at the end of the table when Marco advises us that dinner is almost ready. He insists I sit beside him, and once I do, he grabs my hand. He seems nervous and that's not like him. I'm sure it's whatever he's planned for us tonight.

We enjoy dinner by candlelight and it's straight out of a book. It's dreamy and peaceful, while the sight of him in that suit has me wanting to be tossed over his shoulder and carried to the bedroom. He stares adoringly at me and butterflies flutter in my stomach. My mind swirls with countless questions, but I don't want to douse the flame burning brightly between us. My surprise dinner was pizza and pasta, all a girl needs in life. When he set it in front of me, I burst out laughing. After dinner, he mentions we should get ready for the next part of the date. We change into sweats, grab our passports, and board the elevator hand in hand. Grey warns that he's going to blindfold me and it's a part of the surprise. It makes me uneasy but I trust him. Once he's tied it, he rubs his thumb over my knuckles to soothe me and resumes holding my hand. The elevator dings and he guides me through the lobby.

A familiar voice greets us outside. It's Eric.

"Alright, bird box. Watch your head," he jokes, helping me into the backseat.

I cackle in response.

Why is he here? Is he driving us somewhere? What is Greyson up to?

Eric speaks when he opens my door, telling me to be safe and he'll see me soon before sweeping me into a hug. When he lets me go, Greyson warns he's going to remove the blindfold and I brace myself. I'm shocked that we're standing on a tarmac with a private jet waiting for us. I don't have to guess who was responsible for this one. I'm just not sure where we'd be going that requires this. We board the jet and the flight attendant makes sure we're all set before takeoff. I cozy up in my seat and rest my head on him once the plane takes off. I dozed off for a bit and thankfully it was a short flight.

Did I just hear the pilot say we're in Buffalo, NY?

Did he do all this so I could see Niagara Falls?

You've gotta be kidding me?

"Greyson?"

He glances over at me and lifts his brows in question.

"Why are we in Buffalo?"

"I'll answer that question in the car, baby. We don't want to be late."

There's a black SUV on the tarmac and a driver waiting. He's broad-chested and wears a suit, tattoos coat his brown skin and are visible on his neck and hands. He introduces himself as Royce, a regular driver of Avery's and he shares that he will be driving us to Niagara Falls and back to the airport this evening. After we settle into the backseat, I look over at Greyson and he's got a goofy smile on his face. I give him a few minutes into the drive to start talking, and I get antsy when he doesn't.

"Will you tell me why we're going to Niagara Falls now?"

"Honestly, I can show you better than I can tell you." He wraps his arm around me to pull me closer to him and says softly, "I know you hate surprises, but I need you to trust me."

"I do trust you," I whisper back and rest my head on his shoulder.

When we reach The Falls, Royce tells us he knows where to

get a good view, and we've got good timing. When we park and he lets us out, he locks up and walks with us.

"I'm going to let y'all have some privacy, but I took this gig specifically so I could see this show. I drove six hours from Philly," he says excitedly.

"Alright, man," Grey says with a chuckle and glances at his watch.

"What is he talking about? There's a show?" I ask.

He quickly stands behind me and holds me close. I relax into his touch as we take in Niagara Falls at night.

"Wait for it."

A lighthouse shines onto The Falls, illuminating it with an array of colors and it's staggering. It's unlike anything I've ever seen.

"This is what I wanted you to see."

I'm mesmerized by the vibrant colors dancing across the waterfall. Eye-catching patterns and transitions brighten the attraction, and I cannot look away until the show is over. I'm overwhelmed with emotion right now. The sheer thoughtfulness and planning that went into this is amazing. I'm at a loss for words.

This is the love I deserve.

"Where did you come from?" I ask dreamily.

"Brooklyn."

We burst out laughing. He leans in close, pressing his forehead to mine. "I love you, Sunflower."

He takes my lips in a mind-numbing kiss and glances at his watch again when we take a breath.

"Let's go home. My birthday girl needs to be worshipped," he says matter-of-factly.

Yes Sir.

6

Once we touch down, Eric is waiting for us, leaning up against a black SUV with a toothpick hanging from his mouth.

"Happy Birthday, baby," Greyson says in my ear as we approach the vehicle.

"Thank you for making it special."

"Oh, I'm not done yet," he adds with a kiss to my cheek.

Eric helps us into the car and wishes me a happy birthday. Grey is teasing me with a still hand on my thigh, occasionally kneading it.

I'm going to make him pay for that.

Greyson and I rush into the lobby with hurried steps, still holding hands while we wait for the elevator. It dings and opens to a completely empty car. He gives me a mischievous look before I follow him inside. He taps the twelfth floor, and then his lips are on mine, desperate and hungry for more. He devours my moans as soon as they escape me, deepening the kiss until we come up for air. We don't stop until the elevator opens. We dash to his apartment and barely get through the front door before he presses me against it. He trails his tongue along my neck and nips at my jaw, hovering his hand over my aching pussy.

"Can I taste you?"

"Yes, yes," I breathe.

I kick off my shoes and start slipping out of my pants when he tuts.

"I didn't give you permission to take off your pants, baby. Pull them back up."

I scoff as I do what I'm told.

"Good girl."

75
selah for dessert

Greyson

Manhattan, NY | May 6, 2024

I PEPPER kisses along her neck and jaw as I cage her in. I won't touch her yet. I want to so badly, but I'm dragging this out. She's finally mine, and she loves *me*. We've celebrated her all night, and that won't stop now.

My Selah.

My sunflower.

I'm so in love with her.

I slowly raise her shirt and trail my tongue from her navel to her chest. When she whines, I chuckle against her skin. I love how frustrated she gets when she's eager for me. I lift the shirt over her head and hold eye contact with her as our chests rise and fall. I lean in to take her lips between my teeth with a gentle bite and resume my torture. I remove her bra and drag my tongue across her breasts, eagerly taking her stiff peaks into my mouth before the fabric hits the floor. She throws her head back in pleasure, and I decide not to give her a hard time. My hands generously knead and explore her soft curves as her whimpers fill my apartment.

When I slip off her sweatpants to reveal a lacy blue thong

that matches her bra, I curse at the sight of it. I can't get over the fact that she looks amazing in every fucking color. I have her turn around to give me a full view, and when she faces the wall, she extends her arms above her head and then pokes her perfect ass out, expecting a smack. I give her exactly what she wants, and she moans against the door.

I drop to my knees to soothe the sting with a gentle kiss. I instruct her to turn around, and once she does, I tug at her thong. I groan at the sight of the lace as it clings to her wetness. I slip it further down her thighs to reveal a needy pussy, impatiently waiting for my attention. Trailing kisses down her legs, I drag the fabric down to her feet. I ball the panties in my fist and take in her lovely scent before tossing them behind me.

When I place one of her legs on my shoulder, her eyes widen. Languid strokes of my tongue greet her entrance, and she arches her back in response. My hands travel up her thighs, squeezing her ass as I hum against her. Desperate to have her closer, I bury my face into her center, giving that sensitive bud the attention it deserves. I twist my tongue around her other hole, and she wails. What once made her shy has her digging her nails in the door and begging for more.

My eyes are locked on hers when I suck her clit into my mouth, and she bucks against my face. I reach up and pinch her taut nipples, one at a time, to drive her wild.

"Fuck, Daddy. Please don't stop," she sobs.

That's my dirty fucking girl.

When she reaches her brink, she throws her head back and balls her hands into fists. Her screams echo through the room as her thighs squeeze around me. I lap at her pussy while she shudders on my tongue.

"Fuck," she exclaims with a chuckle, looking down at me with hungry eyes. "You had enough?"

"Not even close."

I carefully set her leg down and rise to stand. She wraps her arms around me and claims my lips in a devouring kiss, loving to taste herself on my tongue. My hands roam her body until I grip her thighs and pick her up. She giggles against my lips as I carry her further into my kitchen. I set her naked body on the marble island, and she gasps at the coolness, leaning back on her hands to watch me undress. I remove my shirt, toss it behind me, and kick off my sweats, leaving on my boxer briefs. Her eyes drop to my straining erection, and I reach for my wallet to pull out a condom, but she stops me with her hand.

"I want to feel you. I don't want anything between us."

I'm trying to process what she said, but it's really hard to understand when she's sitting on my counter naked. I think she said she doesn't want to have anything between us. I haven't gone bare since I was married. I want nothing more than to feel her too. *Fuck.*

"Are you sure?" I ask, searching her face for any hesitation.

"I'm sure. I know we already talked about it, but nothing's changed on my end. I've only been with you, and I have an IUD."

"Nothing's changed here either. I've only wanted to be with you."

"Good. Then fuck me," she orders with flames stoked in her irises.

She hops off the counter and bends over, spreading her ass to reveal that glistening pussy for me. I murmur curses in approval and drop my boxer briefs, pumping myself twice. I tease her entrance, rubbing and slapping my dick against her aching core.

When she begs, I finally line myself up and thrust inside of her tight heat. She gasps as I hold onto her hips and her back arches. My hips crash against her plump ass as I pound into her from behind.

"You feel incredible, baby. Fuck."

She grips the edge of the counter as she throws her ass back onto me. She knows how much I love that. There's a silent plea for more, and I oblige with merciless thrusts.

"Such a good girl for Daddy."

I spank her ass, and she moans louder. Her orgasm rips through her, and I feel her pussy spasm around my dick. She digs her nails into me as she rides it out. I follow behind, spilling warm jets deep inside of her. I wrap my arms around her waist and hold her from behind as we catch our breaths.

I slip out of her slowly and pick her up. She nuzzles into my neck as I carry her through the hallway and into the en-suite. I set her on the counter and clean us both up, stealing kisses in between. I give her privacy and wait for her to join me in bed. She climbs in bed beside me, resting her head on my chest, and she hums contentedly.

"Do you still hate surprises?"

"Ask me tomorrow. Something tells me you've still got plans." She chuckles.

I glance up at the clock on the wall, and it's after midnight.

"Happy birthday."

"Thank you." I feel her smile against me. "I love you," she says softly as her finger gently traces the *durumi* tattoo on my arm.

"I love you too, Sunflower."

76
selah for breakfast

Selah

Manhattan, NY | May 7, 2024

THE SUN FILTERS IN, and I blink my eyes open. Greyson's arm is draped over me, caging me in. I lean into him and feel his erection poking my back. Flashbacks of last night are fresh in my mind, and I wiggle closer to his chest, getting poked again. A moan escapes me, and as I reach to cover my mouth, Grey grabs my hand. "Don't hide your moans from me," he asserts.

My panties dampen at the rumble of his voice in the morning. Still feeling his hardness jutting my back, I roll over to look at him, and there's pure hunger in his eyes. "Happy birthday, Princess."

I know I'm gazing at him like a lovesick teenager, but I can't help it.

"Thanks, Daddy."

"C'mere," he urges, enveloping me in his arms while he peppers my forehead with soft kisses. I indulge in the attention and his scent.

"Do you mind if I take care of this?" I ask, looking down at his straining dick in his boxers.

"I do mind. Did you think I was lying when I said I didn't want you lifting a finger today?"

"But I want to, and you're supposed to let me have whatever I want today. Your words, not mine."

"Well, I can't argue with that. What do you want, baby?"

"Right now? You. Then I want breakfast and to relax with my pets today."

"*Your* pets? You're adopting my son now?" His eyebrows shoot up in surprise.

"I sure am."

He leans forward, taking my chin in his hands, and says, "I will fuck you, feed you, pick up *our* kids, and do whatever you ask for the rest of the day. How's that sound?"

"Whatever I ask? A girl could get used to that kind of treatment."

"Get used to it, Sunflower."

I lean in to meet him in a soft kiss, and as we pull apart, I lock eyes with him and whisper, "I love you."

I still can't believe it.

I'm in love.

"I love you, too," he assures me, adoration in his gaze. I aim my chin up, and he steals a kiss that silences my thoughts. It's rough and passionate—he squeezes the back of my neck, and I let out a moan as I reach out for him. I tease my fingers over his bulge, signaling how desperate I am to taste him. He growls into my mouth, and I capture it, nipping at his lip when we come up for air.

I drink him in, and I'm enraptured all over again.

Greyson loves *me*.

I plan to cherish this, but right now, I want to enjoy this time before our day begins. I lay back, lifting my hips to slide my panties off. His gaze sets my body on fire.

I move to toss them on the floor when I get an idea. I'm reminded of the time he threatened to gag me with my panties, and I'm intrigued. I stretch forward as if I'm going in for a kiss when I demand he opens his mouth for me. He obliges, and I ball up the panties in my hand and place them in his mouth. He feigns surprise but moans with a full mouth.

"Good boy," I say, taking a page out of Audrey's book, and he whimpers as he waits for my next move. I sit up on my knees and crawl down the bed, making a show of it before I settle between his legs.

I curl my fingers into the waistband of his boxers, and his dick springs free. My mouth waters at the sight. I shuffle around on the bed as I tug them off. He lifts his hips to make it easier for me, and I toss them aside.

He lays back, folding his hands behind his head. I bend over and arch my back, giving him a nice view of my curves. I wrap my hands around his dick, stroking softly as I flatten my tongue, working him into my mouth. He throws his head back as his muffled moans fill the room. My thighs become slick with arousal from how vocal he is. I love how he responds to me when I take charge. I remove my mouth and spit on his dick, stroking it with one hand and taking him deeper into my mouth. His hips jut up as he fucks my throat. I'm overwhelmed with the need to touch myself, and my core is throbbing.

I don't fight the urge to gag because he loves it. He slows down his movements, and I take him deeper while gradually moving my lips up the shaft, sucking harder as I reach the tip. I reach down to my core to rub soft circles around my clit and moan around him. His fists ball up with the sheets, and his moans grow louder, giving me the silent praise I crave.

I remove my mouth again and twirl my tongue around his tip when I hear clattering in the kitchen. My eyes widen in shock, and I stop abruptly. Concern etches across Greyson's face once I sit up and listen harder. "Um, baby?"

"Yes?" he attempts in a muffled response. When he hears himself, he removes the panties and holds them in his hand.

"It sounds like there's someone in the kitchen."

His thick brows wrinkle when he asks, "What time is it?"

I glance over at the clock on his nightstand and see it's 10:15 a.m.

"Oh, that's the chef making us brunch. I told her to get here around ten," he responds calmly, like that was a normal thing to say.

I whisper-shout, "Are you being serious right now? Grey, what chef has a damn key to your house?"

"The *Elena* chef, who also doubles as my best friend," he adds matter-of-factly. His eyes rake over me, satisfied with my outfit choice. I'm only wearing a shirt, *his* shirt.

A devious smile stretches across his face. "Now, where were we?"

"Grey, what if she hears?"

"She isn't going to care. Trust me. Since when do you care if someone hears, Princess? You think Estelle doesn't hear what I do to you? She's right next door."

I feel myself blushing. "So *that's* why she looks at you like that."

"She hears me do filthy things to her neighbor and flirts every chance she gets."

"Is that right? I suppose I need to work on my volume then. I'm certain she's more experienced than me," I say teasingly.

"You don't need to work on anything." He ponders, then adds, "in fact, if you're open to feedback, I—"

I silence him when I toss a pillow at his face.

"Okay, okay," he says while chuckling, raising his hands in surrender. "I was just going to say I think you could benefit from making even more noise for me."

"Sure, you were," I answer with an eye roll.

"Are you really going to start lowering your voice when I'm inside you from now on?"

He looks at me with sad eyes and a pout to match.

"No. I don't think I have much control over my volume when you're touching me," I admit.

"That's what I thought. You like being loud for me anyway."

I scoff. "Now, who's the brat?"

He winks and challenges, "Remind me how well you take me in that pretty fuckin' mouth."

His eyes are heated, and I've never been more anxious to please him.

"Put those panties back in your mouth, and we've got a deal."

"I love when you boss me around," he says before quieting himself with the panty gag.

Wet heat pools from my core as I peek over my shoulder at the door again and hear the faint music coming from the kitchen.

Fuck it.

If he says she doesn't care, then I won't either.

I bend down to lower my mouth on him, hollowing my cheeks and inching closer to his base. I inhale and exhale deeply as I guide him further into my throat. I bob my head up and down as my hand strokes him, watching his eyes roll back while he whimpers and moans in pleasure, praising me in a way only he can.

His grip on the sheets is unrelenting and I know he's close. I take a second and decide I'd like to savor this moment of him relinquishing control to me.

I stop abruptly, removing my mouth and peppering kisses along his dick, trailing them over his thighs. I wear a mischievous grin, taking a play out of his book to deny his orgasm. The look on his face tells me that I'll be paying for that later.

I can't wait.

I climb up the bed toward him. Once I'm close enough, he grabs my hips, placing me on his lap. He guides me forward until his dick is pressed against me. I grind into him, seeking my pleasure, and I can't help the moans that escape me.

His eyes darken as he watches me use him, pinching my nipples as my rhythm increases.

"Oh, god," I cry out.

He encourages me silently, his chest rising and falling. I lean forward, removing the panties from his mouth, and he lets out a sigh of relief but never takes his gaze off me.

"Use me to make yourself come, baby."

I nod in understanding and pick up my pace as I feel the sparks building in my lower back, the brink of my orgasm intensifying.

"Fuck," I wail.

"Give it to me, Princess. You're doing so fucking good," he urges.

My body thrums at his praise as if it's all I need to hear to finally let go. The wave rushes over and takes me entirely. He digs his fingers into my hips while I scream his name, then sits up and wraps his arms around me. I slump into him, catching my breath in his neck.

He rubs my back with one hand, kneading my ass with the other. He presses soft kisses across my shoulder and coos in my ear, "Such a good fucking girl."

If I could come from words alone, that would certainly do it.

I lean back to take him in, and when our eyes meet, he greets me with a soft smile. I think back to last night, and I'm in awe of the fact that this man is not only real, but he's *mine.*

"Hi," I say softly.

"Hey." He leans forward, placing a kiss on my nose, and I giggle in response. "You're breathtaking. Do you know that?"

"I didn't know that," I state, sarcasm heavy in my tone.

"You and that mouth." He nips at my lip playfully. "I love when you're a brat."

"I know."

He slaps my ass hard enough to leave a mark, and I nuzzle into his neck and moan through it. His large hands smooth over it to soothe the sting. "I suppose I earned that," I say, muffled against his skin.

"Sit on my face, Selah," he orders in my ear.

"But what about breakfast?"

"Your cum on my tongue will hit the spot," he says playfully.

My jaw drops, and I gape at him as he lays back to assume the position.

"C'mon, birthday girl," he commands before reaching under my thighs to guide me forward, my wetness trailing across his stomach. I remove my shirt, tossing it on the floor.

He tries to pick me up and place me on him, but I argue, "Stop using your weight against me. I can climb you all by myself."

"Then do it. Now."

I sit up on my knees and lower myself over him, grabbing onto the headboard for leverage. I feel his breath on me and goosebumps erupt all over. I take a deep breath to prepare myself as I've never done this before.

He grumbles beneath me and chides, "You're hovering. I said sit on my face. I won't tell you again."

"But I don't want to hurt—"

He grips my waist and hastily seats me onto his face, stopping my argument as quickly as it began, greeting my entrance with a plunge of his tongue.

"So eager," I taunt, repeating his earlier words, and he chuckles against my clit, sending vibrations through my body.

He devours me, and I start to lift myself off him, overwhelmed with pleasure, when he stops me by holding my thighs in place as he carries on. He moans between my legs as he consumes me.

My legs begin to shake, and I hold onto the headboard for leverage while he laps greedily at my pussy as if he hadn't had enough of me the night before.

I don't think he could ever get enough of me.

Nothing compares to Greyson's tongue on me. As it swirls around my clit and flicks it, my moans and cries fill the room. Wrapping his lips around my sensitive nub, he sucks eagerly, not letting up.

"Grey, please?" I manage through shaky breaths before I sob, "please don't fucking stop."

I dig my nails into the headboard and begin grinding against his face. He groans in approval and spanks me.

"Ride my face, baby. Be a good girl and come on my tongue."

Lifting his hold on my thighs, he reaches up to tease my stiff peaks with a brush of each thumb. He pinches them hard, and I cry out in response.

My orgasm hits me like a freight train, and I succumb to it. My grip on the headboard doesn't waver as my vision blurs and my senses heighten. When I come down, I see stars and hear my screams of pleasure.

He relentlessly feasts on me as I grind absentmindedly on his tongue. Hoping to restore my breath, I breathe deeply and try to rise up, but my legs are weak. I lean onto the headboard to relieve him, and I whine in defeat. He follows with a teasing laugh.

"Remember when you told me to stop using my weight against you? I bet you'd really appreciate it now, huh?"

I snort. "You're a jerk. You know that?"

"I'm actually rather nice, and since you need my help, ask for it, Princess."

I roll my eyes and ask in a seductive tone, "Would you help me, Daddy? Please?"

"That's my good girl."

He grunts as he lifts me up and sets me down beside him. I notice his erection, and when I return his gaze, I know I'm in for it.

"Remember when you edged me earlier? Because I do."

I giggle. "It's not so fun when it happens to you, is it?"

He pins me with a playful stare. "I distinctly remember you asking me if you could take care of my needs. I wanted you to bounce on my dick, but since your legs are weak, I'll let you take a break."

"I don't want to take a break," I protest. "I can handle you just fine."

I lie on my side and scoot closer to him, arching my back

until I feel him pressed against my ass. He leans in closer 'til he's flush against me, leaving soft kisses on my shoulders. I hold my leg up, granting him access, and I'm greeted by his hard dick slapping against my aching core.

"You're so fucking wet for me, baby," he says as he wraps his corded arm around me, resting his hand against my soft stomach.

He slips into me, and I gasp, giving me a moment to adjust to the fullness before he starts pounding into me. His thrusts are determined, hitting the right spots as I claw for the sheets. I throw my head back and cry out for him.

He sinks his teeth into my shoulders as he drills into me, and I grind back. His other hand reaches for my neck and holds me steady. I chuckle as he applies pressure, and he hums against my skin.

"That's my dirty fucking girl." He pulls out and slaps himself against my pussy again before plunging back inside of me. His hand on my stomach inches down and skates across my clit. His fingers caress me, gently swirling my sensitive bud in contrast to his punishing thrusts. Pressure builds within me, and I dig my nails into his arm. "Oh my god, Grey. Please?"

"Please, what?"

"Please don't stop," I beg.

His grip tightens on my neck as he whispers in my ear, "I'm not stopping. Give me one more, Sunflower." I clench around him, and I mewl into my shoulder as my body trembles in his arms.

"Fuck. I'm going to fill that pretty pussy up. Is that what you want, baby?"

"Y-yes," I manage through heavy breaths, digging my nails deeper into him.

"That's right, baby. Come for Daddy."

He continues his pace, and I gasp when I reach my crescendo, arching my back into him. He roars as he spills into me our names on each other's tongues as we descend. I collapse onto him, and he holds me tightly as we lie there, sated and lovestruck.

I shuffle around, and he scoots back to give me room to get comfortable. I shift onto my other side, and he's staring longingly at me with admiration in his gaze.

I suddenly hear music when the aroma of brunch wafts into the room and am reminded that we are not alone and have been exceptionally *loud*.

I glance at the clock and see that it's 11:30. We've been at it for over an hour.

Footsteps approach on the other side of the door, followed by Elena's voice. "You've gone quiet, so I'm going to assume you're all finished. Don't step out of this room unless you're cleaned up. I started cooking slower when I heard y'all going at it, so it'll still be hot."

I cover my face in embarrassment, and he cradles me into his chest.

"Don't be shy now. I love how you receive feedback, by the way." I slap his shoulder and bury my face deeper into him. He rubs soothing circles across my back.

"We'll be out in ten, Elena. Thank you!" he shouts out.

"I hope you know I'm adding a fee for this," she says, her footsteps descending.

"I'll pay it. You know I'm good for it!"

"Yeah, yeah. Hurry up! I'm lonely without Clifford."

"I miss him, too," I say, looking up at him as I rest on his chest.

"Me too, baby. C'mon, Let's get cleaned up," he orders before pressing a kiss to my forehead.

We climb out of bed, and I watch him as he steps into the en-suite. I hear the sound of running water and the grumble of his voice when he emerges with a smile and something in his hand. He gushes over a new shower cap he found for me.

"It's silk lined. Do you like it?"

I smile up at him and think to myself how lucky I am to have found him.

"I love it, Grey. Thanks for thinking of me."

"I always think of you," he assures me.

"Why is that?"

"Because I love you, silly."

He picks me up and carries me into the shower.

Turns out he was serious about me not lifting a finger today.

Once again, I'd like to thank the woman who wrote Grey.

Happy birthday to me.

77
i love surprises

Selah

Manhattan, NY | May 7, 2024

TODAY HAS BEEN unlike any birthday I've ever had. I woke up thirty years old with a clean slate, in the arms of a man who adores me as I am. I couldn't be more grateful. I know I just wanted to relax today, but he kept his word and gave me what I wanted. After brunch, we curled up with our pets, and I caught up on my current read before he sent me out of the house for pampering. He's taking me out for a nice dinner tonight, and he was still firm about me not lifting a finger today.

He made me a hair appointment with Chess for a wash and style. I wanted my curls straightened with a few inches taken off. My curls always look so much better when they're not weighed down, and she took the perfect amount off. As much as I love to embrace the curls, occasionally, I like to switch it up. I was a little nervous about what Greyson would say, but it's safe to say he was more than happy with the outcome. When I got home, he kindly asked if he could wrap it around his fist just to test my new length. How could I deny such a reasonable request? It wrapped around *three* times.

6

I complete my look as I zip myself into a backless yellow maxi dress. Open-toe heels peek through my low slit. I'm secretly hoping that eggs aren't cooked at the table tonight. I've asked for hints as to where we're going, but he won't budge.

I step out into the hallway to model for him, and he growls in approval when he sees me. He's in a navy, silk button-down with dress pants, paired with a belt I can't wait to watch him take off later. I honestly didn't think we'd get out the door, but he insisted we had a reservation to make.

We're on our way to the restaurant, and the ride has been nice. He drives with one hand and holds mine with the other. As I take in our surroundings, I begin to wonder where we're really headed once it seems like we're entering SoHo. I raise my brow and keep staring out the window until the very townhouse I expected to see comes into view. Greyson slows down the car, letting go of my hand as he settles into a parking spot on the street in front of *Audrey's* house.

I whip my head over and give him a quizzical look.

"Reservations, huh? What are you up to? More importantly, are we overdressed?"

"I'm not up to anything, and we are not overdressed," he assures me, helping me out of the car.

He's right behind me as we head up the stairs, but it appears that no one is home. I hesitate at the door when he boldly turns the knob and motions for me to enter the house. I stand in the quiet foyer, and when I feel my anxiety heighten, I ball my fists and breathe deeply through it, rooted to the spot. Grey leans down, resting his forehead on mine, and rubs his thumb over my knuckles.

"Trust me, baby," he whispers with a kiss to my cheek.

"I do," I breathe out.

When we continue walking, he guides me with his hand on the small of my back. There's no sign of anyone here, not even Ghost, who we should've seen by now. I pass through her huge kitchen to the front of a door that leads to her dining room. I pull the doors open, and I'm startled by a collective song of various voices shouting *Surprise!* with one rumbling from right behind me, and it's Greyson's.

The light flicks on, revealing a full spread on the table and familiar faces standing around, including my mom's. Tears well in my eyes at the sight of her and the thoughtfulness of him. I didn't mention it to anyone, but I was dreading spending my thirtieth birthday without her. We'd already spent so many years apart when I lived in West Chester, and now that we're closer, I want to celebrate everything together. I planned to fly her in, but she said that she wouldn't be able to get off work until next week.

Before I can speak, she yells, "Happy birthday, baby!" and rushes to greet me with a warm hug. After a moment, I hear her whisper, "*Thank you*" over my shoulder to Greyson. The girls come over to hug me, and Chess finally meets Greyson. I realize now that I never updated them about how much has changed in the past few days. I'll need to sneak off to update them later, mama too.

When I introduce him as my boyfriend, the room erupts in whoops and cheers. I admire him over dinner, and my heart swells at how well he fits with us. He's charming everyone and really hitting it off with Mom. The guys seem to approve, and I really love this intimate family dinner over going to a restaurant. He includes my family because let's face it—that's what they are to me.

I tell Greyson to meet me out on Audrey's terrace to steal a moment away. I realize how quickly things have changed over the last several days, and I just want a moment to talk with him.

"Selah, why was your mom quizzing me about pinochle when I picked her up from the airport yesterday?"

I inquire, "She's been in town since yesterday, and I'm just now finding out?"

"Don't change the subject. She was fully aware of these plans and has been living lavishly at *The Woodward* since I dropped her off. You do not want to see that bill."

"Good for her."

He continues, trying to hide his smile. "Back to my question. Why does she think I'm an expert pinochle player?"

"Umm—I may have mentioned that as a joke when she was accusing us of having sex and we weren't."

"When was this?"

"Thanksgiving. She saw how you looked at me, like you'd swallow me whole. Mama knew it was going to happen anyway and told me to call whenever it did. If I said 'pinochle' three times you were a good neighbor and just once if you were a bad one."

"So, the whole time, it's a code word. I was looking it up and hoping to impress her," he says, shaking his head.

I can't hold back my laughter, and he eventually joins me.

6

I bring my eyes to his with a thought. "Greyson, when did you know you loved me?" I ask with a shaky breath.

"I could ask you the same," he challenges. "On the count of three?"

I nod. He keeps eye contact, holding my face in his hands. Tears fall down my cheeks, and his thumb swipes them away.

"One, two, three."

"March eleventh," we say in unison.

He takes my lips in a demanding kiss, capturing my moans, and I quickly remember we have a party we need to return to. When we come up for air, I remind him of that, and he lights up as if he has an idea.

"Dance with me."

"There's no music."

"There's always music," he counters, holding up his phone.

He turns on *Lay It Down* by Allen Stone. I place my hand in his and take his lead as we softly sway across the terrace. Meeting my gaze, he sighs contentedly as his free hand travels my bare back, stopping just before my ass.

He guides me across the terrace effortlessly and mouths *I love you,* and I mouth it back. It's funny, like we're still adjusting to the words and how they sound out loud. I break our gaze for a moment to peer reluctantly at the night sky or lack thereof. It's darkness. with faint signs of light. I love living in Manhattan, but I really miss stargazing. It was something small that brought me joy on even the worst day.

On nights like these, I wish I could see the stars.

"Wishing we weren't in New York right now so you could stargaze?"

Seriously, how does he do that?

"How'd you know?"

"A wise woman once told me, 'Everything is obvious when you're paying attention.'" He dramatically dips me, and my eyes widen. He smirks and pulls me up, resuming the slow dance. "To know what's going on inside your head is a gift, an honor that I don't take lightly," he adds with a sweet kiss to my forehead.

The song changes, and we don't stop moving. I could get lost on a dance floor with him for the rest of my life, and I hope I do. I'll never know the time, allowing me to make the best of every moment.

"Don't look, but everyone's watching. Tissues are being passed around."

I chuckle into his chest, and we keep on for one more song in front of our spectators. I eventually look up and see Mom and Chess crying. Audrey, Daya, and Eric are cheering, as expected. Rome, August, and Avery, the brothers I never had, stand there with soft smiles. If they cried, it would be in private. We head back inside to rejoin the party when Greyson stops me.

"Do you still hate surprises?" he asks.

"Yes, but only when you're not involved. I love it when *you* surprise me—you leave no stone unturned. You are something else, Greyson Park."

"You are everything, Selah Bailey."

THE END

epilogue

Selah

Sandyston, NJ | 3 Months Later

WE'VE BEEN DRIVING for two hours, and Grey refuses to tell me where the hell we're going. I eventually stopped asking and dived into a book, occasionally looking up to enjoy the scenery. This town reminds me of a place not far from where I grew up. Here's a fun fact: I've developed a kink for watching Greyson drive, so I must avert my eyes often. Though I catch him glancing over at me every once in a while, and that spark between us magnifies.

Three months into this *real* relationship and he hasn't let up on the surprises, romance or grand gestures. He's really living up to book boyfriend expectations and I fall deeper in love with him every day. The Hapless In Love Book Club is proud to announce our discovery of not one, but two men restoring faith in the male population, three if you count Eric.

"You're not taking me out here to bury me, are you? This was fun while it lasted, Grey."

He scoffs, keeping his focus on the road.

"If I needed to know where to hide a body, I'd ask Audrey."

"Why would you say that?" I ask, shifting to face him.

"I'm just joking, baby. Though, she did threaten me once. Said if she was wrong about me, she'd make me disappear."

It's very likely she said that. She loves a good threat.

"That sounds about right. Sorry," I say with a wince.

"You don't need to worry. I plan to make you happy as long as I live. You're going to be stuck with me for a long time. Is that alright with you?"

"I guess. You're not so bad. Eric and Aud were right. You really don't scare easily."

He chuckles. "Sunflower, I'm from Brooklyn. Ain't shit for me to be scared of," he says, leaning over to kiss my forehead. "Ready to find out where we're going?"

He turns down a long dirt road, and by the looks of it, my fingers are crossed for a cute bed and breakfast. It's quaint, and there's miles and miles of farmland. I bet the stars look amazing out here. A good distance down the road, crops come into view, and my breath catches when I spot a sea of familiar yellow petals standing tall.

I don't need to look at him to know he's smirking. Once we reach our destination, my heart swells. I'm still staring, slack-jawed, at a sunflower field. I've never seen one in person before, and it's remarkable.

"What are we doing here?"

He tilts my chin and gapes at me. "I want to get photos of my Sunflower during golden hour. Then I have something else planned. Does that sound good?"

I grin from ear to ear. "Of course."

He drapes his camera around his neck, and we walk through the field in search of the perfect spot. It doesn't take him long to find it. It's a hot day, but Greyson will get the shots he needs quickly, *if* I cooperate.

He tells me where to stand, and I pose with his direction. I love watching him in his element, but today I agreed to be the model and must focus on the task at hand. I admire his concentration, the little way he bites his lip in victory when he takes the perfect shot, and I don't mind how silly he looks trying to get the best angle. He praises me in front of the camera as he would in the bedroom, and I resist the urge to blush. I swear that I don't blush, but he's managed to get it on camera a few times.

The sky looks like cotton candy by the time we're done, and I could go for a snack. We start walking through the field of sunflowers and a question dawns on me that I've never considered before.

"Why do you call me Sunflower?"

He stops in his tracks. "Good question. It's a long story."

"Lucky for you, we have a long drive home," I challenge.

"Fair enough."

He continues walking with my hand in his.

"Why do you always open my curtains when you come over? Why won't you let me enjoy the dark?"

"Sunflowers thrive in sunlight," he says casually.

"W-what do you mean?"

He squeezes my hand while leading the way.

"I like to think I do a pretty good job of keeping you watered, but I'm always open to feedback. While they don't demand as much attention as *you do,* they need plenty of sun and room to grow. As long as I'm alive, you'll never hide in the shade again, so get used to being in the light, Sunflower."

He turns to me with a teasing smile, and I tug his hand.

"How do you know so much about sunflower care?"

"Wouldn't you like to know?" he teases.

"I would, actually."

"I promised myself if I got ahold of another flower, I'd tend to its every need. I'd read every book, provide enough light, and pour back into its soil. If I could prove I was worthy of a beautiful garden, I may be lucky enough to keep it alive. Might even have a family to share it with."

I'm taken aback by that. We haven't discussed kids much. I'd love to have a family with him. I'd love to build a life together. *I love him.*

"I love you," I croak.

"I love you too, baby. C'mon," he says, pointing to the SUV that's now in our view.

We were lucky to find the parking lot without getting lost in all the flowers. He gets me situated, starts the AC, and says he'll be right back. I take sips from my steel water bottle and sigh in relief as the cool air hits me. His words from moments ago repeat in my mind.

If I could prove I was worthy of a beautiful garden, I may be lucky enough to keep it alive.

I think back on the woman I was three summers ago to now and I don't even recognize her. I was a prisoner of the storm, desperate for solace. When I escaped, I was armed to the teeth and looking for a fight. A woman weathered, alarmed, and full of rage. Grey and I, we are the balance of opposites. He is a rush of calm after the storm. A place of refuge. When the dust settles, he remains. A strong, resilient hero with open arms who is patient, fearless, and kind. Loving him isn't a threat to the life I created for myself because he contributes to it. I don't fight to survive with Greyson because he breathes life into me. I believe it's mutual. I didn't lose my independence, and he didn't give up his success for us to be together. We *have both.* We just didn't know that was possible until we found each other.

The locks flick upward and release me from my thoughts when he returns, holding ice cream cones and a sunflower bouquet tucked into his elbow. His smile is contagious, and I'm in awe of him. I roll down the window to free his hands when he disappears to the trunk, returning with blankets he tosses in the backseat. I watch him when he climbs in beside me, smiling softly to himself as he backs out of the spot.

I never know what he has up his sleeve, and I've grown to love that about him.

We enjoy our ice cream, getting familiar with dirt roads as the sun sets and darkness creeps in. We're driving for about thirty minutes when he turns down a short path, seemingly to nowhere, and parks, the road still in view. He hands me a blanket and gets out of the car, rounding to my side. I take his hand when I step outside. We're beneath a beautiful night sky filled with twinkling stars. I gaze in amazement as my eyes well up.

I love this man so much it hurts sometimes.

"I figured before heading back to the city, we could see the stars. Is that okay?"

"Of course," I say tearfully. "I love you."

"I love you too, Sunflower."

He picks me up and sets me on the hood of his SUV. He joins me, draping the blanket over our legs as we admire the starry skies.

"I have a fun fact for you."

"Lay it on me."

"Did you know that you're the love of my life?"

"I do now," he says with a smile.

A year ago, an audacious man interrupted me reading on an elevator, and I fell in love with him.

epilogue - part two

Greyson

Austin, TX | 1 Year Later

"AND THE WINNER IS...*SOULBLEND*!"

The crowd erupts in applause, and my staff is seated at surrounding tables, cheering like it's a sporting event. My eyes widen in shock and Selah squeezes my arm.

"Baby, did you hear them? You just won a Techy award. You gotta go up there and give your speech." She beams with pride.

"Are you okay with me professing my love for you on national television?"

"I'd be offended if you didn't," she says with a chuckle and a peck to my lips.

I rise and swallow as I stride toward the stage, where the presenter awaits with a smile and my award. It's a gold plaque of a hand holding a smartphone in the air. I greet her with a bow and she hands me the award. I take my place on the floor marker and breathe deeply before I speak.

"I'm sure many of you have read this about me, but *SoulBlend* was a passion project I tried to keep myself busy. I never imagined it would become...this," I say, holding up the award.

"I created the code and had the plan, but I can't take credit for what we've become. To my support system, the incredible minds and software engineers at *SoulBlend*. I have the best team on earth and without them, I wouldn't be standing here today. We're celebrating six years and countless love stories with a Techy. I couldn't be prouder.

Down The Aisle Magazine's 2025 Jewelry and Engagement Study named *SoulBlend the* most successful dating app for marriage with forty-eight percent of meet cutes starting with us."

The crowd roars and my eyes search for my Sunflower. She isn't hard to find as her gorgeous smile is wide and a silk yellow gown clings to her curves. I take a quick breath and continue.

"I created this app to restore my faith in love and I needed a project to dive into amid my divorce. The app helped my ex-wife find her person, who was on the other side of the world. And my person was actually a neighbor, who lived in my building for months before we met. I'm certain we would have noticed each other sooner if we hadn't been so engrossed in our phones *or* in her case, e-reader." My eyes stay focused on her. "She was using the app and I had some competition. I eventually had to pull out the big guns to earn her attention. Donuts from *Artie's* on 43rd. Tell them I sent you," I say, my accent thickens and I don't rush to stifle it. A few whoops in the crowd prove that somebody agrees with me.

"So, I suppose you could say that *SoulBlend* indirectly led me to Selah. Except we matched in *real* life. I managed to find a love that defeated my expert coding. You could find love on *SoulBlend*, at a party, the bookstore, or even in an elevator. Just prepare to be surprised.

"Thank you all for nominating us this year. I'm so honored to be in the same room as my heroes in tech, and to have *SoulBlend* be recognized among some of the best to ever do it, has truly made my year. I'd like to thank my parents, Henry, Elena, Selah, and the *SoulBlend* global teams. Lastly, I'd like to thank my first investor and my best friend, Alexander Evans. When I showed you this app I created, you took it seriously and invested. Even said, 'you can thank me when you get your first techy.' I did it. *We* did it," I say, holding up the award. I swallow the emotion building in my throat before I continue.

"Now, if you'll excuse me, I've gone far too long without holding her hand, and I'd like to get back to it," I say, gesturing to Selah. "Thank you for not running the music on me. You all have a wonderful night, and thanks for believing in a little Korean boy from Brooklyn who just couldn't get off that damn computer." The audience roars in applause as I exit the stage and return to my seat.

I'm congratulated with pats on the back and loud cheers, but when Selah's eyes meet mine, they silence. Her smile illuminates the room like a beacon calling me home. I quicken my pace and once I wrap my arms around her, I am renewed. She settles into me with an exhale that sends sparks throughout my body.

She's silent, but I cherish the gift of reading the endless story that is her. I sense pride in her touch and the love in her gaze as she took in my speech. The show goes on, but she and I are still fused. Our heartbeats thump in tandem as excitement buzzes through our veins. *SoulBlend* may have won a Techy tonight, but nothing compares to Selah Bailey, the perfect blend for my soul.

afterword

Elevator Pitch is a love letter to myself. There are a lot of parallels between Selah and I. We both are neurodivergent Black women, born and raised in St. Louis, MO, who are anxious homebodies. We're both survivors of domestic abuse and our lives began in our late 20s when we started over. The *'Fuck It List'* is real. I wrote my first one in 2022 and never stopped.

Selah's tattoos are inspired by songs and artists that saved my life. Selah's love for Harry Styles is because his music brought me solace when I didn't know where to turn. Music was my first love and we reconnected through this project. Some of you have already discovered my music and are streaming it. Some will after reading this. For that, I thank you and hope you enjoy.

The Hapless In Love Book Club is inspired by friendships I cherish in my life. How easily you can feel seen and safe with people that share your interests. I wouldn't be who I am today without my support system and I hope you love this little found family based on them.

Selah's navigating corporate America as a neurodivergent Black woman with anxiety was important for me to share and I know it's very relatable. Skye symbolizes a group of dear friends

I made working from home when I was alienated from my loved ones. I found a sisterhood during the loneliest period of my life–the pandemic–and they've healed me more than they even realize. Not to mention my childhood friends who've always shown up and loved me for me. There are little nods to each one of them in this novel and others to come.

Selah's hibachi date from hell is loosely based on a real date. The egg incident really did happen and my date tipped the chef well at the end of the night. I wanted to forget about it and hadn't told anyone out of embarrassment. One night I told one of my best friends about this date and they insisted it was just too good of a story to take to my grave. He was absolutely right.

I hope you enjoyed the Hapless In Love crew because they aren't going anywhere!

acknowledgments

Let's do this, shall we? Thank you to my family for supporting me and never being embarrassed to claim me as a smut pusher. First it was music and now books. Mom, you'll tell anyone who will listen about my accomplishments, no matter how big or small. Your daughter wrote a romance with over fifteen chapters of smut! Gram, I know you're not interested in the spice, but if you do get around to reading the sweet stuff, keep tissue close by. Bubbie, I love you, kid. Thanks for sitting with me for hours to help me map out the first two MMCs of this series. I can't thank you all enough for always being there for me. Your love and support was crucial throughout this process as we all know how difficult it was for me to share this story.

To my dearest friends and support circle: BreAnna, Ashley, Ken, Amber S., Tati, Ess, Kendra, Teeny Tina, Giu, Cass, Olive, Amber Fawn, J.S. Jasper, Miah, Oona, Cynthia, and Kath. I cannot thank you all enough for your love, light and kind words throughout this journey. Even when you didn't know I needed it, you were there. I am happy to finally write this because we made it!

Thank you to my amazing team: Treshell, Shay, Deb, Sam, Aida, Renee, Mia, Lindsey C., Cassidy, AJ, Lindsey and Shaye. I am so blessed to have found you all and look forward to creating more magic for round two. To my sensitivity and beta readers: Guiliana, Annie, Kylie, June, Khushi, Kyra, Court, Olive, Lana, Ess, Kendra, AJ, and J.S. I appreciate you all so much for taking the time to share your culture, experiences and feedback with me. I look forward to teaming up with you all again! To my cover reveal and street teams, you've been so integral in spreading the word about this book and I cannot thank you enough for your support!

Gang Gang - The sisterhood I found in an unlikely place. I met you all in my darkest hour and you shined your light on me. You all saved me in more ways than you know and when I finally found my voice, you listened and encouraged me. I hope every woman gets to experience a sisterhood like ours someday.

Hercules, Hercules! There's so much I can say but I'll keep it short and sweet. You were the first person I told I was writing a romance novel because I knew you wouldn't judge. You are the Eric to my Audrey and my best friend. You've said yourself you don't think you're book boyfriend material and I disagree. So much so that I created a fictional version of you to test that theory. I look forward to proving you wrong for *once*. Even though men aren't supposed to be right. ;) I don't know how we survived without each other, but we're inseparable now.

Court, my sweet baby. I cannot thank you enough for your support in everything I've done so far. You are the true definition of a friend and I am so grateful to have you in my life. You never read romance before this and dove headfirst to be prepared for this series. I fear I've corrupted you, but I must admit, I love sharing this with you. You were an early reader and the first person I shared this book with. You inspire me so much and I can't wait for you to see my ode to you in future books. It's criminal that we've never met and that will change soon. We're long overdue for hugs. I love you so much.

Amanda, to think we met as kids on twitter and look at us now. I am so blessed to know you and to have always had you in my corner. I know you haven't read sucia books before and will be starting with mine. My debut novel will be your first romance purchase and read of the genre. You have no idea what that means to me. You bring so much light into my life and I'm excited to continue writing about our friendship. I love you!

Kyra, I am so happy you slid into my DMs to strike up conversation about books and smut. We were friends for a few weeks when I told you I was doing this and you couldn't be more thrilled. You were an early reader and I am so appreciative of you for sharing your honest feedback. You understand my work as if you were in my head when I wrote it. I value our friendship and the person I get to be with you. You love loudly and I am grateful to receive it. I'm proud of you and can't wait to read your acknowledgements someday.

Teeny Tina, I absolutely adore you and our talks give me life. You've become such a major part of my life in such a short time. I appreciate you for always keeping me grounded and being a safe space. You're incredible and such an amazing friend.

AJ, you slid into my DMs and my life forever changed. You are one of the most beautiful people I've ever met and you believed in me before you'd even read a single word. I saw more dark days than anything and you were always there for me. The friendship we have is exactly the kind I wrote about. Sisterhood. Thank you for being you, simply amazing.

Giuliana Victoria, (You should read all her novels, btw. Quiver and Tremble are out now.) I was obsessed with you and your book long before we became friends. Then I had the pleasure of reading your work and fell in love with you too. Sorry, Mr. Giu Giu! I can honestly say I don't think I'd be at the finish line without you. Thank you for always thinking of me and doing book boyfriend things behind my back. I'm so proud of you and am grateful we found each other.

Cassandra Diviak, My Gemini Twin and dear friend. Your writing led me to you and I'm so glad it did. Thank you for believing in me and for listening to my ramblings all hours of the day. I appreciate your openness, understanding and kind heart. Thank you for always encouraging me and holding me accountable. You just get me. I want you to know I'm so proud of you! (Everyone should read her novels! The Lies We Tell and The Games We Play, which just came out, btw.)

Treshell Fisher, you are such a beautiful person with incredible talent. To go from being a fan of your art to collaborating with you on my debut was a dream come true. You always see my vision and I cannot thank you enough for capturing the beauty of this story on the cover. It is as beautiful on the outside as it is on the inside. I am looking forward to you reading it and cooking up more magic together!

Lastly, THANK YOU TO MY READERS, Booktok and Bookstagram friends! Many of you have been on this ride since the very beginning and the team has grown exponentially since. I am so thankful! Your excitement, commentary, voice messages and live reactions give me life. You've welcomed me into this community with open arms and I'm so happy to be here. Thank you for reading *Elevator Pitch*!

about the author

Evelyn Leigh is an indie romance author based in the Midwest. A multifaceted Gemini who's lived a thousand lives both in and out of books. Writing worlds for you to escape to using the imagination she never quite outgrew.

Evelyn loves creating underrepresented characters that are relatable for you to live vicariously through. She likes sharing fast paced stories sure to make you laugh, cry, swoon and blush. After reading countless happily ever afters, she has decided to try her hand at writing her own. Here's to her next chapter.

authorevelynleigh.com

www.ingramcontent.com/pod-product-compliance
Lightning Source LLC
LaVergne TN
LVHW102131170926
848365LV00032B/410

* 9 7 9 8 9 9 1 5 3 5 8 0 9 *